The Wrath of Monsters

by

Dan Rice

The Allison Lee Chronicles, Book 3

The Wrath of Monsters

Contact Information: info@thewildrosepress.com

Cover Art by *Debbie Taylor*

The Wild Rose Press, Inc.
PO Box 708
Adams Basin, NY 14410-0708
Visit us at www.thewildrosepress.com

Publishing History
First Edition, 2024
Trade Paperback ISBN 978-1-5092-5467-5
Digital ISBN 978-1-5092-5468-2

The Allison Lee Chronicles, Book 3
Published in the United States of America

Dedication

Dedicated to Frank Lambirth and The Puget Sound Writers' Guild for all the invaluable critiques.

Chapter 1

Remote school is deadly…for my mental health. So is being locked up in my room. Of course, I choose to be locked up in my bedroom, but still. I never chose to have security agents, some of them actual magicians, stalking me through the house twenty-four by seven. I never asked for any of it, but here I am, staring at my laptop's screen, trying to do pre-calculus homework. The problem is I can't make heads or tails out of linear equations and logarithmic functions.

My hand strays from my wireless mouse to my camera on the study table beside the laptop. My fingers brush against the device's cool metallic and rubberized body. I'd love to go outside to take pictures, but I need permission to leave the house from Agent-in-charge Leroy McAllister. Sometimes I wish that man had his neck twisted like fusilli, I really do, but then I remember Agent Deveraux's neck misshapen like that, and acid rises up my throat. My hand goes to my chest. My throat and back of my mouth burn.

I stand and reach for the laptop to close it but stop myself. Dalia promised to help me with my math homework. She might video call or message me any time now. Instead, I wrap my fingers around the camera's grip and enjoy the tactile nature of the rubber. My go-to photographic subject is a precarious stack of dirty dishes on the tabletop behind the computer. The acid on my tongue turns me off from photographing anything remotely related to food.

I try to take all my meals in my room; it's the only place I won't have an agent watching my every move. I glance around the bedroom, eyeballing every corner. Presumably, they don't watch me while I'm here. I wouldn't believe them, except I've scoured every nook and cranny of the room with my prosthetic eyes, zooming in and out, and searching for heat signatures or the lack thereof in IR mode. Never found anything. I wouldn't put it past the magicians from the UN Draconic Task Force to surreptitiously observe me by magical means, but my father, who is the last remaining archmagus, ensures me they aren't watching. If I can believe him after sixteen-plus years of lies.

Sighing, I pick up my camera and cross the room, stepping on dirty and clean clothes to the head of my unmade bed. Next to the pillow, a giant kitty cat stuffy stares at me with unblinking eyes. I flip the cat around, so it stares at the wall. I pull up the blind shading the window on the wall behind the head of the bed and am greeted by another day of March gloom: endless gray clouds and drizzle. Nothing inspiring to photograph, but at least the crowd I hear from the street in front of the house protesting my existence probably numbers less than twenty instead of closer to one hundred. The increased security since I was kidnapped by a team of magician commandos led by none other than my nemesis Gore, a drug-crazed magic-wielding assassin, has the wonderful silver lining of keeping most of my detractors and fans at bay.

The room is stuffy, so I open the window. The cold outside air caresses my cheeks, bringing with it the scent of rain and automobile exhaust from the main drag a quarter mile up the street. Nose crinkling, I slam the window shut.

A sharp rap comes from the door. "Is everything okay in there?"

I wince at the high-pitched voice of Valentina Lopez, Draconic Task Force agent and a magician of unknown ability. As long as she keeps her magic to herself and her mouth shut, Valentina is tolerable. But whenever I hear her overly feminine voice, I wish she was sucked down the kaleidoscopic black hole displayed on the poster adorning my door.

"Just airing out the room."

I cross the room and flop down in my chair. Placing my elbows on the desk, I massage my temples and stare at the linear equations on the screen. My eyes lose focus, the numbers, letters, and mathematical symbols slithering into pen and ink faeries, dragons, and skaags. The creatures whorl into a true monster, a doctor with her face hidden behind a mask. Gasping, I slam the laptop shut. The sleeper ripples inside me, making my skin feel like it crawls from the inside out. The beast wants out to rend flesh from bones, but I can't allow that. My half-skaag form, a cross between a super-sized alligator and a gargantuan eel, is small compared to a full-blooded skaag, but it is still large enough to destroy my room and probably bring the entire house down in the process.

No! I can't do that. I can't transform. She's dead.

The sleeper's deadly desires still ooze through my mind, making my heart race and mouth water—*ewww*—but my bestial side settles itself.

"She's dead," I say out loud for both sides of me to

hear, the human and the skaag. "She can't dissect you. She's dead."

I lose track of how many times I've repeated this to myself when my ancient flip phone vibrates, rattling across the desk. I pick up the phone and flip it open. A text from Dalia.

—Tried video calling you...ready to hit pre-calc?—

I chicken peck out a response with my index finger, cursing my dad the entire time for not allowing me a proper phone. *—No, but I need your help, or I'm going to flunk—*

Dalia responds instantaneously. I can imagine her thumbs flying over her phone's pop-up keyboard. *—Call me. I'm online.—*

I open the laptop and start up the video chat app, placing the call by clicking on an icon that is a close-up of Dalia's face with pink bangs and a golden hoop nose ring prominently displayed. My BFF picks up after the first ring.

"Sorry I'm late. Track tryouts went a little long," Dalia says, smiling and bubbly and apologetic all the same time.

"How did you do?" Before The Incident, we ran cross country together, and Dalia was always the faster runner. Now, with my half-skaag prowess at my disposal, I can set world records at any distance.

"Pretty good. I don't know." Dalia flashes an uncertain smile. "I finished second in the two-mile after Leslie. She's so fast. I didn't do as well at the other distances. Hopefully it's enough to make varsity."

"I'm sure you'll make varsity." I stifle a pang of jealousy. She has nothing to complain or worry about. At least she's allowed to attend school live and in person. Meanwhile, I'm told by my innumerable government minders I should count myself lucky I'm not locked away on a military base or a secret supermax prison.

"I hope so. I'll die if I don't make varsity." A sound comes from offscreen. Dalia looks toward the noise. "Would you leave? I'm doing homework." She moves off-screen, expression harried.

From the laptop's speakers comes the sound of a door being slammed super hard. Dalia reappears on screen, sighing as she sits. "Sometimes I can't wait to move out."

"At least you can head to the bathroom without Valentina watching you," I say.

"Oh geez, I know, you have it so much worse."

I inwardly scold myself for being waspish. "I haven't been sleeping well and being cooped up all day…"

"More nightmares?" Dalia whispers.

My eyes go wide, and I give Dalia a meaningful glare. Yes, I've had more dreams, but I don't want to talk about them using laptops we both know are monitored by the government. To be honest, I don't want to talk about my dreams with anyone, ever. I just want them to stop.

"Is Leslie still pissed at Jason?" I ask, hoping to change the subject.

Light glimmers on the edge of Dalia's nose ring. "That's putting it mildly."

Dalia fills me in on what's happening at school for thirty minutes or more before we move on to tackling our math homework. With my friend guiding me through the problems, I don't know if I understand the mathematics better, but at least the numbers and symbols aren't morphing into monsters.

Dalia is in the middle of explaining a particularly gnarly problem when an explosion shakes the house.

"What the…" I mumble and twist in the chair to stare out the window. I don't see any sign of the explosion. Outside in the hallway I hear Valentina talking. With my preternatural hearing, I should be able to eavesdrop on the conversation, but the words are muffled. I wonder if the agent is using magic to prevent me from listening in.

"Allison, what was that? I heard a loud boom."

I turn back to the laptop. Dalia stares, nervously chewing on the tip of her thumb. "Explosion maybe? I'm going to check it out," I say.

"Be careful. Text me," Dalia says.

"I will." I close the video app and shut my laptop.

Standing, I grab my phone, stuffing it into my front pocket, and swing my camera over my shoulder by the strap. I march to the door and throw it open.

Valentina blocks my path. "Stay in your room."

Her voice is like fingernails scratching a chalkboard, but I manage not to cringe.

"I'm going to photograph the aftermath of the explosion or whatever." I heft my camera.

Agent Lopez gives me her best condescending smile. At least we're about the same height, so she doesn't look down her nose at me while she does it. "No leaving the house without McAllister's approval. You know the rules, Allison."

"Your rules, not mine." I barge past her, shouldering her aside, gently, of course.

"Agent McAllister and Dr. Radcliffe will hear

about this, young lady!"

"Don't I know," I call as I head downstairs for the entryway. I hear Valentina following, but she doesn't try to stop me.

In the entryway, Agent Haskell guards the front door. He stands well over six feet and is about as wide as a silverback gorilla, so he looks down his nose when speaking to me. "Allison, you don't want to go out there. Believe me." He placatingly spreads out his arms. "Honest, you'll find it upsetting."

I look the giant up and down. "Is that a new suit? It'd be a shame if you got blood on it."

Haskell steps aside, giving me access to the door. He whispers as I grab my raincoat from a hook beside the entrance. "Be careful. Valentina will report you for threatening me."

I open the door and step outside into the cold, damp afternoon to a flurry of activity. Security agents and soldiers have corralled and silenced the protesters on the sidewalk. People speak on their cell phones or walkie-talkies, and some snap photos. Most everyone stares at a dark cloud rising over the houses a few blocks away in the direction of the home of the first boy I ever kissed and one of my best friends in the whole world.

"Oh my God!" I gasp. "Haji."

Chapter 2

Pulling on my raincoat, I step out into the wet and blustery evening. I do my damnedest to ignore the agents and the protesters, who start screaming vitriol when they spot me. I'm pretty good at it because I have tons of practice.

It's only a little past five, but already the city is dark under the ominous clouds, promising a night of rain pounding against rooftops. My fire engine red hair is matted down before I manage to pull up my hood. I wrap my jacket around my camera to keep the device from getting soaked. It's water resistant, but I don't need to test that out.

Agent Haskell follows me down the crack-riddled concrete path through the front yard toward the street. The branches of the cherry tree sway in the wind and creak as we pass beneath them. In the vicinity of my friend's house, dark smoke continues to billow.

"Sir, she's leaving the house."

Haskell speaks into his phone behind me. Getting permission from McAllister, evidently.

"Yes, sir. I understand."

Gnawing on my lower lip, I pull out my ancient flip phone and dial Haji's number. The call goes immediately to voicemail.

"Haji, why is your phone off?" I whisper as I hit the speed dial for Dalia.

She answers on the second ring. "What happened?"

"An explosion. I think it might be Haji's house."

"I'll be right over," Dalia says.

"No. Stay put for now. Try to contact Haji. I called him, but he won't pick up."

"I'm on it. Call me if you find out anything."

"I will." I end the call, closing the moisture-slickened device and thrusting it into my pants pocket.

"Allison, let me drive you." Haskell nearly shouts to be heard over the howling wind. He doesn't need to. He could whisper, and I'd probably hear him despite the noise.

"I can get there faster on foot." I need to run. I need to know what happened and to make sure Haji is safe. I must because if anything bad happened to him, anything at all, it's more than likely my fault.

"Hear me out, Allison," Haskell says, a pleading edge to his voice.

Clenching my jaw, I slow my pace. I don't want to hear anything Haskell has to say. He's part of the government protection detail I don't need or want that makes my life miserable, but I owe him. I hate feeling like I owe him, but I do. He took a bullet to the chest trying to rescue my friends and me from Gore and his cadre of super magicians. The agent's bulletproof vest stopped the bullet but hadn't kept him from bonking his head so hard he lost consciousness. That had saved his life, I have no doubt. Bullets and magic had slaughtered every other agent who tried to help me.

"What?" I snap.

"McAllister doesn't want you going anywhere, but he knows we can't stop you. He's giving me permission to drive you over to the site as long as we take

Valentina along."

"Does she have to come?"

Haskell rolls his eyes. "This is how we both stay out of trouble. Plus, your camera won't get any more wet than it already is." Haskell fishes a key fob out of the pocket of his damp sports jacket and dangles it before my face. "It's an electric."

The vehicle being electric convinces me. I don't think I could stand riding in one of the oversized gas-guzzling SUVs the agents typically drive. "Fine. Let's go."

****

Emergency vehicles with their lights flaring line the street in front of the remains of the Patel house. Half the house is smoldering wreckage being doused with water by firefighters. Haskell pulls up behind a small crowd gathered at the edge of a security cordon.

"Stop so I can get out," I say.

"Settle down," Haskell says, pointing toward the crowd. "I think I see the Patels."

"Do you see Haji?" My chest erupts with tension. Inside me, the sleeper stirs, eager for release to sate its savage desires. My prosthetics zoom in on the crowd where the agent points. I spot the crying, rain-soaked Mrs. Patel being comforted by her husband, but no sign of my friend. "Let me out."

Haskell pulls in behind a police cruiser. I burst from the car, heading for the gathering crowd. Valentina exits the front of the vehicle with an umbrella in hand.

"Don't cause any trouble," the magician calls after me.

Weaving my way through the crowd toward the

Patels, I call Dalia.

She picks up on the first ring. “Are you there?”

“Oh, damn,” I snarl under my breath as I veer away from the scene toward the road, hoping the entire time the reporters setting up their equipment near the Patels didn’t see me.

“What?” Dalia asks, voice taut. “Are you at his house? Do you see Haji?”

“One sec. Reporters are staking out the scene.” I pull my hood over my damp red mop. There’s no longer a deluge, but it’s sprinkling so I won’t attract attention with the hood up.

“Did they see you?” Dalia asks.

I glance over my shoulder. The news crew is filming the devastation, and a tall female reporter from Channel 5 speaks to the Patels. Mr. Patel is agitated, telling her she should ask the security people why they can’t see their son.

“Thank goodness,” I breathe.

“What?”

“I think Haji is alive.”

“What happened, Allison? Tell me?” Dalia says.

“I’m not sure. It’s bad. Half the house is in ruins. There’s a fire, but it’s under control. I see Haji’s parents, but I don’t see him.”

“How do you know he’s alive? Allison—”

“I’m going to look around. I’ll call you back.” I end the call.

I weave my way to the front of the crowd, keeping my head down. A handful of security agents and a squad of national guard troops with long rifles keep the curious and reporters at bay. I move toward the blockade. A security agent in a dark trench coat steps in front of me. From behind me come the voices of agents Haskell and Lopez. I ignore them.

"Stop right…" The agent's gaze flicks away from me, then back again. He squints, staring at me hard. "Hey, you're—"

"You're going to let me by, aren't you?"

"Miss Lee, I can't. Or—"

I give the agent a tight smile. "I electrocuted the last person who called me that."

The agent's mouth drops open. Clearly, he's not used to dealing with seventeen-year-old females, who can literally bite his head off.

"It's okay. We'll handle her." Haskell comes between the agent and me. "The blast site is off-limits, even for you."

"Can we go back to the car?" Valentina says from behind me. "The rain is starting to pick up."

I sniff the air. Most of what I smell is what I expect. Burned wood with chemical undertones, possibly from the paint or household cleaners consumed in the fire, the ever-present body odor of those around me, and Valentina's flowery perfume permeate the air. But there is another scent. One I know well—cooked human flesh.

"Who burned to death?" I demand.

"I don't know," Haskell says.

"Who burned to death?" I yell at the security around the house.

Off to my left, someone says, "Is that Allison Lee?"

I glower at Haskell. "Let me by, now."

The agent looks ready to concede, but Valentina comes up next to him with the umbrella held over her head. "You need to start learning to listen. No means no."

In my peripheral vision, I see a cameraman train his camera on me. The tall reporter from Channel 5 lopes toward me like a predator smelling blood.

"Make me." I stride past Valentina. She reaches for me, but Haskell stops her with a shake of his head.

"Let her by," Haskell tells the security.

I march across the Patels' front yard strewn with blackened, smoking debris. The smoke clogs my nostrils and makes my eyes water. The remains of rosebushes caught in the blast crunch beneath my feet. I'm vaguely aware of shouting behind me.

"What's that girl doing?"

"Stay back. Stay back!"

I'm not concentrating on the din surrounding me. Instead, I'm focused on voices and soft crying from behind the ramshackle house. I sniff the air and have my sinuses burned by acrid smoke. Crinkling my nose, I hack, expelling the fumes from my lungs. Still, I catch a whiff of the disturbing aroma of burned human flesh. It's coming from the backyard near the voices and sobs.

I try to interpret the conversation of the unseen speakers, but the racket of activity is too loud. Ahead of me, firefighters spray down a few hotspots, but as best I can tell, the fire is under control. A firefighter not manning the hose waves and lumbers toward me.

"Hey, you can't be here." The firefighter heads me off and places his hands on his hips, equipment clinking.

I'm forced to a standstill before this large man, made all the more domineering by his bulky gear. If he knew my hide is far more fire-resistant than his coat and pants, he might not be so pushy.

His nostrils flare above a bushy red mustache speckled with gray. “The same goes for the two of you. This is an active scene.”

I’m well aware the “two of you” he refers to are agents Haskell and Lopez. Even with all the ambient sounds, I can tell the agents follow about four feet behind me by their footfall and breathing.

Ignoring the firefighter, I imagine my surroundings in a vibrant splash of rainbow colors. My prosthetics switch to IR mode. Much of my vision is distorted by the heat from the extinguishing fire, but I make out five humanoid shapes beyond the building. My heart feels like it will burst from my throat. Two of the figures are on the ground and aren’t moving.

“Who’s back there?” I demand, blinking until my vision switches from IR back to normal.

“You need to…hey, stop!”

The firefighter grabs for me as I dart past him, but he is only human, and I am so much more. His hand grasps air. More shouting comes from the other firefighters when I burst through the stream of water from the hose. The blast of H2O knocks me sideways and makes my drenching from the rain seem like a light sprinkle, but I remain on my feet. My pants and shoes are sopping wet, and goose bumps rise on my thighs, but at least my raincoat continues to repel moisture.

I round the house for the backyard, driven to panic with worry at what I will find. If Haji is seriously hurt or…or dead, guilt will suffocate me. He pursued magic to impress me after I broke up with him for discussing my personal, private life with podcast host and bottom feeder ’n chief Devin Montoya, who happens to be

Dalia's ex.

Behind me, Haskell and Valentina deal with the firefighters, a task they are certainly up for since one is a federal agent the size of a small bulldozer and the other a magician. Ahead of me, hidden from the street by the half of the house that wasn't blown to smithereens, are agents led by none other than Agent-in-charge McAllister. Kneeling over a prone body are two agents. They don't seem to be doing anything other than observing the victim. Approximately ten feet beyond the first victim is a body covered by a dark trench coat. A sobbing woman sits next to the body.

I break into a run. "Where is Haji? Is that him?"

No sooner than the words leave my mouth, I see my friend is the first victim and is breathing. Relief slams into me like a murderous rogue wave, washing away pent-up energy and my inhuman prowess. I'm worn to the quick as if I sprinted across the Sahara under the noonday sun during a sandstorm.

When McAllister blocks my path, I've already slowed to a walk. I stop before him and use my dwindling reserves to crane my neck to look into his intense gaze. Everything is intense about the Agent-in-charge. He wears a black trench coat for the rain but appears unperturbed at the water beading on and running down his bald, ocher head.

"Allison, I've been expecting you," McAllister says, voice sharp enough to dice steel.

"What's wrong with Haji? What happened?"

"I'm not sure. I can speculate, but I won't. What I do know is this. A Draconic Task Force agent assigned to Mr. Patel is dead. Likely killed in the explosion that destroyed half the house. The surviving magician believes magic use preceded the explosion."

Oh, no, Haji. What happened? What have you done? "What is being done for Haji? Is he even conscious? Why isn't he being taken to a hospital or something?"

McAllister gives me a condescending look that oozes "oh, really." "Mr. Patel is unconscious but otherwise unharmed as far as we can tell."

"Unharmed as far as we can tell?" I scoff and stride toward my friend.

McAllister raises a long arm, his trench coat unfurling like a batwing, impeding my path. I nearly collide with his arm.

"Let me see him." My voice quavers with anger, sweeping away my tiredness and brushing against my abysmal prowess.

"Be my guest. He's no longer my problem, but you, Allison, remain my problem." He drops his arm. "Remember that."

I swallow the lump in my throat. "What do you mean he's no longer your problem?"

McAllister's cell phone rings. He retrieves the device from the interior of his trench coat and checks the screen. "I have to take this. I'm serious when I say you can see your friend. I won't stand in your way."

The Agent-in-charge turns away. I'm tempted to listen in on his conversation. There's a good chance I'll be able to hear both sides of it, but my bubbling concern for Haji's immediate wellbeing takes precedence. The agents, two hurly-burly men of indeterminate ages of over thirty but under fifty, stand and move aside as I approach but remain hovering uncomfortably close when I kneel beside my comatose friend.

"Haji," I whisper, touching his hand. His skin is insanely warm, like he suffers from a deadly fever, a sure sign of recent magic use. But at least he breathes. As long as he's alive there is hope. "Why can't you leave magic alone?"

Why can't he be an ordinary, human boy without magic or monstrous abilities? Why can't he be satisfied with being my friend? This isn't the first time his taste for magic has gotten him in trouble and resulted in him being in a coma. If it weren't for him, I never would've been held prisoner on Golden Shoal, a tropical island on the edge of Singapore's territorial waters, and nearly been dissected by a mad scientist.

Conversely, Bria would still be held prisoner on the island, being experimented on against her will, her blood used to turn human magicians into super-powered magic wielders enthralled to the faeries. At least we rescued her. That's one good outcome from our Singapore misadventure…or is it? Now, as far as I know, the poor faery girl is locked away on Joint Base Lewis-McCord against her will.

I withdraw my hand from Haji's, ball it into a fist, and punch the damp grass.

Once.

Twice.

"Allison. Is something wrong?"

I unclench my hand at the sound of the burly agent's voice.

"How long has he been like this?" I ask, never taking my gaze from my friend's dusky face. Since our return from Golden Shoal, I've seen Haji a handful of times and then only over video chat. He's been confined first on base and then at home for his and the public's safety. Tears moisten my eyes. He looks as gaunt and wan in person as he did on the screen.

"Since we found him. Not more than thirty minutes ago. Maybe less."

"What's being done for him?" I demand. The last time he was like this, it took an injection of faery blood, a.k.a. the Juice, to revive him. Of course, last time, he was convulsing. He's not now. Is that good or bad? I gnaw on my lower lip.

"McAllister's handling that," the other agent replies.

I break my gaze from my friend's countenance, unable to shake the niggling fear that he might stop breathing. The Agent-in-charge is no longer on the phone. He kneels beside the surviving magician, offering hushed words of comfort. The covered corpse draws my attention like a siren's poison song. My vision momentarily goes out of focus as my prosthetics zoom in like camera lenses on the body. I'm transported to the white corpse hall deep underground on Golden Shoal. Dozens of charred bodies littered the floor, some burned beyond all recognition.

My kills.

My fault.

My vision zooms back to normal, and I turn to Haji. "I hope this wasn't your fault."

Taking a deep breath, I gather my thoughts before pulling out my phone and dialing Dalia. "I'm with Haji. He's alive."

"Oh, thank goodness!"

I wince at her shrill scream.

"Is he okay? Can I talk to him?"

I sigh. "He's in a coma or something."

"What? Allison…"

A rumbling growl of an internal combustion engine comes from behind me. I lower the phone, glancing over my shoulder. Knobbly tires plowing deep grooves into the grass is a four-wheel-drive but otherwise nondescript black van. Overflowing the van's sides are a white dragon's translucent body parts. Its serpentine neck rises a good fifteen feet above the van's roof, flickering in and out of existence. Only I can see the dragon while she rides the slipstream, a highway system interconnecting all the universes in the multiverse. The beast's wide, pink eyes pin me like a butterfly to a specimen board. All the glimmering draconic body parts project out of a shriveled woman with long snowy hair sitting in the passenger seat. Of course, the woman isn't human. She is a golem made of clay animated by the dragon's magic.

Although I haven't seen her in over a year, I know this dragon far better than I care to, and I don't trust her. The van rolls to a stop not more than five feet from where I stand next to Haji. The growl of the V-8 engine dies when the ignition is cut.

"Allison! Allison!" Dalia squawks from my phone.

I hear the groan of doors opening. Two men in blue hospital scrubs, one so obese his garb can barely contain his girth, and the other thin enough to make a scarecrow look fat, rush around from the back of the van carrying a stretcher. They appear to take no notice of the rain dampening their clothes. McAllister strides quickly toward me. The passenger side door of the van creaks as it swings open.

I lift the phone to my ear. "I have to go. Tanis is

here. I think she's come for Haji."

"What? Tanis—"

"I got to go." I end the call and slip the phone back into my pocket.

"What are you doing?" I demand of the men in scrubs, who ignore me, going directly to Haji's side. They lower the gurney to the ground and kneel beside my friend as if preparing to move him. "I asked, what are you doing?"

I reach for the obese man. I don't know who or what these men are. They might be medics or magicians or both. All I know for certain is that they're with Tanis, and that's not good for Haji. The two agents nearest interject themselves between the men in scrubs and me.

"Please, don't interfere," one says.

I drop my arm to my side. "Get out of my way, or I will go through you."

A hand firmly grips my right shoulder, and I go stiff. A glittering draconic foreleg passes through my head and torso, coming out at my abdomen. One moment the leg seems so substantial, I will burst like a shot watermelon, and in the next, it fades away as if it never existed, only to reappear again with my next breath. Rain passes through the leg as if it is insubstantial as air.

"Allow me to help Haji, Allison. You know I can."

"What? You'll use magic on him? Like you did to me?" Her magic woke the sleeper within me, the half-skaag who had been held in check for sixteen years by my mother's magic. If Tanis had never awakened the sleeper, I'd still be the semi-anonymous girl struggling to survive high school. Instead, I'm a global celebrity, hated or adored depending on who you ask. "Oh, I know what you'll do. You'll lock him up on base like you have Bria."

"Did my magic hurt you?"

"You ruined my life."

"I'm sorry you feel that way. Believe it or not, Allison, I'm helping Bria and learning valuable information about what her people are plotting."

One of the medics produces a hypodermic full of dark, purplish liquid.

"No! Stop!" I cry, my entire body going glacier cold. Images of the vile magician Gore injecting me with drugs and the dragons working blood magic on me slice through my mind.

Chapter 3

I bolt for Haji, but Tanis wraps her arms around my waist. Her humanoid limbs might look spindly but are as strong as steel girders. Her glimmering draconic forelimbs flash before my eyes with headache-inducing intensity.

"Let go!" The sleeper's prowess gushes through my veins like rocket fuel, as does the beast's innate hate for dragons. Tanis's golem might be inhumanly strong and tough, but I can tear it to pieces. I clamp my hands down on the golem's thin wrists and slowly but inexorably begin wrenching its arms aside.

The agents between us and Haji exchange worried glances and back away. They may or may not know what Tanis is, but they have a theoretical understanding of what I am capable of. The scarecrow in scrubs depresses the hypodermic a fraction, causing purple fluid to bead at the needle's tip. I redouble my efforts to free myself. What they're about to inject Haji with might not be the Juice, but it sure looks like a mixture of dragon blood and who-knows-what that will give Tanis power over Haji she can't be trusted with.

"Don't interfere with the medics, Allison!" McAllister bellows.

"Allow me to help Haji," Tanis whispers into my ear. Despite her straining to contain me, her voice is calm.

"No!" I snarl and throw her arms aside.

The rotund medic's mouth goes unhinged, and he shouts a warning at his compatriot. The scarecrow drops the hypodermic and crabwalks backward across the damp grass. I dart forward and smash into something when I'm less than a foot from my friend. My right hand goes to my nose and comes away with blood. I reach my left hand forward a few inches before it comes up against resistance. I press my hand into the invisible force, straining. My fingers slide forward another inch or two as slow as desiccated earthworms. I might as well be facing a brick wall.

"Calm down, Allison, please," Agent Haskell says.

I try doing a one-eighty to lock my wrathful gaze onto Haskell, but more invisible barriers impede my movement. The best I can manage is a glimpse of him out of the corner of my eye. Next to the mammoth agent is the ever-so-annoying Valentina. Only it's Valentina as I have never seen her before: hair a matted down bird nest from the rain, make-up running down her cheeks, eyes glazed, and her skin luminous with lime-green bioluminescence. Agent Valentina Lopez dares to use magic against me? My body quivers.

I try moving in every possible direction to discover the translucent barricade surrounds me. Jumping rewards me with a bonk on the head. I catch an eyeful of a second magician, who apparently decided to stop mourning her fallen comrade and join in the fun of trapping me inside an invisible box. She stands next to Agent-in-charge McAllister, emitting the same lime-green glow as Valentina.

"Release me!" Inside me, the sleeper thrashes, eager to destroy the cage holding us. "I can transform.

This magic won't trap me then."

It's a bluff, of course. My skaag form might only be a quarter of the size of my mother's, but it's still large enough to squash those around me like roadkill flattened by a semi. Transforming is out of the question unless I want more deaths on my conscience. Ghosts don't keep odd hours; they keep all hours and are relentless.

"There's no need for threats or dramatics, Allison." Tanis walks around from behind me.

She faces me, both the human and the white dragon, that is invisible to everyone but me. The dragon lowers its head. Saucer-wide pink eyes split by vertical black pupils stare into mine with hypnotic intensity. The beast stops appearing and reappearing, becoming more substantial while remaining translucent. It's an indication the real Tanis, the decrepit, ancient dragon steeped in lore and powerful in magic, will emerge from the slipstream in a storm of lightning. But I don't think she will. She might crush someone if she does.

"You know I can help him," Tanis says.

"By locking him up on base again? What's wrong? You don't get enough jollies torturing Bria? How is holding her on base any different than what she experienced on Golden Shoal?"

"I'm not experimenting on her. I'm helping her." Tanis points to the half-demolished house and the dead magician. "Allowing Haji to leave my care was a mistake. A Draconic Task Force agent is dead. His parents could have easily been killed in the blast and even his neighbors."

"You don't know what happened," I say. "You're speculating."

The golem's lips twitch upward in an infuriatingly condescending smile that reminds me of my mother.

"Don't I? The magicians guarding him didn't do this. In your heart of hearts, you know that too. An agent is dead, and it is his fault. On base, he will be under my care. By extension, he'll be in the custody of Dr. Radcliffe. Frederick can protect Haji, but only if the boy is in custody. Do you understand and accept these statements?"

Dr. Radcliffe is the head of the Draconic Task Force and leader of the three dragons who claim Earth as their home. If anyone can keep Haji from being locked away on manslaughter charges or worse, it's him. Not that being confined to a military base under the oh-so-tender care of Tanis is any better than solitary confinement. I don't trust either dragon, but Radcliffe did help us survive Golden Shoal.

I nod to Tanis in the affirmative.

"Are you done causing trouble?"

I take a deep breath and slowly release it. "Yes."

"Release her," Tanis says.

"Is that wise?" McAllister asks.

"I'm confident Allison won't cause more trouble," Tanis says.

Tanis turns toward Haji and kneels next to my friend. The invisible cage holding me dissipates in a rush of air. I flash Valentina a you'll-pay-for-this stare as I join the dragon beside Haji. Tanis retrieves the hypodermic from the grass and holds it before her eyes. Light from her dragon form glitters along the needle's length. She lowers the needle toward my friend.

"What are you injecting him with?" I ask.

"A mixture of my blood cut with a small amount of

faery blood. You need not worry. I've given this to him before."

"What will it do to him?"

Tanis's dragon form stares down at me, but her humanoid face remains fixed on Haji. The needle hovers millimeters from his neck. "My blood will give me a certain level of influence over him. Not control, exactly, but near enough to keep him from doing anything dangerous with magic."

"Control," I scoff, recalling how Dr. Radcliffe and my mother have exerted mental control over humans. Mother had turned the Agent-in-charge before McAllister into a marionette dancing to her every whim. I inwardly wince at my last memory of Deveraux with her neck broken by a rogue magician's magic. "It's always about control."

Tanis ignores my remark. "The faery blood should be enough to rouse him from the coma but is not a great enough quantity to enhance his magical ability."

"You're sure this is what's best for him?" I ask.

"It would have been better if he had never pursued magic in the first place," Tanis says, and I swear her dragon form smiles, revealing teeth the length of daggers that glitter and fade from existence like ephemera.

"We can both agree on that," I whisper.

****

I watch the black van with flickering dragon body parts projecting out of it as it drives past the growing crowd on the sidewalk and pulls out onto the street, unable to determine if I should feel some degree of solace or soul-devouring despair. Haji was conscious but listless, strapped down to the gurney by thick leather restraints when they loaded him into the back of the van. With a V-8 roar, the van accelerates and quickly disappears from view.

"Allison."

Blinking, I come out of my stupor, acutely aware of agent Haskell looming next to me, the reporters at the front of the crowd shouting my name, an insistent buzz, and something vibrating against my hip.

"I better give a statement before this gets more out of hand." McAllister strides past me, heading for the crowd. He pauses and gives me a firm glare. "Whatever you do, don't talk to the media. Head straight home." He turns away without waiting for my reply.

"Allison, your phone," Haskell says.

"Oh." I remove the device from my pocket—it's Dalia. I flip open the phone and lift it to my ear.

"What's happening? I'd be there with you, but the damn agents won't let me leave the house!" Dalia's voice is shrill with anxiety.

"She took Haji away."

"Who took Haji away?"

"Tanis."

"What? He's going to be a prisoner on base again?"

"She claims she can help him. Dr. Radcliffe can help him." The words taste like ash in my mouth.

"And you believe that," Dalia snaps, then continues sorrowfully. "I don't blame you. I know there's nothing you could do to stop her."

"He might've killed someone, Dalia."

There's a sharp intake of breath followed by silence.

"The explosion was caused by magic. One of the

Task Force magicians guarding him was killed."

"So the other magician survived. Did you ask the magician what happened?"

"No, she left with Tanis. I didn't even think about asking her. I was so worried about Haji and then Tanis showed up."

"Haji is not a killer. He's not."

"I hope not, I really do. But you know Haji is different since Golden Shoal. The indoctrination changed him."

"But he was getting better. Allison, you know he's not a killer."

I never imagined I'd become a killer, but I am. "Listen. I have my camera with me. I'm going to take some photographs before my babysitters make me leave. Maybe I can capture some evidence proving Haji is not responsible for the explosion."

After a long silence, Dalia says, "I hate feeling powerless."

I don't know how to respond. She's told me many times the last time she felt powerful was on Golden Shoal when she had a scalpel pressed to Dr. Kihl's throat and was prepared to kill him. Not a day goes by that I'm not overjoyed Dalia didn't kill the doctor, but sometimes I think she regrets Bria ripped out the doctor's throat before she had the chance to slit it.

****

At home, I sit at my study desk inspecting photos I took at the disaster site on my laptop. I'm not sure what I'm looking for. So far, I've attached a dozen photos to an email addressed to Mauve, one of my best friends in the whole world and a dragon. She's the only dragon I trust, despite her divided loyalties, because she knows what it's like to be me: a being caught between two worlds. I hope she will look at these photos and see something proving Haji didn't cause the explosion.

After selecting several more photos, I compose a brief message to my dragon friend. I read through it several times to make sure I haven't included anything that will reveal her true identity. The government monitors all my communications but hasn't learned Mauve is a dragon yet, at least as far as I know.

I'm about to hit send when I hear the front door open. My gaze flicks to the time in the upper right-hand corner of the screen. Nine ten p.m. Too early for the agents to be changing shifts. It must be Dad, finally. I have a bone to pick with him about Haji and magic since he is an archmagus, after all.

After hitting send on the email, I lock my laptop and stalk toward the bedroom door decorated with a poster of kaleidoscopic color swirling down a black hole.

Chapter 4

No sooner than I exit my room, I go stiff. I firmly shut the door, refusing to meet Agent Valentina Lopez's venomous brown-eyed gaze. I head for the stairs, hoping to avoid confrontation.

Valentina blocks my path to the stairs. "I was friends with the agent your friend killed."

I meet Valentina's gaze, noticing her eyes are rheumy. "I'm sorry about your friend. I really am, but you don't know Haji killed anyone."

Valentina blinks back tears then sneers. "Her name was Katrina, and Haji murdered her."

Her words are shrill klaxons ringing in my ears. Haji can't be a killer. He can't. "I'm so sorry. I wish Katrina hadn't died. I feel horrible about it. Whatever happened I'm sure it was an accident."

"Accident?" Valentina scoffs. Her left hand briefly emits a lime-green glow. Inside me, the sleeper uncoils, ready to annihilate any threat. "Don't go trying anything. That's the reason I'm here instead…instead of mourning my friend. To make sure you don't step out of line again."

I swallow my retort, which goes down my throat like broken glass. She's grieving, and I don't need to have the last word.

****

I find Dad in the dining room sipping what smells

like herbal tea from a steaming mug with a maroon T embossed on the side for Tahoma University. That's where he works as a computer science professor. He is streaming the local news on the large flatscreen TV affixed to the wall at the foot of the table. He sits at his usual spot to the right of the head of the table. The head of the table is reserved for Mother, who has been missing since she helped rescue my squad and me from Golden Shoal. She is the skaag who quite literally made me what I am today, a half-human, half-skaag monster unable to fit in anywhere. She managed to do that despite not having anything to do with me for the first sixteen years of my life. Then out of nowhere, she decided to rejoin the family. Lucky me. Let's just say it turns out I didn't miss anything not having her in my life for all those years. Now, she's disappeared again without a word. Honestly, that's par for the course and for the best.

"Allison, you're still up. I thought I heard you speaking with…Valentina. Am I right?" Dad says, setting down the mug. He reaches for the television controller, probably to mute the newscaster droning on about improvements to the Seattle waterfront.

I stand over him, trying my best to look down my nose at him. It's tough. Even sitting, he's almost as tall as I am. "You probably want to turn that up. I want to tell you all about my day."

Dad raises an eyebrow and increases the volume. "Sure, Allison."

"Did you hear about what happened to the Patel house?" I ask while silently reminding myself to keep my voice down.

Dad swallows. "I did. I know you want to talk

about it, but maybe that's best left until the morning. After we've both had a good night's sleep and are refreshed."

I pull out a chair and sit down next to him. "Haji might have killed someone. You have to help him."

Dad turns the TV volume up almost to the max. "What do you expect me to do?"

"Valentina or someone else isn't listening in?"

Dad utters a mirthless laugh. "I'd know if anyone was. At least, if magic is at play. You know as well as I, the security detail might have listening devices anywhere."

I lean toward him, smelling the tea's herbal concoction on his breath. "You're an archmagus. There must be something you can do to help him. Whatever the dragons are doing, it's not helping. He's slipping away." My voice rises an octave. "He might've killed someone."

Dad leans toward me until our foreheads are nearly touching. "I am the last archmagus."

"So what? Haji needs help."

Dad leans back in the chair. "I haven't survived as long as I have by taking needless risks."

"A needless risk! Is that what Haji is to you?"

"Your dragon friends will kill me if they find out what I am." He wrings his hands, then twists his wedding band, making it do 360s on his finger. "That's if I'm lucky. More than likely, they'll toy with me first. Torture me. In an attempt to learn my magic. The magic of the archmagi."

I smack my palm against the table. "How do you know that?"

"Because that is what happened to all the other

archmagi."

"What?" I wish I could deny his words, but I can't. I don't want to believe Mauve would torture anyone to learn their magic, but I know Radcliffe and Tanis would be happy to. "There must be something you can do. I mean…"

Dad takes my hand and shakes his head. "I'm sorry."

I wrench my hand free and I'm ready to make an angry retort when the doorbell rings, and the ever-annoying English butler voice comes from a speaker in the hallway. "Unknown person at the door."

Dad looks up, and our gazes meet. We never have guests this late in the evening anymore—not that we ever did. From the entry hallway comes the soft footfall of the agent stationed by the stairs.

"It looks like Dr. Woolworth," the agent calls.

I'm out of my chair and into the entryway before the agent even finishes another sentence. Dad is almost as fast.

The agent looks up from a small LCD on the side table. "Should I send her away?"

"No." I nearly yell, making a beeline for the door.

"We'll handle this," Dad says.

I reach the door first and fling it open. "Dr. Woolworth! What a surprise. Do I have another appointment already?"

Dr. Jane Woolworth is the genius scientist and medical doctor who created the prosthetic eyes allowing me to see. Almost a year and a half ago, my nemesis Gore struck me on the head, blinding me. Back then, Gore was a faceless attacker, and I couldn't see dragons riding the slipstream. After Dr. Woolworth installed the prosthetics, I started seeing the dragons. I didn't have an inkling why my prosthetics allow me to see dragons until I learned my dad is an archmagus. He did some of the particularly gnarly programming the prosthetics rely on. Although I haven't confronted him about it yet, I suspect he did more than write code. He must have woven magic into the hardware, somehow. I only have the most rudimentary understanding of how magic works. The same goes for my prosthetics.

Dr. Woolworth nervously wrings her hands. Her blonde hair, which is just shy of a disaster on a good hair day, is a rat's nest. She wears baggy pink pajamas beneath a gray raincoat even her natural supermodel good looks can't make stylish.

"Jane, come in," Dad says, standing at my shoulder. "Come in. Come in and sit down. What brings you by so late? Can I offer you tea or water?"

"No…I…" Dr. Woolworth shakes her head. "This could have waited till morning."

"Nonsense. You're always welcome." Dad takes her by the upper arm and guides her inside.

I step aside to give them room to maneuver and shut the door. The agent watches us from the staircase as Dad leads Jane into the living room. Dad manages to get the doctor seated on the couch and sits next to her. I sit down on the floor before them.

"You're sure I can't get you anything?" Dad asks.

Woolworth shakes her head. "I received a caller this evening. Someone I wasn't expecting, but…not unexpected either, I suppose."

My shoulders tense. "Was it Gore?" We've warned her about the magician assassin. "Or Jett?" The faery was one of my captors on Golden Shoal and is all bad business.

"Jett?" Jane asks quizzically.

I'd forgotten she doesn't know the details about the faeries. I'm about to jump into an explanation when she continues.

"No." Dr. Woolworth shakes her head. "It was a US marshal."

"What? Why?" Dad asks incredulously.

My mouth drops open. I might not know exactly why a US marshal visited Dr. Woolworth, but I'm sure it has something to do with me.

"I've been subpoenaed by the US Senate. The Homeland Security Committee, to be precise. They want to know all about the technology behind your prosthetics, Allison," Dr. Woolworth says. "I suspect you'll be subpoenaed next."

Chapter 5

As the end of the school day approaches, my eyes cross as I strive to read *The Odyssey*. Stifling a yawn, I blink until the words are no longer black, squiggly lemmings hurling themselves into a white vortex. Twenty pages. I need to get through twenty pages of dactylic hexameter. I have to get the work done and make good grades too or I might miss out on admittance to a decent college. With everything that's happened since The Incident, the euphemism for the series of events that included me discovering I am a shapeshifting monster and preventing an invasion of giant alien alligator eels, I hardly have time to do homework, let alone obsess over college.

Five minutes or an hour later, my head bobbles like a drunken sailor.

Concentrate.

I blink, yawn, and squint the words back into focus.

I make it halfway down the page before I realize I'm lost in the verse and don't remember a single thing I've read. My laptop dinging saves me from trying to read more. A message notification fades in the top right-hand corner of the screen. I grab the mouse next to the computer and open the messaging app to read Dalia's latest missive. My gaze flicks to the time—3:41 p.m. School just ended.

—Will we be subpoenaed next?—

The computer dings again, announcing a second query from my friend.

—Will we?—

An emoji with white eyeballs and grinding teeth suffixes the words. My fingers peck out a response seemingly on their own accord. Before banging the return key to send the message, I read it once.

—I have no freaking idea.—

—Same. I'm scared. First, Haji's house blows up. Now this. It's like we're cursed. I used to think everything would go back to normal, but now I think you're right. When you say nothing can ever be the same since The Incident. YOU'RE RIGHT.—

I almost type "told you so," but I hesitate. This isn't the time for snark, no matter how appropriate the zinger.

—Things will get better. Did I tell you Joe is home from the hospital?—

Joe is one of my best friends in the whole world, an Afghan war veteran and formerly homeless. He saved me from Gore that stormy night on the Tahoma University campus. Without Joe's intervention, the assassin would've done more than knock me unconscious and left me blind.

—That's awesome. He's up and walking?—

—Yes. I guess he's not back to normal yet, but at least he's out of the hospital.—

—That's such a relief!! I know it was touch and go for a long time. Now, to be able to walk again. That's awesome!—

No fewer than ten smiley faces follow the words.

—You know what else? I have permission to visit

him after school tomorrow.—

****

Haskell drops me off in front of the red brick rescue mission. I shut the car door and the vehicle pulls away. A crowd of men bundled up in layers of mismatched clothing huddle on the steps leading to the stoop. They stand aside for me, and some offer greetings. They all know who I am, have an idea of what I am, and most importantly, know I am Joe's friend. I try not to judge them for their odor. It's not their fault I have an inhumanly hypersensitive nose.

"You gonna help out on the line tonight, Allison?" an oldster calls, breath steaming in the cold.

"I'll be slinging some beans," I reply.

That gets a cheer from the crowd, and someone shouts about me being a superhero. I force myself not to cringe. I'm nobody's hero. If it were up to me, these men would only know me as Joe's friend.

I mount the stairs and ring the doorbell with a sign below it stating, "Ring the bell once for service." Once is underlined three times. After several minutes, the soft clack of shoes against linoleum echo from beyond the door. Then, the distinct thunk of the deadbolt retracting. The door opens a crack with a loud creak. A jowly, older woman with gray hair in a bun suspiciously peeks through the doorway. The aroma of cooking rice and beans wafts from inside. Behind me, the men stir restlessly, and someone's stomach loudly growls.

"You Joe's friend?" she demands, voice deep for a woman and melodic.

"Yes, I'm Allison."

"Hmmph." She looks me up and down before opening the door wide enough for me to step inside. "I don't know. Guess I expected you to be bigger or something."

"Hey, let us in there. We starving out here!" a man shouts, and at least half a dozen more voice their agreement.

"You can keep on starving," the woman says. "Dinner is at five thirty, not one minute before."

She slams and locks the door on their pleading. Circular tables are laid out around the space with lightweight plastic and metal chairs stowed on the tabletops. Along the back wall is the serving hatch, the vertical door still down. On a corkboard next to the entrance, flyers advertise the services of organizations devoted to helping the needy.

"I'm Henrietta, by the way. Come on. I'll show you up to living quarters."

Henrietta takes a breather at the top of the stairs before leading me to Joe's apartment. A small window next to the apartment door looks out onto an alleyway and a dilapidated warehouse building. She faces the door and raps against the wood with a fist. "Joe, Allison is here. Don't be getting up now. I'll let her in."

Henrietta opens the door and steps aside to allow me into a small studio apartment. From inside comes the enticing aroma of recently brewed coffee. Joe sits in a recliner, legs up on the footrest. His head lolls to the side, mouth agape, drool dangling from his lower lip. I gasp when I see the walker, like those used by decrepit oldsters, next to the recliner.

"Oh, he's asleep," Henrietta whispers. "He does that a lot nowadays. But it's okay. The nurse who visits says he needs his rest. I know he made that coffee for you. Why don't you get a cup for yourself and wait for him to wake up? He don't sleep more than fifteen minutes at a time during the day."

With that, Henrietta waddles from the apartment and softly closes the door. I tiptoe to the kitchenette to find a cream-colored mug on the counter next to a coffee maker. I pour a cup of black brew, but even its rich scent can't distract me from the guilt bubbling through my chest. Joe is crippled, and it's my fault.

Being here while he's asleep makes me feel like I'm snooping. The recliner sits in the middle third of the space. Next to the recliner is a small side table with the television controller and a glass of water resting on a coaster. A reasonably sized flatscreen TV is in front of the recliner along the wall near the entrance. On the far third of the room is a twin-size bed, made so nicely the sheets might be starched. The kitchenette is all-white countertops gleaming as bright as over-whitened teeth. My lips tug upward in a small smile. It isn't much, but I can't help feeling my friend is doing well for himself all things considered.

I take a slurp of coffee, the liquid hot and ambrosial on my tongue. "Wow," I murmur, nearly choking on the fluid. I had expected the brew to be decent, but not this earthy excellence. A bit of the black gold goes down the wrong pipe. I make disgusting hacking sounds, struggling not to spew coffee everywhere. Setting the mug on the counter, I lean over the sink, mitigating the chance I'll spray droplets of coffee all over the pearly countertop.

A half groan, half snore comes from the living area. "Allison, is that you, girl?"

"It's me, Joe," I splutter between heaves that make my chest ache.

"You, okay? You need help?"

I hear genuine concern in his voice and feel terrible. I might be coughing up a lung, but I'm not the one who took three bullets to the chest and uses a walker. When I was shot, the gunman only managed to graze me. Don't get me wrong, being shot sucks, but my preternatural healing made the wound a nonevent in the long run. Far more traumatic was killing my assailant with a single, devastating punch. The event still haunts me to this day, both during waking and sleeping hours.

I straighten and clear my throat. Confident dark fluid won't erupt from my mouth, I turn to my friend. "Some coffee went down the wrong pipe, that's all."

"My coffee so bad it makes you choke, huh?" Joe says, expression wistful. "I knew I should've gone to that joint you like…" He wags a finger in the air. "The Obsidian Roast. I would have, but…" He waves a hand at the walker, and his gaze drops to the floor.

"No, no, no, Joe." I pick up the mug and take a long swig. "The coffee is wonderful. I'm shocked how good it is."

Joe looks up, lips perking upward. "Honest?"

"You know I don't lie about coffee. Can I get you a cup?"

Joe beams. "Wowee. You had me worried there with all that hacking. I studied how to brew a good cup with my machine there. Even had Henrietta buy me some dark roast, the boldest available, from the grocery. You meet Henrietta yet? You can bring me a cup. They're in the cabinet over the kitchen sink."

I retrieve a mug from the cabinet and set it on the counter. "I've met her. She escorted me up here."

"She's been helping out around the shelter and with the cooking. Helping me out too."

I fill the mug with steaming black brew and pick up both mugs. I bring one to Joe, who takes it gratefully.

"There's a folding chair in the closet if you want it," Joe says. "Sorry about being a poor host."

"No worries. I can sit on the floor." I lower myself to the hard floor and sit cross-legged.

Joe yawns. "Sorry…sorry, guess I better drink some of this." Joe takes a long drag of coffee. "Yikes! Hot stuff. You sure it's to your liking? The coffee."

"Joe, it's the best coffee I've had all week."

Joe nods and sighs. "How's life? I haven't seen you since…well, since I was shot."

"I would have come sooner, but the agent who runs my security detail is a real hard-ass," I say and fill Joe in on the joys of remote school and having magicians up in my business all day.

"Don't sound like a cakewalk." Joe blows gently across the steaming coffee, then takes a sip.

I shrug, feeling bad about complaining. My problems don't seem all that horrible compared to Joe's. I can walk. "Remote school isn't my…cup of coffee."

Joe utters something between a laugh and a snort. "Ouch." His free hand goes to his chest. He sets down the cup on the side table, wincing.

"Are you okay?" I scramble to my feet.

He waves me off, but I remain on my toes just in case. Seeing him in pain brings the guilt simmering inside me to a boil. Maybe I shouldn't have come. I'm a monster, a cancer, a curse. Joe is better off without me in his life.

"I'm all right. Just laughing gets my insides hurting."

I sit by inches, worried I might have to go to his aid at any second. "Sorry. I didn't mean to make you laugh."

"What?" Joe picks up the mug from the side table. "Don't you worry about that. Laughter is still the best medicine, period. Don't let anyone tell you otherwise." He takes a chug of coffee. "Now, I want to hear all about what happened to you and your friends after I was…" He grimaces. "Taken out of action."

"It's no secret. My adventures are all over the news and Internet." I take a swig of coffee to calm my nerves. Inside me, the sleeper uncoils like a serpent considering whether to strike.

Joe sets the mug on the side table and lowers the recliner, grimacing as he does. He takes a deep breath and leans forward, placing his elbows on his knees and interlocking his fingers. His hands hang down below his knees. "Thing is, I want to know what really happened. The unvarnished truth. Unless it's too painful to talk about. If it is, just say the word. I won't press you."

My expression curdles, and I set the half-full coffee cup on the floor.

"Don't say a word. It's too painful. That's okay."

"No." I shake my head. I owe him the truth. "I'll tell you."

"You're sure? I'm not one to force someone to speak on something when they aren't ready."

"It's okay. If it gets to be too much, I'll stop," I say.

Joe nods, and I tell my story, trying my damnedest not to relive it. I start with how Gore spirited Dalia and me to Singapore on a private jet. Inside the deepest depths of my being, the sleeper rumbles its displeasure at the mere mention of Gore. I explain how he used a combination of drugs and powerful magic fueled by faery blood to contain me.

Joe's eyes go wide. "Did you just say faery blood?"

I nod, retrieving the mug from the floor and taking a sip to relieve my dry throat. Unfortunately, the coffee is lukewarm.

"So you're telling me there are faeries in addition to dragons, skaags, and magicians running around? I watched the reports about faeries on TV, but hearing you say it makes them real."

I finish off the coffee and place the mug on the floor. "Yeah. I was shocked to learn faeries exist. Or still exist. Dr. Radcliffe told me they were extinct centuries ago."

"Jesus Christ. What's next?" Joe says and makes the sign of the cross. "Excuse my language. I suppose you'll explain how faery blood… how did you put it? Fuels magic."

I nod.

"Do continue this fascinating tale."

I transition to telling about my time as a prisoner in a converted World War II bunker on Golden Shoal, one of Singapore's outlying islands. The official story diverts quite a bit from reality, so Joe appears properly surprised to learn about the torture my squad and I faced at the hands of a mad scientist and a presumably ex-US intelligence agent. I try to gloss over Jett, a sinister faery boy who almost successfully seduced me with magic, because I feel all fluttery when I think about him, and my inner skaag rears, lightning arcing over its body, ready to lash out in fear and loathing.

The space between Joe's eyes crinkles, and his fingers unlace. His hands form big fists with prominent knuckles. "Did that Jett do anything to you?"

I glance at the floor and hope I'm not blushing. Simultaneously, I tamp down the sleeper, rippling beneath the surface. "No. Maybe." Joe grunts like a bull moose ready to charge. I look up. His expression is thunderous. "We never got past second base." At least, as far as I remember.

Joe unclenches his hands. "Well, I'm glad for that."

To the best of my ability, with my limited understanding of magic, I explain how the faeries use their blood to supercharge human magicians. They captured me to decipher my superhuman abilities, especially my body's enhanced healing capability. They believe, however speciously, that combining a subset of my abilities with the enhanced magical aptitude of their super magicians will equate to an army capable of taking on dragons and skaags. I finish the yarn with how Gore, Jett, and my mother helped Dalia, Haji, and me escape. I purposely leave out us helping Bria escape, Haji's ongoing troubles, and the fact I'll probably be subpoenaed to appear before the Senate. Joe doesn't need to get tangled up in my current problems.

"So Haji does possess magic?" Joe asks.

"Yeah."

Joe shakes his head. "Seems like this magic is more trouble than it's worth, heroin or no heroin."

Heroin makes human magicians feel the magic. "Definitely."

"Is Dalia okay after all that? Are you?"

I raise my eyebrows and shrug. "As well as can be expected, I guess."

Joe leans back in his chair and whistles. "Boy, I thought I had it bad being shot and worrying about losing my job. But it's nothing compared to what you kids have gone through."

"Lose your job? Joe, what are you talking about?"

He waves at the walker. "I can get around some, but my recovery is slow. I can't stay on my feet long enough to do the cooking." He shakes his head. "Forget I said anything about it. Don't worry. I'll be fine."

But that's a lie. If he loses his job, he'll be back on the street. I breathe in sharply as inspiration strikes. My lower lip finds its way between my teeth. I might know how to help him, but I don't like the idea, and I don't think he will either.

Joe's oversized digital wristwatch beeps stridently. "Dang! It's time for me to get to my walking already?"

I set the mug down and face the living area. Joe is struggling to stand, both hands on the walker, which squeals under his weight.

"Do you need help?" I ask.

"Thank you kindly, but no. I need to learn to do this myself." With a moan, Joe heaves himself out of the chair. His pained grimace is enough to make me wince. "Now, I need a sec, then it's time to walk the hallway. Were you asking me something?"

"Oh, it's not important," I say. "Can I get the door for you?"

Joe shakes his head. "I need to do it myself, girl.

Don't you worry, I've done it before."

But the grim line of his lips and eyes narrowed in concentration, forming canyon-like crow's feet, tell a harrowing tale. He shuffles more than walks to the door, hunched over heavily on the walker. I never recall having seen him so weak. Unbidden tears form in my eyes, and I almost turn away but don't. It's my fault he's like this. My fault.

Back inside the apartment, I help Joe to his chair and retrieve a glass of water from the kitchenette. He thanks me for the water, takes a long drink, then leans his head back in the chair, closing his eyes.

"Thank you for that," Joe says softly. "I need to push myself if I plan to get around without that damn walker." Joe opens his eyes to slits. "You know, the doctors say I might never walk without a good deal of pain, walker or no walker. I have a medicine cabinet full of drugs in the bathroom. Prescription-strength painkillers." He shakes his head. "I won't take them. I won't."

I nod, biting down on my lower lip. "Joe, what if there is a way I can get you walking and pain-free? Like real fast."

Joe's eyes open wide, and he stares at me. "I'd listen to you, but I'd think you were selling me snake oil or something…" He shrugs. "You know…something that I'd think was the equivalent of snake oil not too long ago."

"Magic," I say.

"Bingo."

"Magic might be able to help you. On Golden Shoal, there was this doctor, Dr. Kihl. He was a medical doctor and magician. He—"

"Nice guy, is he? Trustworthy and all that? This Dr. Kihl," Joe scoffs.

Flustered, I sputter. "No. No, not at all, but that doesn't mean he wasn't right about magic enhancing medical science." I point at my eyes. "He claimed magic imbues my prosthetics, and I don't think he was wrong."

"Sounds like a shortcut. None of the shortcuts I've ever taken in life ended well for me."

"Joe—"

"I'm so fearful I'll lose my job." Straining, Joe sits up in the chair. His gaze bores into me. Anger and desperation overflow his apertures. "I can't end up back on the streets." He hooks a thumb toward the walker. "Not when I'm like this. I'll be eaten alive. Either by my good old friend alcohol or maybe those prescription drugs in my medicine cabinet or…" He snorts. "Maybe one of those dudes who come here for a square meal and a cot will shiv me for shorting them on the beans or looking at them cross-eyed or denying them a bed for a night."

I cock my head to the side. "So you'll consider…"

Joe nods. "I'm not saying I'll say yes to magic or no, but if it can help me, I'll consider it."

****

Valentina comes for me in the evening after I've helped serve beans and clean up after the meal. I follow her outside into the blustery wind and sleeting rain. The magician puts up an umbrella but doesn't offer me cover. I take snarky pleasure in her dismay at a gust mussing her hair and nearly turning the umbrella inside out. In the distance, lights glow from inside towering skyscrapers, dark spires against darker clouds. At the curb before the shelter waits Agent Haskell inside the sedan.

Valentina starts down the stairs, but I don't move to follow. She stops on a step and faces me. "Hurry up. This weather is terrible."

I grind my teeth. Her voice is exceptionally shrill to be heard over the wind's howls.

"I have a question," I nearly shout.

"Can't it wait until we're inside the car?" Valentina waves toward the sedan.

I shake my head. "Haskell doesn't need to know." The last thing I want is this request to get back to Agent McAllister. Valentina still might tattle on me, but she doesn't have to. Haskell would feel it is his duty to report on me to his boss.

Frowning, Valentina nods.

"Can you help Joe? His wounds. Can you heal them? Take away his pain? Help him walk again?" I ask. I despise the pleading whine in my voice.

"You couldn't ask me this in the car?" Valentina rolls her eyes. "Human magic doesn't work that way. I know they were doing weird stuff on Golden Shoal. Okay? I know that, but that's far-out magic, and nobody understands it yet. Not even Dr. Radcliffe. I'm sorry. Even if I wanted to, there's nothing I can do for him."

Valentina strides to the car, heels splashing in small rivulets on the steps. Soaking and with drooping lips, I follow her, wishing nothing more than to liquefy and follow the rain down the storm drain.

Chapter 6

After the torturous car ride, arriving home is a relief even though I find the security detail, nearly as impassive as Grecian statues, waiting for me. Dad doesn't appear to be around, so I check the garage and see the hybrid is missing. He must be working late, which I decide is a good thing. If he were around, I would undoubtedly ask him if he could help Joe. His response would likely push me to say words that would make living with him even more uncomfortable than it already is.

My stomach roars like a famished dragon, so I raid the refrigerator for a package of chicken sausages. I heat my meal in the microwave and pour myself a glass of orange juice. As soon as the microwave dings, I grab my food and head upstairs to my room. The entire time I feel monitored by the semi-anonymous security agent stationed by the base of the stairs. I stop dead on the first step and stare at the woman, my heart palpitating. In my mind's eye, the maniacal funhouse grin of Ms. Bergman, the hulking woman who had used Dalia and me as punching bags on Golden Shoal, encompasses my entire field of vision. I grip the glass of orange juice so tightly my hand begins to shake. The sleeper erupts from its stupor, gushing adrenaline through my veins with the energy potential of moon rocket fuel.

"Can I help you, Allison?"

I blink, the image of my tormentor fading and my true surroundings return to focus. The voice doesn't belong to Ms. Bergman. The agent next to me isn't that vile woman. I let out a long breath. My prosthetics zoom in on the prominent nose of the agent's otherwise nondescript countenance. The protuberance is mushed to the left like it had been broken and not properly set, just like Bergman's.

I blink until my prosthetics zoom out like camera lenses. "Your nose?"

"Oh, that." The agent smiles self-consciously. "It was a softball accident in college. A wild pitch hit me right on the nose."

I retreat to my room, and I scarf the sausages without tasting them. The orange juice possesses all the flavor of heavily filtered water. The plate and glass join the leaning tower of dirty dishes behind my laptop on the study desk.

I have schoolwork to attend to, but instead, I snatch my camera off the table. I hit the play button that brings up an image on the LCD on the back of the device. Using my thumb on the touchscreen, I flip through the photos of Haji's decimated house while doing 360s on my study chair. I don't know what I'm looking for other than a clue as to what happened, obviously. I'm just not sure what. After inspecting each photo at least twice, I set the camera on the desk.

Flipping open my laptop, I use the Internet browser to navigate to my email. A quick perusal of the inbox shows no response from Mauve to my message regarding Haji. I suppose I shouldn't be surprised. What could she say that wouldn't out her as a dragon?

A lot, actually.

I hope he's okay.

Is there anything I can do to help?

Are you okay?

How are his parents doing?

I massage my forehead with the fingers of my right hand. All those responses, of course, are human. Mauve is a dragon. She's my friend, and she's been masquerading as a human for who knows how many decades—centuries maybe—but she's still a dragon with divided loyalties, at best. When push comes to shove, can I expect her to choose me over loyalty to her people? To her leader?

My gaze migrates to the well-worn cover of Homer's *The Odyssey*. Grimacing, I pick up the epic poem. I have over fifty pages to read by tomorrow a.m. I toss the book onto my bed and turn back to my laptop. In the Internet browser, I search for the US Senate website. I use the website's internal search to find the Homeland Security Committee's page. Quickly, I locate a listing of upcoming hearings. Dr. Jane Woolworth is listed to appear before the committee on Monday in a closed-door hearing.

I screenshot the hearing schedule. I open the messaging app and paste the schedule into a message to Dalia. Below the image I type *—check this out—*. I move the pointer over the send button and hesitate. Should I send the message, or will it draw the eyes of my government minders? Honestly, who cares. I'm allowed to browse the Internet. I hit send.

I spend five minutes or more staring at the screen, waiting for a response from Dalia. Often her replies are instantaneous. I glance at the time in the top right-hand corner of the computer screen, 8:11 p.m. That's way too early for her to be in bed. Stifling a yawn, I close the computer and snatch my phone off the tabletop.

Surrendering to a jaw-straining yawn, I slink from the chair to the bed, knowing I better get my reading done before my eyelids are too heavy to keep open. After adjusting my kitty cat stuffy to act as a back rest, I open the epic poem to read up on Odysseus's time as a captive of the nymph Calypso. Seven years is a long time to spend as a prisoner. I can't imagine being held that long in the stinking underground cell on Golden Shoal. Just thinking about how much that room stank makes my nose twitch.

An insistent dinging followed by soft buzzes drags me out of slumberland. My eyes flitter open to my bedroom, brightly lit by the overhead light in the center of the ceiling. *The Odyssey* lies on my chest, my hand still resting on the book's spine. To my right, on the edge of the bed, is the flip phone dinging and buzzing. Moaning in disgruntled sleepiness, I pick up the diabolical device and flip it open. My gaze flicks to the time on the tiny screen, 10:32 p.m. Not late by my standards, but not early either. I do, however, feel like I was ripped from a deep and satisfying sleep. I press the button for messages, discovering ten new texts from Dalia. I read the first five, but in my stupefied state, all I manage to take in is that she has made the varsity track team.

I hit reply on the last message and chicken peck out a response. *—Congrats on making varsity. Going to sleep. Will talk tomorrow.—*

My eyes droop closed as soon as I shut the phone. I feel like I've only been out for seconds when a dull roar startles me awake. When I open my eyes, I know I'm dreaming because there is no way I'm floating in the eerie yellowish glow of the slipstream, the highway between dimensions. Yet I am. I start hyperventilating, and my heart beats so hard it feels like it's climbing up my throat and will explode from my mouth in a red torrent of viscera.

My hair stirs in an unfelt wind. The yellowish cylinder I float inside possesses the diameter to allow a semi to pass through it. Far in the distance, perhaps at the cylinder's terminus, is blackness as complete as a black hole's mouth. Beyond the slipstream's cylindrical walls is a darkness as vast and indecipherable as time itself. Yet somehow, that void is not as complete or dreadful as the gaping mouth at the slipstream's end.

Wake up.

Wake up now.

Inside me, the sleeper thrashes, and I know it's too late.

Wake up, I scream, but despite forming the words, no sound emanates from my mouth.

Come to me.

The voice echoes through my brain, rendering it to jelly and detonating my free will.

Come to me.

The words resonate through my bones to the sleeper, who responds in an instant longer than a lifetime. Exquisite pain ensnares my very being as an origami master rearranges my organs. My bones split asunder. Muscles and connective tissue stretch and rip, then knit together. The torment crescendos until the pain is so great I will die. The heartbeat before I surrender to the endless sleep, the skaag bursts free.

I wake up thrashing, nearly hyperventilating. The

scream rising up my throat dies stillborn. Instead of staring at the abysmal blackness and listening to the booming voice calling me, a bright overhead light makes my head hurt, forcing me to blink, and from outside comes the rumble of vehicles racing along on the main drag.

Taking a deep breath, I gaze around the bedroom as my prosthetics adjust to the brightness. Am I awake or still locked in a dream? Is there any difference when my life is an unbroken nightmare? Clean and dirty clothes litter the bedroom floor. My camera, my lifeline to sanity, sits on the study desk next to my laptop. I sniff the air, detecting my body odor, which, luckily, I'm inured to despite my hypersensitive nose.

My skin is slick with sweat, and the bedsheets are drenched. Pressed against the wall is *The Odyssey*, the cover torn and moist. Sighing, I roll my eyes. I'll probably have to pay to replace the book.

My phone, which I remember having next to me in bed, is conspicuously missing. I lean my head over the side of the bed and find the device on the floor, resting atop wrinkled denim. I pick it up and set it on the bedside table, my gaze lingering on the alarm clock as I do. Bold red numbers read 4:35 a.m.

Groaning, I throw my head back against the kitty cat stuffy—my head throbs. I don't want to be awake, but I don't want to face the haunting dream either. From the hallway comes the creak of a door opening, followed by soft footfall. After a moment of consideration, I realize the noise is Dad preparing for his morning run. An activity I have explicit permission from Agent-in-charge McCallister to participate in as long as I don't leave the protection detail in the dust.

Valentina claims human magic can't help Joe, but she's not an archmagus. Of course, regardless of his ability to help or not, I'm sure Dad will refuse to do anything. He's too concerned about Dr. Radcliffe uncovering his powers if he does any "big magic." Still, this is too good an opportunity to waste. I know from experience the agents will give us a bit of leeway to get ahead of them. That will be the perfect time to have a little chat.

Chapter 7

I roll out of bed, feet pounding onto the floor. My ample supply of running gear from before The Incident when I used to run cross country is folded with military precision in an icky plastic drawer in the closet. I quickly dress in dark leggings, a participant T-shirt from a local race I had run several years ago, and a white windbreaker with yellow reflective racing stripes. For good measure, I free all the running gear from the drawer, tossing the garments onto the floor to join their brethren. I kick the drawer shut and slam the closet door.

In the hallway, a Draconic Task Force agent guards my bedroom door. The sound of movement comes from the entryway downstairs. I'm about to dash for the stairs when the agent stops me.

"Where are you going at this hour?" he demands.

Letting out a loud sigh, I round on the agent. "Running. With my father. It's one of my few pre-approved activities outside of the house."

The agent harrumphs. "Don't leave your escort behind. I don't want to be out looking for you in this weather."

I roll my eyes and dart for the stairs, shouting, "Daddy, wait up!"

****

Our feet patter against the wet sidewalk, splattering

droplets. A cold drizzle falls from the dark sky, dampening down everything. My hair is a matted mess against my scalp. If only I had thought to bring a hat or a jacket with a hood. With every exhale, my breath steams from my mouth like smoke from a dragon's maw.

Next to me, Dad sets a swift pace and seems unperturbed by the dour weather. From the pounding of their sneakers against the sidewalk and huffing breaths, I know the security detail trails roughly twenty feet behind us like a pack of incompetent wolves on the hunt. Still, I wait until we hang a right onto the main arterial with its ample traffic noise before speaking.

"I need your help," I say.

"With a math problem?" Dad asks, voice strained due to exertion.

"No, a magic problem."

Dad looks behind us and stumbles, windmilling his arms. I almost grab him, but he regains his balance on his own.

"Pay attention to what's in front of you. I'll know if the agents are within earshot."

"Of course, you have your mother's hearing. I told you I don't dare work magic. If Dr. Radcliffe learns I'm the last archmagus, I'm a dead man."

He must be exaggerating. I know he's been working magic underneath the dragon's nose without being detected. "Are you going to hear me out or not?"

"Of course. I'll help any way I can. It's just…you know the dragons will kill me slowly if they learn what I am."

Ahead of us, a crosswalk signal turns red. We stop at the intersection and fall silent as the security detail catches up to us. Vehicles speed by, sending up road spray and spewing stinking exhaust, making my oversensitive nose twitch. When the light changes, we're off like jackrabbits, quickly outpacing the agents.

"Joe needs help," I say. "I thought maybe you could do something for him. You know, like you did something to my prosthetics. You did something to them, right? Something magical? That's why I can see dragons riding the slipstream."

Dad laughs. "You finally decided to bring that up. Your prosthetics restoring your sight is purely the work of Dr. Woolworth. The most important aspect of your treatment was the nanobot therapy that halted and reversed the nerve damage caused by neuropathy. I had absolutely nothing to do with that. However, over the years, I worked with her on the software components of your prosthetics, I had access to her lab, including the prosthetics' hardware components. I admit, I imbued the components with magic. I hoped the devices would reveal the dragons riding the slipstream to me. I—"

"Wait! Reveal the dragons to you? You honestly intended to blind yourself?" Having been blinded, I can't imagine doing it to myself. It's horrible. I'm grateful to have the prosthetics, but I'd much rather have never been blinded in the first place. Then I'd never have known about dragons and skaags and had my life turned into a living nightmare. Not that it's been all bad. I've met Mauve and Jett…I shake my head. Any positive or lustful feelings I have about the faery boy are due to his magical manipulations. They aren't real. They aren't!

"I did. I never got around to planning what I would do to blind myself, but I'd make it seem like an accident. You see, your mother had tracked down Radcliffe, but his associates remained a mystery. She wanted to use him to find the other rebels. He was always cautious, but we knew he was staying in contact with them somehow. I hoped, using the prosthetics, I could follow Radcliffe to one of the many conferences he attended on medieval history. We always suspected he had contact with his kind at the conferences. I planned to identify the dragons at the conferences, so your mother could eliminate them one by one. With all the rebels dead, Mark Cassidy would no longer have any use for your mother. He would release her from service, and we could live together without his interference. I grant you it was wishful thinking. He would've never freed your mother. She's too powerful and proficient a killer for that."

"You used magic on the prosthetics. You used magic and weren't detected," I say. "You could be helping Haji. You can help Joe."

"I imbued your prosthetics with magic over the course of years. I was very careful to mask my spells to prevent detection."

We stop at another light. An urban assault vehicle with oversized tires roars through the intersection to beat the light. Its knobby tires splash through a mud puddle sending up a dirty spray. I leap backward a good five feet to avoid the muck. But Dad ends up with his bare legs and shorts covered in brownish liquid. He glances at me and shrugs, a half smile tugging at the corner of his lips. Then the light changes, and we're off again, setting a fast pace to stay ahead of the security detail.

"Joe's not recovering from his wounds," I say. "He

can barely walk. He's going to lose his job and end up back on the street. Can't you do something magical to help him heal? Just a little magic the dragons won't detect?"

"I sympathize. I really do, but there is nothing I can do."

"You can't, or you won't?"

In my peripheral vision, Dad is straining to keep pace. I throttle down.

"Magic…human magic, even mine, can't heal your friend."

My shoulders sag. "That's what Valentina said."

"I suggest you request the dragons help Joe. Their blood is potent and, in conjunction with their magic, might help him recover."

As Dad says this, I clench my jaw so tight my teeth hurt. When I speak, my jaw muscles ache. "I had been hoping to avoid asking them for help."

After all, Dr. Radcliffe's assistance always comes with a hefty price tag. I fear the amount will be too high for either Joe or me to pay.

Chapter 8

After the disappointing run with Dad, the school day plods like a donkey cart mired in mud. I have lectures to watch, materials to read, and assignments to finish, but each time I start listening to a pre-recorded lecture on my laptop, my mind wanders to what Dad said: "Ask the dragons for help." Soon, I'm not interpreting a single word droning from the device's speakers.

I know what kind of aid the dragons would offer. Help at a price, and even then, no help at all. Haji and Bria are being "helped" by the dragons. What has that got them? Tickets to a lockup hidden away somewhere in the vastness of Joint Base Lewis-McCord under the tender care of Tanis, the very dragon who freed the skaag inside me. I trust her less than I do Dr. Radcliffe, and he offered me up to Mark Cassidy, who intended to kill me, in exchange for the location of an interdimensional gateway.

What excuse did he give for offering me as a sacrifice? The greater good, Allison, the greater good. And to think, I saved that dragon from certain death at the fangs of Mark Cassidy when things went sideways. At least there is Mauve. I can trust her. Can't I?

"Stop obsessing," I murmur.

For a change of pace, I shut the laptop and switch to reading *The Odyssey*. Odysseus outwitted monsters;

maybe he can give me some pointers. My brain disengages before I read a single word. The text on the crinkled page swirls into a black vortex. The swirling stops and the blackness forms an oval of impenetrable darkness. Deep in the recesses of my bowels, the sleeper quavers, shrinking from the gluttonous mouth.

I want to close the book, run across the room, throw open the window, and cast the epic poem into the elements. But I can't. I'm drawn to the infinite nothingness like a fly to a Venus flytrap.

Come to me.

The words are simultaneously soundless and emanate from the oblong aperture, echoing in my mind. Cowering, the sleeper mewls. Intermingled with the beast's fear, I know its desire to plunge headlong into the opening.

Come.

The sleeper uncoils, obedience supplanting trepidation.

"No." I want to sound firm and decisive, but all I manage is a labored gasp.

Obey. It is your purpose.

The words sink into me like a fishhook. I lean, no, I'm pulled, toward the gateway to nothingness, until the voracious orifice encompasses my unblinking vision.

I'm closer, closer, until my nose is ready to pierce the cyclopean eye. The sleeper surges within me, yearning to burst forth.

Ding.

The strident sound cuts the line to the fishhook. My nose presses into the puckered, moldering pages.

Ding.

The sleeper recoils in confusion. I blink, thrusting

the book an arm's length away. The gateway is gone, leaving behind dactylic hexameter.

Ding.

Taking a deep breath, I lower the book and tear my gaze away from it. The laptop and ancient flip phone both emit another alert. I drop the book to the desk and snatch the phone. I flip open the device as I stand and begin pacing the room.

—A US marshal just served me. I was called to the office in the middle of English Lit and there she was at the front desk! OMG, so embarrassing. Glad she didn't barge into my class. I have to be in DC by Monday—

—WHAT?—

I don't think I've ever banged out a text faster on the archaic device. I mean, we expected to be subpoenaed but still.

—Homeland Security Subcommittee of the US Senate. I take it you haven't been subpoenaed yet.—

"Holy cow," I murmur, then type out:*—Homeland Security Subcommittee?!?!?!—*

—You'd think we're terrorists.—

I can totally see Dalia's eye-roll.

—That's crazy.—

There's a soft knock at my door. I glance up from the screen in annoyance. "What?"

My phone pings and vibrates in my hand.

Valentina's shrill voice. "Allison—"

"I'm busy," I bite out, turning my attention back to the phone screen. I read the text: *—Do I really have to go to DC? I don't want to testify.—*

—I don't know.—

—Can you ask? Like Dr. Radcliffe?—

The door creaks. I spin in my chair until I face the

entrance to see Valentina poking her head in. "Hello? Privacy? Can't you see I'm busy?"

Valentina does an exaggerated eye roll that puts Dalia's to shame. "You need to come with me."

I spin the chair until I face the table. "Whatever."

"This is serious, Allison," the agent says.

I pointedly ignore her. *—If I see him, I'll ask.—*

Valentina steps into my room, her overly flowery perfume preceding her. I look up from the phone, glaring at her. This room might be a prison, but it's mine. I wave a hand dismissively at the agent. "Get out of my room."

Standing her ground, Valentina places her hands on her hips. "Dr. Radcliffe is waiting for you outside."

I wince. Her voice is like a buzz saw.

After flexing stiff fingers, I peck out a text. *—I'm going to meet Dr. Radcliffe right now. Will update.—*

Dalia's response is nearly instantaneous. *—OMG! Serendipity.—* The words are followed by beaming smiley emojis.

****

The interior of the electric sedan is cozy warm, which is good because I'm soaked from a midday squall. Rain pings off the vehicle and sheets down the windscreen as the car rolls down the street toward the main drag with draconic body parts only I can see filling the vehicle's interior and overflowing onto the roadway like tens of thousands of twinkling Christmas tree lights. Valentina has the windshield wipers turned up to the max, but they can barely keep up with the deluge. Riding shotgun is a Draconic Task Force agent I don't recognize.

"Why so silent, Allison? Are you not curious why I

am here?"

Radcliffe sits next to me in the back. His humanoid form looks like a college professor turned politician in a blue three-piece suit reeking of starch. Affixed to the tie is an enameled golden dragon with green wings. It's a fairly accurate depiction of his draconic form when he emerges from the slipstream, if about a million times smaller. The sedan softly hums as it pulls out into traffic. Ahead of us is a sluggish anaconda of taillights that is part and parcel of driving in Seattle.

"You're here to tell me I should expect a subpoena from the US Senate." The skaag inside me thrashes and salivates. A dichotomy of fear and excitement pulses through it, through me. Skaags are dragon hunters, dragon slayers. That is the sleeper's calling, my purpose. The insatiable desire is impossible to ignore in a confined space this close to the draconic leader.

"Not exactly." Radcliffe gives me a smile that puts game show hosts to shame. "I knew Dalia would likely inform you that she had been subpoenaed earlier today."

"Less than twenty minutes ago," I say with faux cheer. There's so much I want to ask him—about Haji, about Bria, but I know I can't trust anything he says. If I ask him how they're doing, he'll give me that cheesy game host smile and inform me they're great. If I ask him to help Joe, will I be dooming my friend to confinement on a military base like Haji and Bria? I squeeze my hands so tight my nails cut half-moons into my palms.

"What is wrong, Allison?" Dr. Radcliffe blinks, and his draconic head peers down at me through the car's roof. Green tubes droop from either side of the beast's snout like a mustache. "Are you worried about testifying? Do not be. That is why I have brought Taylor."

The young man in the front seat twists around until he faces me. He smiles and gives me a little wave. The wave is actually kind of cute. "Hi."

I quizzically stare at him and remain silent. Taylor's cheeks flush, and he shrinks in the seat as he faces forward. He might be gorgeous, but he's still a magician, and that's one thousand strikes against him in my book.

"No need to be rude, Allison," Radcliffe says, frowning. "Taylor is not a magician. Like I said, Tay, Allison is prejudiced against magicians."

"I can tell," Taylor replies.

"He is, however, a wizard of a personal assistant. He will help prep you and Dalia for the committee hearing." Radcliffe stares at me, the human and the dragon. "We would not want any information coming out that is better kept secret. Would we?"

"Better yet, why don't you intervene and keep us from having to testify at all," I say.

"And why would I do that?" Radcliffe frowns. "I want the humans as allies; therefore, I must treat them as equals. I must respect their rules. I will not intervene to prevent your testimony or Dalia's."

"You follow the rules when it's convenient for you," I say.

Radcliffe smiles. "Who knew we are so much alike?"

Sighing, I throw my head back against the headrest. So much for avoiding having to testify altogether. But then a sly thought enters my mind. My lips perk upward in not quite a smile. I can use Radcliffe's desire to keep Tanis and Mauve anonymous to my advantage. Of course, I'd never out Mauve, but the good doctor doesn't need to know that.

"You expect me to keep your secrets?" I shrug. "I might be able to do that."

Radcliffe's frown deepens, and his draconic head comes farther inside the cabin until its cat-like apertures stare into mine. It's disconcerting having that dragon head flash in and out of existence inches before my eyes. The draconic orbs are twin boring machines drilling into my skull to extract my every thought.

"What do you mean by that, Allison?" Dr. Radcliffe asks.

"Joe needs help recovering from the gunshot wounds. Can you help him?" Even as the words tumble out, I dread I'm going to regret striking this bargain.

"I help Joe in exchange for you keeping my secrets at the committee meeting?"

I nod. "Exactly. When I say help Joe, I don't mean lock him up on base somewhere. I mean, heal his injuries and let him go on living his life."

"As long as you prep for the committee's questions with Taylor and keep my secrets while testifying and behave like the perfect gentlewoman you are, I will do everything in my power to ensure Joe recovers from his injuries."

"It's a deal then."

Radcliffe gives me a smile that's a bit condescending. "It is a deal. Valentina, please take us back to Allison's abode. She has much preparation to do before Monday. By the way, Allison"—he raises an index finger—"your flight to DC is on Sunday morning. A US marshal will be delivering your summons within the hour. Try not to bite his head off, my dear."

Radcliffe chuckles at this last bit. I simply smile and nod. I'd never bite off the head of a US marshal, but I'd enjoy transforming into a skaag and attempting to bite off the doctor's draconic head.

Chapter 9

The pilot's voice comes over the loudspeakers. "We are approaching Reagan International. I'm turning on the fasten seatbelt sign. Please, stay seated with your seatbelt fastened for the remainder of the flight. Thank you."

"Finally," I murmur, fighting back a yawn. Despite having downed two sodas, I have a hard time keeping my eyes open. Dalia helpfully put in her earbuds and promptly fell asleep less than an hour after takeoff. Taylor…let's just say Taylor isn't much of a conversationalist unless you're a baseball fan, which I most definitely am not. I fought to stay awake, but still fell asleep several times only to wake up nearly gasping from nightmares of the voice calling to me in the slipstream.

"Dalia."

Agent Lopez's voice is as melodious as an out-of-tune piano. She stands in the aisle and shakes my friend by the shoulder.

Dalia groggily blinks and removes her earbuds. "What?"

"We need to switch seats."

"Switch seats?" my BFF says, slurring her words.

Valentina mouths the word magic, which wakes Dalia and puts me on edge. I have not been looking forward to the magician refreshing the spell keeping me incognito.

Valentina standing in the aisle draws the attention of a flight attendant, who tells her to sit down. Next thing I know, Dalia is in the row ahead of me next to Agent Haskell, and Valentina slides in beside me. I grip the armrests and my entire body goes stiff.

"Relax, or you'll destroy the seat," Valentina says.

"I don't find anything relaxing about your voice," I say through clenched teeth, but I loosen my grip on the armrests.

I'm sure she gives me a look that could kill, but I'm keeping my eyes focused one hundred percent on the seatback in front of me. Inside me, the sleeper darts back and forth like a caged animal. The skaag loathes magic being used on us as much as I.

Stay calm. She's trying to help us.

But the sleeper wants to lash out.

I want to strangle Valentina.

"I'm going to take your hand."

Her palm is warm against the back of my hand. Warm like Gore's was when he cast the magic that ensnared the sleeper. I don't know how many times the assassin used magic on me, but the first time I remember was on a plane. His hand was hot and glowed orange.

Valentina mumbles. Her words are lost in the rumble of the jet engines, but her voice is as grating as ever. Her hand heats up as she speaks until my skin burns. Inside me, the sleeper shrieks for blood and flesh to sate its hunger. I turn my prosthetics in their sockets until I see her hand in my peripheral vision. Her hand emits a soft lime-green glow that even I can barely see.

My gaze shifts to the magician's face. Her eyes are

scrunched up in concentration, and her lips move in a frenzy. I gasp. My hand is aflame. I try to draw it away, but Valentina tightens her grip. My insides coil, and the sleeper roars, sending tremors through my body. My free hand reaches across my chest of its own volition, fingers twisted like talons.

She's keeping me incognito. Otherwise, the reporters will mob me at the airport.

A hunger pang makes my stomach rumble and mouth salivate. I'm ready to wrench my hand out of Valentina's grip and do something unspeakable to her.

"Allison."

My clawed hand drops to my lap, fingers uncurling. I face Taylor, who sits beside me in the window seat, smiling. He taps his finger pads together.

"Dr. Radcliffe told me you like soccer. Did you watch any of the playoff games?"

I take a deep breath. My hand is roasting, but I'm able to relax. My insides unwind with the sleeper. Taylor is as much a threat as a smashed snail. "I saw a few games," I lie because I want Taylor to keep talking. Dad tried to convince me to watch the postseason action with him, but I was too angry after learning he's an archmagus.

Taylor's grin broadens. "Did you see the game last night? It was a doozy."

The inferno burning my hand to a crisp reaches a fever pitch, and I wince, squirming. "I missed that one. Tell me about it."

"I didn't watch it either. But I saw the highlights. There was this goal." Taylor fishes out his phone from a pocket. "You have to see it!"

He continues blathering away as he searches up the

highlight reel. I focus on him, on his innocuousness, while doing my damnedest to ignore Valentina and the fire spreading up my arm.

****

It's nighttime on the East Coast when the plane lands, and we deplane at Reagan International. As we lug our carry-on baggage through the wide hallways—our only luggage since we're in DC for two nights—the spell Valentina refreshed allows me to glide past frustrated news crews stationed strategically around the airport to watch arriving passengers. They're definitely looking for me. More than once, I chomp down my lower lip after hearing a camera operator or reporter call out my name, but each time they're calling to someone else who they have misidentified.

We follow Agent Haskell to the arrival pick-up area, where a large black van waits for us. The air is cool, on the verge of being cold, and drizzle moistens everything. All in all, not that different from Seattle. We pile into the back of the van. The agents sit in the row behind the driver. Haskell speaks softly to the driver and the agent riding shotgun. Valentina stares out the window, apparently too tired to utter a word, thankfully.

That leaves Dalia, Taylor, and me in the back as the van zips along the 395 across the Potomac. Taylor points out the landmarks along the way: the Jefferson Memorial, the Lincoln Memorial, and the Smithsonian, all lit up by floodlights. I try not to be impressed, but I am.

"Do you think we'll have time to catch some of the sites?" Dalia asks.

"I hope so. I want to photograph them," I say.

****

The Hotel Europa is a quaint multicolored building nestled on a tree-lined street on Capitol Hill. We check in inside the small lobby and are given our keys. I carry my luggage and Dalia's to the room we share on the third floor. The agents have rooms on either side of us, and Taylor is in the room right across the hallway.

Our room is small and clean. I place my suitcase by the bed next to the rain-speckled window and flop down on the mattress. Dalia sprawls on the other bed, which squeaks under her weight.

Dalia yawns. "Can you believe we have to testify tomorrow? I can't wrap my head around it."

"Don't remind me." I reach for the controller on the table between the beds that operates the thirty-inch flatscreen affixed to the wall across from us.

"What do they expect to learn from me? I mean, you're the special one. I'm just…just along for the ride. You know?"

I look at my BFF with a raised eyebrow and a smirk. Light from the bedside lamp makes her nose ring twinkle. "Along for the ride? Says the girl who tore me from the slipstream. Seriously?"

Dalia rolls her eyes. "You know what I mean."

"Really, I don't." I turn on the TV.

The local news comes up. The reporter, a man with an intense gaze and square jaw, stares into the camera. I recognize the hallway he's inside from Reagan International Airport. "That's right. Still no sign of Allison Lee. There is one more flight from Seattle that's running a bit late. It's due to arrive at 8:45 p.m. If she's on that flight, I'll be sure to get a statement from her."

"God." I switch the channel.

"Just along for the ride," Dalia says.

"You don't have to rub it in my face," I say, flipping channels. "I better turn this off." Sighing, I turn off the TV. "The news will drive me nuts and make it impossible to stay on good behavior. One misstep means Radcliffe won't help Joe."

Dalia listens sympathetically while I fill her in on the deal I struck with Radcliffe to help Joe recover from his wounds. I finish up the story when there is a soft knock against the door.

More knocking, this time insistent.

"It's probably Taylor." Dalia bounces out of bed and heads for the door. "Last-minute prep for tomorrow."

Dalia and I sit cross-legged on the edge of my bed, and Taylor takes the one chair in the small room to the TV's right. He holds a tablet in his left hand, which he uses his right index finger to manipulate. For the second time, he shows us pictures of each committee member and offers insight into the questions they might ask. He also provides us with a rundown on what questions not to answer.

"What do we say when they ask something we shouldn't answer?" Dalia looks between Taylor and me.

"Just tell them you won't answer the question," Taylor says. "Don't lie. Don't prevaricate. Say something like, I won't answer that question. That's all you have to do."

"Are we going to be under oath?" I ask.

"No, Dr. Radcliffe fought hard to ensure you won't be put under oath. Plus, you're minors, so grilling you is already a bad look for the committee. Politically it looks better for them to wear kid gloves."

"So we could lie," I say. Taylor looks askance. "Hypothetically."

He shakes his head. "Don't do that. Assume they know the answer to any question they ask."

I nod. "Okay. Sure. Double checking, that's all."

Taylor sets the tablet on the table underneath the TV. "I think that's all for tonight. Do you both feel confident about tomorrow?"

I shrug, and in between chewing on her thumb, Dalia says, "I guess."

Taylor leans forward and runs a hand through his hair. The floral scent of shampoo wafts from his head. His hair is thick and wavy, and gold highlights sparkle in the brown when the light hits it right.

"Listen," he says, "you're both going to do great."

"Really?" Dalia asks.

"Yeah. In fact—" Taylor pulls a deck of cards out from his pants back pocket. "—all you need to do now is relax. Either of you know any magic tricks? I can show you some."

Taylor puts on a magic show. He's quite good. Even with my prosthetics zoomed in on his hands, it's difficult to track his sleights. Regardless, he's quite a performer, his awkwardness fading with each trick. An hour later, it's nearly eleven o'clock, and Taylor bows out, reminding us that we need to get a good night's sleep to be on our game tomorrow.

Taylor pauses as he heads for the door. "Oh." He turns back to us. "Valentina asked me to remind you that there are enchantments on this room and the entire hotel. If either of you tries to leave the premises without her, all the Draconic Task Force Agents in DC and Dr. Radcliffe will know."

I glower at him.

He raises his hands overhead. “I’m just the messenger.”

“Control freaks,” Dalia murmurs after Taylor leaves.

“Tell me about it.”

It takes us twenty minutes at least to get ready for bed and turn out the lights. Sleep doesn’t find me, though. Instead, I stare at the off-white ceiling that might as well be lit by the noonday sun due to my prosthetics’ light-gathering capability, listening to Dalia’s deep breathing. My insides whirl in time with the sleeper’s restless movements. I dread facing the committee tomorrow almost as much as I do sleep.

I slink out of bed despite feeling zonked as soon as the digital clock on the table below the TV displays six a.m. I didn’t sleep a wink after being tormented by a nightmare. That voice. Who is it? What is it? I don’t have a clue. Dr. Radcliffe might know, but I don’t dare say a word about it to him. It’s more than not trusting him is my baseline. I’m afraid if I say something out of the ordinary about anything, he’ll refuse to help Joe for one reason or another. I can envision him telling me he’ll help Joe as soon as my nightmares are sorted out. Only the nightmares will never be sorted out.

I unzip my small suitcase millimeter by millimeter so I don’t wake Dalia. I strip off my T-shirt that’s still damp from my sweat and catch a whiff of my BO that’s nearly enough to make my eyes water. Scrunching up my nose and dropping the shirt to the floor, I gaze toward the bathroom. A shower would hit the spot, but then my prosthetics focus on Dalia in peaceful slumber. My BFF is so beautiful and innocent I don’t dare do anything to disturb her. I'll suffer my stench for an hour or two and shower after she's up.

After carefully setting aside my clothing for the hearing, I pull on black jeans and a T-shirt emblazoned with our pale blue dot and the slogan Only One Planet. As I slip on my sneakers, my gaze rests on the power suit I agreed to wear at the committee meeting, and I frown. I'm going to be dressed exactly like my mother. *Eww.*

I pad quietly from the room, careful to be as silent as a mouse while opening and shutting the door. As I had hoped, I find freshly brewed coffee in a giant thermos in the quaint dining area next to the lobby. I grab a periwinkle mug and press the plunger on the carafe. Black brew waterfalls into the mug, steaming and smelling delectable. The fresh fruit, organic yogurt, and croissants on a side table look appetizing but won't satisfy my half-skaag hunger. I head to one of the small square tables with beautiful cut flowers in small vases at their centers, surrounded by four chairs. I face purposely away from the television in a corner near the ceiling, tuned to a 24-hour news channel. Thankfully, the volume is so low I can ignore the reporters if I concentrate.

I take a sip of the brew and nearly spit it out. Awful. Grimacing, I gulp down the coffee. Bad or not, I need to drink a pot of the stuff to keep my eyelids propped open. I set the empty mug on the table and stare at the handful of coffee grounds adhering to the cup's interior. Stifling a yawn, I grab the cup and lurch back to the side table for a refill. From the lobby comes the ding of the elevator and people chatting about grabbing food before heading out. I traipse back to my table and morosely sip the hot, brown water.

I need to get a handle on the nightmares plaguing me, or I'll never get a good night's sleep. Superhuman or not, I still need my shut-eye.

Do you know why I'm having these dreams? I ask the sleeper.

The response from the half-skaag is an ambivalent mixture of fear and longing that doesn't tell me anything useful.

"Can I join you?"

I look up at Taylor, standing next to the chair across the table from me. He holds a mug with steam rising off it, and a plate piled high with fruit. Despite the early hour, he is dressed for success.

"Sure…ummm…be my guest." I set down the mug, blinking. People queue at the side table for food, and nearly half the tables are taken by patrons in quiet conversation or stuffing croissants in their mouths. How in the world did Taylor walk into the dining room without me realizing it? I knew someone approached my table, but I didn't know it was Taylor. How is that possible? I can detect the distinct chemical odor of his hair product quite clearly despite the coffee, food, body odor, and perfumes permeating the air.

Taylor sets down his food and sits across from me. "Is something bothering you?"

"I didn't sleep well, and the coffee is horrible."

"Ahhh, butterflies in your stomach. Don't worry. That's not unusual for someone who has to testify. You'll do great. Too bad about the coffee. I was looking forward to it." Taylor spears a melon slice with a small fork. He chews, then swallows. "Hey, do you want to go over the questions you might be asked or—"

He sets down the fork and reaches dramatically into his sports jacket pocket and pulls out a thick deck of black cards held together by a worn rubber band. "—would you rather play this?" He spins the deck in his hands so I can see the logo on the back of the cards. "You know how to play, right?"

His antics bring a genuine smile to my face. "Of course, I know how to play."

"Alrighty then." Taylor removes the rubber band and shuffles the cards with a dealer's expertise.

I nod in approval. Anything. Anything that distracts me from stewing on my nightmares is worthwhile.

Later in the morning, Taylor takes us around to the DC sites under the watchful eyes of Valentina and Haskell. The Washington Monument, Lincoln Memorial, and other monuments to our collective history are impressive. I take dozens of photographs, most featuring Dalia posing in front of a landmark, but my enthusiasm is dampened by the dreary weather.

Chapter 10

Dahlia and I sit at a polished rectangular table before a raised crescent table with seating for the fourteen senators who will soon be grilling us. I chew on my lower lip as I try to take in everything. The seating area is already full of reporters and other onlookers. Dr. Radcliffe sitting in the back row, surrounded by reporters fighting for his attention, draws my gaze. Radcliffe, the man, speaks with the reporters, seemingly unaware of my presence, but the semitransparent golden dragon, flickering in and out of existence, and encompassing nearly the entire committee chamber, stares at me with unblinking eyes. I give the beast the barest of nods, and it returns the gesture before winking out of existence, only to reappear heartbeats later.

I sit at the midpoint of the table's length, which means all the senators will be able to stare down at me like I'm a fascinating bacterium on a microscope slide. On the table before me are a name plaque, microphone, and plastic water bottle.

I frown at the water bottle. "Pacific trash vortex."

Dalia is to my right, shifting in her chair as if finding a comfortable position is an impossibility. Oddly, there isn't a chair, microphone, or bottled water to my left, but there is a name plaque.

The room is warm in the unfortunate power suit I

agreed to wear. Making matters worse, the jacket includes shoulder pads. Shoulder pads! Didn't those go out of style decades before I was born? The suit is forest green, which is my favorite color and only reason I agreed to wear it, but now, I wish I had refused. I'm dressed exactly like my mother, and I feel rivulets of sweat running down the sides of my forehead and my armpits are swamps. My stench permeates the air around me, an odor of unease overwhelming the deodorant I applied after a shower. Apparently, I'm not as inured to my stink as I thought.

I'm tempted to crack open the bottled water. But it's only a mild temptation. I'd rather dehydrate myself to the point of desiccation than add to the plastic detritus overwhelming the planet.

I pick up the placard in front of me and flip it around. White letters against a black background spell my name: Ms. Allison Lee. Ms.? Why can't I be Allison, the girl who flies below the radar most of the time?

"What are you doing?" Dalia gnaws on the tip of her left thumb while eyeing the room like she expects the FBI to burst out of the wood paneling and arrest us for disturbing the nameplate. "Taylor said we should sit quietly and relax."

I shrug, catching a whiff of my skanky BO. I seriously hope my BFF doesn't smell me. "Chill. I'm investigating."

"What can you possibly be investigating?" Dalia rolls her eyes.

I set the name plaque on the table. Standing, I reach for the plaque to my left. The metal is cold against my fingers as I pick it up and flip it so I can read the name. I swear my heart skips a beat and the coldness at my fingertips spreads through my entire body like quicksilver. Spelled out in white letters is the name: Mr. Haji Patel.

"Do you see this?" I hold the placard, so Dalia has a view of the name. "No one said anything about Haji being here."

Dalia scrunches her eyes. "He's here? In DC?"

A growl rumbles in my chest. The sleeper ripples inside me in response to my consternation. "He'll fall apart if he's berated by the senators."

"Maybe…maybe he's improved." Dalia's voice drops to a whisper. "Maybe Tanis was able to help him."

Snorting, I flash my friend a look oozing "Oh, really." I turn to glare at Dr. Radcliffe's dragon form. His draconic head peers down on the proceedings from the ceiling. I dramatically wave the plaque to get his attention, then point to the name on it. The dragon's head fades to nothingness but doesn't rematerialize. Apparently, his head has withdrawn through the ceiling. The other dragon body parts continue flickering around the chamber.

Dr. Radcliffe stands and breaks away from the reporters surrounding him in the back of the public seating area. He strides purposefully toward me, weaving between people in conversation and responding tersely to questions from the press. I drop into the chair to wait for the former professor's arrival, wondering if I'll suffer a lecture or his excuses. I squint, a draconic foreleg enveloping me. Golden glitter falls around me, fading like ephemera only to reappear, as he closes in.

Radcliffe fixes me with a condescending smile and takes the placard from my hand, placing it on the table. "Haji is a late and unexpected addition."

"Seriously? You expect me to believe you didn't know he'd be here?"

"I found out this morning, and he is not here. At least, in a physical sense."

"What do you mean?"

"I mean, he will testify remotely. Ah, here comes the teleconference equipment now." Radcliffe points to the back of the chamber.

I twist in the chair until I glimpse a cart being guided through the crowd by two porters. Atop the cart is a wide flatscreen monitor.

"So he's still on base. A prisoner." I glower at Radcliffe.

He places his hands on the table and leans over until our eyes are even. In a whisper, he says, "He is on base under the expert care of Tanis and medical doctors. That, however, is a fact neither the committee nor I want exposed. Is that understood?"

"Why shouldn't the world know our government keeps children as prisoners," Dalia whispers. Her gaze blazes with righteousness. "Not just Haji either. What about Bria?"

I face forward, lean back in my chair, and cross my arms before my chest. I smirk at Radcliffe. Behind rimless spectacles he doesn't need, his eyes are as dark as thunderheads. His lips downturn in a severe frown, accentuating the wrinkles around his mouth. His draconic head looms overhead and green tubes on either side of his snout dangle. His humanoid gaze drops, and he smacks the table with an open hand.

I draw my head back a few inches, and inside me, the sleeper stirs. “Temper. Temper.”

Dr. Radcliffe looks up. His frown is replaced with a grin showing off blindingly white teeth. His glimmering draconic head lowers on a long sinuous neck until it’s superimposed upon his humanoid face. The dragon’s eyes, shimmering gold with black oval slits for pupils, narrow ominously. Within me, the half-skaag quivers with the desire to emerge and feed. The purple blood of dragons is the most delectable ichor of all.

He ate the last skaag he fought, I remind the sleeper and myself. The skaag’s hiss of displeasure slices through my gray matter, and before I realize I’m doing it, I run my tongue over my upper lip.

“You will both be on your best behavior,” he whispers. “Joe’s recovery depends upon it.”

Smirk turning into a grim line, I swallow a lump in my throat. My gaze flicks to Dalia. She stares at me wide-eyed and nods.

If I do anything, Joe will suffer the consequences, I snarl at the sleeper and say to the dragon, “Best behavior. I promise.”

Dr. Radcliffe straightens and looks at each of us in turn. “Good. Glad to hear it.” His draconic apertures remain locked on me even after disappearing and reappearing. “Here we go. The video conferencing equipment will be set up in a minute.” The porters maneuver the cart up to the table in front of the placard displaying Haji’s name. “I best find a seat.”

Radcliffe meanders away, pausing to rest a hand on Dalia’s shoulder, causing her to shudder. His dragon form smiles at me, flashing curved teeth as long and sharp as scimitars, before blinking from existence.

I shift in the chair, the sleeper lashing about, desiring nothing more than to emerge and meet the threat with lightning and fury. *Dr. Radcliffe isn't an enemy. Not really.*

The sleeper doesn't buy what I'm selling. I'm not sure I believe myself.

When the translucent dragon reappears, the sinuous neck extends into the ceiling, and the head is out of sight. The half-skaag sulks, still ravenous and angry but no longer threatening to burst forth from my insides.

"Allison, look." Dalia is standing and leaning over the table. She points to the left.

I look to where she points and glimpse Haji on the flatscreen. I lean forward in my seat until I can see him clearly. He's sitting at a table in a dark suit jacket, including a red tie over a white button-down shirt. A small American flag pin is affixed to the tie. The clothes seem too big for him by several sizes. His haunted eyes are sunken, and his cheeks are hollowed out like he's on the verge of death from starvation. Even his wavy, dark hair has lost its usual sheen.

I stand, reaching for him, then drop my hand. "Haji. Haji, are you okay?"

He turns toward the sound of my voice, movements halting like he is in pain or drugged or both. Goosebumps rise on the back of my neck. He might be under the influence of magic. I suspect he can't see me, so I start sidling to my left when the senators enter the chamber from a doorway behind the crescent table.

Chapter 11

The senators march in led by a tall Black woman dressed in purple with graying hair. She must be Senator Williams, the committee's chairwoman. Indeed, she sits in the middle of the crescent table behind the name plaque stating Sen. Williams. As she sits, she meets my gaze and smiles reassuringly. Just as Taylor claimed, she possesses the air of being genuinely kind-hearted. On her right, sits a stout man with a ruddy complexion. His small eyes glare at me from above a bulbous nose with prominent pores. Senator Offenbach is well-known for his aggressive questioning and pugnacious personality. Taylor warned us he has made statements to the media indicating he plans to come out punching.

I glance at Dalia, who chews the tip of her thumb and drums her knees together. Her gaze is locked on Offenbach.

"Dalia," I whisper, "relax. It will be okay." I hope. With his red face and beer barrel build, Offenbach looks like a powder keg ready to detonate at any provocation.

Still chewing on her thumb, my friend looks at me.

"Your thumb—" I mime removing my thumb from my mouth. "You're chewing on it."

Dalia's cheeks flush as her hand darts away from her mouth. "Thanks."

The last senator to take her seat farthest to the right of Senator Williams looks gorgeous in a black and white dress. Her long dark hair frames her heart-shaped face to perfection, and her big brown eyes are full of warmth, seriousness, and a bit of mirth all at once. Before I even bother reading her nameplate, I know two things: if I ever wear a dress, I want to look as elegant and powerful as her, and she is Senator Mamani, who, according to Taylor, will be sympathetic toward our plight, perhaps even an ally.

Senator Williams calls the meeting to order. "We have recently learned we face new threats. Faeries, creatures once only thought to exist in children's tales, walk the earth. Their agenda is unknown, but we have disturbing evidence faeries are not friendly toward humans. In fact, as you will hear in testimony today, these creatures have imprisoned humans, including children, to experiment on."

Shaking my head, I grimace. The senator sounds so self-righteous when she's, in reality, a hypocrite. The faeries aren't the only ones who have imprisoned Haji and me. I'm held under house arrest, at least on paper. Haji is locked away on base, and so is Bria. I wouldn't put it past Tanis and military scientists to be experimenting on Bria as I sit listening to this garbage. Even Dalia isn't allowed outside her house without being followed by a bodyguard.

"Most disturbing and frightening of all, we have learned some humans are capable of magic. I'm not talking about the magic tricks performed at a child's birthday. No." The senator shakes her head. When she continues speaking, her voice rises an octave. "I'm talking about something destructive, even sinister. I'm talking about the magic you only read about in fantasy books or see on the big screen as CGI-generated special effects. Some humans possess magic of enormous destructive potential and fuel their magical ability with heroin, a Schedule I substance under the Controlled Substances Act." Senator Williams looks up from her prepared remarks. She looks around the room and says gravely, "I think we can all agree people on heroin are not in their right mind and need help. What they don't need, and what society does not need, is for them to have access to power that can blow up a single-family dwelling with…with—" She waves a hand overhead. "—a wave of a hand and of the utterance of a few words."

"That's not how magic works."

Haji's voice cracks as he speaks, but his words carry. By the senator's bemused expression, she's as surprised by Haji's outburst as I am. Dalia and I exchange a brief look. I raise an eyebrow, and she shrugs. The senators possess a smorgasbord of expressions. Several, all men, look annoyed. Others run the gamut of bored to intrigued, except for Senator Offenbach. He sits up, leans forward, places his elbows on the table, and interlaces his fingers. His lips twitch upward in a smile like he's impressed Haji has the gumption to interrupt Senator Williams. It's his eyes though, that draw my attention. They possess the unblinking intensity of a predator patiently waiting for the optimal moment to strike.

"Mr. Patel, you will have an opportunity to speak. For now, I ask you to remain silent for the remainder of my opening remarks," Senator Williams says.

"But that's not how magic works." Haji's voice is

insistent.

"Mr. Patel, do I need to have you muted for your own good?"

I lean forward to get a view of Haji. His eyes are as wide as shot glasses.

"No, Senator. I apologize."

The senator drones on in the same vein. Regretting the quantity of coffee I had drunk this morning, I squirm in the chair, even crossing my legs. A recess can't come soon enough.

"Senator Offenbach will have five minutes to ask questions." Williams glances at her colleague. "Senator Offenbach, please proceed."

Offenbach puffs himself up like a banty rooster. "Thank you, Madam Chairwoman. I also thank you for the opening remarks." His voice is low and gravelly. "Your words capture many of my and my constituents' concerns regarding recent events. I am particularly concerned about human magicians and their use of drugs. Mr. Patel, you are a magician, are you not?"

"Yes, Senator." Once again, Haji's voice cracks as he speaks.

"Have you ever used heroin?"

Haji hesitates before answering. "Y-yes."

"And were you aware at the time it is a controlled substance?" Offenbach leans forward and folds his forearms on the table before him. His eyes narrow, becoming nearly lost in folds of skin. "An illegal drug?"

"I knew heroin is an illegal drug when I took it," Haji says in a tone that is all self-recrimination.

"Knowing this, why did you use heroin?" Offenbach growls, flashing teeth. I'd like to show him my half-skaag teeth.

"To feel the magic."

"And what does that mean? For all of us who have never felt magic with or without illicit drug use." Offenbach's expression is somewhere between a smirk and a sneer.

"It's hard to explain. It's something…something you have to experience to understand."

"Well, try your best to explain it to us anyway." Offenbach's words drip condescension.

Offenbach's decapitated body falls forward onto the table, spraying arterial blood. His head rolls across the floor like an errant basketball. I blink, and the vision is gone, but my mouth still waters.

Stop that! I silently scream at the sleeper.

Dr. Radcliffe's draconic head descends from the ceiling to hover above the committee. The green tubes drooping from his snout sway to and fro, passing straight through Senator Offenbach and Senator Williams. His judgmental gaze rests on me, waiting for me to step out of line, to misbehave. I won't. I'll stay in control for Joe.

"We're waiting, Mr. Patel," Offenbach says.

"Without heroin, it's difficult to feel the magic inside you. While under the influence of the drug, you can feel the magic coursing through your veins. You can see it—a faint glow. It's the most beautiful thing I've ever seen." The fervor in Haji's voice is frightening. I have never even heard him talk about sports with such fanaticism.

"There is time for one more question," Senator Williams interjects.

"Sounds addictive," Offenbach remarks. "Is there

any other substance that allows you to feel the magic course through your veins?"

"Yes, faery blood." The yearning in my friend's voice is palpable.

A collective gasp comes from the audience, and even the senators appear perturbed by the admission. Offenbach smirks. I hate him for how he exposed my friend to a national audience as an addict desperate for magic. I know what it's like to be seen as an abomination. Now, they will see Haji as a dangerous addict capable of wielding power beyond his control and their understanding.

Offenbach bounces in his chair, his eyes briefly going wide and his lips parting into a menacing smile. The sleeper recognizes a fellow predator enticed by the scent of blood. The beast coils, ready to test its mettle against any comer and yearning to sate its insatiable hunger for raw, bloody flesh.

Offenbach's jaw works, and he raises a hand, pointing accusingly at Haji. Dr. Radcliffe's dragon form watches the senator with an inquiring gaze. A purple forked tongue shoots from the dragon's mouth, like a lizard tasting the air, passing straight through the senator's body before fading to oblivion. Seconds later, the beast flickers back into existence, still appraising the senator. From the audience of reporters and other onlookers comes excited conversation regarding the connection between human magicians and faeries.

"Order. Order!" Senator Williams cries in a stern schoolmarm voice. She glares around the chamber as quiet slowly descends in fits and starts. "I will have order, or I will be forced to clear the chamber of all visitors." She waits for several beats; the only distracting sound a human can detect is a hoarse cough. "Thank you. Up next, Senator Branson—"

"Madame Chairwoman, if I may ask one more question of Mr. Patel?" Offenbach queries, although his tone indicates the sentence is not a question. He seems oblivious to Senator Williams's annoyed glower.

"No, you may not," the chairwoman says. "Senator Branson, you have five minutes for questions."

Offenbach goes purple in the face but remains silent, slouching in his chair. Senator Branson, a tall man with a square jaw, takes up the questioning. One after another, the senators probe the connection between human magic and faery blood, albeit in a gentler manner than Offenbach. Eventually, the questioning turns more generally to our time on Golden Shoal. A few questions go to Haji, and I hope to finally gain some insight into his experiences on the island. But his answers are vague, often trailing off into silence, or he claims to have no knowledge of what is asked. Soon, Dalia and I are responding to queries. The questions quickly become penetrating with a focus on Dr. Rah and Dr. Kihl, and their treatment of me. It seems the committee doesn't want to explore the role of the ex-government spook, Felicia Bergman, at all.

Dr. Radcliffe watches me intently as I answer question after question regarding the two maniacal doctors. With every answer, images of Dr. Rah with a bone saw held millimeters above my chest flash in my mind's eye. By the time it's Senator Mamani's turn to question me, sweat streams down my face; I hold the armrests of the chair so tightly I might crush the wood in my grip, and it feels like the sleeper is causing an electrical storm in my abdomen.

Mamani smiles at me, and I am reminded she, at least, takes pity on our plight. "Ms. Lee, I'd like to know about Jett. Specifically, explain to me how you determined he is a faery."

I'm thrown by the question and take a moment to collect my thoughts. Until now, the questioning has focused on the medical doctors' interest in my half-skaag physiology and the torture Dalia suffered while captive. I had hoped to avoid discussing Jett and resurfacing my ambivalent emotions for him.

"Jett was in the holding cell with us. We thought he was a prisoner, but that was just—"

"Ms. Lee, I understand he pretended to be a prisoner. How did you determine he was a faery?"

Mamani sits straight backed, and her expression is as imperious as her tone. So much for kid gloves.

"I saw faery dust floating around him." I give a brief description of the dust. "He used magic to mask it, but eventually, I saw through the illusion."

"And how is it you saw through the illusion? Is it your physiology? Or your prosthetic eyes?"

The senator's words ring in my ears so reminiscent are they to the demands of Dr. Rah and Ms. Bergman. The air around Mamani shimmers as if with heat. What is going on? I scrunch my eyes shut, and when I open them my jaw goes unhinged. In Senator Mamani's place sits Dr. Rah, a rictus grin contorting her face. She holds a bone saw in her right hand, and blood oozes from a gash on her neck. My pulse goes supersonic, and I swear my abdomen bulges as the half-skaag battles me for supremacy.

No. No! I can't transform. She's not here.

Dr. Radcliffe's draconic head shoots toward me,

stopping inches from my face. His green tubular mustache sways back and forth. The beast looks between me and Dr. Rah, who fires up the bone saw, the blade whirling with blinding speed, then abruptly turns it off. Radcliffe touches the tip of his chin with a long talon. The dragon fades into the void and reappears seconds later with the talon still resting against his chin. His reaction dispels any lingering doubt that I'm hallucinating. If magic was somehow involved with my vision, Radcliffe would detect it.

She's not real. She's…she's a hallucination!

I blink, and the mad scientist is gone, revealing Mamani in her place. The sleeper is held in check for now, but I'm afraid the next time the beast tries to spring forth, I won't be able to hold it back. Dr. Radcliffe's draconic head returns to its place behind the committee, but his gaze bores into me like he can strip away my flesh and see directly into my soul.

"Can you repeat the question?" I ask.

Mamani huffs. "How did you see through Jett's illusion? Your physiology? Or your prosthetic eyes?"

"I'm not sure," I say.

Dr. Radcliffe's draconic eyes narrow, and I realize my waffling answer wasn't the best. I'm nearly caught off guard by my urge to release my bladder. I cross my legs so tight my groin muscles hurt.

Mamani pounces. "You're not sure? Dr. Woolworth was explicit that she has no idea why you can see dragons or anything else otherworldly. Please elaborate on what you're not sure about."

Part of me wants to out my dad as an archmagus on national TV. It would serve him right for all his years of lies. "I prefer not to speculate, Senator."

I think my response would make Taylor proud. Mamani becomes increasingly self-righteous as she continues questioning me, but I ride out the storm. Soon, her five minutes are up, and Senator Williams dismisses us after profusely thanking us.

Dalia and I head to the exit under the watchful gazes of the senators and the media. A staffer turns off the flatscreen displaying Haji. I make a beeline for the nearest restroom.

"Allison," Dalia calls.

"I can't talk right now," I say.

Chapter 12

I sit up against the pillows in the hotel room bed, trying to read *The Odyssey*. I can't get over how Odysseus's trials are mirrored by those facing Haji and Bria. They're held captive on a modern-day Ogygia by a sorceress as wily as Calypso. Without help, they may well be prisoners for seven years or longer.

From the bathroom comes the sounds of the shower and fan. I open my mouth, about to speak loudly to Dalia but think better of it. She won't be able to hear without me yelling, and if we're going to plan to break Haji and Bria out of a lockup on a military base, we need to be secretive. Haskell, Valentina, and Taylor are all nearby, and any one of them will turn us in if they even catch a whiff of what I'm considering.

I redouble my efforts to plow through the verse and am proud I've made it through eight pages by the time Dalia turns off the shower. I've read four more pages when she strolls out of the bathroom wearing pink and white plaid pajamas, still toweling off her damp neon-pink hair. Whether or not I'll retain anything I've read is strictly TBD. Bookmarking the page, I toss the paperback onto the bedside table. It skids across the smooth surface until it bumps into the table lamp.

"Engaging read?" Dalia asks.

I roll my eyes. "I've read worse." I turn in bed so I'm facing her. We haven't had a chance to talk in private about the committee hearing, having spent the remainder of the day after the congressional interrogation in the presence of Taylor and Dr. Radcliffe. I whisper, “Did you get a good look at Haji?”

Dalia’s lips form a grim line, and she sighs. “One sec.”

Dalia scampers back to the bathroom and returns without the towel. She hops onto the bed; the springs creak under her weight. I’m about to speak, but she holds a finger to her lips for silence. She grabs the television controller from the bedside table and turns on the TV. After flipping through the channels to a professional basketball game, she turns up the volume almost to the max. She sets the controller on the table and leans toward me.

“Just in case,” she whispers and points to her ear.

“Big brain idea.” In case Valentina or Dr. Radcliffe are using magic to listen in, or Haskell has bugged the room, the drone of the fan and the roar of the basketball game will hopefully mask our conversation. Emphasis on hopefully because I wouldn’t put it past any of them to be able to filter out the ambient noise. “Did you get a good look at Haji?”

Dalia grimaces. “He looked haggard.”

I nod. “Like he hasn’t slept in days or eaten in weeks.”

“Keep your voice down,” Dalia says so faintly even I have a hard time hearing her.

“Sorry,” I whisper through clenched teeth.

Dalia dismisses my apology with a wave of her hand. “What’s the plan?”

I smile. It’s good to know we’re already on the same page. “We need to rescue Haji and Bria. I haven’t worked out how. The base is huge. They could be held anywhere. Plus, we can't do anything until Dr. Radcliffe helps Joe."

Dalia looks thoughtful and gnaws on the tip of her thumb.

"You're doing it again. Your thumb."

Dalia lowers her thumb, flashing an embarrassed smile, then her expression turns serious. "You're right. We need to do something, but maybe we don't need to break them out."

"What do you have in mind?"

"I was thinking in the shower about how the senators and Dr. Radcliffe want to keep it hush-hush that Haji is held on base. What if we expose that? Put it out in the media: a child and teen are held on a military base against their will. They'll have to release Haji and maybe even Bria."

I take a deep breath, frowning. Her idea has merits. Basically, it doesn't involve me doing anything drastic, which is a big plus. If I want to go on living in civil society, I can't be a monster who attacks military bases, no matter how justified I am.

"It's worth a try," Dalia says, her tone wheedling.

"I don't know. Maybe the media spotlight will pressure them to release Haji, but Bria…she's a faery, and the hearing today made faeries public enemy number one."

"That's true. They might not release her. But she's still a child, faery or not. I can't believe people will sit around and let a child be locked up on a military base and experimented on."

"What about the children they threw in the cages along the US-Mexico border a few years ago?"

Dalia throws up her hands and shakes her head. "Maybe I'm being naïve. But if more people know what's going on, we have a better chance of being able to help Haji and Bria. What else are we going to do? Do you think Tanis will allow you to waltz in there and walk off with Haji and Bria? What if she tries to stop you? Are you willing to fight her? Will you go toe to toe with Dr. Radcliffe next? Are those fights you can win? What about Mauve? She's our friend. We can't put her in a position where she has to choose between us and Radcliffe. I'm willing to fight, believe me I am, but we should pick fights we are willing to have and know we can win."

I sigh. "You're right. We should exhaust every option before doing anything extreme."

Dalia leans over and puts an arm around my shoulder, squeezing. "Good."

"Does this mean Devin will be interviewing me again?" I ask.

"Maybe…sorry."

****

"Our political and national security analysts will break down Allison Lee's congressional testimony after the break," the newscaster says.

An ad for kitty litter featuring a cat that could pass as a small tiger flashes across the TV screen to a banal yet catchy jingle. Seems I can't escape the media spotlight even at home. I set my knife and fork on the dining room table next to the plate with half-eaten chicken sausages. Despite their savory smell, my appetite is quickly going the way of the dinosaurs. Even the cup of coffee that I brewed myself has lost its usual appeal. I'd like nothing more than to go back to bed and wake up several hours later—restart the day.

"Can you at least change the channel? I don't need to see a news story all about me," I say to Dad, who sits across from me, chowing down on his oatmeal.

"Oh, of course." Dad turns off the TV. "We didn't get a chance to talk about your time in DC last night. How was it?"

I roll my eyes. "How do you think?" I shrug. "The sites were nice, but I could've done without having to testify."

I pick up the mug and take a slug of coffee, wincing as the liquid burns my tongue. If I don't caffeinate, I won't be able to stay awake for school.

"I thought you and your friends did great. I watched the entire hearing," Dad says, setting the spoon in the bowl, picking up his coffee mug, and blowing across the fluid's surface. He takes a slurp of the brew. "Wow! This is superb coffee, Allison."

"Went well?" I set down my mug with a loud thump. "Did you see Haji?" I lean forward, placing my palms on either side of my table setting. "Did you get a good look at him?"

Dad gives me an ingratiating smile. "I was paying more attention to you, and most of the time the cameras were focused on you and Dalia. The cameras love her pink hair."

"You could help Haji. I know you can. You can help him, and you refuse to."

Dad sits up straight, sips coffee, and squares his shoulders. He sets the mug down next to the bowl of oatmeal. He whispers, "I've been thinking. Maybe I can help Haji."

My eyes are wide as my jaw unhinges. "You're

willing to help him?"

He raises his palms before him. "Maybe. I'd have to evaluate him. For that, I need access to him."

I stand up and pump a fist. This is good. We get Haji away from base, then Dad can help him overcome his withdrawal from the Juice. I pick up my coffee and take a long chug.

"Daddy, I'm so glad you reconsidered your position." I set the mug on the table. "I need to get ready for school."

"Don't get your hopes up. I might not be able to do anything for him. And as long as he is on base, there's nothing I can do."

I flash him a ten-gigawatt smile. "No worries. I have a feeling everything is going to work out."

****

The morning progresses at a sloth's pace, punctuated by hunger pangs and my eyes drooping from lack of caffeine. I refuse to leave the bedroom for food or coffee because I don't want to face Valentina or any other smirking magician. I count myself lucky I haven't drunk so much coffee I have to pee every hour.

As lunchtime approaches, my hunger pangs tie my entire torso into a tangled ball of power cords. I can't concentrate on the pre-calculus video playing on my laptop's screen. Instead, I weigh my hunger and urge to use the bathroom against facing the agents stationed around the house. I heard Valentina be relieved a half hour ago, so I won't have to risk a conversation with her. Still…

My phone tap-dances next to my laptop, disturbing my reverie. After pausing the video—I will have to rewatch it from the beginning anyway—I pick up the phone and flip it open.

"Huh." A text from Dr. Radcliffe. I can count the number of texts I received from him on one hand. He's more of a face-to-face kind of dragon.

—I have taken the liberty of contacting Joe. He has agreed to accept my help. I have arranged to have him undergo treatment on Wednesday. He has requested your presence. If you agree, I will arrange to have you taken to a secure location on Wednesday after school.—

"Oh, wow," I murmur in equal parts excitement and trepidation. I fat-finger my response twice before finally texting: *—YES!!!—*

I stand and slip the phone into my pants pocket, ready to face the day.

****

Rain drums against the metal roof, the beat echoing through the enormous, dilapidated warehouse. It's not a location that fills me with fond memories. Deep inside Seattle's industrial zone, the ramshackle structure is the same one Dr. Radcliffe and his draconic followers held Dalia, Haji, and me captive in after abducting us from Tahoma University's Chapel Library. This place is where Dr. Radcliffe and Tanis used magic to unleash my inner half-skaag. So yeah, I'm back in the place where my perfectly ordinary life, one where I wasn't a monster or the subject of the national news, was flushed down the toilet.

In roughly the center of the space, Joe lies on a wheeled stretcher beneath an LED bulb dangling from the ceiling by a long wire. His chest is bare, exposing the scars left by the bullets. I stand next to the stretcher with my hands on my hips, doing my best to glare at both Mauve's humanoid and draconic faces.

"Joe has to join the Draconic Task Force? That's bullshit! That was not part of the deal," I scream, spittle flying from my mouth. "Radcliffe promised if I behaved at the hearing, he'd help Joe. He never said anything about forcing him into indentured servitude."

"Servitude?" A puzzled half smile zips over Mauve's face. "I assure you he will be given the same compensation package as every other agent. I understand the salary is competitive."

"That's not the point! He's supposed to put this life"—I shake my head—"of dragons and magic and monsters behind him. Forcing him to join the Task Force is dragging him in deeper." And keeping him under Radcliffe's tooth and claw where the dragon can always use Joe's well-being to keep me in line.

"Ladies. Ladies," Joe calls from the stretcher. His voice is weak. "I'm right here."

We turn to my friend. With him supine before me, I realize how much Joe seems to have shriveled up since being shot. I can count the ribs beneath his dark skin. He was never a hefty man, but he was powerful, and all that physical strength is gone.

"Allison, I know you're all worried about me getting caught up in some nonsense involving these dragons. Hell, maybe even dying facing down a drug-crazed wizard in a back alley. That might happen. But it's worth the risk. Dr. Radcliffe is giving me back my health and a job with a purpose."

"But—" I say.

"There ain't no buts. Let's get this magic bit over with."

I clench my hands into fists at my sides. There's so

much I want to say. Instead, I keep my mouth shut and merely nod. Mauve motions for me to back away, and as soon as I do so, her dragon form stops flickering in and out of existence, becoming solid, substantial. Bolts of lightning arc through the warehouse as the lithe, coppery dragon emerges from the slipstream.

Mauve's golem goes still as a statue. The dragon carefully picks it up and moves it out of the way with a foreclaw. Then, she looms over Joe, mouth agape.

Sweat sheens on his face, and I smell the fear rolling off him in waves. Mauve's forked tongue lolls from her mouth, and she pierces it with a long ivory talon. Purple ichor wells up from the wound. The blood oozes down her tongue, finally dripping onto Joe's chest. With every drop, there is a sizzling sound, and Joe wails in agony. The scent of cooking meat follows. I close my eyes, fighting off the sleeper's hunger and attempting to ignore the sounds of Joe's thrashing.

****

Mauve and I stand outside in the rain underneath the umbrella I hold overhead. Her dragon form spreads out above, before, and behind us. It's dark out, and a brisk wind has joined the downpour, but not enough to turn the umbrella inside out. Joe is unconscious on the stretcher, being loaded into the back of an unmarked black van by a man and woman in blue scrubs.

"Will he recover?" I ask.

"From the blood magic?" Mauve shrugs. "Most likely yes, but there are no guarantees. He knew the risk. So did you."

"It was worse than I expected." Not all my experiences with draconic blood magic were quite that intense. The van doors slam shut, my friend locked inside. “Will I ever see him again?”

“Assuming he survives, I imagine that will be his decision…with input from Frederick, of course.”

I nod. It’s depressing to know that the best outcome for Joe is he’s part and parcel of Dr. Frederick Radcliffe’s machinations. “You’ll tell me though…if—” The words hurt as they come out. “If he doesn’t recover.”

“Yes.” Mauve wraps a warm arm around my shoulder and draws me in close. “I’ll tell you. I promise. Honestly, I think he will survive the blood magic. He will walk again without pain and be stronger than ever before.”

I lean my head against Mauve’s shoulder and sigh. “Either way, I need to know. I can’t be held in suspense forever.”

“I’ll inform you, Allison, even if Frederick orders me not to. Some things are not meant to be kept secret.”

The van pulls away with the roar of a V8 engine.

Tears form rivulets on my cheeks. “Thank you.”

Chapter 13

My computer dings and my phone vibrates across the table, announcing another text from Dalia. After making sure I save my essay on *The Odyssey*, I alt-tab to the messaging app. I know Hemingway said something about writing being the act of bleeding on paper. I'm not bleeding, but my brain has liquefied and is leaking out of my ears. Practically every time I consider a scene from Homer's epic, I'm either bored to near death or suffer a PTSD-ish flashback to my hellish misadventures.

I read through the text twice and click on an embedded URL. A webpage opens about the upcoming event. I lean back in my chair and stare at the ceiling. "That could work."

****

I find Agent Haskell stationed at the base of the stairs. It's easy enough to lure him into the dining room with the promise of conversation and the ambiguous need to show him something on my laptop. I don't know; maybe he thinks I need his help with my schoolwork. I wouldn't say no to him writing my essay for English lit.

"Habitat restoration?" Agent Haskell stares at me in puzzlement.

"Am I speaking in a foreign language? Yes, habitat restoration. As in removing invasive English ivy. Near

Magnuson Park," I say.

Haskell raises an eyebrow. "I didn't know you did that kind of stuff."

I blink and crinkle my nose. "You know I'm involved in the climate movement. I participated in CO2 Free Seattle, and I put in a request to McAllister nearly every week to attend some kind of climate event." I huff. "Not that he's ever signed off on anything."

"Well, those marches and whatnot are like parties at best or ways to mask criminal activity at worst. Habitat restoration sounds like actual work. I didn't think your generation was willing to do physical labor."

My eyes go wide. Haskell's face splits into one of his toothy grins. I take a deep breath, realizing that he's baiting me. "Oh, ha, ha." I glower at him. "Can you put in a good word with McAllister or not?"

"Sure." Haskell shrugs. "No guarantee he'll say yes, but I'll put the most positive spin possible on your request."

"Here are the deets." I set my laptop on the table so Haskell can view the webpage.

"Just a sec." Haskell pulls out a glasses case from the interior of his sports coat. He removes a pair of granny glasses that he perches on the tip of his nose. I can barely hold back my laughter as he peruses the webpage. He glances at me over his glasses. "I get a headache if I try to read without my glasses, okay?"

"I wasn't laughing. Can you help me out or not?"

"Sure. Email me the website." Haskell removes the glasses, placing them in the case and returning it to the jacket's pocket.

"Great! You're the best." I copy and paste the URL

into an email that I send to Haskell, then I shut my laptop and pick it up from the table.

"Hold up. You're not secretly planning something, are you? If you are, I don't want anything to do with it."

"What makes you say that?"

Haskell raises his voice in a poor imitation of me. "You're the best."

"Ever hear of sarcasm?"

Haskell narrows his eyes. "I know what you sound like when you're sarcastic. You're not being sarcastic. You're…overly pleased."

I meet Haskell's eyes and cross my toes. "I'm not planning anything. Seriously."

After staring at me for a minute, Haskell says, "Okay."

****

On Saturday, the Pacific Northwest brings a quad shot of gloom. Rain falls nearly horizontally, driven by a cold wind off the Salish Sea. I wouldn't volunteer to do habitat restoration in this weather under normal circumstances. Even bundled up in my warmest rain-resistant gear, I'm as miserable as a half-drowned cat. The only consolation is Valentina looks like a grumpy clown with her hair matted down and mascara running. She had tried fending off the rain with an umbrella, which the wind turned inside out and destroyed.

The agents watch Dalia and me remove English ivy from a steep slope from positions along a paved pathway near the water. In total, about twenty hardworking environmentalists are removing ivy. We're far enough away from the agents to have some privacy, assuming Agent Lopez isn't covertly using magic to listen in on us. Out on the choppy water, boats at anchor bob. Across the water, huge houses have commanding views of the landscape from a forested hillside.

"Devin should have been here an hour ago," I gripe as I use a lopper with bright red handles to cut vines enveloping the trunk of a Douglas fir.

Every time Dalia pulls the severed vines away from the tree, revealing the trunk, I know we're making a difference. A small difference, but a difference nonetheless.

Dalia sighs. "He'll be here. He's probably waiting for the rain to die down. You know he'll never miss out on a chance to score another interview with you."

"Interview." I snarl the word, snipping the vines while pretending they're Devin's fingers. "I'm giving an interview to a reporter from Channel 5. I don't need to give him an interview this time."

"Well, you know he'll spin this whole thing into an episode for his podcast," Dalia says.

We've nearly cleared the base of the poor tree of vines when the rain diminishes to a light sprinkle, and the blustery wind dies completely. Not five minutes later, Devin shows up decked out in waterproof gear from head to toe. Trailing behind him is assistant Keb in a bright yellow poncho, holding an umbrella over a willowy woman I've never seen before. I pause in my lopping as the newcomers scurry past my security detail and trudge up the slope.

"What's up?" Dalia follows my gaze. "Finally." She drops the vines clutched in her hands into the ample pile we've made near the tree. She waves to the trio downslope. "Over here!"

Devin points us out to his companions and waves. I

concentrate on the woman, who is taller than the males. My prosthetics zoom in on the logo embroidered on the right breast of her blue and black jacket. My shoulders tense, and I clench my jaw. I shift my gaze until I'm zoomed in on the reporter's face. My eyebrows rise involuntarily. Wow. Full lips, wide brown eyes, and a slightly elongated oval face make her striking. Her dark hair is covered by a hood, but I can tell it's fabulously thick and lustrous. There's an intensity about her demeanor that's simultaneously intimidating and attractive.

"The woman with them is wearing a Channel 5 news jacket." I blink until my vision zooms out to normal. "She's going to draw the security detail's attention."

"It's okay, Allison," Dalia says, squeezing my tight shoulder. "Look. They're not paying her any special attention."

"I guess so." I lean the loppers against the tree, and we take a break while waiting for the trio to ascend to our position.

Keb stumbles over the gnarly undergrowth. He throws out the arm holding the umbrella, wildly waving as if trying to find his balance. His other arm shoots out before him to break his fall. For a few heartbeats, his crash to the ground is inevitable, but then the reporter grasps his upper arm and pulls him upright.

Devin trundles upward, oblivious to the drama behind him, flashing an oily smile. "Hey, hey, hey! Allison." He offers me a hand, which I don't take. He drops his hand and says to Dalia with snarky sarcasm, "Your majesty. You know, seems like you'd give me a warmer reception considering I'm here to help you. I get it. You don't like me. But we can have a professional relationship."

He raises his hand again for a handshake, but I leave him hanging. His breath is a disgusting amalgamation of cheese puffs and energy drinks.

Dalia jumps between her ex and me. "Doing us a favor? We're doing you the favor! After Allison's first interview, you got a huge hit in subscribership and endorsements."

Keb approaches with the reporter by his side. "Whoa. Whoa. I thought we were supposed to be hush-hush and go about some environmental restoration work. And, Devin, she's right about your subscribership going nuclear after the last interview."

Devin shrugs, conceding the point.

I point to the Channel 5 emblem on the woman's coat. "Explain to me how that is incognito?"

Keb looks ready to speak, but the reporter beats him to it. "You must be Allison Lee. Nice job testifying to those uptight senators. I watched the whole thing online."

My hostility drains a little at the snark in her tone when she says "uptight senators."

"Unfortunately, this is the one rain jacket I have, and I wasn't going to come out in this weather without it. Contrary to what you might believe, cub reporters barely make enough to scrape by in this city."

"Okay, are we all groovy then?" Devin smacks his hands together, glancing around. He raises a finger. "Intros. Allison, Dalia, this is Bexley, and ditto. Let's get to work."

"You can call me Bibi," Bexley says.

We quickly settle into a rhythm of physical work

and conspiring. To my surprise, Devin works harder than anyone else and takes great pleasure in clearing the English ivy. Best of all, by the time we're done plotting, we have a plan that maybe, just maybe will free Haji and Bria from the clutches of the military and Tanis.

Chapter 14

I'm exhausted Sunday night as Dalia and I study for Monday morning's pre-calculus test. Despite Dalia's game effort, I'm not retaining anything.

"Maybe you should brew yourself a pot of coffee."

Dalia's voice piping from the laptop speakers startles me, and my eyes pop wide open.

"Did I nod off?" The words come out mushy.

"Ummm…yes."

I lean forward in my study chair and sigh. "I don't know if I can pull an all-nighter. I haven't been sleeping well."

Dalia's face pixelates on the screen before resolving into a mask of concern. "More dreams?"

"Yeah—"

"Maybe we should talk about your dreams."

I definitely do not want to talk about my dreams. "It's not the dreams…I don't know. Do you think we can trust Bexley? I mean…"

"I checked her out," Dalia says. "Despite being associated with my bottom feeder of an ex, she's legit. She's a total newbie. I think this is her first job as a journalist, and she's hungry for a big story. Keb says she's into social justice issues, being an immigrant and all."

"That's good to know. Anyone associated with Devin is sus in my book."

"Keb."

"Yeah, you're right. Keb is good people."

We study math for another hour before my inability to keep my eyes open gets the better of me and I go to bed.

****

"Transform, or I will dissect you to decipher how your physiology functions." Dr. Rah hefts a bone saw with a whirling blade as arterial blood sprays from her neck.

Red droplets shower me. I back away from the maniacal doctor, and she swings the saw, missing my chest by inches. Blood smears the white walls and forms an expanding pool at her feet. An enticing coppery aroma fills my nostrils, and my mouth waters. The soles of my zebra-striped sneakers splash down in the fluid as I spin and run full tilt away from the doctor as much to escape my hunger as the humming blade.

"You can't outrun yourself, Miss Lee!" Rah hollers after me. "You can't outrun Ms. Bergman either!"

Dr. Rah's cackling laughter pursues me down the hallway. This must be a dream. Rah wasn't half as talkative in real life, and I don't think I ever heard her laugh. I slow my sprint, but instead of coming to a graceful stop, I slide across the floor on blood-slickened shoe soles. Windmilling my arms doesn't keep my feet from flying out from under me, and I land on my butt with a bone-jarring thud.

"Ouch." Am I supposed to be able to feel pain in a dream?

Laughter still echoes through the hallway. I look back the way I came, glimpsing bloody footprints and red smears where I skated across the floor. God, the blood is enticing. I sniff the metallic scent, and my tongue runs over my upper lip.

"Stop." I hit the sides of my head with open palms. "Dr. Rah is dead. I watched her die. This is a dream. I can wake up."

I pinch myself hard on my left forearm. All I do is leave a purple gouge in my skin. Wincing, I massage my self-inflicted injury. So much for physical pain slaying nightmares.

Thump.

I glance down the hallway in the direction I came. No, not her.

Thump.

No way. I put my hand to the floor. I swear the surface vibrates.

Thump.

"There you are, Ms. Bergman. It took you long enough," Rah chortles.

"Need to follow the bloody footprints, do I, Dr. Rah?" Bergman's voice sounds tinny.

"You are the hunter, Ms. Bergman."

"Indeed, I am, Dr. Rah. Don't go anywhere. This won't take long."

Thump. Thump.

"Don't kill her, Ms. Bergman! It's ever so much more fun if they squirm while I cut open the chest cavity!"

"That depends entirely on how much Miss Lee resists."

Thump. Thump. Thump.

Fight or run. Fight or run. I call the sleeper. Nothing.

Thumpthumpthumpthumpthumpthumpthump.

I scramble to my feet. "Of all the times to ghost me."

Thumpthumpthumpthumpthumpthumpthump.

I break into a run, or rather try to. The soles of my sneakers are so slick I skid across the floor, staying upright by catching myself against the wall with my right hand.

Thumpthumpthumpthumpthumpthumpthumpthumpt humpthump.

The floor quakes. I lean against the wall, and my right hand quivers as I pull off and toss aside my sneakers.

Thumpthumpthumpthumpthumpthumpthumpthumpt humpthump.

My eyes go wide. Any second, Ms. Bergman will appear in the hallway, bearing down on me and out for blood.

Thump. Thump.

She's not far now. I run; my sock-encased feet make me as graceful as an ice-skating elephant. Before I've gone ten feet, I'm hurdling face-first toward the floor. I catch myself with my right forearm a mere heartbeat before doing a faceplant.

Thump. Thump.

The stomping footsteps are nearly deafening. In between each footfall, the distinctive whine and whirling of gears are audible. A new stench overwhelms the delicious scent of blood—acrid smoke.

Thump.

Help me. I call to the sleeper. *I need your strength.*

Thump.

The floor jumps beneath me. I glance behind me to Bergman's hatchet face leering from behind her battle armor's thick glass faceplate. The exoskeleton fills the hallway. Black smoke puffs from the shoulder of the arm holding a black sword etched with glowing orange veins forming fractal patterns. The other arm possesses three gun barrels stacked on top of each other instead of a hand.

I work the sock free of my right foot, but it's slow going because the damp material adheres to my skin.

Bergman's rictus smile widens. "Time to die, Miss Lee."

I pull the sock halfway down my foot.

With a grinding of gears and a puff of sooty smoke, the sword arm raises. The blade's tip pierces the ceiling.

"Wait. Doesn't Dr. Rah want me alive?" I rip the sock from my foot.

"Heh. Dead will have to do. I've been waiting for this moment for a long time, Miss Lee, a long time. I will have satisfaction!"

Gears grind, and smoke spews from the shoulder of the sword arm, but the blade doesn't slice downward. The tip is stuck in the ceiling. Bergman snarls in frustration and the armor rattles.

I run. Every time my left foot hits the floor, I feel like my feet are about to fly out from under me, but then my right foot lands, and I'm steady again.

"You can't escape, Miss Lee! You can only make the hunt more enjoyable!"

I haven't gone twenty feet when I see a door on the left side of the hallway. I skid to a halt, staring at it.

Thump.

Ms. Bergman has freed the sword from the ceiling.

"Why can't I wake up?" I throw open the door and

enter a gargantuan stainless-steel chamber.

It's identical to the room I was locked inside on Golden Shoal, except in its center, where there should be an industrial strength examination chair, is a gash in the floor emitting an eerie yellowish light—an opening to the slipstream.

"Where are you going to run to now, Miss Lee?"

Bergman stands in the hallway outside the doorway. The battle armor is too large to fit through the opening. With a metallic shriek, the black blade's tip stabs through the wall. It won't take Bergman long to slice her way inside.

I cross the room to stare at the opening into the slipstream. The lambent path forms a mineshaft through the void.

Come to me.

The stentorian voice rumbles through my skull. Suddenly, I'm aware of the sleeper stirring inside me. Before I can stop myself, my legs move at the sleeper's command, and I step out over the opening.

I'm in freefall for a few seconds, with the slipstream's dull roar filling my ears and the voice reverberating through my gray matter, when pain explodes through me, starting deep in my bowels. My vision goes white, then black, and then I don't see anything. My organs are torn asunder and rearranged. My skin bulges, and broken bones burst out. The agony crescendos to a fever pitch, and I'm fading as the skaag subsumes me.

When the torturous pain subsides, I'm left as excess baggage inside my monstrous skin. The sleeper is the pilot driven entirely by the desire to obey the voice that grows in power, even vibrating the skaag's bones, as the beast speeds toward the distant wall of ominous black at the slipstream's terminus.

Come to me. It is your purpose.

Dread slithers down my spine, leaving behind slimy residue. Whatever is happening, it isn't right. The sleeper is many things, but it's about as obedient as I am. *Don't listen to the voice. This isn't like you, like us.*

I can't even tell if the sleeper notices my pleas over the deafening voice spurring the skaag onward. In desperation, I try wresting control from the beast, demanding my body stop undulating toward the voracious blackness and…and just levitate. But the sleeper brushes aside my inept attempts while at the same time extending an offer to truly become one.

I recoil because I know that entails accepting all the beast's primal desires and sacrificing my humanity in the process. The sleeper forces me into the back of our mind like a child sent to time out. Now, I'm truly an observer without recourse. Maybe now I'll find out if the darkness at the end of the shimmering path is as ominous as I fear and discover who or what is behind the unrelenting voice exhorting the skaag.

Stop this. Don't do it. You don't want this.

My pleas fall on deaf ears. But a distant voice penetrates the slipstream. I strain to make out the words over the cacophony urging the sleeper onward.

****

Hands grip my shoulders and shake me.

"Wake up, Allison! Wake up."

My eyes open to Dad standing over me with his hands firmly gripping my shoulders. I blink several times as my prosthetics adjust to the brightness of the overhead light.

"Mr. Lee, do you need help?"

A female voice. One I recognize as belonging to a Draconic Task Force magician.

"No. She's awake." Dad's brow creases with worry.

"I'll be right outside if you need anything." The door shuts.

"Can you let me up?" I'm becoming increasingly aware that my bedsheets and blankets twist around me in an uncomfortable array. Everything is soaking wet from my sweat. Even my hair is matted down against my scalp.

Dad lets me up and pulls my study chair over, castors squeaking. He flops down in the chair that creaks beneath his weight. His expression morphs from concern to pure exhaustion.

I sit up in bed. My bedsheets and blanket are more than twisted and stinking from my sweat. At least one is torn, and my kitty cat stuffy is on the floor with one of its forelegs conspicuously missing.

"Holy cow," I whisper, not quite believing my eyes.

Dad places his elbows on the chair's armrests and massages his temples. "You were screaming and thrashing in your sleep. The agent came and woke me up. I had fallen asleep in my chair downstairs. When I entered your room…" He glances over his shoulder at the bedroom door. He turns back to me and leans in close. His whisper so soft mere human ears wouldn't understand his words. "I sensed a presence. One I've only felt once before."

Chapter 15

"Presence?" I whisper. "What are you talking about?"

Dad grimaces. "Magic—"

My hands ball into fists. "A Task Force magician put a spell on me. I'll…"

Dad shakes his head. "No, the magic is distinctly draconic in nature."

My jaw works as an angry response rises up my throat.

Dad puts a hand on my right fist and shakes his head again. "It's not what you think. It's not Radcliffe or his followers."

My fist dissolves as puzzlement replaces my anger. "If not Radcliffe or the others"—I shake my head—"then who? What about the Task Force magician? Can she detect it?"

The implications whirl through my mind like startled starlings. There are more dragons on Earth, and the ones we know about, including Mauve, have kept their existence a secret.

"I believe detecting this magic is beyond an ordinary magician's capabilities. As for who put a spell on you?" Dad shrugs. "I'm not sure. Before your mother left us after giving birth to you, I felt the same magic radiating off of her. The signature is distinctive. I'm certain the spell that ensnares or ensnared her entangles you."

I shake my head. Mother is the most powerful sorceress on Earth. The dragons and my dad acknowledge her supremacy as a master magician. Not only is she an expert in skaag magic, she possesses mastery of human magic as well, having been taught by Dad. My knowledge of magic wouldn't fill a thimble, but I know mastering another species' magic is rare. Radcliffe and his followers can use a smattering of human magic, but they are far from masters.

"I need you to tell me what happened, Allison. Can you do that?" Dad squeezes my hand.

"I can't believe Mother would ever allow someone to place magic on her. I mean…you know how she is. She's a total control freak."

Dad laughs but his eyes brim with worry. "We haven't talked much about your mother or anything else since you returned from Golden Shoal. I know it's my fault. You're angry at me for keeping secrets from you." He withdraws his hand from mine and shrugs. "We always did what we thought was in your best interest."

"That's laughable," I scoff. Mother condemned me to live as a freak of nature and abandoned me at birth. At least Dad stuck around, but he still lied to me every day about my mother, his double life as an archmagus, and my true nature. As if any of that was ever in my best interest.

"We made mistakes, but we tried our best, Allison." Dad takes a deep breath. "What have the dragons told you about the Empress and General Bane?"

I recall Dr. Radcliffe speaking at some length about

the Empress, the ruler of dragonkind against whom Radcliffe and his compatriots are rebelling. Mark Cassidy had mentioned General Bane. He's a skaag leader, Mom's old boss. Cassidy was afraid if Bane showed up on Earth and I was alive, the general would be displeased because I was an experiment not meant to survive. I tell Dad what I know, adding, "General Bane is probably dead. There were skaags in the slipstream when I collapsed the portal."

"Perhaps, but unlikely. Generals rarely lead from the front." Dad stares at the ceiling. Sighing, he faces me. "I think we're both in the same boat. We don't know much."

"Didn't Mother tell you anything?" I demand.

"I could ask you the same thing."

I raise an eyebrow.

"You're the one who spent time in the wilderness training with her in all things skaag."

My mirthless laughter sounds like a snort. "The torture sessions, you mean? Like when she shot me in the head sixteen times."

Dad's expression sours. "At least she waited until you transformed."

I cross my arms before my chest. "She never told me anything about her life before coming to Earth or even on Earth. The training sessions always focused on me transforming from a human into a skaag and back again and controlling my electrical attack. Sometimes she'd test the durability of my skaag form by shooting me in the head or biting me or wrapping herself around me like an anaconda and squeezing until I couldn't breathe. She never once mentioned the Empress or General Bane. I suppose everything she subjected me to was for the best, right?"

Dad is downcast. "I admit, when you put it that way, her methods sound extreme. Know that she, that we, only wanted you prepared to defend yourself if the skaags or dragons ever came for you." He looks up, meeting my gaze. "Turns out, she was right to push you. You escaped the faeries on Golden Shoal and saved your friends."

I roll my eyes. I'm not going to have that discussion. "You're the one who lived with her before I was born and stayed in contact with her after she abandoned me. You knew she wasn't human. Did she tell you anything about her time before coming here?"

Dad shakes his head. "I didn't know she wasn't human at first. When we first met, I only knew her as the most interesting and beautiful person I had ever encountered. On top of that, she possessed an extraordinary predilection for magic. She knew a bit of human magic already.

"I was besotted. Against my better judgment, I started teaching her magic. I quickly discerned that not only had I met the love of my life, I had also found a human capable of becoming an archmagus. I was such a fool. I became suspicious that she wasn't human when she refused to pursue magic that required the caster's blood. By then, I knew her desire for magical knowledge and power was as insatiable as mine. There was no good reason for her refusing to attempt the spells. We argued, and I lost my temper. I became physical. I'm not proud of that. She was more than my girlfriend at the time. She was my apprentice by then. The traditions of the archmagi are ancient and include corporal punishment for certain offenses. You can guess how that went for me."

"Not well, I imagine."

Dad laughs, and surprisingly, it sounds genuine.

"She put me in my place. I reacted rashly with magic—a defense mechanism drilled into me by hundreds of hours of training at the hands of harsh masters—which she countered with skaag magic. The skaag was out of the bag, so to speak. She either had to kill me to keep me silent or…choose love."

"Love! That woman isn't capable of love," I splutter before bursting with laughter.

It's Dad's turn to roll his eyes. "I know you struggle to believe this, but your mother loves you very much. We both do. Now, are you going to tell me what happened tonight? Were you dreaming?"

"Tell me about the presence first."

Frowning, Dad sighs. "There's not much to say. The first time I sensed the presence was seventeen years ago, mere weeks after your mother gave birth to you. I immediately knew what I sensed was draconic magic, but it wasn't something I had ever felt from Radcliffe. The magic rolled off your mother like a bad smell. I asked her about it. All she said was that it was a summons she could not resist. She refused to say anything else. By then, I knew her skaag heritage was off-limits. For the rest of the day, she made plans for her departure, including devising a means for us to secretly remain in contact. The next morning, she left."

My throat is dry. "She left to answer a summons." Hearing him speak of her abandoning me, even in the most abstract terms, is still like picking at the scab of a half-healed wound. But what sets me on edge is that she was summoned.

I tell Dad about my dreams, leaving out most details except for the voice calling me and the skaag's desire to answer the summons. He listens intently, occasionally asking pointed questions that I dodge unless they pertain directly to the voice.

Dad puckers his lips and leans back in the chair. "So you enter the slipstream, and this voice calls to you?"

I nod. "Then I transform."

"You resist transformation but unsuccessfully."

"Correct."

Dad leans forward, eyes narrowing. "It's as though the skaag must obey the voice?"

"Yes. It's strange. The sleeper—that's what I call the half-skaag—is as obedient as I am. But when it comes to that voice…" I shake my head.

"I see. We cannot know definitively the magic at work in your dreams is the same that called your mother all those years ago, but we should proceed with the assumption that it is. Tell your dreams to no one, especially the dragons. In case my assumption they have nothing to do with them is wrong. Agreed?"

I nod vigorously in the affirmative. I don't tell him I've mentioned the dreams to Dalia. He doesn't need to know that.

"Good. Good." He looks at me sharply. "When did the dreams start?"

"I don't remember. A month ago, maybe."

He smirks like he doesn't believe me, but he doesn't press.

"From now on, I want you to keep a dream log. In the morning, write down any dream you can remember from the night before in a notebook. Any dream. In detail."

Yeah, right. I want to stop dreaming, not recall them in detail. "Sure. I can do that."

"Make sure you do. If I'm going to be able to help you, I need details. They might give me insight on how to counter what is happening to you. In the short term, I have a tea that might help."

My prosthetics feel like they'll fall out of their sockets. "I'm not going to drink a magic tea."

Dad raises an index finger and smiles. "It's not magical. It's a concoction of herbs known to the archmagi that dull the effect of spells acting on the mind. It's effective against draconic magic. I have a small supply of the ingredients, but I can order more. Come on. You have school tomorrow. Let's go downstairs and I'll prepare some of the secret sauce."

"No dreams? I'll drink it."

****

Wednesday afternoon, Agent Haskell and Lopez drive me to my regular appointment at the Robotics Technology Center or RTC for Dr. Woolworth to give my prosthetic eyeballs a once-over. For once, even Valentina's squeaky voice fails to irritate me too much. After I started drinking Dad's concoction, I've slept better than ever since returning from Golden Shoal. The herbal cocktail tastes like mud mixed with liquified slugs, but it does keep the nightmares at bay—at least for now.

Haskell parks the electric sedan in a nearly empty visitor lot, and we enter the RCT. The modern interior is hot with warm air blasting from vents after being outside in the cold. Students sit in egg-shaped chairs at low-slung tables sprinkled throughout the space. I head for the stairs trailed by my useless bodyguards.

I make a beeline for the open doorway to the medical robotics lab. I knock on the door frame, and Dr. Woolworth, sitting on a stool, looks up from a widescreen monitor on a table full of gadgets that may or may not be prototypes of prosthetics.

Woolworth stands and walks to the door. "Come in, Allison."

I enter and move aside as the doctor addresses the security agents. "I'm going to remove Allison's prosthetics today. The appointment will take about an hour."

"Gotcha, doc," Haskell says. "We'll be right outside as usual."

Dr. Woolworth shuts the door, leading me through the lab crowded with computers and various robotic devices that are either freestanding, laid out on long tables, or stashed on shelving. Some contraptions are shaped like human appendages; one looks remarkably like a human lung. Unlike my previous visits, the lab lacks graduate students.

Woolworth stops at a door in the back of the lab and whispers, "The female agent…is she a magician?"

I nod.

"Can she hear us? See inside?"

"I don't think so."

"You're sure? When your friend came…Leslie…to arrange this. Well, since I agreed to this, I've been worrying myself sick." Woolworth's face pales as she speaks.

Honestly, I don't know how Dalia convinced Leslie to help set up my under-the-radar interview with Bibi. The last time I saw Leslie, we didn't exactly part on the best of terms—I had threatened her and her boyfriend, Jason. So embarrassing.

I wave a hand dismissively. "Believe me, the magicians only pretend that they can hear and see everything."

"I'm not getting cold feet. I'm…nervous," Woolworth says.

She opens the door to a cleaning closet illuminated by a single LED in the center of the ceiling. Bibi sits on an overturned plastic bucket with a notepad and pen in hand and a phone balanced on her knee. The reporter smiles, and the light twinkles in her dark brown eyes. My breath catches in my throat as I step inside the closet.

"You girls have fifteen minutes. Then I must start servicing Allison's prosthetics," Dr. Woolworth whispers and gently shuts the door.

Chapter 16

I smile nervously at Bibi, drowning in her beautiful brown eyes. She even smells good, a subtle mixture of jasmine and lavender wafting from her hair. Realizing that I'm staring, my cheeks warm and my gaze drops to my zebra-striped sneakers. "Hi."

Jeez. I'm such a dork.

"Have a seat." Bibi indicates an overturned orange plastic bucket to her left.

I pull the bucket over, which scrapes loudly across the tile, and sit down across from the reporter. Her graceful fingers with perfectly manicured nails stained a vibrant purple brush against my knee. I look up and again find myself mesmerized by her eyes. I hope she does break into TV news. When she's on the screen, people won't look away.

"Relax, okay. Fifteen minutes will be over before you know it."

Bibi reaches into a pocket of her Channel 5 parka, pulls out two bright red balls, and offers them to me. I raise an eyebrow.

"Stress balls. Devin said they might help you relax."

My initial reaction is to reject the balls and make a snide comment about Devin, but Bibi's smile is so warm and authentic that I can't without feeling needlessly petty. Instead, I take the small red globes that could easily pass off as clown noses—one for each hand. I squeeze the balls to see if they squeak. Not a sound.

"Wow." My anxiety drains as my fingers compress the balls. "Thanks."

Bibi hefts her phone. "Is it okay if I record our conversation?"

I squeeze the ball on my left hand until it bursts with a pop. We both startle. White grain leaks from the ball onto my knee and the floor.

"Relax, okay?" Bibi's smile is brittle, but her eyes remain kind.

I grip the remains of the ball in my hand so tightly it bulges between my fingers. "Sure. I'm relaxed."

Bibi starts recording with the flick of her index finger. After stating our names and the date, she asks the first question. "So, Allison, can you tell me how your life has changed since The Incident?"

"I learned I'm an alien-human hybrid with the ability to shapeshift," I say and summarize how my life has changed. I focus on the protesters who stake out my house and remote school, as those topics will keep me away from anything better left unsaid. Bibi gently asks follow-up questions as she takes page after page of notes. She's so easy to talk to that I'm worried my tongue might wag too much.

"Allison, pardon my interruption, but I think it's best we move on. There's something you want to share with our audience about your friend Haji and a young girl named Bria?" Bibi says.

I nod and find myself smiling. This is the meat of the interview, which will hopefully lead to the release of my friends. "Definitely. Haji and Bria are held against their will on Joint Base Lewis-McCord. Haji is a US citizen and a teen. Bria is a little girl, a child. It's…it's wrong! If the government can lock up a child on a military base, they can do that to anyone, at any time, for any reason. Do you know why Haji testified to the Homeland Security Committee via video conference? Because he's locked away somewhere on base. The government doesn't want you to know that. They're embarrassed and know holding children as prisoners is wrong. I'm not locked up on a military base because they know they can't hold me there. Not if I want out." Uh, oh. I chomp down my lower lip before saying something else I shouldn't.

"Please, keep going," Bibi says.

I squeeze the ball in my right hand so hard it pops. This time neither of us is startled. "I shouldn't have said that last bit."

Bibi looks up from her notes. "About the military not being able to lock you up?"

I nod.

Bibi crosses out several lines of notes with flourishes. "No worries. I'll leave it out." She adds with a smile. "But it is juicy…"

I must look aghast, eyes bursting wide and mouth drooping open.

Bibi waves aside my concern with her hand holding the pen. "Okay. I read you loud and clear. Is Haji being locked up related to the destruction of his house?"

I explain Haji is a magician, but there is no proof that he had anything to do with the explosion at his family's home. I add, "Even if he did do something, where is the due process?"

"Tell me more about Bria. Is it true she is a faery?" Bibi asks.

"She's a child," I say and explain how I rescued her while escaping from Golden Shoal. I purposely leave out that her blood is the key to creating the Juice that human magicians need to superpower their magic.

A soft knock comes at the door. "Allison, Bexley, it's been fifteen minutes. I need to start servicing Allison's prosthetics now," Dr. Woolworth says.

Bibi stops recording and gives me a thumbs-up. "You did great. I have enough for an eye-popping article."

"When will it be posted?" I stand.

"Start checking tonight around…" The reporter glances at the time on her phone. "Seven."

****

That evening I check the time on my flip phone about every three minutes. If time moved any slower, I'd be in stasis. Next to my phone on the table sits a plate full of steaming linguine slathered in creamy alfredo sauce—a favorite food before my inner half-skaag dramatically altered my diet. Dad took the liberty to slice up my savory chicken sausage and mix it in with the pasta and sauce. In between checking the time, I carefully spear chunks of sausage with my fork, avoiding consuming any pasta and as little sauce as possible. As the sleeper and I become more in tune, food other than meat doesn't satisfy my hunger and has lost most of its flavor.

Across from me sits Dad, interrogating me between bites of food. "Are you sleeping better?" He drops his voice to whisper. "Since drinking the tea."

"Yes, Daddy. Just like I told you this morning." I

separate the sausage from the pasta.

"Great. That's great. What about the dream log?"

"I haven't had anything to record."

"You should journal about your previous dreams."

"I haven't had time. Pre-calculus and English lit are kicking my butt."

The look Dad gives me tells me he suspects I don't plan to journal about my dreams. He's right. No need to relive my dreams, especially since the tea is working. For one thing, I don't trust the sleeper not to try something if I start reliving the dreams.

Dad shrugs. "How did your appointment with Dr. Woolworth go?"

At the mention of Dr. Woolworth, I check the time on my phone again: 6:58 p.m. Time to check the Channel 5 website! "Crap!" I grab my phone off the table and head for the hallway. "I need to get upstairs. I have a homework date with Dalia."

"Allison, your tea," Dad says sharply.

"Oh, right." I slip my phone into my pocket to pinch my nose shut with my thumb and index finger while I chug the hot, dream-slaying liquid. The flavor almost doubles me over to retch, but I manage to swallow my medicine and keep it down.

****

I shut the door to my room and scamper to my study desk. Sitting down, I flip open my laptop and navigate to the Channel 5 website. I drum my fingers against the desk as the website loads at sloth speed. Banners advertising used cars splash across the top of the screen, and a sidebar displays the seven-day forecast—cold and liquid sunshine, of course. A spinning blue wheel appears in the center of the screen with the subscript loading.

"What is going on." I spin in my chair.

After a minute, I try reloading the page with the same result. Odd. It's unlikely to be my network connection. Dad only allows me an archaic flip phone, but he spares no expense when it comes to fast Internet speed. I pick up my phone and text Dalia.

—Can you access the website? I get a loading message.—

As soon as I send the message, my phone rings and I answer it. It's Dalia.

"Oh my God, Allison. I'm reading the article right now."

My pulse quickens for all the wrong reasons. "What? What did she write?"

"You're going to love this," Dalia replies and begins reading the article out loud.

My jaw goes unhinged as Dalia reads. The article is better than I ever hoped. Bibi paints me as a social justice crusader and my imprisoned friends as young people abused by the government regardless of their magical abilities or species.

"Allison, are you there?"

"Yeah, I'm blown away. The article is so lit!"

"You know, maybe the reason you can't get on the Channel 5 website is because the article is going viral. I just checked my socials. It's already trending."

Chapter 17

The next morning I'm awake before my alarm, listening to the rain hammering against the roof and the wind shuddering the downspouts. Excitement propels me out of bed. I want to read Bibi's article for myself—despite refreshing the page dozens of times before I went to bed, the post never loaded—and see if the story has gained any traction on the national news networks.

Yawning, I collapse in my chair and open the laptop, squinting against the screen's bright luminescence. The web browser displays the Channel 5 website complete with the spinner in the center of the page, indicating the content is still loading. Groaning, I hit the refresh button. Seven agonizing seconds later, the page loads with Bibi's story at the top under the headline Local Teen and Child Held on Military Base.

"Yes." I pump my fist.

I'm about to open the article when I hear a voice from downstairs. "Where is she? I want to see her right now."

"She's still in bed, sir. She won't be up for another hour," the security agent at the base of the stairs replies.

"Guess she won't be getting her beauty sleep."

The distinctive thumps of someone—no, several someones—stomping up the stairs resound in the wake of Agent-in-charge McAllister's angry words. Grimacing, I close the laptop and spin in my chair to face the kaleidoscopic swirling color of the poster decorating my bedroom door. Even with the lights out, I can clearly see the words Dark Matter Electrica in the center of the chromatic storm.

"Come in, agents. I'm already wide awake."

"Well, shit," McAllister mutters, then opens the door. He towers in the doorway in a dark, wet trench coat. Flanking him are two equally damp and rather miserable-looking agents. "Is it normal for you to sit in the dark by yourself?"

I point to my eyes. "Prosthetics have advantages."

"Huh." McAllister flips on the overhead light and slams the door on his backup.

I blink several times as my prosthetics adjust to the light. McAllister stares down his nose at me, eyes disturbingly wide. Rain droplets dot his dark skin. He points a long, claw-like finger at my laptop.

"Admiring your handiwork?"

"You're making my clothes and carpet wet." I indicate the water dripping from his trench coat onto the floor and scattered clothing.

McAllister gives me a condescending half-smile. "That's the least of your problems. Your interview is causing me heartburn. Hell, by the time I'm done dealing with the fallout, I'll probably have an ulcer."

"And why should I care?" I clamp my mouth shut and wince. I shouldn't have said that.

McAllister puts his hands on his knees and bends down until his eyes are level with mine. "When you do something like that, Allison, something you know you shouldn't, you're making life miserable for both of us. The shit is going to roll down the hill all the way from DC on this one. You have embarrassed and created political complications for some powerful people. They will want answers. Like how is it the reporter got access to you? Hmmm…let me think…that's a tough one. Oh, I know. She spoke to you while you were at the RTC under the tender care of Dr. Woolworth."

My mouth drops open, and inside me, the sleeper stretches, limbering up for violence, undoubtedly. I swallow. "Talking to a reporter isn't illegal."

McAllister straightens. "That's true for as far as it goes. But…life's going to get miserable for Woolworth, that reporter, yourself, and anyone else involved."

I burst from the chair, getting right up into McAllister's personal space and craning my neck to glower at him. Inside me, the sleeper hums with pent-up energy and transgressive desires. "You shouldn't threaten me, Agent McAllister."

McAllister backs up to the door, startling when he bumps into it. "I'm not threatening you. I'm reminding you of the reality we share. If you don't like it, transform into a monster and go live in the wilderness somewhere."

I stare at McAllister in stunned silence. How can this man who hardly knows me peel back my defenses to deliver a pinpoint strike?

"Not too keen on that, are you?" McAllister shakes his head. He turns for the door, then stops and faces me. "Let me level with you. I sympathize with you. Your life got turned upside down through no fault of your own. Hell, I think you got the shaft. Being a Black man, I know what that's like. I'm a federal agent, but I've been pulled over for driving a nice car in a nice neighborhood. Makes me mad, real mad.

"But I keep my cool. On the outside, at least"—

McAllister's posture tenses—" 'cause I don't want to get shot. So I know what it's like to get the shaft. I might not know exactly what it's like to be you. But I know the shaft. I know it real well." McAllister waves an index finger at me. "We both know there isn't a prison in the world that can hold you, at least not for long. But you keep going down the path you're on, these people you're messing with might decide to try building a cage capable of holding you for the rest of your natural life. I know you don't want that, and I'm pretty sure you don't want to go live in the wilderness like some wild beast. I think you want to live in civilized society, and that means toeing the line, Allison, toeing the line."

****

After McAllister leaves, I stew. His speech struck closer to home than I like, much closer. Sighing, I reopen the laptop and read Bibi's article. It makes me feel good, but I also wonder if Dalia and I are naïve, believing this one story, this one brief interview, will start the avalanche of events ending with our friends' release.

I'm about to check the national news sites when my stomach rumbles. McAllister bursting into my room disturbed the sleeper, and the beast is always ravenous. I check the time in the upper right-hand corner of the laptop's screen—nearly seven a.m.

"I wonder..." I spin in my chair until I face the door.

After heading downstairs and brewing a pot of coffee, I sit at the dining room table with a steaming mug of aromatic coffee in one hand and a plate with six chicken sausages in the other. I set my burden on the table and turn on the TV. After a second, the flatscreen starts up, already tuned to Channel 5.

The morning news host, a middle-aged woman with dark, lustrous hair wearing a red dress, smiles into the camera. I take a slurp of java. Hot and flavorful, just how I like it.

"After the break," the newscaster says, "reporter Bexley Aziz will speak to us about her exclusive interview with none other than Allison Lee, who makes disturbing allegations against our government. Stay tuned. You won't want to miss it."

Some coffee goes down the wrong tube, and I start hacking violently as an advertisement for boxed macaroni appears on the screen, and a catchy ditty plays from the speakers several decibels louder than the newscast. I slam the mug on the table as I continue coughing with chest-bursting intensity.

A security agent appears in the doorway to the dining room. "Do you need help?"

I wave off the agent the very instant the fluid rushes up my throat, spraying all over the table. The agent returns to her post, but not before giving me a snooty smirk. I rush to the kitchen to grab a rag to clean up before the news resumes.

"Welcome back. Thank you for spending your morning with us. As promised, reporter Bexley Aziz is here to discuss her interview with Allison Lee. So, Bexley, I understand it was quite a cloak-and-dagger routine to gain access to Allison. Is that true?"

I go on high alert, pulse thrumming like an over-revved engine, at the mention of cloak and dagger.

"You could say that. The interview took place in a supply closet, a very cramped supply closet. Seemed like something from a spy novel."

The news host titters and asks a follow-up question. I'm not listening because I'm blown away by how gorgeous Bibi is made up for television. She's dressed conservatively, including a tan-colored hijab, which is strange since I hadn't seen her wearing one before, but still, she is stunning. Her make-up, her eyes, the shape of her face—I can only dream of being so beautiful.

The front door squeaking open and thudding shut breaks my hypnosis. That will be Dad returning soaking wet from his morning run. I start back up wiping the coffee droplets sprayed in front of my place setting, but I can't take my gaze off Bibi; I nearly overturn the coffee mug.

"Is Allison's story credible?" the host asks.

Bibi looks thoughtful. "Yes. For example, she could have denied Bria is a faery, but she didn't. Given the chaos the faeries caused in Singapore and all the negative coverage they're receiving in the national news, I think her openness adds credibility to her story."

The host speaks, but I'm distracted by Dad entering the dining room. "You're up early, but I'm not surprised. McAllister called me when I was out on my run. Told me all about what you did. Is this the reporter?"

I nod and give him a dirty look for talking over the TV. His hair is matted down from the rain, but the rest of him is dry. He must've left his rain gear hanging in the entry by the front door.

Spill mopped up, I sit and listen to the remainder of the news story. It's a recap of what I told Bibi at the

RTC, and she paints me as a social justice warrior like she did in the article. Dad sits across from me at his usual place.

The host closes the interview. "We plan to reach out to officials at Joint Base Lewis-McCord today to get to the bottom of exactly what's going on regarding a teen and faery presumably held on base. Tune in at eleven for an update or anytime at our website."

"I hope you know what you're doing," Dad says.

I pick up the coffee cup and turn to him. "Helping my friends."

Dad checks the entrance to the dining room, then leans forward in his chair. "Did you give the interview at…" He glances at the entryway again, then whispers, "…the RTC."

I nod.

Dad throws himself back in the chair, which creaks under the strain, and stares at the ceiling. "Did Jane know about it?"

"Yes. It's one of the only places I can go without Haskell and Valentina up in my face all the time."

"It won't take them long to figure out that's where you did the interview. They'll pull security footage. The lab doesn't have any security cameras I know of, but cameras cover the entrance to the RTC, the stairs to the second floor, and the elevator bay."

My stomach clenches when I think about Bibi entering the RTC in her Channel 5 jacket. I'm a complete dunce. Why did I put Dr. Woolworth in the government's crosshairs? "McAllister already suspects that's where I did the interview. Isn't a subpoena or something needed to get the security footage."

"I suppose." Dad crosses his arms before his chest.

“I didn’t do anything wrong. Neither did Dr. Woolworth.” I pound the tabletop with a fist, causing the plate and mug to rattle.

“Don’t split the table in half,” Dad says.

“It’s so unfair.” Inside me the sleeper quivers as images of lightning and destruction flit through my mind’s eye.

Chapter 18

I can barely concentrate during the enlightening pre-calculus lecture. Taking the class remotely doesn't help, but I can barely resist opening a second tab in my browser to check for updates on the Channel 5 website and a third tab to check on the national news. After breakfast, I had perused several national news sites and half a dozen major papers; two had already picked up Bibi's story, but none offered anything new.

"Allison."

"Yes, Mrs. Turnbull," I reply to my teacher, a middle-aged woman with a perpetual squint. Realizing my microphone is muted, I click on the icon along the top of the screen of a mic with a red slash through it. "Sorry. I was muted."

Turnbull frowns. "I asked if you could lead the class through solving the problem on the whiteboard."

My cheeks redden as I read, given that the equation for a circle is $x^2 + y^2 = 49$, find the radius. I chew on the inside of my lower lip.

"This will be on Friday's quiz," Mrs. Turnbull says.

"I don't know," I say through clenched teeth.

"Make sure you study, Allison. The quiz is five percent of your grade."

"Yes, Mrs. Turnbull." As if I don't know. I barely eked out a B minus on the last quiz, and that was with

Dalia helping me study.

The teacher calls on another student who talks the class through the solution to the formula. I try to pay attention, but it's all I can do not to start opening multiple browser tabs to check the various news sites. In my defense, I can barely track pre-calculus when I'm not distracted.

As soon as the class is over, I open a tab and type in the Channel 5 website address. After the first three letters, the site's complete URL appears in the address bar, and I click it with the pointer. I know I should be studying, but I can't help feeling that is less important than checking up on my plan to free my friends.

"Dammit." The page is painfully slow to load, but maybe that's a good thing. Perhaps that means thousands, no, millions of people are reading Bibi's article and becoming righteously angry about Haji's and Bria's plight.

Someone knocks on my door.

I look up from my computer; the website still isn't fully loaded. "I'm studying."

"Dr. Radcliffe wants to talk to you. Now."

I scrunch my eyes and draw a deep breath at Valentina's strident voice. I turn my laptop, so the screen won't be visible from the doorway. I stand and march to the door.

I open the door a crack. "What?"

Valentina gives me a dirty look over the phone she holds about half a foot from her face. "Here she is, sir."

"Thank you, Agent Lopez," Radcliffe's voice pipes from the phone.

I snatch the phone out of Lopez's hand and slam the door in her face. Her sharp retort is barely muffled by the door. On the phone screen, Dr. Radcliffe stares at me with his disappointed professor face.

"There is no need to be rude to Agent Lopez, Allison," his tone as patronizing as Valentina's is piercing.

I start pacing the length of my room. I'm sure I'm about to get chewed out by the dragon, and I'm in no mood for it. "She's the most annoying person in the world. Couldn't you assign a different magician as the lead Task Force agent?"

"She is the best human magician I know, and her loyalty is unimpeachable."

I snort. "Loyalty to you."

"Loyalty to the cause of protecting humanity from skaags."

I almost ask him about my nightmares and the Empress and General Bane, but I don't. Dad's tea continues to keep the dreams at bay, for now.

"How's Joe?" My voice cracks.

The dragon resonantly laughs, but the mirth never reaches his eyes. "I anticipated this question. I checked in with the facility where he continues his recovery. He is up and walking regularly without a walker. In another month, two on the outside, I am told he will be ready to begin his training as a Task Force agent."

"There's one thing I still don't understand." I grip the phone so tightly my hand shakes. "I thought all the Task Force agents are magicians?"

"We are always looking for ways to expand the Task Force's capabilities. Joe will be part of that."

"Whatever," I say, knowing the wily dragon won't reveal any details even if I push.

Radcliffe toothlessly grins. "Whatever, indeed.

Whatever were you thinking when you gave the interview to Ms. Aziz?"

It's my turn to grin. "What? Am I giving you heartburn?" After McAllister's speech, I do feel a bit bad for giving him heartburn, but I have no issue with causing Radcliffe grief. He's given me more than a little acid reflux in the time we've known each other. In the back of my mind, I'm still worried he might make threats against Joe to keep me in line. If he's going to pull something like that, it's best to find out now.

"Not at all. Your friends, on the other hand..." Radcliffe's lips form a lopsided frown, and he raises his eyebrows as if in a shrug. "You are making it difficult for Tanis to help them."

"Tanis help them? Give me a break. They're prisoners."

"They are both improving under Tanis's care."

"Last time I saw Haji he didn't look like he was improving. He looked terrible."

"The leadership on the base is seriously considering holding a press conference and parading Haji and Bria out in front of reporters. I have informed them that would be utter foolishness, but they are facing considerable media and political pressure. Some in the media and Congress are asking if children are being sent to die on military bases. You know, Allison, your shenanigans might reveal Bria's location to the faeries. If they learn her location, they will come for her. People will die. That will be on you."

I shake my head. "No, no. The faeries are on the run. My mother is hunting them down as we speak."

"My dear, dear girl, no one has heard from your mother since she disappeared over Golden Shoal. I underestimated the faeries once—I thought they were extinct, after all. I will not make that mistake again. In all likelihood, they are watching, and if they learn your friend's location, they will come for her. I wish I were on the base right now to help deal with the fallout of your antics, but I am stuck in New York at the UN through Saturday."

A rumbling growl rises up my throat. I end the call and hurl the phone against the wall. The device careens off the wall, leaving behind a divot, and crashes to the floor.

****

After the conversation with Radcliffe, I feel like a ticking time bomb. Inside me, the sleeper squirms, and stray images of terrible violence and gore keep flicking through my mind like the outtake reel from a D-grade slasher movie. I can't stay still. I can't keep myself from pacing.

"Forget about what he said. It's working. The pressure campaign is working."

By the time I calm myself down enough to join my next class—English lit—I'm five minutes late. Fortunately, Mrs. Achebe doesn't call me out for being late, instead continuing to lead the class discussion about whether or not Odysseus is held on Calypso's island against his will.

I surprise myself by turning on the mic when there's a break in the conversation. "I think Odysseus is ambivalent."

"How so?" the teacher asks.

The sleeper presses against my insides like it wants out. I swallow a lump in my throat, wishing I had stayed quiet.

"Allison, don't you have more to add?" Achebe prompts.

"Ummm…there are consequences either way. Odysseus has to choose which consequences he's willing to deal with," I splutter, then turn off my mic.

I breathe easier when other students take up the discussion. Surprisingly, I find myself tracking the dialogue, although I don't offer my thoughts again. The class ends with us finding out we have to finish *The Odyssey* by the following Monday, which brings groans from the entire class. I turn on the mic, adding my voice to the expressions of dismay.

The period ends, and I log out of the classroom. I switch to the tab with the Channel 5 website. The page has finally loaded, and scrolling across the top of the page are the words BREAKING NEWS: Officials from Joint Base Lewis-McCord will address youths held captive on base at 11 a.m. today.

I check the time—just a little over an hour.

****

I spend the physics lecture staring at the digits in the upper right-hand corner of the screen slowly advancing toward eleven a.m. This is easily the longest hour of my life, no exaggeration. The monotony of the lecture on Newtonian physics is broken up at 10:43 when my phone buzzes. At first, I think it must be a text from Dalia, but the phone continues vibrating, advancing toward the edge of the table.

I turn off the laptop camera and pick up the phone—it's Dad. That's odd. He never calls during school hours.

"Ms. Lee, your camera is off." The teacher interrupts the lecture to chide me.

I turn on the mic. "Bathroom run. Sorry." I turn the mic off.

"Make it quick. This is important stuff," the teacher barks, then returns to the lecture.

I flip open the phone and raise it to my ear. "Hello, Daddy. What's up?"

"Don't leave the house. I'm coming home right now. I should be there in twenty minutes. Maybe less if the stoplights cooperate."

"What are you talking about?"

"Don't leave the house."

"Daddy…" I lower the phone. He ended the call. "What in the world?"

I set the phone on the table and mute the physics lecture. I listen, for what I don't know. All I hear is what I expect on any run-of-the-mill day: the creaks and groans of an old house, the regular breathing of the security detail, the trill of a robin from somewhere down the street, and in the distance the rumble of automobiles on the main drag.

Frowning, I recheck the time—10:50. Dad's call must have something to do with the press conference, but what? Magic? If Dad detected magic at the base all the way from here in Seattle, why isn't the magician outside my door losing it? Forget physics. The press conference is about to begin.

Chapter 19

I open the door to find Valentina blocking my path with her right hand in front of her at chest level, palm up. “Can I have the phone back?”

I suppress my urge to barge past her. “Sure. I’ll get it.”

I back up and gently shut the door in her face. I scan the floor for the device. I spot a glint from a corner of the phone screen jutting out from beneath black underwear. Retrieving the phone, I check the screen for damage, half expecting a spiderweb of cracks, and note the time. No damage, but I need to get downstairs fast to watch the start of the press conference.

Exiting the bedroom, I hand the phone to Valentina. “No need to thank me.”

I pound downstairs to the dining room and turn on the TV, which of course, is already tuned to Channel 5. A strapping reporter with broad shoulders and thick blond hair sits behind the news desk.

“I heard from the reporter on base that the news conference is about to begin. Bexley, what do you have for us?”

Bexley appears on the TV bundled up in her Channel 5 rain jacket with the hood pulled over the hijab I saw her wearing earlier in the day. Water beads on the jacket.

“I’m here on base. You can see they’re going to

hold the press conference outside despite the weather. Behind me is a small shelter over a podium. Behind that, a Humvee pulled up about a minute ago."

Even dressed for the elements, Bibi is absolutely gorgeous. Her voice contains the right amount of excitement to make my heart thump a little faster for all the right reasons. I can't look away from her, and the thimbleful of dread lingering in the back of my mind evaporates. I'm happy for her. She deserves this breakthrough. The broadcast cuts back to the studio.

"We'll return to Bexley as soon as the news conference starts. For now, it's time for a weather update on the fives."

I drum my fingers against the table as the weatherman gives the rundown of the weather for the rest of the day—drizzle, showers, downpour at rush hour—and cracks a not-funny joke when the technology doesn't display the Doppler radar on command.

"Oh, gosh. Sorry to interrupt, Tom." The voice of the midday reporter cuts in. "The news conference at Joint Base Lewis-McCord is beginning."

The coverage cuts to a man in a camouflage military uniform standing behind the podium. My jaw goes unhinged. On the spokesman's right, flanked by four burly soldiers, stand Haji and Bria. Behind my friends I catch sight of Tanis's white hair and wrinkled face. My hands form fists, nails cutting half-moons into my palms.

"What's going on? The girl. The faery girl." Bibi's voice comes from the TV.

Bria, her wings out of sight, struggles against two soldiers. Only a few stray spindles of colorful fairy dust float around her. Her thin arms look like they might break in the soldiers' hands. I know better. I'm sure she could escape if she wanted to unless she's drugged, or Tanis's presence gives her second thoughts, or both.

"What are those things overhead?" Bibi's voice again. "Get a shot of those black…no way…are those people flying?"

The image zooms out and in as the camera angle changes to a view of the gray sky. The sleeper reacts before I do, cowering like a cornered beast, ready to lash out with deadly intent.

"No. It can't be." The sleeper and I both know what the dark shapes are—faeries and humans encased in battle armor.

****

I exit the dining room ready for a fight. The agent on duty at the foot of the stairs calls after me as I make a beeline for the front door, but I ignore him. Instead of trying to stop me, he warns the agents outside I'm heading for the door.

I'm moving through a tunnel, vision going black around the edges. All I see is the front door, painted white with nicks around the edges betraying its age. I'm not sure what I'm going to do. I'm not certain what we're going to do, but I know I need to get out of the house. We need room to transform. That's the reasonable thing to do and what we should've done in the first place. Show them all our true nature and demand our friends' release.

I throw open the door and step onto the damp concrete of the front stoop. I let out a little yelp and almost retreat inside the house. Even through my now wet socks, the concrete feels damn cold. My reverie breaks, vision brightening around the edges until the tunnel vision completely dissipates. Everything about the outdoors is moist and chilly.

Blocking the concrete path leading from the house to the sidewalk are half a dozen agents led by Agent Haskell. The drizzle is quickly dampening down their trench coats and hair.

Haskell flashes his patented toothy grin. "Why don't you slow down, Allison? You can tell me what's bothering you. I want to help."

I don't have room to transform in the front yard without crushing the agents. If they don't get out of my way, I'll have to move them. I need to get to the base now before people die. My friends and Bibi might be hurt, and it's all my fault.

The front door squeaks behind me. Over my shoulder, I glimpse Valentina. I step down from the stoop. "Stay back." I face Haskell. "Tell your people to clear the front yard."

The big man raises his meaty hands before his chest. "Allison, come on—"

"Tell them to move, or I will move them!" I hear the door shut behind me and footfall on the stoop. "I told you to stay back, Valentina."

"Why don't you tell me where you want to go? I can get it cleared with McAllister and I'll drive…"

Haskell swivels toward the street at the whine of an approaching car. It's my dad in the hybrid, and he must have the accelerator jammed to the floor. The vehicle jumps the curb onto the sidewalk with a squeal of braking tires. Swerving into the front yard, the car cuts tire tracks in the grass and sprays dirt. The security agents scramble to avoid being chopped down by the oncoming vehicle. Several pull their sidearms, but Haskell calls for calm as Dad throws open the driver's door and gets out.

"Allison, thank goodness you're still here. There's magic—"

I run to his side. "On the base. I know. I have to go there."

His face curdles with anguish. "You don't know what you're getting yourself into. I can't lose you to the faeries like I did your mother."

"I have to, Dad."

He visibly deflates while, at the same time, his expression hardens. "Okay. I can get us there…close at least."

He steps away from the car and slashes his arm through the air, creating a black gash about half his height, hovering next to him. My eyes go wide, although I shouldn't be surprised he can cast the same magic Gore used to escape the campground by Forks approximately one and a half years ago.

Dad extends his hand to me. "Let's go save your friends."

I take Dad's warm hand. "Thank you."

"Wait! Stop!" Haskell screams.

The hulking agent lurches toward me. Dad steps into the black gash, and I follow.

Chapter 20

I plunge into darkness as absolute as the void beyond the slipstream. Even with my prosthetics' superior light-gathering capabilities, I can't see a thing. Not even Dad, who I know is less than an arm's length away because I grip his hand like it's a life preserver. The heat radiating from his palm is the only warmth I feel. Otherwise, it's like I've been plunged into a vat of water a degree or two above freezing.

Wherever this is, I want to escape it. To run, to sprint, or at least walk faster. In the direction of our movement, there is resistance similar to walking through water. And I'm not the only one panicking. Inside me, the sleeper thrashes, making my insides bulge. If we don't leave this place soon, my inner half-skaag is coming out whether I want it to or not.

Something brushes against my neck, tracing an icy line from my jaw to my clavicle. Fear pounds through me causing my muscles to seize up, and I hold my breath. If I dare breathing, whatever brushed against me will enter my body and possess me.

Dad tugs sharply, and I lurch forward through the resistance and into blessed light, and a steady drizzle falling from a slate-gray sky wets me down. But at least the dread chill is gone.

"Where were we?"

"It's known as the Unseen World. Little is known

about it."

"Something…something touched me. I think it wanted to enter me."

Dad takes my hand and squeezes. "What you experienced isn't uncommon. I know next to nothing about the denizens of that plane, but everything I've observed tells me they can't survive in our world. You're safe. Now, let's rescue your friends."

Nodding, I release his hand and take in my surroundings. The rumble of automobiles comes from the left beyond a tall chain-link fence topped with concertina wire. We stand inside the fence in a narrow clearing running between it and a dense woodland. I do a double take at the massive thoroughfare beyond the chain link.

"That's I-5." I point to the freeway. "Are we on the base?"

Dad nods. "Your friends are in that direction based on the magic I detect." He points at roughly a forty-five-degree angle into the trees. "I think I see a clearing up ahead where you can transform. Then we can fly to your friends' aid."

I follow Dad through the trees and thick undergrowth that scratches at my jeans. Pine needles and twigs poke at my feet through my socks, and my damp T-shirt adheres to my skin. Shivering miserably, I wish I had taken the time to throw on a pair of sneakers and rain jacket.

Emerging onto the meadow Dad alluded to, I quickly survey the dimensions. This will do. "Can you move out of the clearing and turn around?"

Dad stares at me with evident puzzlement.

"I'm not going to strip in front of you."

His cheeks flush a shade of crimson I don't usually see on an adult. "Sorry. Of course."

Dad lopes for the trees, quickly disappearing from sight. I strip, turning my T-shirt, socks, and jeans inside out in the process. Everything is sodden, so I don't bother stashing the clothes in the trees to keep them dry. Instead, I leave my threads in a pile.

Teeth chattering and arms crossed before my chest, I jog to the center of the clearing, trembling the entire time. Every raindrop striking me feels like a pinprick of ice. I lower my mental barriers holding the sleeper in check and concentrate on transforming into the half-skaag.

I expect my body to be shredded and expanded in an instant of blinding pain.

Nothing happens.

"Why now?" I mutter between chattering teeth. *What's wrong?*

The sleeper remains coiled like a rattlesnake ready to strike. I don't understand the beast's hesitation to emerge. Usually, it's all I can do to hold the half-skaag, with its desire for wanton violence and insatiable appetite for raw meat, at bay.

"Can I turn around?" Dad calls.

"No! Absolutely not!"

"Is something wrong? Why is it taking so long?"

"Just…just shush. Okay? I need to concentrate."

Thankfully, Dad falls more or less silent, but I can still hear him muttering to himself about this being a mistake. My senses have gone supersonic and it seems like I can hear every drop of drizzle, birdcall, and distressed squirrels for a quarter-mile or more. The scent of the woods and the rain are full of earthy goodness.

What's wrong? I demand of the beast again, putting all my impatience and fear for my friends into the query.

My knees buckle when Ms. Bergman's face twisted into a rictus smile fills my mind. The dread accompanying the image is so powerful I'm stunned and fail to stop myself from falling to my knees. The image shifts, revealing Bergman encased in ultrahigh-tech battle armor. Her left hand clasps a black blade highlighted by orange fractal patterns. Her right arm is a gun with three barrels stacked on top of each other. The gun barrels flare with blinding light. The half-skaag's dread twists my innards and my back ignites in fiery pain. One hand going to my abdomen and the other to my lower back, I involuntarily cry out.

"Allison! What's happening? Do you need help?" Dad yells.

The pain dissipates to a tingle, and I growl through clenched teeth. "Stay back."

You're afraid. That's okay. I'm scared too, but we can't allow our fear to stop us from helping Haji and Bria.

A winged black body highlighted with orange fractal patterns being torn into by razor-edged teeth fills my vision. Hot, orange blood sloshes inside my mouth, and entrails spill over my snout. It's so real I can taste the blood and smell the gore. Then, in a blink of an eye, it's gone.

I know the sensations for what they are—a question.

Maybe, I reply.

The pain of transformation is immediate and all-consuming as my body folds and expands as I'm remade. My next conscious thought is annoyance at the raindrops burning my eyes as I hover over the ground with all my monstrous might at my disposal.

****

As a skaag I hear the distant gunfire and explosions and know exactly what direction to head. My first impulse is to take to the air and fly heedlessly into battle. The sleeper and I are simpatico on this. If anything, the beast is even more eager for action than me. It wants to force me to make good on the promise to consume faery flesh.

Dad emerges from the trees, beaming, and stumbles at the clearing's edge. He teeters but regains his balance without breaking his smile for even a millisecond. As he approaches, it slowly dawns on me that he's smiling so broadly out of pride. But pride for what? Pride for me? That's not something I've ever associated with my skaag form. Mother made sure to disabuse me of any inclination I might have toward that attitude, informing me time and again of how weak and malformed I am.

Dad reaches for my head above my right eye. I tamp down the simultaneous urges to either flinch or bite his arm off. He caresses my hide above my eye, wiping aside the rainwater.

"I know the water burns," he says, then bends at the waist and walks beneath me to my right foreleg without hesitation or any outward sign of trepidation. "I'm ready."

I clasp him to my underbelly with my short, powerful leg, much like an alligator's, only several orders of magnitude larger. It's odd how calm and accepting Dad is of my skaag form. I haven't had any creature, human or otherwise, react to this body without fear or, in my mother's case, disappointment.

I shoot skyward, the drizzle burning like acid every time it runs into my eyes. The base is a sprawling expanse of twining roads, massive warehouses, housing, and grassy fields. Gunfire and the sirens of emergency vehicles ring out from up ahead, punctuated by explosions. My insides clench. If my friends are hurt, I don't know if I'll be able to control myself.

In the distance, I glimpse the firefight consuming a rectangular grassy field with a roadway along the perimeter. Near the center of the field is the canopy shelter I saw on TV. People run from it in every direction as orange fireballs spill from overhead, launched by faeries buzzing through the air like a swarm of angry wasps. A handful of soldiers with long guns shoot ineffectually at the zipping faeries. Blackened bodies with dark smoke rising from them speckle the grass. Panic and rage power through me, and I surge headlong toward the fight.

The action around the shelter draws my attention. Tanis's draconic form is captured in the same orange netting that had ensnared Mauve and Dr. Radcliffe on previous occasions. I'll have no help from her. But the dragon isn't what captures my focus and the sleeper's attention. Before the shelter, a faery slashes a glowing orange sword indiscriminately at people fleeing—even at a distance, I can tell it is Jett by his once handsome face disfigured by the gnarly scar on his right jawline.

Jett isn't the reason we slow our charge toward the battle. It's the half dozen armored figures methodically advancing on the dispersing crowd, carefully targeting anyone in a military uniform with blinding blasts of plasma from arm-mounted cannons. From above they look like ten-foot tall humanoid-shaped mechs ripped from the pages of a manga. My vision clouds, and I plummet.

Chapter 21

Bergman raises her triple-barreled gun arm at point-blank range until it's aimed between my eyes. She cackles, her mouth going horrendously wide like a snake about to consume prey.

"I told you I'd have revenge for Dr. Rah, Miss Lee!"

The top gun barrel burns bright as the midday sun. I scrunch my eyes shut, but it's too late—they're already sizzling like frying eggs.

"Allison! Pull up!"

Dad's caterwauling splinters the waking nightmare. I'm not sure if the ground rushes up to meet me or I fall to meet it, but either way, I'm about to smash into the green grass and crush my dad like a stomped slug. My body ripples, and I pull up as hard as I can. My vertebrae pop, and my tail end brushes the moist grass.

My heart thuds like a kettledrum booming at forte. Do I feel Dad's blood splattered against my chest or seeping between my talons? Panic besting me, I shout, "Daddy, are you okay?" My words come out as an ear-splitting shriek.

Until the shriek, the faeries strafing the ground like psychedelic World War II fighter jets hadn't taken notice of me. Now, they wheel in the air to confront me, the collective buzz of their wings like a vintage prop plane. Several dart toward me, black bodies aglow with orange light and surrounded by colorful dust. Their hands are aflame. Half a dozen, maybe more, hover in place and hurl fireballs. The flaming globes range in size from softballs to jack-o'-lanterns.

I shoot upward into the blue sky to avoid the projectiles, twisting so my back faces the oncoming fire. I don't want Dad burnt to a crisp if he's not already dead. The faeries chasing me continue their pursuit without hurling fireballs. Instead, they dart after me with their fiery arms outstretched like kamikaze pilots hell-bent on destruction. Fortunately, I can outrun them, at least in the short term, but I'm not sure who will tire first, me or the faeries. What do they plan to do if they catch me? They can roast Dad with a touch. My leathery skin has proven practically impervious to their magical fire.

The sleeper, however, isn't concerned about Dad. The beast is in full-on fight or flight mode, having selected, of course, fight followed by a gluttonous feast featuring a side of faery as the main course. It's all I can do not to go into a dive with the intent of slamming into my pursuers like a runaway freight train.

"Let go of me! Allison, let go!"

Relief rushes through me at Dad's voice over the roar of the wind. One thing is for sure, I'm not going to let go of him. I don't know our elevation, but it's a high enough drop that he'll splatter like an overripe tomato.

I twist my neck to dare a downward glance. I've outdistanced the fireballs, glimpsing two falling back to the earth to briefly flare when they strike the rain-soaked grass and then extinguish. The faeries launching the fireballs at me have turned their attention back to the ground, picking off the remaining soldiers and newly arrived police officers. The three pursuing me haven't given up, although I'm still outpacing them.

"Let go of me, Allison. You can't fight effectively

while carrying me, and neither can I! The fall won't hurt me. I have magic. Hurry! Drop me. I can save people."

It's his final sentence that almost convinces me. That's why we're here. To save people. To rescue my friends. But I can't drop him even if he has magic that will protect him from the fall. What about the faeries? One touch from them, and he'll be a human torch.

"Allison, I am an arch—"

Dad's words morph into a surprised yell when my foreleg releases him. Entirely on its own volition or, more accurately, the sleeper's. Part of me wants to rail against the beast for acting against my will, but I don't have time for that. I twist in the air and dive toward the oncoming faeries. I needn't have worried about Dad falling at all. He waves at me as I plummet past him, by all appearances standing atop an invisible magic carpet.

The faeries converge on me: one straight down the barrel at my face, one on my left, and one on my right. An electrical tingling courses over my hide. I struggle against the urge to unleash an electrical attack. While it will surely fry my three opponents at this range, it's about as refined as a rutting bull moose in a china shop. There's a fifty-fifty chance I'll fry Dad and even people on the ground.

My skin heats, and I glimpse a jagged yellow arc in my peripheral vision. The electricity is ready to be released in a heartbeat.

No! We can't. The risk of collateral damage is too great.

Still, the faeries close with their appendages extended like flaming lances. Over the wind, gunfire, and occasional explosions, I hear the roar of their fires.

An image fills my mind of the faeries forcing their fiery hands into my eyes and up my nostrils. The picture fades, and another takes its place. Electricity blasts from my body in every direction. Bolts sizzle into the faeries, and they drop from the sky like zapped mosquitoes. This time when the lurid film dissipates, the faeries are so close I feel the heat from their fire hands.

No! I won't risk killing my father!

Reality disappears. In human form, I ride the half-skaag's back like a dragon rider from a fantasy novel. The meaning is clear—take a seat and let the sleeper run the show in exchange for the beast not emitting a devastating electrical storm.

Yes. Do it. Take control. I hate myself for surrendering my agency. The last time this happened, the sleeper had wrested control of our body from me. I was thrown into a liminal state, beyond semiconsciousness, yet not quite unconscious. The half-skaag had electrocuted dozens, scores perhaps, of enthralled super magicians to death.

The sleeper brushes me aside, and I don't resist. This time, I'm not thrown into an abyss. This time, I have a front-row seat to a violent melee so swift I struggle to track what's happening. One instant, a faery, colorful dust cascading from its mouth to swirl around its body, is so close I see its black pupils surrounded by sclera highlighted with ocher veins. Fire burns my mouth, then my jaw snaps and I taste a bloody tang.

Somehow, I snatch the faery on the left out of the air with my short, powerful foreclaws. She struggles against me, and the orange fractals etched into her skin flare like bonfires. Burning hands press into my foreleg, but the flames register as little more than an annoyance. My talons compress, piercing her torso and legs. She keens, then explodes into a spray of orange fluid and gore. I want to retch, but the half-skaag licks the stringy flesh from our snout.

Heat presses down on the right side of our head, scorching our eye. An enraged shriek shears from our mouth, and we roll through the air in a desperate attempt to shake the faery from us, but its claws are barbs jammed deep into our hide. Electrical tingling builds over our body again.

No! You can't. It's too dangerous. Dad nears the ground, but by my estimation, he's still in the range of a stray bolt.

A flaming hand appears in our peripheral vision, lowering closer and closer to our oculus dexter. I'm so hyped up on fear and adrenaline I can burst at the seams. I want that hand away from my eye now! The temperature is quickly passing from barely tolerable to unbearable.

A bolt arcs up my assailant's arm. The flames engulfing the black hand sputter and die, and the glowing fractals etched into the dark skin like molten lava fade. The hand falls away, and I feel the faery's lifeless body dangling from our side.

The sleeper possesses control over our body I can only dream of having. Is this what Mother tried to teach me all those weekends spent training in the wilderness? That the only way I can master my monstrous abilities is by surrendering to the half-skaag?

I don't have time to contemplate what happened. Not yet. I might be riding shotgun, but I can still act as a navigator, or at least, a backseat driver. The sleeper whips about to a trajectory bringing us in behind the darting faeries bombarding the ground with fireballs. I don't comment because dealing with them would be my next course of action.

For one thing, the faeries concentrate half their firepower on Dad. He seems to have erected a translucent bluish dome large enough for the people on the ground to cram inside. People can scramble inside the shield's perimeter, but the fireballs explode against it with reverberating thumps.

The mechs advance slowly on the shield, meticulously gunning down soldiers and police officers in their way. The shield repels the few stray plasma shots that slam into it, but with each plasma burst strike, there is a long hiss and a bright blue flare. Even more worrying, what's to stop the mechs from marching across the magical perimeter like everyone else?

The sleeper issues a bloodcurdling shriek as it closes in on the faeries. The winged humanoids burst from our flight path like a flock of startled birds. Instead of regrouping to meet the attack, the faeries retreat, their dragonfly wings buzzing blurs. The sleeper's first impulse is to pursue fleeing prey.

Wait. They aren't the priority. We need to help the people on the ground and rescue Bria. Assuming she isn't already taken. In all the chaos, I can't be sure. But the armored super magicians are reforming a perimeter around the shelter. I wish I could see what's going on inside, but while in skaag form, I don't have access to my prosthetics' IR mode. All I can see is the canvas canopy with Tanis's draconic body projecting out in all directions. The orangish netting still traps the dragon.

Sometime during the fight, a klaxon had started,

sounding like an air raid siren from an old war movie. More police cars and Humvees have arrived and are converging on the tent in the field's center. We need to act now, not just to save my friends but to prevent a further bloodbath.

Still, the sleeper hovers, indecision palpable.

Please. We can save people. Prove we're not a monster!

Bergman's smiling face flashes in my mind. She shot me with a plasma bolt while I was a skaag. The blast had wounded me terribly, and it took me weeks to recover.

You ate some of that faery. We ate some of it. If I had control of my body, I'd puke right now. *I fulfilled my side of the bargain. Now it's your turn. Bria, Haji, and Bibi are down there and need our help.*

Chapter 22

The sleeper continues hovering in place as if frozen by past trauma. I don't know what to do. The onrushing police vehicles and Humvees are forming a perimeter approximately thirty feet from the tent. Police and soldiers exit the vehicles, taking positions behind doors, trunks, and hoods. Some carry gnarly-looking rifles that, I suspect, will barely scuff the mechs' armor. The mechs' plasma cannons will make short work of the newcomers.

We have to do something. More people are about to die.

My pleading falls on deaf ears. The sleeper doesn't care. Why? Because the half-skaag sees lesser beings, who are food, and the deadly threat posed by mechs. The scent of charred meat rising from the blackened corpses set our mouth salivating and twist our stomach with hunger. It's horrible. I want to suppress the insatiable desires, but I can't.

What should I do? Do I dare try to reassert control of our body, or will that see me thrown into the liminal state again?

My friends are down there. Dad is trying to save people. What about our bargain? We can't do nothing.

Still, the sleeper doesn't budge. I have a bird's eye view of the ensuing standoff. Maybe a hostage negotiation? A man in camo stands on the flatbed of a

Humvee. He speaks into a megaphone, demanding the intruders release any hostages and surrender—fat chance of that. The mechs have stopped gunning down people and hold position maybe ten feet or less from the tent.

Dad leads the survivors under his shield away from the scene toward long white buildings across the road. I hope Bibi is among those crowded around him and not dead or one of the wounded calling for help as they crawl across the grass.

I never knew you were such a coward. I thought you were a hunter, a warrior.

Bergman's leering face replaces my view of reality and disappears in a flash.

She's not here. If she were, she wouldn't be down there. She'd be trying to kill us right now. Listen to me. We must go down there and save my friends before the faeries return. This is our chance to save Haji, Bria, and Bibi. We need to…oh my God! Bibi!

A figure wearing a tan hijab and a blue-and-black parka crawls away from the line of mechs before the tent. That must be Bibi. I could die when I see smoke rising from her shoulder.

Go! Now!

The sleeper doesn't move.

Then give me back control!

Without preamble, I'm thrust back into the driver's seat. I reorient myself, then I'm plunging toward the mechs. I don't have time to consider what I should do other than get between them and Bibi because they could start indiscriminately firing again at any second.

When the battle-armored soldiers start shooting, there's nothing random about it. They're aiming at me.

The sleeper cringes every time a burning plasma shot blazes by. The bolts fly past close enough that my hide heats. These have to be warning shots, or at least one would've grazed me already.

Seconds after the opening barrage, gunfire erupts from the gathered police and military vehicles. The bullets ping off the armor with no effect other than to draw the attention of several of the enemy. They turn their plasma cannons on their assailants, quickly turning a handful of police cars and Humvees to slag. The police and soldiers retreat under the withering assault while continuing to return fire.

Plasma shoots by so close it singes my skin. The sleeper slams into my consciousness, battling for control of our body like a cornered animal. I'm knocked off balance, teetering on the edge of the abyss. One misstep, and I'll fall. But then I see Jett, his body glowing with orange light and surrounded by variegated faery dust, emerge from beneath the shelter. In his right hand he clasps the grip of a black sword decorated with the same orange fractal patterns as his body. His left arm clamps an unconscious Bria against his chest.

No. You had your chance. Through sheer willpower, I step back from the abyss and cast the sleeper into the darkness.

Three armored figures break off from the firing line to form an escort around Jett. One armor-clad fiend continues under the tent. Now would be an excellent time for Tanis to escape the magical netting ensnaring her, but the dragon remains motionless.

Plasma burns through the canopy, and the frame collapses, revealing burned bodies, a smashed podium, and Haji's supine body with an arm cannon pointed at his head. I pull up from my helter-skelter dive, levitating a few feet before the line of mechs. They have stopped firing at me but keep the triple barrels of their gun arms trained on me. If they open fire at this range, I'm charcoal. A few mechs still exchange fire with the retreating soldiers and police.

Jett smiles at me from behind the line of armored thralls. His smile hideously twists the ruined flesh along his right jaw. Faery dust sprinkles the mangled skin, but the wound seems beyond the magical dust's ability to heal.

"Allison, a pleasure to see you again, especially in your true form. You'll forgive me if I don't stay and chat." He points the sword toward Haji. "Your friend will remain alive as long as you don't pursue me." His dragonfly wings flutter, quickly becoming a blur, and he lifts off the ground with Bria clutched to his chest. "Don't bother saying anything. I know all you can manage is the most horrible shrieking as a skaag."

I tremble with my desire to do something, anything. But I don't dare. I know Jett can't be allowed to escape with Bria, but I don't doubt his threat that any interference on my part will lead to Haji's execution.

Jett puckers his lips and blows me a kiss, then shoots skyward on buzzing wings. Rage pulses through me at his amorous gesture, and I shriek.

With a deafening rumble, like the afterburners from fighter jets, the mechs take to the air, flames blasting from their heels. Through the fire and smoke, I see the rearguard, the mech with its gun arm trained on Haji.

I look skyward, and drizzle strikes my eyes, burning like citric acid. A growl rumbles in my chest. I pine to chase Jett down and force him to relinquish Bria. The problem is I want Haji to survive this day even more. I scrunch my eyes, promising Bria I will save her one day soon and make Jett pay for all he has done this day.

A crack rings out over the patter of rain and the moans of the wounded and dying. I whip my head around, glimpsing the mech standing over Haji. Blood and gore paint the battle armor's glass face plate. The gun arm slides listlessly to the mech's side, and it teeters precariously, threatening to topple over onto Haji.

Pulse thrumming in my ears, I streak over the ground, careening into the armor with a bone-jarring thud. The mechanical contraption topples backward away from my friend, tumbling head over heels for fifteen feet or more before coming to a clattering rest.

Breathing hard, I hover protectively over Haji, fearing the mech will rise like a horror movie villain back to try to kill the final girl one last time. But through the increasing rain, a sizeable hole is visible in the side of the armored head, presumably caused by a large caliber round. Along with all the sounds of the approaching soldiers and police, I hear Haji breathing, slowly and deeply, like someone in a fathomless sleep. A swift inspection of him shows no outward sign of trauma, but his state is eerily familiar to ones I've seen him in before.

Blinking against the rain, the glow from Tanis's still dragon form, and the orange netting holding her, I see Jett and the mechs are specs against gray clouds. Soldiers and police fan out around me. Some level their guns at me, while others point their firearms at the ground. Several speak, but I care nothing for their words. I let out a hiss, a warning sound, because I fear if they shoot at me, they might hit Haji by mistake. But the boy beneath my bulk isn't the only person I'm concerned about. What about Dad? What about Bibi? I had seen smoke rising from a wound to her shoulder.

I shriek, sound weaponized. People recoil, some fall to their knees, others drop their weapons, and many combine all three actions, but Haji doesn't stir. I writhe skyward, scanning the grass for Bibi. I spy her prone on the ground with her hands covering her ears, and I hate myself for what I've done. I've hurt her. I dart to her side, coming around until we face each other. Her dazed eyes go wide, and she screams, a piercing sound of absolute terror that impales my heart.

My transformation into human form is immediate and wrenching, but the pain of rending flesh, sinew, organs, and bones cannot compare to the suffering caused by Bibi's scream. I kneel next to her.

"Bibi, it's me. Allison," I say.

I might see recognition in her eyes before they roll back into her head and she passes out. The noisome stench of burned flesh and singed fabric fills the air. Her left shoulder is blistered and bloody.

"Help!" I scream. "My friend is hurt!"

Chapter 23

Soldiers and police officers close in with their guns trained on me. Their expressions are grim and determined, except for a few who look horrified. None approach to provide Bibi medical aid.

"Please, she needs help," I say.

They keep their distance, nervously shifting. Their collective fear is a palpable musk hanging in the air as thick as the Great Smog of London.

"What do we do? She's that monster!" a soldier says, bouncing on his feet with pent-up energy.

"My name is Allison," I say, my tone betraying my anger at their inaction. I point at Bibi, unconscious on the grass. "My friend needs help. I don't know what to do. She was conscious"— my voice cracks—"then she passed out."

The soldiers glance at each other, clearly waiting for someone to take charge. The eyes of several bug out so far, it looks like they'll roll right out of the sockets. Bibi's breathing is shallow, and her usually tan skin has taken on an unhealthy pallor. My throat constricts, and I can't breathe. When I look away, my breath comes in a ragged gasp.

"She's that monster," the soldier bouncing on his feet says, voice rising octaves as he speaks. "Do we shoot her?"

"She's just a girl, man," a soldier growls. His trembling finger rests against the trigger of his rifle. "And she saved us."

"Well, shit." The bouncing soldier lowers his

weapon. "If we ain't going to shoot her, we should get her a blanket or something. She's naked."

"And a medic," I say.

"Don't worry. We'll make sure the civvie gets medical attention."

****

I sit on the bottom bed of a bunk bed inside what I'm told is an old barracks. The building smells musty, overhead lights buzz like a swarm of bees, and every time I shift on the thin mattress, the bed's worn metal frame creaks loud enough to wake the dead. I'm alone except for my guards—a man and a woman armed with rifles and wearing camo with an MP patch on their left shoulders standing near a wall of peeling white paint.

I wear ill-fitting gray sweats, which beats being naked. I wish I could shut off my brain for a few minutes. I can't rid myself of the image of Jett shooting skyward with Bria clutched to his chest. Recalling how on Golden Shoal I had kissed him and yearned for his sensual touch leaves ash on my tongue. He's a monster, and now he has what he wants—Bria's blood, a.k.a. the Juice. With that, the faeries can transform more human magicians into super-powered thralls.

I pound the mattress with a fist. The bedframe squeals in protest. "This is all my fault. I'm so stupid."

That's why I'm here instead of breezing by the guards to find my friends and Dad. I don't trust myself. If I hadn't staged the media blitz, none of this would've happened. Jett would've never known Bria's location.

I punch the mattress again, and the springs squeal. Standing, I pace the considerable length of the barracks. I can't even blame Devin for this as much as I might like to. In the end, I greenlighted the plan. I put my hands on the sides of my head. Now, that monster has Bria, and Haji is in a coma again. And Bibi. Poor Bibi. She wouldn't be involved in this if it wasn't for me.

I've paced the length of the barracks at least a dozen times when McAllister shows up, veins on the side of his bald head bulging, flanked by Valentina and two other Draconic Task Force agents I don't recognize.

"You really screwed the pooch on this one," McAllister announces as he stops in front of me. He looks down his nose, face scrunched up in a frown. Valentina glares daggers at me from her position behind his right shoulder. McAllister puts his quivering index finger under my nose. "You remember that yet-to-be-built super prison we spoke about? Do you? Well, I think it might get built after this."

I combat the temptation to bite his finger. "You came all this way to say that?"

"No." He lowers his hand to his side. "But I feel better having said it. I'm here to tell you that you're not to leave this building until Dr. Radcliffe arrives."

"When will he arrive?"

"I've been told he's on a flight back from New York. That's six hours, give or take."

I gaze at the ceiling. "Can you tell me about Haji, Bibi, my dad?"

McAllister gives me a quizzical look. "Bibi?"

"Bexley Aziz. She's a reporter. She was wounded."

McAllister shakes his head. "I'll ask around. There are so many burn victims they're being sent to all the hospitals in the region. Your friend Haji is awake." I let out a breath, and my hands go to my chest. "He's still messed up, but Mr. Lee is a miracle worker. I heard

Radcliffe is astounded to learn he's a magician. I have to say, Allison, your family is full of surprises. Valentina and these agents are here to keep you company. Now, if you'll excuse me, I have to go deal with your mess."

I watch McAllister leave, my heart and mind racing. How long will it take Radcliffe to discover Dad is an archmagus, one of the magicians he hunted down and killed for centuries?

****

Time rolls by like it has stopped. I sit on the bunk and ignore Valentina's stink eye.

I don't know if five minutes or five hours have passed when a coppery glint streaming in from one of the evenly spaced square windows along the wall disturbs my ruminations. Mauve?

A minute later, Mauve's dragon form enters the barracks, passing through the guards, walls, ceiling, and bunkbeds with equal ease, painting everything in a copper radiance. The light diminishes and brightens in time with the flickering of the lithe dragon. In contrast, Mauve's humanoid golem is the dictionary definition of frumpy, from unstylish clothing to disastrously hacked hairdo. She nods to the military police and Draconic Task Force agents as she walks over to my bunk.

She stops in front of me, arms crossed before her chest. Her unblinking eyes bore into me. I immediately feel judged guilty.

"How is Tanis?" I ask, hoping a show of concern for the elderly dragon will short-circuit any ill will Mauve feels.

"Recovering." Mauve sits next to me on the mattress. The springs squeal in distress at the added weight. Mauve stares at me, eyes as large as eggs behind circular glasses she doesn't need. "I helped free her from the disruptor field. She's old, Allison, and the attack has left her in a fragile state."

My hands go to my mouth. "Will she be okay?"

Mauve sadly smiles. "Like elderly humans, ancient dragons don't always recover from trauma."

"Oh, no…I'm so sorry. I know words aren't enough."

"Haji is doing better. Your father is a magician of unusual skill. Frederick will be interested to speak to him when he arrives. Very interested."

I lower my hands. "Is Haji talking? McAllister gave me an update earlier. He said Haji isn't one hundred percent yet."

"That's difficult to say," Mauve says with a slight frown. "He is under the influence of your father's magic. Magic more complex than I've ever known a human magician to perform."

Chapter 24

The rain stops late in the afternoon. A break in the clouds allows golden sun beams to stream through the small square windows. I wish I had my camera with me.

My nose twitches at the distinctive scent of beef in the air—*eww*. Simultaneously, my mouth salivates, and my tummy rumbles. I shift on the squeaking mattress, careful not to upend the tray with my so-called dinner. It doesn't look bad for institutional food—a hamburger with an attractive bun and french fries tempt me. Next to the food is a clear plastic cup full of a sparkly yellow beverage that's probably some kind of soda. Meat will satisfy my inhuman hunger, but I refuse to eat beef. Before The Incident, I was on the cusp of going vegan.

The sleeper stirs deep within me. As always, the beast is insatiable and curious to try beef, even if it is cooked. Licking my lips, I tear the bun and lettuce from the beef patty. I pick up greasy ground meat, mouth hanging open ready to chomp down. A golden radiance plays over the patty, giving it a magical sheen.

"I did not know you eat beef. Good for you. You need the iron."

I look up, realizing the golden light sparkling against the grease is the luminescence from Dr. Frederick Radcliffe's dragon form. The sleeper retreats from the draconic presence, and our curiosity to sample beef extinguishes. I unceremoniously drop the ground meat onto the bottom half of the hamburger bun, rattling the plate against the tray.

"Thanks. I don't think I could forgive myself for eating beef." A hunger pang cramps my abdomen. I grab a french fry slick with oil and bite it in half. The crispy combination of salt and fat explodes in my mouth. I won't be eating just one.

"Your hunger will not be satisfied until you consume meat." Radcliffe smiles.

"You know I don't eat beef. The—"

"Yes, yes. The environmental impact is too great." Radcliffe indicates the bunk bed with a wave of a hand. "May I?"

I nod my assent, and he sits down next to me. The dragon's humanoid golem is dressed to the nines in a dark blue three-piece suit. I can smell the starch from his white button-down shirt. Around his neck is a red tie with an American flag pin prominently positioned. Below the flag is the pin portraying his dragon form in miniature. Golden light sparkles against the pins and his rimless glasses.

"Did you know there are companies growing animal protein in laboratories?" Radcliffe smirks. "While in New York, I was told about one on the cusp of seeking FDA approval for lab-grown chicken meat. Presumably, you cannot tell the difference between their product and meat from a slaughtered chicken."

My expression curdles, and I drop the handful of fries onto the plate. Lab-grown meat brings back images of the cavern on Golden Shoal, where the faeries harvested blood from genetically altered infants.

"Meat from a lab has a smaller environmental

footprint—"

"Can we skip to the part where you chew me out and then tell me what's going to happen?"

Radcliffe laughs, but the mirth never reaches his eyes. His draconic head lowers through the ceiling, so that his vertically slit dragon eyes stare at me as judgmental as ever.

"I have no intention of chewing you out, Allison. Instead"—he reaches into his suit jacket and pulls out a phone—"I want you to have a conversation with someone—a real heart-to-heart. While you do that, I will deal with your father. I see two possibilities of how he could have kept his magic secret from me all those years. The first possibility is that your mother's magic hid him, but I do not believe that. She was gone for nearly two decades, and I would have detected him unless he was masking his magical ability himself. No ordinary magician could do that. That means he is exceptional."

"Leave him alone. Don't—"

"Hurt him? I make no promises." Radcliffe dials and offers me the phone. "Take it. I know you want to talk to Joe."

I snatch the phone from his hand. In the center of the screen is a blue circle with the name Joe in black letters. Beneath the circle is the message: placing video call…

The golden light fades, and the clap of dress shoes against the floor rings through the barracks. I look up from the phone and glimpse Dr. Radcliffe ambulating toward the exit.

"Allison! Allison, that you, girl? I can't see you." Joe's voice emits from the phone.

Joe's happy face fills the screen. I swear all the pain worn into his features has sloughed away. Maybe I did the right thing when I turned to the dragons for help. But I also know this call is Radcliffe's way of warning me my friend is under his power. "Joe! Wow! You look…you look great!"

"I know." He beams. "Ten years younger, the nurses say."

I nod, absentmindedly. I want to be present with Joe, but I don't trust that dragon not to harm Dad.

"I know you're worried Doc Radcliffe might do something to your daddy. He told me all about it. He suspects your daddy is a…archmagus or something."

My breath catches in my throat, and I swear my heart palpitates.

"I know you're worried that something awful is going to happen. Now, I ain't going to tell you not to worry. The Doc told me he wouldn't lie to you. He told me he wasn't sure what he'd do if he found out your daddy is one of these archmagus types. But I'll tell you what, Allison, I don't think he'll do anything rash. The Doc don't strike me as the rash sort, and neither does your daddy."

"You can't trust Dr. Radcliffe, Joe. He—"

"I know the Doc ain't no angel. But God's honest truth, I think he has humanity's best interests at heart. I really mean that. Since the procedure and my recovery, I've been talking to him every night. He's convinced me about the skaag and faery threats to our world and his sincere desire to protect all life on our planet. Now, I know you've been up to some nonsense. Nonsense that might have some bad consequences. I tell you what. You're a soldier now, Allison, and that means being part of a team. You got to tell your teammates what you're doing and follow the leader. You can't be going maverick. That's how bad things go down."

Joe sounds sincere, and it tears my heart asunder to tell him the truth. "Joe, Dr. Radcliffe helped you and gave you a position in the Task Force to keep you close to him. So he can threaten your well-being to keep me in line."

Joe's expression turns stormy, then clears with a smile that's all sunshine. He speaks in between chuckles. "Allison, I can walk now without pain and feeling like I'm going to pass out. Every day, I'm stronger. At this rate, I'll be stronger than ever. Stronger than I was as a twenty-year-old macho man in the infantry. Bet you didn't know I already started my training ahead of schedule, did you?" I shake my head. "There's something I want you to know. The Doc didn't want me to tell you this, but he didn't strictly forbid me from telling you either. Their magic, the dragons' magic, did more than heal my wounds. It changed me. I can smell magic now. All kinds of magic. I'm learning to distinguish between the different types. It's—"

"What? That is not okay, Joe! That is not okay!"

"Hush. Hush." Joe shakes his head. "I'm telling you this, so you know not everything revolves around you. I'm something new. An experiment. A human augmented by dragon magic. That's why they agreed to help me. Your friend Mauve contacted me and told me about what they wanted to do. I agreed, Allison. I agreed."

I'm gobsmacked. Enraged. My jaw works, but I'm at a loss for words.

Without warning, the overhead lights click and go out, and the image on the phone screen goes blank.

Chapter 25

I blink.

The phone remains dead in my hand. The lights don't buzz or flicker.

"What the…" I bite my lower lip, hoping Joe isn't worried about me.

Valentina's phone appears to have powered down too. The screen's glow no longer illuminates her face, and she looks at her compatriots with puzzlement.

"Did you feel that?" the magician asks, her lips quivering.

Her companions nod. The male magician *ratatat*s his foot against the floor. The woman standing next to him swats his upper arm.

"Stop that," she hisses while nervously glancing around the barracks.

I stand from the bunk. "Feel what? What's going on?"

Valentina points at me. "You stay here." She turns back to her companions. "Go find Dr. Radcliffe. We need to know what that was." The female magician strides for the exit, head rotating as if trying to look everywhere at once. Valentina turns to her male companion. "Check the sky. Just in case…" Her voice drops an octave. "…those faeries have come back."

"Yes, ma'am," the male magician says smartly and heads for the exit.

The soldiers standing guard appear only slightly less anxious than the magicians. They murmur, curious why the power went out and wondering when the backup generators will kick in. One tries a walkie-talkie that's dead, and the other has her cell phone out. Both devices might as well be bricks. I can see why they're perplexed. The weather calmed down as the light of day faded from the sky. There's no blustery wind to knock out the power, and from what can be seen out the small windows, the rest of the base is without electricity too. And there's the odd fact that everything powered by batteries is dead.

"What did you feel? Magic?" I ask Valentina.

She glares at me, shakes her head, and then goes back to staring out the window. I'd like to throttle the woman, and the sleeper reasserts itself at the thought. Black emotions ooze through me, and my hands curl into bone-pulverizing fists.

No, I tell the half-skaag. *I'm not going to do anything to Valentina. Now, if you can't tell me what's going on with the power, go away.*

I force myself to flop onto the mattress. The springs bounce and squeal under my weight. The sleeper refuses to withdraw to the recesses of my mind, peppering me with visions of absolute blackness slowly resolving into the barracks.

What are you trying to tell me?

In my mind's eye, everything goes black.

Okay? And?

Slowly, the scene brightens until I see a pair of eyeballs on a white table. What the…? A person in lab gear, including a face mask, materializes next to the table. My throat constricts and pulse doubles.

"She's dead," I gasp. "Dr. Rah is dead."

The deceased doctor picks up an eyeball in a gloved hand. She turns toward me and extends the hand holding the eye—the prosthetic eye—like she's about to shove it into my eye socket.

"Allison. What's going on?"

Valentina's shrill query shatters my rumination. I blink. The annoying magician stands in front of me, squinting.

"I can see. That's what the sleeper was trying to tell me," I say and feel approval bubbling from the half-skaag.

Valentina's mouth forms an O. "Your eyes are tech. Why can you still see? Your father…" Valentina snaps the thumb and middle finger of her left hand. "Magic caused the power outage." She starts pacing before the bunk. "But he shielded your prosthetics against magic somehow. I don't know how. His magic must be…like nothing I've ever encountered."

She stops pacing and looks at me, shaking her head.

"Maybe?" I say uncertainly.

Did the faeries cause the outage? I ask the sleeper and receive no response.

****

I open my eyes at the thrum of electricity and sit up on the mattress. The overhead lights flicker back on. I'm not sure how long we've been without power, but I'm guessing no more than thirty minutes.

A few seconds later, the phone vibrates in my hand. It has rebooted and displays a lock screen. A message displays missed calls from numbers I don't recognize. None have local area codes, but that doesn't necessarily mean anything in this age of cell phones. Names are associated with a few of the calls, which I scan through—no one I know.

"Wow," Valentina says, her eyes glued to her phone.

"What?" I ask.

She looks up from the screen for a second then her gaze flicks back. "The power outage…it was pretty widespread. I need to make some calls." Valentina turns away, bringing the phone to her ear. She catches her companion's eye. "Don't let Allison out of your sight."

The male magician, back from having checked the sky for faeries, ambles over, all casual as if he's pretending not to watch me. I can't stop myself from a dramatic eye roll.

"If I was going to leave, I'd already be gone."

He gives me a sheepish smile and shrugs. "Orders."

Dr. Radcliffe's phone vibrates in my hand again. A number splays across the screen. No name is displayed and I don't recognize the number, but I am able to answer the call even with the phone locked.

"Hello?"

"Allison! What happened? Are you okay?" Joe's voice is so loud I have to hold the phone away from my ear.

"Not so loud, Joe. I can hear you. I'm fine. The power went out, and the phone died."

"But you're okay? You can still see? Nothing happened?" His words are rapid-fire.

"I can see. I didn't have any problems with my prosthetics. I still don't know what happened other than the power went out and all the electronics, even those with batteries, lost power. What do you know?"

"They think the whole West Coast lost power. That it might've been some kind of attack. Things are sketchy on the news, but one of my handlers—you know, a Task Force agent—got some special communication from the government or something. They don't know if it's the Russians or Chinese or something else"—his voice hushes—"something magical."

"The magicians felt something. I heard them talking after the power went out."

"Have you seen Dr. Radcliffe? He'll know something."

"Not yet. I've been staying put like you told me. It's horrible, Joe. I can't even trust myself anymore. Not after what happened to Haji and Bria. It's all my fault." My voice cracks with the final sentence.

"You can trust yourself. You have to remember to be a team player and trust others."

"Like Dr. Radcliffe," I scoff.

"I'm not saying trust blindly." I hear other voices over the phone. "What? Seriously. Hold up. I hear you." Joe sighs. "I got to go, Allison. Something's up. Comms blackout. Probably won't last long. Call me if you find out anything."

We say our goodbyes, and Joe ends the call. About thirty seconds later, a call comes in from a different number which I answer. The female voice on the other end of the line demands to speak to Dr. Radcliffe and abruptly ends the call when I say he's unavailable, but I'd love to know any details about the power outage on the West Coast.

"I better take that for safekeeping," the magician

says, holding out a hand.

Reluctantly, I hand him the phone, giving him a glower for good measure. This whole being a team player routine is already wearing thin.

****

It's well and truly dark out when Dr. Radcliffe, Dad, and Haji finally make an appearance. I'm overjoyed Radcliffe, who has a phone superglued to his ear, hasn't killed my father, but it's Haji I sprint to embrace.

"Haji! I was so afraid you would never wake up!"

I'm within Radcliffe's translucent dragon form, but for once, I don't mind the ache behind my eyes. Haji is alive. Even better, he's up and walking around. I spin him around in a 360. I don't know if I've ever been more excited to feel someone alive next to me.

He smiles toothlessly and doesn't return my embrace. "Good to see you too."

I release him and retreat a step to get a better look at him. He looks dazed and tired. His cheeks are hollowed out, and the shadows are so dark beneath his eyes that they could be bruises.

Dad steps forward and says to Haji, "Why don't you sit down, lad?"

Haji nods without a word and retreats to a bunk.

"Is he going to be okay?" I ask.

Dad shrugs and sighs. "I'm doing what I can to help him, but he is addicted to faery blood. The dragons are trying to wean him off it…" Dad shakes his head.

Sighing, I shut my eyes. If I had been a little kinder to Haji, maybe he wouldn't be messed up right now. I look at Dad. His shoulders are hunched and his features drawn. I'm not sure if it's from battling the faeries or facing down Radcliffe or both.

My gaze flicks between Dad and Radcliffe. “Do the two of you have a truce?”

Dad gives me a half smile. “For now. We have bigger fish to fry.”

“Thank you, Mrs. President. Yes, ma’am. I will be on the plane as soon as it is ready. Yes, I will handle this personally.” Dr. Radcliffe lowers the phone and slips it into the inside pocket of his suit jacket. “What have you told her?”

“Nothing yet,” Dad says.

“Where you on the phone with the president?” I demand.

“I speak with her weekly,” Radcliffe says nonchalantly. “She is a remarkable woman. Now…” Radcliffe takes a deep breath and his expression turns deadly serious. “An opening has been torn in the slipstream by the faeries.”

My jaw goes unhinged. “What? Why would they do that?” An opening in the slipstream could give skaags and who knows what else access to Earth. I know from Jett the faeries have little love for skaags. That is if I can trust anything the lying faery boy has ever told me.

“We do not know why. We have an approximate location of the opening. It is on or near the Hawaiian Islands,” Radcliffe says.

Joe said to trust myself, so I go with my gut. “What are we waiting for? Let’s go.”

Chapter 26

Dad and Dr. Radcliffe exchange an adult look as if what I'm proposing is naïve or plain stupid. Not true. I know how to collapse the slipstream. I go inside, transform into a half-skaag, and discharge electricity—been there, done that. Just ask the expeditionary force Mark Cassidy invited to Earth. Oh, wait! They never made it to Earth, did they, because I collapsed the slipstream on them.

"What are we waiting for? We have to close it. The sooner, the better." I glance between Dad and Radcliffe. "We can fly, right?" I'm not sure how far I can fly as a skaag without resting, but I know Mother has flown to Hawaii in skaag form.

"Conceptually, I agree with you." Radcliffe steeples his hands under his chin. "But we must be cautious. Rushing in could prove dangerous, even fatally so."

I throw up my hands. "Fatal for who exactly?" I start counting off the fingers on my left hand. "First, we have you, Dr. Radcliffe, a dragon and magician of immense power. Second, we have Mauve, another dragon and magician of—"

"Mauve will not be joining us," Radcliffe says.

"What? Why?"

"Tanis's condition is fragile since being freed from the phase disrupter. Mauve will not want to leave her mentor's side, nor will I command that of her."

That's an odd attitude for a dragon who was willing to sacrifice me for the greater good, but I keep that point to myself. I don't want Mauve commanded to do anything she wouldn't do willingly. "Okay. Second—" I wave my fingers under Radcliffe's nose. "—you have me. A half-skaag with the proven ability to collapse the slipstream." I tick off a third finger. "We have the last remaining archmagus. Admittedly, I don't know the full extent of my father's powers, but I know he practiced magic right under your nose for decades without you knowing. That counts for something, right?" I lift a fourth finger. "You can call upon the Draconic Task Force. How many magicians is that? Dozens? Hundreds?"

"I admire your enthusiasm. I do. But we need to be careful," Dad says. "The magic that was used…" He shakes his head. "It's powerful, like nothing I've ever felt before."

"What will we do if skaags or something worse come through the slipstream?" I place my hands on my hips and glare at both of them. "It took three dragons working together to take down Mark Cassidy. And he was only one skaag." I point at Dr. Radcliffe. "You're the one who said the skaags will use humans as food stock."

Radcliffe nods. "We do need to move quickly. On that, we agree. We will fly to Hawaii by military transport. If the faeries spot a dragon or skaag over the ocean, undoubtedly, they will know we are coming."

"What about the weird power outage? What if that happens again while we're in the air? The plane will fall out of the sky."

"We think the power disruption is a side effect of the magic the faeries used to open the slipstream," Dad says, "not a weapon."

“If something happens to the plane, we will reveal ourselves and fly under our own power.” Radcliffe’s smile is predatory. “I believe for this mission less is more. The three of us—”

“And Haji,” Dad adds.

“Haji? Seriously?” I glance at my friend, who looks closer to needing twenty-four-hour medical care than being ready to go on a dangerous mission.

“My magic keeps him from slipping into another coma,” Dad says.

“Can’t we leave Haji here? Under Mauve’s care?” I ask.

Dad shakes his head. “I need to refresh the magic stabilizing him regularly. I believe we’ll find him greatly improved by the time we reach Hawaii.”

“Maybe you shouldn’t come then. You can stay here with Haji,” I say.

Dad takes a deep breath. “I’m coming. If there’s even the slightest chance of finding your mother, helping her…” He shakes his head. “I have to be there.”

I look to Radcliffe for support. “This is insane. You don’t agree to bringing Haji, do you?”

Radcliffe frowns. “The four of us will find and infiltrate the faeries’ base, discover the location of the gateway, and destroy it.”

“For the record.” I throw up my hands. “Bringing Haji along is nuts. When do we leave? The sooner we close the gateway, the better.”

“A C-130 Hercules is being provided to take us to Hawaii. I have been told it will be ready in the morning,” Radcliffe says. “For now, I suggest you rest, Allison.”

****

Dad and Haji stay behind with me in the barracks while Dr. Radcliffe leaves to go about his important business as the head of the UN Draconic Task Force. Dad paces near the entrance, repeatedly glancing at something in his hand.

Haji sits on a nearby bunk, staring listlessly at the floor with his shoulders slumped. I don't know if he's lost in thought or completely zoned out in the space between consciousness and sleep. Part of me wants to go to him, but he's not the only person I am losing my mind over.

I approach Dad. "Can I borrow your phone?"

He startles and stops pacing, clutching what he holds to his chest. "Umm…sure."

Dad fishes in his front pants pocket with his free hand and pulls out his phone. He offers the device to me, but I don't take it.

"What's that?" I point to the hand clutched to his chest.

Looking sheepish, Dad lowers his hand, revealing the vial of purple ichor he holds.

My mouth drops open and I lean in close to him.

"That's dragon blood," I whisper.

"I need it to make the potion to stabilize Haji long-term," Dad says.

"You're going to use draconic blood magic on Haji?" I glance at Haji who seems oblivious to our conversation.

"Not yet. My magic sustains him for now. But I need this to wean him off faery blood."

"I've seen blood magic…it's been done on me. My friends."

Dad's voice rises. "This isn't that…" Dad shuts his

eyes and take a deep breath. He opens his eyes and continues. "I'm considering what spells to infuse this blood with to create a potent and safe potion." He unlocks the phone with his thumbprint and presses it into my hand. "Now, if you allow me to get back to brainstorming…"

I take the phone and scowl at Dad. "Is Haji still on the Juice or not?"

"Faery blood is a component of the potion." He looks at the vial. "A very small component."

"That sounds exactly like what Tanis was injecting him with!"

"Listen, Allison. I infused the mixture of dragon and faery blood with spells to augment the beneficial properties of the mixture and lessen the…psychotropic effects of the dragon blood. Right now, Radcliffe is retrieving more faery blood and the herbs needed for your tea."

My eyes bug out. "Did you tell Radcliffe about my dreams?"

"No. No." Dad shakes his head. "Allison, I know this is a lot to ask. I need you to trust me. Have your dreams returned?"

I shake my head.

"I've helped you, and now I'm going to help Haji. You're going to see him improve greatly over the next few days."

I back up. "Okay. Fine. But if his condition worsens, I'm blaming you."

"That's fine. No problem," Dad says and returns to pacing.

I walk over to the bunk Haji sits on. "May I join you?"

Haji looks up from the floor. His eyes are glazed. After blinking several times, his gaze focuses. "Allison…sure."

I sit next to him, so close our legs touch. Warmth spreads through me. I haven't been this close to him since he did the first interview with Devin. From what I can tell, Haji doesn't react to my touch. I'm surprised how much that hurts.

"So…ah…my dad put a spell on you?"

"Yeah, I…I think it's helping…with the withdrawal. My mind is foggy, but it's getting better."

"Do you want to talk to Dalia?" I ask.

Haji shakes his head. "Nah, you go ahead. My head hurts."

"Should I—"

"No, stay here." He grabs my free hand. His hand is feverishly hot, like Gore's when he cast magic on me.

"Okay." I type Dalia's number on the keypad and press the phone to my ear. My friend answers after the first ring.

"Hello, Mr. Lee?"

"Dalia, it's me."

"Allison! What happened?"

I give my BFF a rundown on everything that's happened, leaving out the part that we're planning to go to Hawaii to destroy the portal.

"No! The faeries have Bria? Oh, no."

"I shouldn't have done the media blitz…I don't know. Maybe the attack would have never happened. All those people would still be alive. Bria wouldn't be in the hands of the faeries right now."

"You don't know that, Allison. It might all be a coincidence."

"You don't believe that, and neither do I."

"You can't take all the blame on yourself! It's my fault too!" Dalia shouts.

Afraid anything I say will upset my friend more, I remain silent. She softly sobs. I want to say something, but I don't trust myself. Not anymore. Everything I say and do is wrong. At best, people get hurt. At worst, they die.

Finally, Dalia stops sobbing. I'd almost think she had ended the call, but I can still hear her breathing. The bunk groans as Haji shifts his weight. The next thing I know, he's leaning against me with his head resting against my shoulder.

"Haji…" I fall silent when I glimpse his closed eyes. The ripe odor of sweat wafts from his thick, wavy hair. His chest gently rises and falls with his deep, rhythmic breathing. I don't remember the last time I saw him so peaceful. I take a deep breath and fill my friend in on the one aspect of the attack I left out—Bexley Aziz being injured. Dalia gasps at the news. "Can you find out about her condition? I'm worried sick."

"I'll get in touch with Devin. I think he knows her mother."

"Let me know as soon as you find out anything. You can call or message this number."

"Allison."

"What?"

"You're going to close the slipstream. Don't bother denying it. I know that's what you're going to do. You and Dr. Radcliffe. Maybe even Mauve and your dad. I'm going with you."

My lips quiver. "Dalia, no. We don't know what

we're getting into. You'll be—"

"What? Are you worried I'll get in the way? Are you worried I can't contribute? I've proven myself."

Dalia's tone is deadpan like she is stating simple, inalienable facts. Somehow that hurts more than if she were emotional and shrill. Because she's right. I would've died when I collapsed the slipstream if she hadn't reached inside the gateway between dimensions and pulled me out. I would've died because I had given up, but Dalia hadn't given up on me. I owe her, and I will never be able to repay that debt.

The problem is Dalia is all too willing to do things I am reluctant or unwilling to do. She tortured Gore and had been prepared to murder the maniacal Dr. Kihl in cold blood. I know what it's like to have killed. I still swim in that sea of guilt; I almost drown in it many days. I don't want that for her, and I'm afraid that if she keeps putting herself at risk, continues fighting against the monsters in this world, she will become a monster just like me.

"We're a squad, a team. You need me, and you know it," Dalia says. "I need you to be my conscience, and you need me because I'm the one willing to burn everything down to protect those I love."

Trust your team, Joe told me. I hope he's right. "Okay. I have to come get you tonight. We leave in the morning. Be ready." As soon as I say the words, I fear that I will live to regret them. Just because I don't trust myself doesn't mean I should let others put themselves at risk, no matter how much they want to.

"I'll be ready. You better not leave without me." Dalia ends the call.

I set the phone down and carefully extricate

myself. I gently lower Haji's head to the mattress. After retrieving the phone and slipping it into a pocket, I lift Haji's legs onto the bed. He groans softly, and I clench my teeth, but he doesn't wake up. I watch him sleep, hoping he's either not dreaming or his dreams are peaceful.

****

I have to wait hours before Dad and the magician guards nod off. It's another hour, maybe more, until I slink to one of the windows and slip out when the soldiers manning the entrance change over. Easy as pie.

I drop to the ground and scurry between the low, white buildings. A few exterior lights fight back the darkness and create jagged shadows. I crouch behind a building, away from the light, peer into the night, and listen. A cacophony of sound—freeway noise, buzzing lights, snatches of conversation—assaults me, but it's all distant.

"Easy peasy," I murmur, reaching into the pocket of my borrowed sweatpants for my dad's phone. The device's glowing screen is insanely bright in the night. I quickly tap out a message to Dalia and hit send.

I detect a faint increase in the ambient illumination. Jamming the phone into the sweatpants pocket, I glance around and see Dr. Radcliffe's luminous draconic head and neck towering over the building. The dragon flashes out of existence and reappears a heartbeat later staring straight into my eyes. Knowing I'm caught, I stand and wait for his humanoid golem to come around from the side of the building.

"Did you think it would be so easy to sneak away while I am present?" Radcliffe is still dressed to the nines. You wouldn't know he got off the plane hours earlier and had been on the move ever since.

"Dalia wants to come with us. I'm going to go get her."

Radcliffe raises an eyebrow. "Is that so? I think that is a splendid idea." He claps his hands together. "Bring the team back together again."

Part of me wishes he'd tell me no and prevent me from leaving. Then, Dalia would be safe, or at least safer than she would be in Hawaii. "Really? You're not going to stop me? Tell me I shouldn't do it?"

"You should not do it. I say that as the head of the UN Draconic Task Force. Your friend is underage, for one thing. For another, she possesses no special power or skill that will aid us in discovering and destroying the opening to the slipstream. But I also know we will need more than simply power and skill to succeed. We will need something intangible…I believe you humans call it grit, and Dalia possesses that to spare. Also, someone will need to look after Haji while we battle faeries and who knows what else."

"You're not worried someone will intervene? I don't know…accuse us of kidnapping her?"

Radcliffe gives me a knowing smile. "Allison, you are a skaag, and I am a dragon. At the end of the day, we can do as we please, and no one can stop us. All I ask is that when you retrieve your friend, do it quietly and without harming anyone."

Chapter 27

The moon backlights the clouds in the early morning sky when we clamber aboard the C-130 Hercules. After spending half the night retrieving Dalia and the rest convincing Dad not to call her parents by threatening not to drink any more of his herbal tea to block my nightmares, I'm zonked. Part of me wants to sleep through the flight, but since Dalia still has no news about Bibi, I'm too worried to nod off.

A crew member in a green jumpsuit leads us to the cargo ramp into the plane's fuselage. Dalia and I walk on either side of Haji, ready to catch the gangly boy if he stumbles. I know Dad claims Haji will improve, but it's not happening fast enough. He moves like he'll collapse at any second.

Neither the roar of the huge propeller engines nor the vibrations of the aircraft disturb Haji from his sleep. He shifts every time the plane alters course, never once fluttering an eye. Even with the ear protection passed out by the crew, the deafening rumble from the engines keeps me wide awake.

Across from me, Dad's eyes droop as if weighed down by diving bells, but never entirely close. When his neck goes flaccid and his head rolls to the side, he immediately straightens and blinks, followed by an enormous yawn. In contrast, Dr. Radcliffe is wide awake without being present at all, at least in his humanoid form. The capacious golden dragon expands in every direction. I suspect at least half its bulk floats outside the confines of the plane.

Dalia's gaze is transfixed by her phone's glowing screen. Occasionally, her thumbs fly over the screen to type out a message at speeds just shy of sound. I can't shake the feeling that having Haji and Dalia along is a mistake I'll soon regret.

"Allison!"

I blink and shake my head to clear the cobwebs. Something tickles my jawline. Hair from the ten-pound weight resting against my left shoulder—Haji's head. I brush aside his hair, reminding myself to be gentle so as not to wake him.

"Allison! Check this out."

Dalia waves her phone before Haji, indicating for me to take the device. I reach around the slumbering boy and take the device in my left hand.

On the screen is a series of texts between Dalia and Devin, living proof that a human can be as appealing as a mold-encrusted peanut butter and jelly sandwich.

I read the last text from Devin.—*Talked to her mom. Bibi is at Tacoma General being treated for burns. She's expected to recover. That's all I know.*—

My hand drops to my lap. Expected to recover. I never knew three words could bring so much relief.

****

I stand beneath a cobalt sky in a maroon sand and rock sea. The reddish dust could've been cut from an image taken by a Martian rover and pasted into the landscape around me. I might believe I was on Mars if it wasn't for the sky.

In the distance, I see a figure standing on the edge

of a yawning blackness with jagged edges highlighted by an eerie yellowish light. My entire body goes cold despite the sun blazing overhead. That is an opening to the slipstream.

My prosthetics zoom in like camera lenses onto the figure standing at the chasm's brink. The shock of pink hair tells me all I need to know. I break into a run, calling upon all my abominable prowess to sprint over the flat ground. Only the sleeper doesn't answer my call. I'm alone, and soon my lungs are burning, as I stumble over the ground that isn't as level as I thought. The landscape rises and falls like the peaks and valleys of a sine wave.

I stop atop a peak, hands on my knees, gasping for breath. I straighten and shout, "Dalia!"

I can't tell if she hears me or not. She appears mesmerized by the opening before her that, from my vantage, is the grinning mouth of a ravenous beast. Dalia takes a step toward the opening, and the unearthly yellowish light slithers over her ankles like dozens of alien tentacles.

"Dalia! Run!" I dread my warning won't carry over the vastness between us.

I'm ready to run and hope for a second wind, but I never lift a foot. A burning smell I know well captures my attention and tugs my gaze downslope to the valley floor. There on the red sand is a blackened, humanoid shape. The smell of burned meat causes the sleeper to stir, and saliva fills my mouth. I almost turn away, disgusted at the sleeper, at us, but I hear a whisper on the wind.

"Allison…help."

Haji.

My heart reverberates.

Haji's voice came from what is obviously a corpse.

A piercing scream echoes across the landscape. I look up in time to watch Dalia being dragged by the yellowish tentacles into the insatiable blackness. My throat constricts.

"Allison…" Haji's voice is a death rattle.

I'm shaking, being torn down the middle like Rumpelstiltskin.

Come to me. It is your purpose to obey.

****

The C130's wheels touching down jolt me awake. That and Haji's cranium smashing into my shoulder like a wrecking ball. Despite catnapping on and off during the flight, I feel like I've been spin-dried in an industrial washing machine. I remember dreaming, hearing that strange voice commanding me to navigate the slipstream. The memory is like ice water rolling down my spine. I drank Dad's disgusting tea before boarding the plane. That should block the magical presence causing the dreams. I consider telling Dad, but reconsider upon seeing Dr. Radcliffe sitting across from me broadly smiling as his draconic form flashes in and out of existence. I trust that dragon about as far as I can throw his fully materialized draconic form and don't want him knowing anything about my dreams.

I push Haji off me, and he bends at the waist until his head rests on his left knee. I'll say one thing for Haji, he might look fit as a gulag inmate, but he hasn't lost any flexibility. Dalia looks at me with unfocused, tired eyes. I give her a tight smile. Dad looks reasonably well-rested, considering the accommodations and practically eardrum-bursting din from the Hercules's massive props.

Once the plane trundles to a halt, a crewmember tells us we can disembark. He leads us to the rear of the plane and lowers the ramp. We head out onto the tarmac with Dr. Radcliffe and Dad leading the way. Dalia and I bring up the rear supporting Haji between us. Heat and humidity reminiscent to what I experienced in Singapore blast into us as soon as we step off the plane.

Waiting for us about twenty feet from the ramp is a Humvee. A tall woman dressed in a camouflage uniform stands next to the passenger side door.

"I'm General Lovelace," she calls. "I hope you can tell me what in the world is happening atop Mauna Kea."

Chapter 28

General Lovelace slides into the front passenger seat of the Humvee. The rest of us pile into the back, which is more spacious than I imagined. Dalia and Haji get into the third-row seats along with Dad. To my surprise, the gangly boy scrambles inside the military vehicle without assistance. Radcliffe and I sit behind the driver and Lovelace. The dragon is directly behind the general, so his flickering draconic form engulfs her in glittering golden light.

The Humvee speeds along the tarmac toward low white buildings with red tile roofs beyond a high chain-link fence topped with concertina wire. The general twists to face us.

"How up-to-date are you on the situation?" she asks.

The general's attention is focused on Dr. Radcliffe. I might as well not even exist.

"You asked about what is happening on Mauna Kea," Dr. Radcliffe says. "Perhaps you can enlighten us? We know magic has been used somewhere on the Hawaiian Islands or close by, but not much else."

Lovelace frowns. "We believe whatever caused a power outage on the West Coast originated atop Mauna Kea."

The Humvee slows to a stop at the gate with a guard station manned by two soldiers armed with rifles.

The soldiers salute the general and wave the vehicle through.

"Do you have any photographs of what happened?" Radcliffe asks.

The general's frown deepens, aging her by a decade. "No. The drones we've sent disappear without a trace. All we get from satellites are pictures of an impenetrable fog over Mauna Kea."

"Have you been briefed on the slipstream?" Radcliffe asks.

Lovelace nods. "We all have. Is that what we're facing? An alien invasion?"

"Are you aware of the attack on Joint Base Lewis-McCord?" Radcliffe asks.

Lovelace's expression darkens. "I know generalities. No details. Is that connected to the power outage?"

"I cannot say for certain, but I suspect the answer is yes." Radcliffe gives Lovelace a rundown of the assault at Lewis-McCord, Dad and I add pertinent details. Dr. Radcliffe concludes, "We believe the power disruption was caused by the faeries opening a portal to the slipstream. Was the power disruption purposeful? Was the timing so soon after the attack significant? We do not know. However, I can say with confidence, the faeries are the culprits."

"So faeries are to blame for all this." Lovelace shakes her head. "That's not something I ever expected to say. No posting on social media or telling anyone about what I'm going to tell you. Is that understood?"

We agree to the general's stipulation.

"We had drones and fighter jets fall out of the sky. We scrambled more jets once the power was restored.

Those were taken out. Maybe by the faeries. But we're not sure. That's the military losses. Airliners fell out of the sky too. Casualties are in the thousands."

"Oh, no." I raise my hand to my mouth, fingertips brushing my lips. Devastation and death on such a vast scale makes the battle at Joint Base Lewis-McCord seem like an insignificant skirmish.

"Wow," Haji says. "That's bad."

I throw a quick glance over my shoulder at Haji. Even under the circumstances, it's good to hear him talking again. He meets my gaze for a moment and nods.

"Jesus," Dalia says. "At least one hundred thirty airliners and an unknown number of small planes fell from the sky last evening."

Lovelace's gaze is intense. "I said no posting on social media."

"I'm not. I was checking my feeds." Dalia's eyes are glued to her phone's screen.

"Good. Keep it that way," the general says.

The Humvee pulls up to a two-story white building with a red tile roof. Jutting from the roof are all kinds of communication equipment.

"The president is going to address the nation this morning. I fully expect the president to declare that we're at war. With the faeries, I suppose? Do you think Knights of Magic are involved?" As Lovelace speaks, she seems to age even more.

"Knights of Magic?" I exchange clueless looks with Dalia and Haji.

"Researchers for the Draconic Task Force recently uncovered the name of the shadowy international organization the faeries are allied with, the organization

Felecia Bergman belongs to, is Knights of Magic," Radcliffe says. "We must assume they are receiving material aid from that group. That is why we are here. To help you decipher who is making war on the United States and how to beat them."

****

Lovelace leads us inside the building, past armed guards in the front office area where harried soldiers answer phones and pound at keyboards. Everyone sounds professional, but I can hear the nearly imperceptible quivering in their voices. Beneath their stoic demeanors, the soldiers are as taut as rubber bands ready to snap.

The building's interior is utilitarian, with unadorned white walls and recessed light fixtures that softly buzz. The linoleum floor shines like it was recently polished, and a harsh antiseptic scent hangs in the air. We follow the general up a narrow staircase. I'm impressed Haji manages the stairs on his own, although he pauses on a landing, breathing hard. The stairs lead to an even narrower hallway on the second floor.

General Lovelace leads us to the door at the end of the hall, guarded by two soldiers with sidearms. "We're going into the command center. Usually, civilians wouldn't be allowed anywhere near this building, let alone the room we're about to enter."

"Oooh, the inner sanctum. Did you hear that, Haji?" Dalia whispers.

"I know, cool right?" Haji says.

The general pauses her speech to give Dalia a disapproving stare. My pink-haired friend drops her gaze to the floor.

"Sorry."

Lovelace continues. "Fortunately, the president signed an executive order granting all of you security clearances. Still, I have some paperwork that each of you will need to sign. Also, you all must surrender all electronics before entering."

"I have to give up my phone? Do I get it back?" Dalia asks.

Lovelace informs us our electronics will be returned after leaving the command center. Phones are surrendered to the guards. The general uses a key card to unlock the door, and we enter the command center. She leads us around three rows of soldiers sitting at long desks at computers to a large square table at the front of the room. Taking up the entirety of the tabletop is a detailed map of the Hawaiian Islands and surrounding water. The exterior wall is nearly floor-to-ceiling windows providing a commanding view of the Pacific's azure waters.

An officer with a stack of paperwork and pens is waiting for us by the table. He provides each of us with a memo to sign and a pen, explaining we must keep our mouths zipped about everything we hear and see. He collects the signed paperwork in a manila folder, then sits at an unoccupied workstation in the front row.

Lovelace picks up a laser pointer from the table. "We are here." The red dot appears on the map on the southwest coast of Maui. "We believe the attack's epicenter is located on the Big Island somewhere on Mauna Kea." The red dot disappears and reappears near the center of a large island to the southwest of Maui.

"Aren't there observatories on Mauna Kea?" Dad asks.

Lovelace nods. “Yes. The university manages the observatories. We’ve been in contact with university officials. Unfortunately, no one has heard anything from the facilities. Ground forces were dispatched from the Pohakuloa Training Area and two Apache attack helicopters from Bradshaw Army Airfield.” The laser pointer shines on an area to the southeast of Mauna Kea. “Both the Apaches are confirmed downed. By enemy fire—we think. We’ve lost all contact with the platoon sent to reconnoiter Mauna Kea from the ground. At last contact, the platoon had taken up position here”—the pointer highlights an area south of Mauna Kea—“on the road to the observatories and started evacuating civilians from the area.”

“Was the platoon attacked?” I ask.

Lovelace grimaces. “Unknown. Contact with the Big Island is spotty.”

“When you mentioned the Apaches being downed, you said you think it was enemy fire.” Radcliffe steeples his hands underneath his chin. “Why is that in question?”

Lovelace clicks off the pointer and sets it on the table. “I hope you can help me answer that question. Lieutenant, please bring up the Apache footage.”

General Lovelace leads us to a workstation in the front row. Haji catches my eye, and his lips perk up in a smile.

“This is recording from the camera mounted next to the Apache’s minigun. It essentially records everything the pilot sees. The gun turret moves in sync with the movement of the pilot’s helmet,” the lieutenant says.

In the distance are small dark shapes that seem to

glow. I squint, and my prosthetics zoom in like camera lenses on the darting forms. I bite down on my lower lip. I want to say I'm seeing faeries flitting around the screen, but I can't tell in black and white. And being zoomed in extenuates the image's graininess. I blink until my eyes zoom out to normal perspective.

"Can you add audio from the cockpit?" General Lovelace asks.

"Yes, ma'am." The lieutenant brings up a smaller window next to the video and presses the play button. Then, he opens up a menu on the video player that decreases the rotor noise. A few seconds later, voices are audible.

"Do you see that? What the hell are those things? People?" A female voice.

The might-be faeries continue darting in the distance.

"I think those are people. People with wings." A man's voice.

"What kind of people have wings?"

One of the shapes breaks off from the group, quickly closing the distance.

"You don't think it could be those…faeries? You know, what those kids testified about."

"I don't know. I'm taking us in closer. Wait a minute…are they glowing orange?"

There's a bright flare.

"Watch out!"

The video jerks as the chopper makes an extreme maneuver. Still, I see the distinctive fireball hurling toward the helicopter with remarkable speed and accuracy. There is an explosion and the video ends.

Haji is the first to speak in a stuttering voice.

"Those were faeries."

General Lovelace looks at Radcliffe for confirmation.

"I concur," he says.

I look around at everyone. "We have to go there. Like right now." Lovelace raises a skeptical eyebrow. "This is confirmation the faeries are on the Big Island. Bria is probably there. We have to rescue her and stop whatever the faeries are doing."

"Damn right," Dalia says, pink hair bobbing.

"We must," Haji says.

Radcliffe looks to the general. "Can you provide us with surreptitious transportation? I fear if I reveal my dragon form and"—he gestures toward me—"Allison transforms into a skaag, we will reveal ourselves to the enemy."

"I can arrange a C-130 to get you to the island." The laser pointer highlights the southern tip of the Big Island. "There is a civilian airfield here. It's large enough for a C-130 to land and take off. To minimize the chance of the enemy detecting the infiltration, the operation will take place at night."

I nod and Radcliff says, "Excellent."

The general continues. "We've had spotty contact with an infantry squad that has access to ground transportation. We will arrange to have the squad meet you at the airfield and provide transport to Mauna Kea."

Chapter 29

We are escorted to the station's nearly empty chow hall by a nervous army specialist. The hall is a large, plain room with a breakfast buffet along one wall. In the center of the opposite wall is a flat-screen TV tuned to a 24-hour news station. The anchor states that the president will address the nation about the power outage within the next half hour. Open windows allow a gentle breeze to cool the room, carrying the ocean's briny scent.

My stomach growls as I hunt the buffet for anything vaguely resembling the savory chicken sausages that are my staple. All I find are scrambled eggs, hashbrowns, and unappealing breakfast meats, but nevertheless, the greasy aromas set my mouth salivating.

Haji piles his plate with eggs and every side of meat available. Dalia eyes the food skeptically, finally opting for fruit and a small single-serving yogurt. My rumbling tummy painfully twists, reminding me I've hardly eaten anything for the past two days. I put several breakfast sausages glistening with fat on a plate. Against my better judgment, I fill a ceramic mug with coffee from an insulated carafe. The black brew steams and smells ambrosial.

Tentatively, I take a sip of coffee and nearly spit it out, tongue smarting. They got the hot part right. I blow across the java, then try it again. My eyebrows and lips perk up. Decent coffee. After another blow across the steaming liquid, I take a second sip. Better than decent. It's damn good.

"Make sure you grab some coffee," I tell Dad, who waits on a toaster to brown a bagel.

"Come here." Dad offers me a mug. I can tell by the smell it brims with the tea meant to keep my dreams bay. "Any more dreams?"

"Nada," I lie. I don't want to discuss my dreams on the plane with anyone right now. "No worries." I pick up the mug and sip the tea, finding the fluid lukewarm. I chug the rest, hoping the dosage will stave off more nightmares.

"Good." Dad nods toward Haji. "Your friend is improving. Like I said he would."

"So far so good." I stride back to the coffee carafe.

I fill a second mug with coffee for Dalia, then join my friends at a long table. I sit next to Dalia, across from Dr. Radcliffe, which means I am within the glowing luminescence of his draconic abdomen. Haji sits on the other side of my bestie, attacking his food with gusto.

"His appetite is back, at least," I whisper to Dalia and set a mug of steaming coffee next to her. She looks at the brew and shoots me a questioning glance. At normal volume I say, "It's good." I slurp from my mug. "Better than good, honestly. Watch out, it's hot."

Dalia picks up the mug and, after blowing across the fluid, has a taste. "Wow. No joke."

Dad joins us, sitting next to Dr. Radcliffe.

I bite down on a rubbery sausage. Lukewarm oil flavored with salt and other spices squirts into my mouth. The meat tastes like what it is, overly processed pork, and I nearly spit it out in disgust.

"That good?" Dad says between bites of bright yellow scrambled egg and bagel.

I choke down the meat, battling my gag reflex the entire time. "I can name a thousand things that taste better off the top of my head."

"I don't know what you're complaining about," Haji says. "This food is a grand slam."

We fall silent as the newsreader on the twenty-four-hour news channel announces the presidential address is about to begin. Everyone turns to face the television except for Haji, who shovels a final forkful of egg into his mouth before leaving the table for the buffet.

The program cuts from the newsroom to a lectern decorated with the presidential seal before a red-carpeted hallway. The president enters the frame from the left and faces the cameras, her expression as forbidding as an undertaker's.

Her tone is equally grim. "My fellow Americans, yesterday at—"

Without preamble, the power goes out. I glance around the chow hall, half expecting the power to come back on at any second. If anything, the handful of soldiers sprinkled around the room eating their breakfast look more surprised than my crew and me. I bite down on my lower lip, a sinking feeling in my gut. This isn't a brownout. This is a blackout. On a military installation. Again. This can't be good. Inside me, the sleeper undulates, disturbed by my heightened tension.

Haji returns from the buffet and sets his plate, heaping with eggs, bacon, and potatoes, on the table.

He looks overhead at the light fixtures. "Did the power go out?"

"Ummm, yeah," Dalia says.

Haji shrugs, sits down, and commences eating.

Radcliffe glances at Dad. "Did you sense anything?"

Dad shakes his head in the negative. "Maybe it's a run-of-the-mill power outage."

I point out the window to the pristine blue sky. "What would cause a power outage? The weather is perfect."

"I did not sense anything either," Radcliffe says. "For now, I suggest we finish our meal and assume the power will be restored."

"I don't know about that." Dalia holds up her phone. "Dead as a doornail."

Everyone else's personal electronics are as dead as Dalia's phone.

"Perhaps we'll fly to the Big Island under our own power after all," Dr. Radcliffe says.

After everyone finishes eating, all the electronics are still dead, so we head outside and after asking for directions, make our way to the beach beyond the runway. The drone of diesel generators resounds from all over the base, but from appearances, the power is out for the most part. A C-130 Hercules is cockeyed on the runway with a score of people in uniform milling around it.

I stop at the edge of the green grass before it gives way to the red dirt. The same bloody red as from my latest dream.

Dalia skips past me onto the sand. "Come on! What are you waiting for?"

Haji trails behind her moving faster than I've seen him go in some time. He grins and waves for me to follow. I hope nothing bad happens to them on the Big Island, but I can't shake the sinking feeling that my dream was a premonition.

Taking a deep breath, I ignore the bloody earth and march onward toward the ocean. The dirt gives way to tan sand and tropical ground cover. A handful of palm trees arrayed in a neat row mark the beginning of the beach proper, a long narrow strip of sand approximately the length of the airstrip, terminating to the right at a headland replete with outbuildings associated with the military installation and to the left a rocky outcrop.

Haji and Dalia already bathe their feet in the blue vastness I can hardly believe is the Pacific Ocean. The sun is uncomfortably warm, combined with the humidity, causing me to sweat. The contrast with the beaches of Washington is astounding. Biting wind, slashing rain, and water so cold it can cause hypothermia are what I associate with the ocean at home.

I kick off my sneakers and run for the cerulean water, but my muscles seize up, and only my preternatural reflexes keep me from falling face-first into the sand. The fear permeating my body and mind is not mine. It's the sleeper's.

Leave me alone. This is my body. Not yours.

In response, images of me almost drowning as a skaag flood my mind until the tropical beach before me becomes as clouded as a wilderness beach on Washington's coast. I gasp for air and flail my arms. My lungs burn. I taste salt on my tongue as icy water fills my mouth and rushes down my throat.

As a skaag I can't hold my breath or swim.

But I'm not a skaag. I'm human.

Leave me alone.

Our wills crash together like battling bulls. If it was the battle of wills alone, I might've won. But the sleeper's fear of water is primordial down to the cellular level. We come to an uneasy truce. I sit on the beach and watch the waves. As long as I don't try to approach the water, the sleeper remains calm and keeps the fear at bay.

I don't like the sleeper's hold over me. After the skirmish at the military base, I thought our roles were set. I was in the driver's seat, and the sleeper was a passenger. Maybe a copilot? But I was the pilot. I was in charge—no ifs, ands, or buts. Now I'm not so sure.

After about an hour at the beach, we're summoned back to the general's presence in the command center by a squad of soldiers. Inside the command center, men and women in uniform work quietly to resuscitate computer equipment without avail. Lovelace leads us to a table with the map of the Hawaiian Islands and the surrounding ocean. On the table is a large, softly crackling radio, complete with a mic. The contraption looks like it could've been ripped straight from a 1950s sci-fi movie. The power cord is connected to an extension cord from a rumbling gas generator sitting on a table next to the now-open floor-to-ceiling window.

"Any idea what caused everything requiring power to fail this time?" The general stares at Dr. Radcliffe and my dad in turn.

"We detected no magic," Dr. Radcliffe replies and Dad nods.

Lovelace shakes her head in exasperation. "From

what we've been able to determine, an EMP device was detonated on the Big Island. Everything with an electronic circuit was fried. Fortunately, this relic was stored inside an EMP bag." General Lovelace points to the radio on the table. She picks up the mic, depressing a button on its side. "Lieutenant Gilmore, do you read me?"

Lovelace releases the button, and the static returns. About fifteen seconds later, a voice comes from the speaker. "Loud and clear, general."

"Is he on the Big Island?" My pulse thrums with excitement.

Lovelace nods. "Listen up, lieutenant. Our guests are with me. The C-130 is a no-go after the EMP." The general leans over the map, indicating a point of land on the southeast coast of Maui with an extended finger. "Fortunately, I have some Force Reconnaissance, who can help get them to the Big Island undetected. Here's the plan."

Chapter 30

I stand on a beach next to Dalia, the bitter aftertaste of the tea that is supposed to hold back my nightmares still on my tongue. I had downed it earlier in the evening before our nighttime excursion. With any luck, we'll soon close the slipstream, and Dad will be able to free me from the mysterious magic causing the nightmares. Wishful thinking, I know.

Ahead of us, a squad of six marines charges toward the crashing waves carrying a black zodiac with an enormous outboard engine. The sound of the surf sets the sleeper stirring within me, and my heart pounds so hard I swear my sternum rattles.

I'm in control.

Me.

Not the sleeper.

"Are you okay with this?" Dalia whispers. "When we went down to the water by the base, you didn't come. Is it…the skaag?"

"I'll be fine."

Dalia takes my hand, fingers unballing a fist I hadn't realized I made.

"You'll do great. No worries."

The marines lower the raft into the choppy water. Haji and the adults stand behind us, the light of Radcliffe's dragon form painting the sand in golden light. The only other light on Maui's Kamanawa Point is from the stars and the moon, partially obscured by high wispy clouds. The last remnant of the day is a purple tinge to the clouds barely visible with my prosthetics. Even with my superior vision, I can't see the Big Island from the beach. The Maui Strait, thirty forbidding miles of dark, deep water, separates us from our destination.

The squad leader issues a terse command for us to scramble aboard the zodiac.

Dalia squeezes my hand. "I'll go first. Follow right behind me."

My bestie enters the water and is swept off her feet by a wave she probably didn't see. My heart thunders into my throat. I intend to rush to her and catch her before she falls, but I remain rooted with the sleeper coiling inside me. Luckily, a marine catches her around the waist and heaves her over the raft's side.

Damn you, I curse the sleeper and receive no response.

Haji brushes past me, seemingly eager to climb aboard. He looks over his shoulder as the surf inundates his feet. His thin lips move, but he doesn't say a word. His eyes are cavernously sunken in the dim light. He shouldn't be here, nor should Dalia for that matter. I clench my jaw until my teeth almost crack. I'm such a fool for allowing them to come.

Haji boards the zodiac without incident.

Near the craft's stern, the squad leader waves to us. "Come on. Double time!"

A hand resting against my shoulder startles me. I should've expected Dr. Radcliffe to be beside me from the glimmering radiance of his dragon form.

"I understand you are fearful," Radcliffe murmurs.

"Do not be. Always remember that you can swim while human."

I understand that, but the sleeper either doesn't or doesn't care. I'm not sure which.

The one-time university professor scampers onto the boat with an agility that belies his aged appearance. Several marines exchange impressed looks, but they should know better. Radcliffe is a dragon, and his humanoid form is a façade. His dragon form overflows the raft, bathing everyone in light only I can see.

"Hurry up," the squad leader calls again.

I try to force myself toward the inky blackness of the Pacific Ocean, but to no avail. The half-skaag's fear is sour against my tongue.

Dad stands beside me, squinting against the darkness, and takes my hand. "It's okay, Allison. I won't let anything happen to you. You can trust me. The skaag can trust me."

He strides toward the water, our arms extending. I want to go with him, but the sleeper is having none of it, refusing to budge one millimeter. Dad stops and throws me a reassuring smile over his shoulder.

I need to do this. I'll be in a boat, not the water.

To my surprise, when Dad moves toward the ocean again, I follow—my gait is jittery and halting, but I'm moving. The sleeper is still fearful, but for some reason the beast trusts him. Maybe because I do? Or the sleeper understands my mother, a full-fledged skaag, trusts him? I don't know, but I can approach the water and don't retreat even when the surf runs over my feet.

Once I'm close enough to board the zodiac, I'm out of the water like it's boiling, pulling Dad along behind me. We cram together like sardines in the raft that must be filled well past its maximum capacity. The marines push the craft farther into the waves, then haul themselves aboard, packing us in even tighter. A marine in the stern lowers an outsized outboard engine into the water.

He fiddles with the engine. I fear it might not start up, and we'll be forced to fly to the Big Island after all, but then the engine rumbles to life, and soon the craft bounces over the water.

****

In less than an hour, the Big Island looms on the horizon, dark and foreboding. Deep in my bowels, the sleeper is a knot of quivering anxiety. I battle nausea and taste bile in the back of my mouth. The air temperature drops out on the open water, and the wind shear is downright cold. Dalia and I sit pressed shoulder to shoulder as close to the center of the craft as we can in a futile attempt to stay warm and dry. Occasionally ocean spray from the ship's hull thumping into a wave splashes us. To call the journey miserable is the understatement of the decade.

Dad's face takes on a sickly greenish hue. As far as I can tell, he keeps his eyes clenched shut and his arms around his midsection the entire time. Unsurprisingly, Dr. Radcliffe appears indifferent to the wild ride. His draconic head lifts skyward as if he admires the constellations peeking out from breaks in the cloud cover.

Haji takes every crash over the choppy sea with an enormous smile, whooping when a huge wave makes the craft feel like a roller coaster. Eventually, one of the marines politely but firmly tells him to keep his lips zipped. I can almost believe Haji is back to the way he was before Golden Shoal, before The Incident. But I can't shake the feeling that what I'm observing is a façade ready to crack and shatter when put under stress.

After another hour, maybe a little more or a little less, the rocky, reddish-brown cliffs of Upolu Point rise above a narrow, sandy strand. The cliff face mesmerizes me. That color. It's so reminiscent of the bloody earth from my dreams. My gaze flicks to my friends, first Dalia, then Haji. I gasp as eerily glowing tentacles slither from the dark waters to snatch my friends in their slimy grips.

"Allison, what's wrong?" Dalia asks.

I shake my head. "Nothing. Nothing."

The glowing tentacles are in reality the golden light of Radcliffe's draconic form sparkling against the waves. I'm left with the uncomfortable feeling that my dreams are seeping into my conscious reality. Are they omens, or am I adrift above an abyss of madness? Most disturbing of all, I have no sense of the sleeper stirring inside me, so I have only myself to blame for what I'm experiencing.

When the zodiac finally bottoms out on the sand, it's still night out, probably close to two or three in the morning. Dalia and I are the last to clamber out of the boat. My bare feet touch down in the sand and water. I expect to feel immediate relief, but the riptide grips me in its watery hand, and the world spins as I'm shattered by vertigo. I try to walk toward the cliffs, but instead, I move sideways like a punch-drunk boxer. My knees buckle, and I'm going to faceplant onto the wet sand, but Dalia snatches me by the elbow, steadying me.

"Let's get you up on dry land," she says.

"Thanks," I murmur, still woozy. Inside me, the

sleeper already unwinds.

Dalia leads me up the beach to where the others gather in the shadow of the cliffs created by the silvery moonlight. There are shadows only I can see, too, flashing in and out of existence in sync with Radcliffe's appearing and disappearing draconic form.

I sit in the sand, waiting for my balance and strength to return. Neither is in a hurry.

"How do you feel?" Dad asks Haji.

"Fantastic!" The gangly boy points to the zodiac, from which the marines unload a dry bag. "That was one heck of a wild ride."

Dad queasily smiles; the green hue still hasn't entirely faded from his cheeks. "I think I'll pass on another boat ride like that. Seriously though, no withdrawal symptoms?"

Haji shakes his head. "No. I feel great. The treatment is working."

"Can you call upon your magic for me?"

"Sure." Haji extends his hand, palm upward. Light flares beneath his skin, revealing fractal patterns on his extended hand and bare arm.

I gasp. Several of the marines softly curse. They probably haven't seen magic before.

"What?" Dalia asks.

I point, and she looks at the blue and orange light radiating from Haji's skin. I'm familiar with the orange from my time in the presence of the faeries and Gore. It is the color of faery blood and magic. It is the color of the Juice, which Gore and other magicians shoot up to superpower their magic. But the blue. The blue is reminiscent of the glow from the shield Dad erected to protect the civilians from the faeries' fireballs and mechs' blasters.

"That's enough," Dad says.

Haji twists his hand back and forth, expression enraptured, apparently entranced by the luminescence and fractal tracery.

"Enough," Dad says more firmly.

Haji's lips droop into a frown as he lowers his hand, and the light winks out.

Dad leans close to Haji and whispers, "You must listen and comply with commands without hesitation. Do you understand?"

Haji nods.

The squad leader drops a dry bag onto the sand. "Gear up. We don't have much time before the water is pounding against the cliff."

Inside the bag are towels to dry off our feet and our shoes. While I'm putting on my sneakers, a marine brings over a second dry bag. Inside is a backpack full of essential supplies—food, water, maps, and first aid kit.

"I wish they'd give me a gun," Dalia says.

Radcliffe and my dad had been offered firearms, but both declined. Dalia had pointedly requested one but was told no.

"Have you ever shot a weapon?" I stand up and put on the backpack.

"How hard can it be?" Dalia extends her arms and makes a gun out of her hands, aiming at the ocean. "Bang!" She lowers her arms to her sides. "Point and shoot."

The squad leader passes us. "It's a little more complicated than that, but you got the gist of it." He stops in front of the group, facing us. He points to the cliff. "Follow me. There's a trail up the cliff face, but be mindful of your footing. It's narrow and rocky and extra treacherous in the dark."

He leads us up the beach to the escarpment. Radcliffe confidently follows the squad leader, a reminder that he can see in the dark almost as well as I can. Haji and Dad are tight on the dragon's heels, bathed in the dragon's luminescence. Dalia trails behind them, glancing at me.

"Are you still dizzy? Do you want to hold my hand?" she asks.

My dizziness has passed, but I take her offered hand anyway. I'm afraid she and Haji will die on this island, and the only way to protect them is to keep them close.

"Happy hunting," the squad leader says as we pass him and step onto the trail.

Dalia leads the way, her left hand extending behind her to hold my hand. Our progress is slow, probably because Dalia can hardly see all the tripping hazards in the darkness. I don't mind. Just because the lack of light hardly impacts my vision doesn't mean I don't need to be careful where I put my feet. Ahead of us, Radcliffe's dragon form flickers in and out of existence. He sets a fast pace and carries Haji with one hand around the gangly boy's waist.

Dalia lets out a strangled cry and stumbles. Our grips tighten, and I pull back on her hand in time to keep her from teetering off the trail. Her face is as pale as a freshly laundered white linen, and I hug her to me.

"Thank you," she whispers.

I say nothing, wondering if I will be there to save her next time something happens. The marines are already in the zodiac, the rumbling engine propelling them away from the beach.

"Is everyone okay? I heard a scream," Dad calls.

"We're okay," I reply.

We continue up the trail, holding hands the entire way.

Chapter 31

"Stay down," Dad hisses as soon as Dalia and I reach the top of the cliff.

We drop to the moist, close-cropped grass. The others crouch in a small group bathed in Radcliffe's luminescence. The airport is literally splayed out right in front of us. There is a short landing strip with an old plane with a prop engine on either wing sitting at the far end. Across the runway from us is a blue shipping container with the doors wide open. In front of the container are plastic chairs painted the same blue color. Nearby on a pole, an orange windsock outstretches, indicating the wind direction. Besides the crashing waves on the rocks below and the windsock flapping, the airport is silent.

"What is it?" I ask.

"I saw something, perhaps a skaag." Radcliffe points into the distance. "In the clouds."

Goose bumps rise on the back of my neck. The clouds are grayish against a navy-blue backdrop in the predawn. I blink until my prosthetic eyeballs zoom in on the patch of sky Radcliffe indicated. Occasionally, between the puffy clouds, I spot the faint twinkle of starlight.

"Do you see anything?" Dalia asks.

I shake my head. "No."

"Maybe I was wrong, or the beast has moved on,"

Radcliffe says.

"Could it have been Druk?" Dad asks.

The longing and fear rife in his voice are icicles thrust into my heart. I blink until my vision clears and continue inspecting the sky, zooming in and out, for several minutes. I imagine the world in a rainbow of colors until my prosthetics switch into IR mode. I don't register any distinctive heat signatures.

I blink several times and my vision returns to normal. "I don't see anything."

I suspect the dragon didn't see my mother. If she were still alive and free, I'm certain she would have returned home months ago, if only to make my life as miserable as skaagly possible. At the very least, she would have used magic to keep in contact with Dad.

"I hate to point out the obvious." Dalia stares across the airfield, squinting. "But where are Lieutenant Gilmore and his men? Aren't they supposed to meet us here?"

"Maybe they're in the building?" Dad says.

Across the tarmac near the midpoint of the airstrip is a small, blocky two-story building with three single-engine prop planes and a midsize SUV parked out front. The SUV is clearly not the vehicle we expected to find Lieutenant Gilmore and his men driving. Supposedly, they are in possession of a vintage jeep, a functional museum piece dating from shortly after World War II.

"Let's go find out." Haji starts to stand, but Radcliffe grabs him by the arm and pulls him down.

"I suggest we err on the side of caution." The dragon glances at Dad. "I do not detect magic."

Dad shakes his head. "Neither do I."

"Do you see anything, Allison?" Radcliffe asks.

"I'm on it. Wait. I have a heat signature. Behind the building. One person. Maybe in a vehicle. Not moving."

"Heat signature?" Haji asks.

"Her eyes have IR mode," Dalia says.

"That's so cool." Haji's voice rises octaves as he speaks. "Why am I just learning about this?"

"Quiet," Dad says.

"Anyone else?" Radcliffe asks.

"Doesn't look like it." I finish my inspection of the plane at the end of the runway—empty—and turn my attention to the shipping container. "One person. That's it."

We huddle together to devise a plan. We'll approach the unknown interloper in two groups—Haji and Dad with Dr. Radcliffe, and Dalia with me. Our caution is probably overkill. Radcliffe and I should be able to handle anyone we come across blindfolded and pig-tied, but as we tread across the runway, dread oozes over me.

The other group reaches the left side of the building at the same time Dalia and I reach the right. Everyone holds positions as I switch to IR mode once again. I wonder if I'll ever get used to the dappled colors. After I confirm the unknown person hasn't moved, I wave to Dr. Radcliffe's draconic head that overtops the roof, and we continue around the back of the building.

I take the lead as Dalia and I round the building. Parked near the building is a green vintage jeep with a man wearing a ragged camouflage uniform, maybe asleep, slumped in the driver's seat. Sitting across his lap is a rifle. Dr. Radcliffe and the others appear on the opposite side of the building.

"Stay here," I whisper to Dalia. "I think he's asleep, but he has a gun."

"Be careful."

I reach inside me, brushing against the well of nearly infinite prowess that is the sleeper. All my senses become hypersensitive. In a burst of inhuman speed, I sprint for the jeep, unconcerned if I lose the element of surprise. I'll be on top of the man before he can react. Radcliffe is on the move, too, a blur of golden light approaching the vehicle almost as fast as I am.

I smell the man before I reach him, an eyewatering amalgamation of burned fabric, stale sweat, and dried blood. The last is enough to set my mouth salivating and cause the sleeper to vibrate within my bowels. Fortunately, his stench keeps most of my transgressive hunger at bay.

I'm halfway to the vehicle when I hear the rhythmic breathing of a human in deep sleep. At the vehicle's side, I observe the slow rise and fall of the man's chest. This close to him, the stink rolls off him in waves. His camouflaged uniform is torn, burned, and bloody. His neck, face, and dangling left arm are splotchy with red burns.

Radcliffe makes his final approach at a walk, the golden light of his dragon form sparkling across the jeep and man. His draconic head lowers over the soldier, green tubular mustache passing through the man's chest.

"This is Lieutenant Gilmore."

I hear the patter of Dalia's footfall from behind me. Up ahead Haji and Dad cautiously approach.

"Are you sure?" I ask.

Radcliffe uses a long finger to lift the torn shirt collar, revealing a name patch on the man's chest. All in capital letters is the name, Gilmore.

"Is that the Lieutenant? Where is everyone else?" Haji asks in a voice that's anything but a whisper.

Gilmore utters a snore that is somewhere between a snorting pig and a trumpeting elephant. His eyes flutter open as he sits up, squinting in bewilderment.

I reach my hands before me, palms outward. "Lt. Gilmore, we're—"

"Back! Stay back!" His words are slurred, hands clamping down on the rifle and bringing the weapon to bear.

Radcliffe reacts first, wrenching the rifle out of the soldier's hands.

****

The jeep chugs along the narrow and winding Airport Road at nearly forty miles an hour. On either side of the road are slowly rotating wind turbines, spectral in the wee hours. The red warning lights often seen pulsating atop giant turbines are out, a reminder that the power grid on the island is offline. Occasionally, a handful of cattle can be seen grazing beneath the windmills.

The drive would almost be peaceful with two exceptions: the jeep violently jitters every time Gilmore uses the clutch to shift gears, and the lieutenant's constant stream of conversation. Dr. Radcliffe sits in the passenger seat. The rest of us are crammed in the back. Gilmore insists his wounds are superficial and that he intends to see us safely to Mauna Kea as quickly as possible. So far, he's dodged questions about the fate of the squad, although I did hear him mutter about an ambush.

I lean forward until my head is between Radcliffe and the lieutenant. “Tell us what happened, Lt. Gilmore. Tell us about the ambush.”

Gilmore glances at me, eyes wide and wild with fear that I can smell. It excites the skaag like a predator about to make a kill. Involuntarily, my tongue runs over my upper lip.

“Ambush? What ambush? I…I didn’t say anything about an ambush.”

“I heard you murmur something. Under your breath.”

Gilmore looks at me again, then Radcliff, before turning his gaze back to the road.

“I said no such thing.”

“I heard you say something about an ambush as well, Lt. Gilmore,” Radcliffe says.

“What…how?”

Radcliffe taps his left ear lobe with a finger. “I am not human. Allison is not entirely human.”

“My sense of hearing is insane. If I concentrate, I can hear people’s heartbeats,” I say.

“Any information you have about what we’re getting into is crucial,” Dad says.

Radcliffe puts a hand on Gilmore’s arm. “You are shaking. Perhaps you should pull over.”

“Damn. You’re right,” Gilmore says.

The jeep slows to a stop, and Gilmore puts it in neutral, allowing the engine to idle. He doesn’t even bother pulling over, not that it matters. We haven’t seen another soul let alone a car along the road. I want to say something about the detrimental effects of automobile emissions on the planet, but when the lieutenant faces us, he wears the expression of an animal about to be slaughtered and the words drown in my throat.

"You're right. It's my duty to help you. I should tell you what happened." His gaze flicks from Radcliffe to me and back again. "You're a dragon?" Radcliffe nods. Gilmore's bloodshot eyes lock onto me. "You're a…a…skaag?"

"Half-skaag," I say, then add when his expression turns puzzled, "The same thing, basically."

He licks his lips. "Not human."

I nod and give him a reassuring smile. "Yeah."

"I'm a magician." Haji comes up beside me and hooks a thumb at my dad. "So is he."

Gilmore gulps. "Magic as in real magic? Not card tricks?"

"Real as it gets." Haji nods enthusiastically.

Gilmore turns to Dalia. "What about you?"

Dalia laughs. "I'm just along for the ride. I can't do magic, and I'm most definitely human."

Gilmore wrings his hands, but he has stopped trembling. "That makes two of us. The ambush—" He clenches his eyes shut, and his face contorts. When his eyes open, he stares at his hands. "Honestly, I…" He shakes his head. "Sometimes I think it was all a dream. Then my burns hurt like the dickens." He shuts his eyes again, and tears roll from their corners. "They came for us at night. I survived by playing dead."

Chapter 32

Gilmore hangs his head. "I'll never forgive myself for playing dead. I should've done something. I should've thought of something." He looks up, lower lip quivering. "I was their commanding officer. I…"

Gilmore falls silent and faces forward and stares listlessly into space. He's lost in thought or trapped in the nightmare of his past. I know that feeling all too well. My life often seems an unending nightmare since The Incident, one I fear I'll never wake from. Still, I don't know if I can trust him. Not yet. His wounds are real. His fear seems real. But I can't get my head around how his entire squad died while he survived and maintained possession of the jeep.

"Who ambushed you?" I ask, doing my best to keep my voice gentle.

"Was it faeries?" Haji's tone is strident. "It was, wasn't it?"

"You're not helping," Dalia whispers.

"He should tell us," Haji says.

I have to agree with Haji. Gilmore's prevarication isn't winning my trust.

Gilmore turns and twists his neck to gape at us in the back of the jeep. "Do faeries exist? I mean, I watched the hearings, but I don't know…I thought maybe it was all BS."

"Faeries do exist," Dr. Radcliffe says.

The officer faces Radcliffe. "What do they look like?"

The color drains from Gilmore's face as Radcliffe provides a concise description.

"The orange light. Does it form fractal patterns over their body?" The officer's voice is tremulous.

"Yes." My voice twangs with excitement. This is confirmation. Of what we feared, yes, but it also offers a plausible explanation for what happened to the squad.

"And they have wings." Gilmore nods to himself. "Do the wings buzz? Like…like a fly's or"—he snaps his fingers—"a dragonfly's?"

Dr. Radcliffe nods.

"And their magic allows them to shoot fire?"

Gilmore looks at Radcliffe and me. We both nod in the affirmative.

"That explains a lot." Gilmore takes a deep breath. "It was midnight. We were getting ready to head out to the rendezvous. Checking our gear. We were hiding out on a farm outside of Waimea. We had the jeep there in a barn, but we didn't sleep there. We slept and kept most of our gear in nearby trees. We had come out of the trees when Sgt. Pascal—" His voice cracks. "Pascal was a good man. They all were, and I failed them. Pascal said he heard something. Some of the other fellows said they didn't hear anything, but Pascal was insistent and demanded silence. Then I heard it. A buzz from overhead. Not a plane. Not a helicopter. A buzz like a gargantuan fly. Then I saw the orange glow. A bunch of the boys did. Pascal said something about fractals. Then flames. Explosions. Out of nowhere and everywhere."

Gilmore starts sobbing, softly at first, then so

violently his body trembles.

"It wasn't your fault." I place a hand on his shoulder. "You had no idea what you were up against."

Gilmore snorts up snot. "Story isn't done yet." He shakes free of my hand and wipes the tears from the corners of his eyes. "The initial attack must've been over in seconds. But they weren't done with us. There was a second team that wasn't faeries. I'm sure about that. They were men. Geared up in tactical gear, including night vision. Some of my men were still alive. They were shot. Pascal called his daughter's name until they put a bullet in his head. I was hurt, but I could move. I could've fought. Instead, I played dead."

"How did you survive? If they were shooting everyone," Dalia says, accusation in her tone.

"They got a call over a walkie-talkie," Gilmore says.

"Night vision gear and walkie-talkies," Dad says. "So they have working electronics?"

"That's right," the officer says.

"Do you have any working electronics?" I ask more sharply than I intended.

Gilmore glances at me with narrowed eyes and shakes his head. "Just the old radio. That was in an EMP bag. It's gone now. I left it at the farm in my rush to get out of there." He looks around at the others, shaking his head. Everyone is looking at him with mistrust. "Search me. Search the jeep. I don't have anything to hide. They got a call on a walkie-talkie. About trouble. That's the reason I survived. The reason they didn't find the jeep. They got a call and rushed off."

"What kind of trouble?" Radcliffe asks. "Where?"

Gilmore's voice rises as he speaks. "I don't know. I didn't hear. I had been burned." He holds up his reddened arms. "My ears were ringing from the gunshots. I thought I was going to die." He slams his open palms against the steering wheel. "You have to believe me."

A breeze comes from off the water, carrying with it the ocean's briny scent and a waft of the lieutenant's odor. Inside me, the sleeper stirs, intrigued by his scent. I lean close to him and take a good sniff. Gilmore looks at me askance as the sleeper analyzes the odor roiling off the officer.

Along with the stink of sweat and the aroma of dried blood is a smell the predator within me knows well. The musky fear of a cornered animal.

"We can use magic," Haji says. "I know a spell that will make him tell the truth."

"Powerful and dangerous magic," Dad says, "that will give us away to any faeries or human magicians nearby."

Haji shrugs and crosses his arms.

"We can interrogate him." Dalia balls up a fist. "Using enhanced techniques. Like we did with Gore."

I tense. Although Gore had tried to kill me twice, Dalia shouldn't have tortured him.

"I'm telling the truth," Gilmore whines.

"No one is going to torture you." I give Dalia a dirty look, then face Gilmore. "In fact"—I nod to Radcliffe—"I think we can trust him. He's afraid. Pure fear. I don't think he's lying."

Radcliffe meets my gaze. "I agree. We will trust you, Lt. Gilmore, until you prove us wrong. Please, drive on once you have calmed down."

****

We reach Hawi as the predawn light crests the distant horizon. The high clouds blush pink, a harbinger of the coming sunrise. The jeep putters down the town's main street between buildings with colorful façades. Most buildings are two stories and sport large windows on the top floors. The interiors of the buildings are dark, and the few streetlights are out. In the distance comes the rumble of generators.

"This place makes me nervous," Gilmore mutters. He glances left and right, head cocked to view the high windows. "It's a good place for an ambush."

I try to look everywhere at once. I don't see anyone watching us from dark rooms or peeking out from behind doors, but there are too many hideaways for me to scan everything. On top of that, Radcliffe's glittering dragon form flashing in and out of existence messes with my night vision. Someone might lurk inside one of the darkened stores, and I might miss them. I consider switching to IR mode, but Gilmore depresses the accelerator, and with a guttural rumble, the jeep picks up speed.

"Relax," Dalia says, pink hair swishing side to side. She nods toward Haji, who has somehow managed to fall asleep, sandwiched between the side of the vehicle and Dad.

I smile, although I know I won't be relaxing anytime soon. It's more than foreboding over a potential ambush. It's the fact Dalia and Haji are even here in the first place. My dreams might be portentous, or maybe not. That doesn't matter. What matters is that my friends are here, and they're in danger. More than danger from faeries, murderous commandos, and maybe even skaags. Dalia is a danger to herself. She wanted to torture Gilmore. Perhaps it was just a threat to get him to talk, but she tortured Gore and I know she's willing to do it again. I don't want her to be that girl. I don't want her to become a killer. Once she treads that trail, there's no turning back. I know that all too well. The same goes for Haji. Would the boy I had known before The Incident be willing to scramble a man's mind with magic for information? I don't think so.

Gilmore applies the brakes. I turn my attention to the road. Up ahead is a partially blocked intersection. By all appearances, the automobiles had died in the intersection's middle and were abandoned.

"Where is everyone?" Dalia asks.

"It's still early in the morning," Dad says. "They're probably still asleep."

"I don't mean the locals. I mean the stranded tourists. This town is a tourist trap."

"Maybe there's a hotel they're staying at or a community center," Dad says.

"Not everyone is asleep." I point to a black and white mutt eyeballing us before a storefront advertising Hawaiian doodads.

The passenger side front and rear wheels roll over the curb onto the sidewalk. When the wheels roll off the sidewalk, the suspension creaks, and we're rattled like dice. The dog starts barking a gruff "get the hell out of here" warning. Gilmore hits the gas, and the jeep accelerates down the road. Behind us, the dog slinks into the street, balefully watching us.

We reach the edge of town without incident. No shootout at the OK Corral this morning. Leaning back, I admire the brightening sky, a deep blue vast enough to drown in and towering puffball clouds slowly fading from vibrant pink to peach. Soon, the jeep slows again, disturbing my contemplation of the sky and Dalia from her drowsy half sleep. Haji remains slumbering, head lolling against Dad's shoulder. Dad, too, has succumbed to weariness, chin pressed against his chest and eyes shut.

I sit up in time to see that we hang a right on Kohala Mountain Road toward Waimea, where the lieutenant and his men were ambushed, I recall with a sinking feeling. In the distance, the sky is afire with oranges and reds. My breath catches in my throat, and inside me, the sleeper goes on high alert.

"Skaag," I splutter.

"Stop and turn off the headlights," Radcliffe says.

Gilmore complies. The skaag passes in and out of the clouds like a snake slithering through psychedelic grass.

"Why did we stop?" Dalia's voice is gummy with tiredness.

"Skaag." I point at distant clouds. I have no doubt of what I see and neither does the sleeper.

"I don't see anything. The clouds are pretty." Dalia sits up beside me.

"It flew into a cloud."

"I might've seen something, but I'm not sure," Gilmore says. "We're so far away. How can it even see us? We'd be a speck."

"If I can see it, you can it bet can see us." I look to Dr. Radcliffe. Radcliffe the man and the dragon stare at the clouds with unblinking intensity. "Did you see it?"

Radcliffe faces me, but his dragon gaze remains

fixed on the sky. "I saw it. Only a glimpse before it disappeared behind the clouds. We will continue without headlights."

"It's still too dark for me to drive without headlights," Gilmore says.

"If our enemy spots headlights on the road, we will attract unwanted attention," Radcliffe says.

"I know this road pretty well, but without the headlights, we'll end up in a ditch," Gilmore says.

"We have night vision." I point to Radcliffe and myself.

"Fine." Gilmore gets out of the vehicle. "Can either of you drive a stick?"

I shake my head. I've never driven a car, let alone a stick shift.

"I have, but not in a long time," Radcliffe says.

Radcliffe shimmies to the driver seat, and Gilmore tells me to ride shotgun since I have night vision. The lieutenant clambers into the back careful not to wake the sleeping beauties.

Grinding sounds come from under the vehicle as Radcliffe puts the jeep in gear. Dalia utters a startled yelp, and Gilmore curses. The vehicle lurches forward, then, bucking like a bronco, dies.

"What's going on?" Dad's voice is mushy.

"Apologies," Radcliffe says, restarting the vehicle. "I have not driven a stick in years."

I turn to the back and inform Dad about the skaag. He takes the information in stride, or maybe he's too tired to fully process it. Haji, with his eyes shut tight, remains asleep.

On the second attempt, Radcliffe successfully puts the jeep in gear, and soon, we're heading down the road at forty miles per hour. We come to hairpin turns, which require some braking that Radcliffe manages without downshifting. Alongside the road is pastureland, and occasionally I spot a few cows in the distance when I'm not warily watching the brightening sky for skaag activity. I'm looking for skaags on a sharp turn when Radcliffe unexpectedly brakes. From the back, Gilmore screams stop, and Dalia joins in. The jeep shudders and wheels lock, squealing.

I face forward in time to spy the enormous ruddy cow standing in the middle of the road. The bovine unworriedly chews its cud as we careen over the asphalt on a collision course.

Tires squeal. The cow remains statuesque in the road except for its working jaw. Haji's and Dad's confused voices join the cacophony from the back. My life doesn't flash before my eyes, but as the cow encompasses the entirety of the windscreen and beyond, I wonder if my body's supernatural healing ability will save me after colliding with a nearly one-ton animal. Inside me, the sleeper surges toward the surface with the promise of survival and hankering for a good meal.

The jeep screeches to a halt less than a foot from the cow, which flicks its tail and defecates in the middle of the road. The aroma of the manure is strong enough to make my eyes water. Business done, the cow meanders toward the side of the road, hooves clopping against the concrete. Soon, the bovine moves through the tall grass along the road toward the pasture beyond. The half-skaag calms once the cow is out of sight. Radcliffe is about to set off when Gilmore pipes up.

"It's bright enough I can drive now."

Radcliffe and Gilmore trade spots and the jeep rolls

relatively smoothly down the road, the gears grinding a little bit when the lieutenant uses the clutch. I go back to scanning the now baby-blue sky punctuated with popcorn clouds on the lookout for skaags and faeries.

The morning has turned warm and humid when we reach Waimea. The town is larger than Hawi and doesn't possess the tourist trap vibe. A few people, either solitary or in small groups, walk the streets and sidewalks. As the jeep weaves between broken-down vehicles, people watch us, some warily and others with obvious envy for our working vehicle.

Gilmore points down a side road. "The farm where the faeries killed my men is about five miles down that road."

We offer the lieutenant words of comfort and go on high alert. If we weren't in enemy territory before, we are now.

At the edge of town, we come to the turnoff to Mamalahoa Highway. Gilmore slows the jeep nearly to a stop to maneuver around a semi and half a dozen other vehicles ranging from a small EV to a 4 x 4 with oversized knobbly tires clogging the intersection. Sunlight gleams off the windows of a gas station minimart on the opposite side of the road. On a plot of reddish-brown earth sprinkled with grass struts a rooster watching over a clutch of hens and even a few chicks. The rooster is colorfully striking, and the chicks are cute, but the dirt reminds me of my dream where my friends die.

Gilmore successfully maneuvers the jeep onto the highway when a man in baggy shorts and a white tank top bursts from the minimart, waving a pistol overhead and screaming at us to stop.

"Get down!" I scream worried he might open fire.

Dalia and Dad get low, but Haji gawks at the gunman without lowering himself. Finally, Dalia pulls him down. Radcliffe watches the gunman seemingly without concern.

With a growl, the jeep accelerates down the road, leaving Waimea and the highwayman in the dust.

****

By midday, we roll into the parking lot at the base of Mauna Kea. The lot is crammed with vehicles, including tour buses, but eerily devoid of people. Gilmore parks the jeep close to the bathroom facility, and everyone gets out. The pure humans of us use the restrooms while Radcliffe and I stand guard.

A breeze picks up, carrying with it a disconcerting aroma. I glance at Radcliffe. His nose twitches and he nods to me.

"I'll check it out," I say and follow my nose to the edge of the parking lot where tall yellow grasses, green bushes, and small trees spread over the landscape. In the distance is a ridgeline that forms the lower slope of Mauna Kea.

I stop at the edge of the concrete, scanning the tall grass for the source of the stench of decomposition. I'm not sure what I expect to find. Dead people? Dead animals? Whatever it is, it's been baking in the heat and humidity for a while.

I tread through the tall grass. I've gone ten feet or less when I spot the first body in a camouflage uniform. I clamp a hand over my mouth as I start heaving from the stench. I manage not to throw up because my stomach is empty. Straightening, I quickly inspect the surrounding area, finding eight more bodies hidden in the grass, all soldiers with gunshot wounds and stripped of equipment. They must be part of the recon force General Lovelace told us about.

Chapter 33

I head back to the restrooms and tell everyone about the bodies. Gilmore feels it is his duty to inspect the corpses. Despite my warning about the smell, everyone tags along.

"That smell!" Dalia exclaims at the edge of the parking lot, eyes watering.

Haji bends over, hands to his knees. "I'll hang back here."

"Yeah, we'll go over there where the smell isn't so strong," Dalia says.

Dad waves a hand before his nose. "I'll stay with them."

I lead Gilmore and Radcliffe to the bodies. The lieutenant tries his best to put on a brave face, but I can tell he's in a similar boat as me and the stench curdles his stomach. But there's a difference between us. Yes, my human side is disgusted by the smell, but the skaag wonders if there might be fresh meat intermixed with the rotten. I keep my gaze on the ridge in the distance and do my best to ignore the sleeper's stirrings. Radcliffe, of course, is unaffected.

Gilmore confirms this could be the part of the unit Lovelace told us about. "Looks like they were in a firefight somewhere else and dumped here. Had to be those damn mercs who did this."

"What the…" I murmur, prosthetics zooming in on

several black shapes moving down the ridge.

"What is it?" Gilmore asks.

"I see people. They're armed!"

"What? On the ridgeline? Ah, I see them," Radcliffe says.

Gilmore has his rifle raised and looks through the scope. There is a tremor in his voice. "Those gunmen…soldiers…whoever they are. They're outfitted the same as the men who executed my squad."

"Have they seen us?" Radcliffe asks.

"I don't think so. They're…wait." The mercs jog down the slope. The man in the lead points with a black-gloved hand.

Blinking, my prosthetics zoom out a little bit, and I follow where the man points. A woman in a tan outfit leads two children down the hill. She holds each child by the hand, half dragging them behind her. I focus on the new group, and my prosthetics zoom, momentarily throwing the scene out of focus then sharpening until I can see the tears streaming down the children's faces and the fear distorting the women's features. I clutch my hands into fists.

"The soldiers are pursuing a woman and two children." I blink until my perspective changes, giving me a view of both groups racing down the slope. A haze descends, encroaching on the scene from all sides until all I see is a pinprick of the Hawaiian landscape. The mist solidifies into the stark white hallways of the base beneath the sands of Golden Shoal. Dalia and I run through those hallways, desperate for escape, for safety, for survival. Our pursuers' boots echo through the corridor like the throbbing heartbeat of a ravenous eldritch terror. My throat cinches tight, and my next words are a rasp. "We have to help them."

"That might not be wise," Radcliffe says.

"What is that supposed to mean? Children. We're talking about children pursued by men with guns."

"Rendering aid is not the optimal strategy," Radcliffe says. "We will be better off avoiding these people altogether. To maintain the element of surprise."

I blink until my vision zooms out and glare at Radcliffe. "We save children."

Radcliffe appears ready to lecture me, but Gilmore, still looking through the rifle's scope, speaks first.

"Agreed. We have to help the kids, and we need a plan of action pronto. The soldiers captured the woman and kids."

Radcliffe frowns. "Very well. We save the children. I hope this does not ruin our chance at closing the slipstream."

****

I brush against the sleeper as I lope up the hillside with unnatural ease. On the stiff breeze coming down the slope, I can discern the individual scents of my prey, including the rich aroma of recently drunk coffee. I wonder if the ambrosial flavor of java will infuse the man's raw, bloody flesh as I gorge myself on his writhing body. And the young ones…will their flesh be exceptionally tender?

I squeeze my hand so tight my fingernails cut half-moons into my palms, then bloody grooves. *Stop. Stop! Stop!*

The sleeper withdraws, and its gory fantasies fade from my forethought, although the afterimages remain. Luckily, the infinite wealth of physical prowess still courses through my body as potent as jet fuel. Already I have a flanking position on the three mercs holding the woman and children. Keeping low, I move behind a small, twisted tree and crouch. Although perhaps five hundred feet separate me from the mercs and their captives, I listen to the conversation as easily as if I'm among them.

"Stop your whining!" A black-clad man raises his rifle's butt and feigns striking a whimpering boy.

The child cowers, and the woman tries to throw herself between him and the weapon, only to have her movement impeded by her hands zip-tied behind her back. The other captives, a boy and girl too small to pose any threat, have their hands behind their backs too. I nearly burst from my hiding spot to run down the evil men, but I stop myself.

The flickering dragon highlighting his location, Radcliffe has yet to take up his flanking position opposite mine. A coordinated assault is the plan. That will give the captives the best chance of survival. If I move without Radcliffe, I'm sure I can overcome the fiends without suffering harm, but the same cannot be said about the children. So I wait the interminable seconds, minutes, I don't know which, until Radcliffe reaches the agreed-upon position. At least my squad, Dad, and Gilmore remain at the parking lot hidden behind the bathroom.

"Should we call it in?" a trooper asks.

"Why? We have our orders."

"I didn't sign up to shoot kids."

As soon as the words are out of the man's mouth, I'm at full tilt, all pretense of stealth trampled under my sneakers. Radcliffe isn't in position, but I don't care. I'm not about to let a child be executed. I might only be half a human, but I'm not a monster either, and I will never compromise on this.

By the time the soldiers hear my approach, I've cut the distance between us in half. When they face me, I'm already on top of them. Eyes bugging out of his head, the soldier nearest me raises his rifle, but it's too late because I smash into him like a freight train. He crumples beneath me with the crack of snapping bones. In my peripheral vision, Radcliffe has broken cover and charges up the slope with inhuman speed, the man and the dragon in perfect unison.

The soldier who threatened the boy points his weapon at the child. "Stay back or—"

I am the whirlwind, moving faster than my opponent can twitch his trigger finger. I yank his finger from the trigger so hard the digit detaches from his hand with a pop of bone and a spray of blood. His screams fill the air. Dropping the finger, I'm about to punch him with my full power, but I stop myself. If I do that, I'll kill him. Instead, I slap him with an open hand. He's unconscious before hitting the ground, but he'll live.

The children sob, and the woman pleads, "Please don't hurt us!"

The scent of urine intrudes on the otherwise pleasing scent of fresh blood. My gaze falls on the captives, spotting the dampness on the girl's shorts. They fear me as much or even more than the gunmen. My tongue slips from my mouth, stretching for something oozing along my face to the right of my nose. I gasp, tingling with pleasure at the metallic tang of my prey's blood. Trembling, I muster all my human willpower to keep from dropping to the ground to stuff the detached finger into my mouth.

The report of a gunshot echoes across the landscape.

Chapter 34

With the gunshot ringing in my ears, I duck low and maneuver myself over the crying children. The woman, a park employee by her uniform, kicks out at me with her feet inside dusty, heavy-duty hiking boots. She connects with my shin below the knee.

"Ouch!" I'd like to kick her back but compromise at shooting her a thorny glower. Can't she see I'm trying to protect the children?

I glance in the direction of the gunshot. Radcliffe stands about twenty feet downslope over the unmoving body of the final gunman.

"Ouch!" This time the woman lands a solid blow to my kneecap. Pain blossoms up and down my leg as I hobble back a few paces. "Would you stop? We're saving you."

"Stay back, you monster!" she says through clenched teeth and kicks again with both feet. Luckily, I'm already out of range.

That word, though, monster, slices me like a knife punching into my guts. Why is it I always have to be the monster girl? I wanted—my innards twist both with hunger and disgust—to eat that man's trigger finger, but I didn't. I resisted the urge. It'd be nice if the stench of fear didn't roll off them like spoiled milk, and the park ranger stopped assaulting me.

"We saved you from the soldiers." Above the

pocket on her left breast is a name badge. “Lani? Park Ranger Lani, I can snap the zip tie.” I glance at the children, flashing them a winning smile. “For all of you.”

“Stay back,” Lani says, spittle flying from her mouth, then starts shimmying across the ground away from me. The children follow her example.

“Seriously?”

The eyes of all three go wide, and I can’t help noticing they focus on something behind me. Of course, I can hear Dr. Radcliffe’s footfall crunching against pebbles and dirt as he closes in.

Lani’s expression turns from angry fear to terror, and the children switch from half-controlled sobbing to sloppy crying. A quick peek proves Radcliffe is scaring them witless. The right side of his head above the eye is conspicuously missing. Instead of spilling blood and gore, the wound exposes grayish material reminiscent of clay. This doesn’t surprise me because I know his humanoid golem is made of clay and animated by draconic magic.

“Are these humans uninjured?” Radcliffe says. “I am afraid I may have killed the one back there.”

“The kids and Lani are fine. Just scared. I don’t think I killed anyone.” I tap the right side of my skull with a finger. “You’re missing part of your head.”

Radcliffe, the glimmering dragon, inspects the wound before flashing from existence and reappearing a second later, staring at me. “That happens when a bullet passes through one’s head.” He waves to Lani and the kids. “I am not hurt and will not harm you.” His gaze falls on me. “We best hurry. The gunshot may attract unwanted attention.”

We face Lani and the kids. Honestly, I'm glad they haven't managed to regain their feet and make a run for it yet, not that they'd get very far.

"Listen, those men were about to shoo—"

The boy interrupts in a soft, squeaky voice. "You're Allison Lee. You're on TV."

I blink, surprised they choose to suddenly recognize me now. Couldn't they have recognized me sooner and spared me the kicks and incessant crying?

"Yeah," the girl says. "You're the monster girl. Monsterspotting.com! My big brother is always looking at your pictures. He has a crush on you."

Wincing, I nod. "That's me." I hook a thumb in Radcliffe's direction. "That's Dr. Radcliffe. I know he looks pretty scary right now, but he's not human, and he's not hurt. I know you can't see it, but he's really a dra—"

"Dragon," the kids say in unison.

I nod again. "Ummm…yeah. So no need to be afraid. We're here to save you."

Lani squints at me, mouth agape. She points her left index finger at the sky, then at me. "I saw a clip of you testifying. Before the Senate."

The overwhelming fear drains from all three of them, and they let me snap the zip ties binding them. I even learn the children's names, Caleb and Jen. For once, being a celebrity isn't absolutely terrible.

****

I unsling the second unconscious soldier from my shoulder, leaning him next to his equally insensible partner in the odiferous men's bathroom. Lucky for the man missing his finger, Gilmore and Lani possess basic first-aid training. Together they managed to stanch and bandage the wound. We tried interrogating the man while the first-aid was applied, but we didn't get much. He and his compatriots are mercenaries, extremely well paid to do what they're told and not ask questions. Their job was to round up tourists around Mauna Kea, which they had done quite effectively. Only then Lani and the kids spoiled everything by escaping.

We might've gotten more info out of him, but that's when Dalia decided it was a good idea to kick his wounded hand. He promptly passed out from the pain. On the plus side, Lani can lead us to an outbuilding of a radio telescope array where some of the tourists are held.

The man I ran over like an angry rhino breathes raggedly; honestly, it sounds pretty awful, like scary bad. I'm afraid he might die. He was about to shoot the children, so I don't have sympathy for him, but I don't want more blood on my hands, either. I don't need more ghosts haunting my dreams.

I double-check the zip ties binding their hands behind their backs, murmuring, "You don't kill kids. And make smarter choices next time. Your partner. He's in the women's bathroom. He didn't make it."

Shaking my head, I roll my eyes and march out of the bathroom. Why am I talking to these unresponsive men? At least, a soft voice whispers to me, it's better than talking to the dead.

****

"No way! I'm going with you, and I want a gun." Dalia crosses her arms before her chest.

"I'm coming too."

Haji jumps down from the back of the jeep to stand next to Dalia. I shoot him an exasperated look.

Haji raises a hand palm outward. "But I don't need a gun. I have magic."

"You're suffering from Juice withdrawal." I shake my head. This is going about as well as I expected.

At least Gilmore has agreed to stay with Caleb and Jen, who sit in the back of the jeep. He plans to motor to a nearby copse of trees where they will be hidden from view but still close enough to help out the soon-to-be-free hostages.

I need Haji and Dalia to go with Gilmore and the kids, but I don't know what to say to convince them. If you ascend Mauna Kea, you'll die. That will go over like a balloon leaking mustard gas.

"Allison, I need to stay near Haji in case his withdrawal symptoms worsen," Dad says.

"I know. You can stay behind too. Dr. Radcliffe and I can handle this."

Dalia and Haji look at me with disapproval. Dad scoffs and shakes his head. I turn to Dr. Radcliffe, hoping for support but not expecting any. My eyes widen at his deformed skull. Even knowing his humanoid form is not a human at all and a magical machine doesn't make the sight any less disconcerting.

Radcliffe points skyward. His draconic head has been obsessively scanning the sky since the gunshot. "We do not have time to argue, Allison."

I point to Lani, who holds a walkie-talkie liberated from the soldiers. Gilmore has the other in the jeep. "We've listened in on the radio chatter. There's no indication they heard the gunshot."

"Perhaps, but someone will eventually notice the men in the restrooms have gone missing. We started this journey as a team. We should continue as a team,"

Radcliffe says.

Dalia retrieves one of the rifles leaning against the restroom building. “We have a job to do. Free the hostages, then save the world. Let’s roll.”

Chapter 35

Lani, armed with a rifle she admits that she doesn't know how to use, leads the way at a fast pace across an increasingly Martian landscape that reminds me of the reddish-orange dirt and rock from my nightmares. With every footstep, dread scurries over me like hundreds of chittering cockroaches. I glance over my shoulder. Fit from running hundreds of miles in cross country, Dalia keeps pace a few feet behind me, although she does breathe hard. Radcliffe lopes along easily, his dragon form flashing. Like me, he could easily outpace Lani and everyone else. Haji lags behind, his deteriorated physical capacity on full display. Dad stays beside him, offering encouragement every dozen strides or so. Ahead of us the summit of Mauna Kea is cloaked in dense fog.

We've been slogging uphill for the better part of two hours when Lani calls a halt several hundred feet before our path intersects the winding road up the side of the volcano. I'm far from exhausted, but I'm glad to stop for a few minutes as the backpack straps slung over my shoulders have started to chafe. I unsling the backpack and offer water to Lani and Dalia as we wait for Haji and Dad to catch up. Both women gulp down water.

Dalia hands me back the open, half-empty canteen. I take a drink and replace the lid.

When Dad and Haji catch up, they both guzzle the water greedily and return the canteen empty. I offer them more water, which Dad immediately turns down. Haji looks ready to ask for more but then shakes his head.

"Are you sure you don't want more?" I ask.

"I'm good. Ready to take home the bacon." Haji manages a half-hearted smile. His dark wavy hair is matted down to his scalp by sweat. A red blush is visible on his dark cheeks.

When I hear his sports reference—he's told me dozens of times taking home the bacon is attributed to an old-time boxer—and see his goofy smile, I can almost believe the old Haji, my good, good friend is back. But the smile, the mirth, the goofiness never reaches his eyes.

"Come on." I put the empty canteen back in the backpack and take out a full one, offering it to Haji. "You'll be doing me a favor. Less water, less weight."

"All right." Haji smiles and takes a canteen.

"Allison," Radcliffe calls from where the others gather around Lani.

I join the group, followed by Haji, gulping water. He hands the bottle back to me, nearly empty, which is a relief.

Lani points to a hill across the road. The road loops around the base of the landmark to disappear from view. "From the top of that hill, we'll have a line of sight on the outbuilding."

The park ranger gives us a quick rundown of the outbuilding and other structures, making a sketch with the butt of her rifle. "Two men were guarding the building." Lani indicates a square surrounded by a larger rectangle, a fence. "A van was parked out front. They used it to transport the prisoners to the building."

"Once we free the hostages, they can use the van to get away," Dalia says.

People nod and voice general agreement.

"Have we heard anything on the walkie-talkie about the mercenaries we took out?" I ask.

Lani shakes her head. "I haven't heard a thing about them or anything else."

"Does that seem odd?" I look at Dad and Dr. Radcliffe.

Dad shrugs. "Yeah, but I'm not a soldier."

"We still have the element of surprise," Radcliffe says with confidence. However, his dragon head continues to scrutinize the sky and landscape. "If the faeries or skaags suspected our presence, we would already be under attack."

"I don't want to walk into a trap," I say.

"They do not know we are here," Radcliffe insists.

I hope he's right. I point to the diagram at our feet. "Here's what we do."

****

Lani and I drop to our bellies before the crest of the hill. The ground is strewn with rocks and pebbles that press uncomfortably against me. We low crawl the last few feet to the peak. My knee scrapes against a jagged rock, and I wince. Lani fares even worse in her tan shorts, a perpetual grimace plastered on her face.

Reaching the summit first, I poke my head up to discover if what we're dealing with matches Lani's diagram. The dominant landmark is the radio telescope array behind a tall fence. I sweep my gaze from the astronomical equipment to the blocky building behind a barbwire fence, and my pulse goes ultrasonic. My prosthetics zoom in on the figures standing before the building. The sleeper thrashes inside me, ready to fight or flee; I don't know which.

"Gaaah." I scramble backward and grab Lani by the shoulder to keep her from raising her head. My prosthetics are still zoomed way in like a super telephoto lens, throwing my perspective into la la land.

"What is it?" Lani tries to shake herself free. "Ouch! You're hurting me."

I release her. "Sorry. Not so loud. Sorry, I didn't mean to. It's just…" I keep blinking until my prosthetics finally zoom out, and Lani snaps into focus, frowning and rubbing her deltoid. "I saw a faery."

"What? You're not serious?"

"As stage four cancer."

Lani looks toward the crest. "I want to see."

"Slowly. Faeries have sharper senses than humans, and where there is one, there might be more."

Nodding, Lani crawls forward, and I follow. In front of the building beside the entrance is a mercenary dressed all in black, armed with a rifle, speaking to a faery with its dragonfly wings on full display.

"Wow. So that's a faery?" Lani starts to unsling the rifle from her back.

"Hold up. What are you doing?"

Lani stops and hunkers down. "I want to get a look through the scope. I'm not going to try to shoot anyone."

I shake my head. "The faery might see the reflection. They have excellent eyesight."

Lani frowns. "Okay."

I turn my attention back to the outbuilding and the

faery. I can understand why Lani is fascinated by the creature, wearing a form-fitting black jumpsuit with a long slit down the back allowing its translucent wings to sprout from between its shoulder blades. Faintly glowing orange veins etch the wings, forming swirling patterns reminiscent of fractals. The faery's hair, including the eyebrows, is as pure white as freshly fallen snow and stands in stark contrast to his skin, which is as black as crude oil. Even more bizarre, variegated dust surrounds the faery and cascades from his mouth as he speaks to the mercenary. The mercenary breathes in some of the faery dust. I know from experience that breathing the dust makes humans more compliant to a faery's commands.

I try to listen to what is being said, but even with my heightened perception, I can't make out their words. If only I could move closer without being seen, but that seems impossible given the barren landscape.

"What do we do now?" Lani asks.

Two soldiers I could outflank and overcome without any issue. Throw the faery into the mix? I'm not confident I can take out all three of them before a soldier radios for aid. I could trek down the hill to where the others wait and beg Radcliffe for assistance. But no, the dragon would use the faery's presence as an excuse to abandon the hostages. "We wait. Maybe the faery will leave."

No sooner than I say the words, the door to the blocky building opens, and a second mercenary steps out, followed by another faery. My heart feels like it's running up my throat and the sleeper batters against my insides.

Stop! I scream silently at the sleeper. I swear my

abdomen will explode in a shower of blood.

Lani looks at me worriedly. “Is something wrong? You look like you’re going to be sick?”

I shake my head and say through gritted teeth. “I’m fine.”

The second faery is Jett, a scar marring the right side of his face along the jawline. Just looking at him fills me with loathing and makes my abdomen tighten. I don’t know if I want to kill him or feel his caress setting my body aflame.

“Get down!” I hiss and slide down the rise. The park ranger remains rooted in place. “Lani!”

She scrambles back next to me. The color drains from her cheeks. “I swear a faery looked right at me. Do you think he saw…”

I raise a finger to my lips for silence. At the precipice of my hearing, I detect a faint buzz. My breath catches in my throat. That’s the sound of faeries taking flight. If they’re coming for us, we’re fish in a barrel. I’ll have to transform and that will definitely eliminate our surprise advantage.

“What’s that buzz?” Lani asks.

“The faeries are flying.”

But are they flying toward us? I can’t tell. The sound ricochets directionless around the landscape. Taking a deep breath, I crawl toward the rise.

Chapter 36

The buzz of the faery wings seems to come from everywhere at once. The racket fades, then increases without warning. Heart thundering in my chest like a Taiko drum being played by a gremlin on speed, I poke my head up. Inside me, the sleeper dances to the frantic beat, knotting my innards like poorly stowed Christmas lights.

A breath I hadn't realized I've been holding whooshes out of me. I lower my head behind the rise.

"What's happening?" Lani demands.

"The faeries are leaving, flying away from us. They're headed up the mountain," I say.

"Great. That's great." Lani crawls forward for a peek.

"Careful. The guards are still there, and the faeries might turn back."

"I can barely hear the buzz." Lani glances at me. "Now is our chance to free the prisoners."

"Would you get down? The guards might see you."

Muttering, Lani scoots down beside me.

"We need to take our time. Do this right, or people might get hurt."

Lani's gaze goes to her rifle, and her grip tightens on the barrel.

"The wrong people, Lani." Lecturing the ranger makes me feel weird. I mean she must be almost ten years older than me, out of college, and has a real job with responsibilities. She should be calm and collected, instead of chomping at the bit to get into the action.

"It's just…" Lani clenches the gun's grip. For a moment, I think she might flip off the safety and wrap her finger around the trigger, then some of her tension slackens. "The prisoners are tourists, most of them anyway. Part of a tour I was leading. Over half of them are children. I'm responsible for them. Me." She looks up, gaze intense. "I don't want anything to happen to them, especially the children. I know you understand that."

To my relief, the buzz of the faeries' wings continues to fade. What's disconcerting is Lani isn't being entirely truthful. I don't know what's giving her away. Her smell? A smorgasbord of little tics that are all insignificant on their own but put together are a flashing neon sign stating, I'm prevaricating. I don't know. But she's holding something back. I know it, and so does the sleeper. "And?"

Lani looks puzzled. "And what?"

"You're holding something back. What is it?"

Lani's cheeks flush. "Am I that obvious? There's a man, a scientist, Orion Nash. Dr. Orion we call him on the tour because it sounds cool. He's an astronomer at the observatory. He's nice and great with the kids who visit. Academic. I'm gushing, aren't I?" Her blush deepens. "God. Pull it together, Lani. He can get a little intense. He might do or say something to set off the guards. I'm worried about him. That's all. Can we go now?"

Seems innocent enough. "Not yet. I want to wait until I can't hear the faeries. Just in case. Why don't you go tell the others what the holdup is."

Lani cocks her head. "I can't hear the buzz anymore."

"I can. They're not as far away as you think."

****

Despite taking a long route to stay out of sight, I'm behind the blocky gray and tan outbuilding in under five minutes, and I'm not even breathing hard after the sprint. Still, I warily eye the barbed wire topping the tall fence. The obstacle must be fifteen feet tall, well within my ability to jump, but I don't want any mishaps.

Judging by the murmur of their conversation, the guards are still around at the front of the building. I think they're arguing about whose favorite pro football team is better. I jog to each side of the building, crouching low, to make sure the guards are still out front. I pause at the left side of the building to admire the radio telescope array some fifty feet away behind more fencing replete with no trespassing signs and high voltage warnings. Up close, I have a better appreciation of how massive the dishes are—each as big as a semi-truck, at least.

I catch myself whistling one of Dark Matter Electrica's cosmic dance beats. Cursing myself as an idiot, I bite my tongue to stop myself from vocalizing the catchy tune. I scurry to roughly the building's midpoint and eyeball the fence.

"I need to land quietly. No problem." I take a standing leap.

I soar over the fence, landing catlike on the dirt. The impact lances up my legs, terminating at my hips with dull but painful blossoms. Straightening, I raise my hand to brush off the dirt and stop. A chill runs through me despite the heat and humidity and the sweat rolling down my brow. Red dust stains my fingertips. The same color as the ground in my nightmare.

A drop of sweat rolls into my left eye, causing me to blink. That breaks the spell long enough for me to wipe away the dust. I'm still cleaning my hands when boots crunch against the ground from my right. What the heck? How am I being snuck up on? I spin to come face-to-face with a man rounding the corner of the building. He is clad from boots to neck all in black, with various accouterments hanging from his belt and suspenders. A gnarly-looking automatic rifle hangs across his chest by a shoulder strap. He's not wearing a helmet, revealing a bald head burned red by the sun. I'm sure his eyes, hidden behind dark, reflective sunglasses, are as wide as his gaping mouth.

He starts to whip the gun barrel toward me. "Don—"

I pounce, grabbing the left side of his head and slamming it against the side of the building. The entire time my mind is caught in a loop: don't kill him, don't kill him, don't kill him.

His head smacking the building makes a dull thump that I swear his compatriot out front must hear—at least, I hope his cohort is still at the front of the building. I grab the merc as he falls and lower him gently to the ground. The bloody stain left on the side of the building makes my insides twist, and I taste bile in the back of my mouth. Did I kill him? No. He is still breathing, thank goodness.

With the unconscious merc cradled in my arms, I listen for any sound that might betray the other guard approaching. Nada. Good. Maybe fortune is smiling on me.

I sit the guard up against the building. His scalp is split open and bleeding profusely. The blood excites the sleeper. Its coppery aroma sets my mouth salivating.

"You should've worn a helmet," I whisper to the unconscious man.

I unsling his rifle and slide it over the ground out of easy reach, kicking up reddish dust. Searching his utility belt, I find a zip tie which I use to secure his hands behind his back. I loosen the strap fastening the walkie-talkie to his suspenders. I consider breaking the communication device under my foot but decide that might make too much noise. Instead, I hurl it over the fence, estimating it travels a good quarter mile before landing with an explosion of components. A grin alights my face. Maybe I should pursue a career as a quarterback?

I take one last look at the merc to make sure he's still breathing. He is, which is a relief, but what's not is my urge to lap his blood.

No. No way, I tell the sleeper.

I try to move, but my feet might as well be encased in one-ton blocks of concrete. This is not a good time for a clash of wills. This dude's partner might come looking for him at any moment.

Okay. A compromise. Just a taste.

I feel sick.

The half-skaag feels joy.

I hesitate over the man, my right index finger centimeters from the bloody scalp wound. Revolted and excited, I clench my eyes shut and brush my finger pad through the blood. I press the bloody digit to my tongue—ambrosial. A miraculous fire suffuses my body, making every millimeter tingle with euphoria.

I want to puke.

The sleeper wants to feed.

No! That's it. That's the compromise.

The beast acquiesces while giving off a smug vibe. I have to take a moment to keep myself from bursting into tears. My humanity is slipping away.

I creep along the side of the building and catch a whiff of cigarette smoke. Pressing myself against the wall, I take a look-see around to the front. The guard stands before the entrance with a cigarette dangling from his lips.

I charge him powered by all my monstrous might. He barely has time to turn before my open palm slams into his jaw, knocking him out cold. Catching him under the armpits, I lower him to the ground. After making sure he's truly unconscious and alive, I wave to my companions on the hill.

****

"Should I kick down the door?" I ask. "Is there anyone right on the other side of the door? I might bust it off its hinges by accident."

"I can look." Radcliffe, the man and the dragon, steps forward. The dragon lowers its long translucent neck toward the building's roof. His flickering head passes through the roof as though it is as insubstantial as he. "The doorway is clear. Hmmm…by outward appearances, there are only hostages inside the building. I do not see any gunmen or faeries."

Lani looks between Radcliffe and me. "He can see inside?"

"You know the dragon you can't see?"

Lani nods.

"While invisible to you, it can pass through walls." I look around at everyone. Dalia kneels next to the unconscious mercenary, going through his utility belt. "Stand back. I'm going to kick down the door."

"Hold up." Dalia stands, wearing a smile that is too smug by a mile. In her hand, she waves a rectangular key card. "Maybe we should try this first?"

I step back from the door, feeling abashed. "I should've thought of that."

"I guess when you have superhuman strength, you think every obstacle needs to be broken down." Dalia presses the key card to a rectangular black pad on the wall next to the door.

A high-pitched beep comes from the pad, followed by the mechanical click of the door unlocking.

I step in front of Dalia before she can open the door. "Let me go first, just in case. And keep your rifle over your shoulder. No accidents."

Dalia rolls her eyes and raises her hands on either side of her head. "Fine. Fine."

I open the door and step into what, for all appearances, is an oversized storage shed. Recessed fluorescent lights provide illumination. Along the walls are metal shelves full of boxes and containers from floor to ceiling. In the middle of the room is a worktable. A handful of adults and close to twenty children are sitting and standing on either side of the table, staring at me. Near the back stands a tall man with long hair pulled back in a ponytail and wearing aviator-style glasses.

"Don't panic. We're here to rescue you."

Dalia follows me inside, standing at my shoulder. Lani brushes past us, waving to the tall man in the back, who waves back. She swings the rifle over her shoulder and makes a beeline for him. As she moves through the crowd, she fields questions from the adults and children, that yes, we are here to free them. Reaching the tall man, she throws her arms around him. He must be Dr. Orion Nash.

I smile at Dalia. Everything is going to plan, for once. The adults are corralling the children. We're saving them. I didn't even kill anyone in the process. I did sample that guy's blood—I tremble with pleasure. Better not think about that.

"What is that?" a woman hollers, blood draining from her face, pointing at me.

Other people stop what they're doing and stare at me wide-eyed. Great. Identified as the monster girl once again. Wait. They're not staring at me. I notice the flickering golden light suffusing the room and the various vaguely draconic body parts passing through everything. I glance over my shoulder at Dr. Radcliffe standing in the doorway with the right side of his head missing.

"It's okay," Lani says. "It's Dr. Radcliffe. The dragon man from TV."

"Why is he missing part of his head?" a girl asks.

A boy no older than six or seven starts crying. Seconds later, half the children are in tears. People are panicking.

"Everyone, calm down!" Dalia shouts.

All the adults are either shouting or trying to comfort inconsolable children. I'm about to turn back to Radcliffe and ask him to step outside when someone takes my hand and gently tugs. I look down at a little girl with ribbons in her thick black hair, who looks absolutely adorable in a pink summer dress.

"What is it?" I ask.

"You're Allison Lee?"

"Yes."

"You help people."

"I'm here to save you from the bad men with guns."

"And the people with the wings. They're scary." Her lips quiver, then she takes a deep breath and says in a deadpan. "Dr. Orion has a gun."

"What?"

Chapter 37

"Dr. Orion has a gun," the girl repeats, pointing across the chaotic room. "Dr. Orion. He's next to Ranger Lani."

Dalia has stepped in front of me and is trying to calm everyone. People are pointing, crying, shouting epithets, and gaping in horror at Dr. Radcliffe. I take a step to the side to better view Lani and Dr. Orion.

They no longer embrace. Lani kneels beside a gaggle of children, trying to calm them. Dr. Orion stands behind Lani, gaze darting around the room, never resting until he locks eyes with me. An indication he doesn't appreciate my scrutiny? He turns his attention to a child speaking to him.

Fortunately, the astronomer remains standing, so after blinking a few times, my prosthetics zoom in, and I examine him in detail. I start at his waist on the theory I might see a bulge indicating a gun.

"I don't see a gun," I say.

"He does to have a gun," the girl says sternly, her grip tightening on my hand.

I notice Radcliffe's golden glow fades from my peripheral vision. From the scuttlebutt, I take it Dad and Haji have entered the fray, attempting to calm the people we're trying to rescue. Their first move was to ask Radcliffe to step outside—smart.

"What's your name?" I ask the little detective

gripping my hand.

"Zakira," she mumbles.

Even with my preternatural hearing, I might not have heard her had the ambient cacophony not died down after Radcliffe left the building. Dad lectures the crowd in his stern, no-nonsense professorial voice, and they're actually listening.

"Zakira, I don't see a gun."

"He's not holding it, silly. Everyone would see it. It's big and shiny."

"Where is…"

I tense. Dr. Orion reaches around behind him, like for his back pocket. I half expect him to pull out a shiny, space-age gun. Instead, he holds a walkie-talkie, a compact version of those carried by the mercs.

"Hey!" I release Zakira's hand and point at Dr. Orion. "He has a walkie-talkie." I start across the room, my way impeded by children and adults alike. "Lani, he has a walkie-talkie!"

The ranger faces me with a puzzled expression. I wave at Orion as I dance through the crowd. Orion knows I'm calling him out. He brings the walkie-talkie to his lips while backing away until he bumps into the shelving unit behind him.

"Tell Bergman Allison Lee is here. So is that dragon. Dr. Radcliffe. Hurry!"

Orion says more, but I don't catch it over the hubbub. My pulse throbs in my ears and my vision narrows to a tunnel at the mention of Bergman. Her hatchet face twisted by a rictus smile encompasses my field of view. She raises her mech's triple barrel arm cannon. Inside me, the sleeper is a tumult of rage and fear. All three barrels ignite with blinding light, sending my vision white, then red. The sleeper cowers in my bowels like a whipped puppy. Around me, the air superheats, and I await death. At least, it will be fast. In my human form, I imagine I'll be instantly incinerated.

With every breath, the air is so hot it sears my mouth, throat, and lungs. I expect to be turned to ash by plasma at any second. But that second never comes. Children screaming and the smell of burned metal intermixes with the stench of ozone catapult me back into the here and now.

My vision resolves into Dr. Orion holding a polished metal hand cannon above his head. A smoking hole the size of a softball is in the ceiling, charred around the edges. Lani is splayed on the floor next to him, bleeding from a cut on her cheek and with one arm held protectively before her face. Orion lowers the double-barrel gun, swinging it back and forth to cover all the occupants. The children have started wailing again, some cowering in the arms of adults.

"Nobody moves or I'll blast you to oblivion!" Orion yells, eyes bulging behind his glasses.

Dalia raises the rifle in a surprisingly professional-looking grip. She aims at the astronomer, one eye shut tight and the other pressed to the scope. "Drop the blaster, Doc, or I'll give you a third eyeball!"

Someone grabs my hand. I look down to discover Zakira has followed me through the crowd. Her eyes are moist. "I'm scared."

I free my hand from hers and press down on her shoulder. "Get down and stay down."

"Don't test me!" Orion says, voice rising an octave with every word. "You've seen what this weapon can do."

“Don’t test me!” Dalia shouts over the panicked hullabaloo.

Orion moves along the wall until he reaches a break in the shelving where a waist-high crate sits. Dalia rotates at the waist, tracking him with the rifle.

“Haji, don’t!” Dad calls.

I glance over my shoulder, glimpsing Dad crouching low, waving furiously at Haji, who crawls on his hands and knees between adults and children. Magic! They should use magic against Orion. He has already alerted our foes to our presence, so using magic won’t give us away. The element of surprise is already lost.

“Stop fidgeting, or I’ll start shooting!” Orion shouts.

I turn my attention back to the astronomer. His movements are becoming increasingly frenetic. People tell him they won’t resist and beg him not to open fire.

Orion holds up the walkie-talkie. “I’m falling back into the tunnel. They have me outnumbered. They have a gun on me.”

“Hold position, Dr. Nash. Reinforcements are inbound.”

My heart palpitates when Bergman’s voice crackles over the walkie-talkie.

“No! I’m falling back!” Orion screams into the communication device.

I’m ready to spring over the people separating me from the astronomer, but in my peripheral vision, Haji rises, a baseball size fireball bursting from his outstretched hand.

Adults and children alike scream at the top of their lungs. Orion ducks in the nick of time, the fireball flying over his head to burst against the concrete wall, leaving behind a sooty stain.

"Damnit! I could've had him," Dalia says.

Next to me, Dalia fiddles with the rifle, apparently having forgotten to turn off the safety. I leap, soaring over awestruck faces, and land next to the astronomer, who strains to move the crate. Surprisingly, the giant box moves smoothly over the ground to reveal a square opening in the floor with a ladder built into the side.

I grab Orion by the upper arm, spinning him to face me. He tries to bring the gun around, but I bat it aside with my free hand. The weapon flies from his grip, banging off the wall before spinning across the floor, coming to rest at the hole's edge.

"No!" Orion cries, struggling against my grip.

I shake him like a ragdoll until he stops struggling.

****

"What do you mean I need to go back with the kids?" Dalia demands, rifle slung over her shoulder and hands on her hips.

"I mean"—I hook a thumb toward Dr. Orion Nash, sitting on the floor with his hands zip-tied behind his back—"use the tunnels to get the little kids and the dangerous prisoner to Lt. Gilmore."

"How many times are you going to try to leave me behind? I've proved myself more than once, yet you keep saying I shouldn't be here. It's like I'm a burden. How am I more of a burden than Haji?" She points at the gangly boy, who looks even worse after hurling the fireball at Dr. Orion. "How? Tell me."

Dad removes a vial of bluish liquid and hands it to Haji, who downs the concoction under his watchful gaze. "You were ready to kill him." I point at Orion. "If the safety wasn't on, you would've shot him or at least tried to."

"It would have served him right." Dalia turns her glare on the astronomer and shakes a fist at him, then she turns her angry gaze on me. "I wish I had shot him. Shot him dead. And if Orion hadn't ducked, Haji's fireball would have killed him. Why don't you chew out Haji?"

"Well, he did duck, and no, Dalia, you don't wish you had shot him." For one thing, if Orion were dead, he wouldn't have told us about the tunnel system running up to the mountaintop and down to the parking lot below. Yeah, turns out Dr. Orion Nash isn't so tough after he's been disarmed and shaken like a tambourine. "I'm haunted by every person I've killed. Haunted every day."

Dalia drops her hands from her hips. "You're a skaag! You can't blame yourself. You've told me it's a constant battle for control. It's not your fault. Besides. All those people you hurt or killed were trying to kill you. It was self-defense."

"It doesn't matter. I still killed them. I'm a murderer, Dalia. I don't want that for you."

Dalia drops her gaze to her feet and shrugs. "Okay. I'm glad I didn't have to shoot him. Is that what you want to hear?" She looks up. "I won't kill anyone. I promise."

I roll my eyes. "Am I supposed to take you seriously right now?"

Dalia gets right up in my face. "When I said I'd burn down the whole world to protect those I love, I meant it. That's why you need me. Because I'll do whatever it takes to protect you and Haji."

"You know what. You're right." I lick my upper teeth. "I need you. We all need you. Lani needs you to help her get the children and their teacher down to Lt. Gilmore while escorting"—I point at Orion again—"the dangerous prisoner."

"We should've let Blake beat him to death."

Blake is the charmer who riled up some of the angry adults to give Dr. Orion, in his words, an old-fashioned ass-whooping. When Dr. Radcliffe and I intervened, the angry adults and about half the children left in the van parked out front, leaving behind a twenty-something kindergarten teacher and her dozen pupils.

Radcliffe's glowing draconic body proceeds him climbing up the ladder out of the hole leading to the tunnels. "That would have been a mistake." Radcliffe's human head pokes out of the hole. "Dr. Orion knows more about the operation here than he is telling us. Given time, I can extract that information using magic. It may prove to be valuable intelligence."

Radcliffe pulls himself out of the hole, and Dad joins us.

"Based on my reconnoitering, Dr. Orion's description of the tunnel system is accurate. I believe it can be used to ascend and descend the mountain," Radcliffe says.

"Like Dr. Radcliffe, I couldn't help overhearing your conversation." Dad holds up a hand. "My listening was incidental. I wasn't trying to eavesdrop. Promise. You know, Dalia, we have four walkie-talkies now. Gilmore and Lani each have one. You take one, and we'll keep one. We can tune them to the same frequency. That way we can call if we need you while you help Lani escort the children and the dangerous prisoner down the mountain."

"I'll need your help," Lani says from where she stands guard over her one-time friend. She told us they weren't an item yet and won't be now.

"If we need your help, we'll call you on the walkie-talkie," Dad says.

"You'll be our backup," I add, smiling.

Dalia frowns, hands forming fists at her sides. "Fine. I'll do it. But I'm taking the high-tech gun."

Chapter 38

The ladder leads to a cool tunnel of roughhewn stone. At the base of the ladder are several battery-powered LED lanterns. I watch Dalia in the bright light cast by the lantern she carries in her left hand as she brings up the rear of the group heading down the mountain. In her right hand, she holds the high-tech hand cannon pointed at Dr. Orion, who stumbles ahead of her with his hands zip-tied behind his back. Despite her new weapon, Dalia keeps the rifle strapped across her back.

A bend in the shaft takes those in the lead out of sight. Dalia pauses, throwing a sullen glance over her shoulder. The lantern light glimmers along her golden nose ring and casts tall shadows over the floor and walls. Noticing me watching her, Dalia's lips twitch upward in half a smile, and she nods. I return the smile and wave. Then she turns and walks out of sight.

Part of me is relieved to watch her go. Maybe with only Haji to protect, I'll be able to keep him alive. Then again, perhaps I can't outmaneuver my premonition. Am I sending Dalia to her doom?

"This shaft was carved by magic," Dad says.

Dad holds the lantern overhead as he and Haji inspect the wall. Farther up the shaft, Dr. Radcliffe waits, frowning. His dragon form encompasses the entire tunnel, passing through the walls and ceiling as it flickers in and out of existence.

Haji touches the rock almost reverently. "I don't sense any magic."

"It's faint. Residue." Dad looks at Radcliffe. "Faery magic, I believe."

"I concur." Radcliffe nods.

"How long ago was it carved?" Haji asks.

Dad shakes his head. "Thirty to forty years ago. To be more precise—"

"Would take time we do not have," Radcliffe says. "Our enemies know we are here. They are likely in this tunnel. We need to move out and expect to encounter resistance, possibly an ambush."

Radcliffe sets off without waiting for a reply. Dad and Haji hurry after him, and I take up the rear. Carved from faery magic thirty years ago or more? Who knows what deadly booby traps are hidden down here.

After we have traveled for an hour or maybe a little more, the shaft slopes upward, gently at first, but then becomes quite steep. Soon our pace slows as Haji lags. I'm tempted to sweep him off his feet and throw him over my shoulder because I want out of this shaft. I can't shake the feeling we're being watched even though my continuous inspection of the walls and ceiling fails to detect any surveillance devices. Maybe we're being observed by magical means? Presumably, Dad or Dr. Radcliffe would detect magic, so that's probably not the case. Still, dread scurries up and down my back, gnawing at my spine like a cantankerous rat.

Finally, we come to an intersection. The others rest while I quickly explore the right-hand tunnel, which according to the information provided by Dr. Orion Nash should terminate at a dead end. After one hundred and fifty feet or so, the tunnel ends at a solid rock wall. I return to the others and after a brief confab we decide to trust Nash's directions to continue up the center shaft and ignore the other tunnels.

As the upward slog continues interminably, I wish we had avoided the tunnel and scaled the mountain in the humid air under the burning sun. Rationally, I know that is potentially the more dangerous path. We must assume until proven otherwise the skaags and faeries are working together. Trekking over the side of the volcano would expose us to attack by skaags and faeries from above. Down here, we need not fear that. The tunnel is too narrow to accommodate even my malformed half-skaag body or for an aerial assault of any kind.

I've lost track of how long we've been in the tunnel when Radcliffe whispers, "Wait here."

Up ahead, Dad and Haji trundle to a halt. Radcliffe's tail materializes, flicking to and fro, at the edge of the lantern light. On high alert, I come to a stop behind them. Radcliffe is out of sight beyond the bend. His visible draconic body parts stop flashing and glow bright, momentarily illuminating the tunnel in a golden brilliance only I can see. Then the luminescence fades like the lights dimming inside a movie theater. The *ratatat* of quick footfall proceeds Radcliffe's human form appearing at the bend.

The one-time university professor holds a finger to his lips for silence, then waves for us to gather around. Somehow Haji trips over his feet, cracking his head against the jagged wall. Making a half-stifled garbling sound, he falls onto his butt, hands going to his forehead and coming away bloody.

"Ouch," Haji says, eyes glazed.

Dad sets down the lantern and kneels next to Haji. "Let me see. Oh, we need to bandage this."

Radcliffe stalks over to them with a stormy expression. I, however, have grown roots into the rock, not daring to approach my bleeding friend. The scent of blood in the air reminds me of its coppery tang and the fire that flavor ignited throughout my body. Deep inside me, the sleeper lurches into frenzied locomotion, and the beast's desires commingle with mine. I force myself not to gaze at the blood running over Haji's forehead and dripping to the ground.

No. That was a one-time-only deal. Never again.

The sleeper withdraws to the edge of my consciousness, pacing like a caged tiger. At least if it comes to a fight, I can brush up against the half-skaag's prowess. But will I remain in control? The copper aroma in the air makes me shudder and, shutting my eyes, roll my tongue over my upper lip. My grip on humanity seems more tenuous than ever.

"Allison," Dad says.

I open my eyes, but I don't dare look up. The aftertaste of human blood still lingers on my tongue, enticing. Intrigued, the sleeper wants more of everything.

"Keep your voice down," Radcliffe whispers. "Although, undoubtedly, we have already been heard. Around the bend, the tunnel opens into a large cave used to store equipment. Hidden in the cave are half a dozen people armed with the same weapon Dalia now carries."

Silently, I curse myself for allowing Haji to come on the mission. He should've stayed back in Seattle, even if that meant Dad stayed too. Even before suffering withdrawal from the Juice, he wasn't a fighter. Now, despite what he did to help overcome Dr. Orion, he's a liability. I don't know how I will keep him alive when he can't be trusted to walk in a straight line without tripping over his feet.

"Allison, I need a first aid kit from the backpack," Dad whispers.

I unsling the backpack from my shoulders, feeling like a dolt for not being more on the ball. Crouching, I unzip the main compartment and push aside water bottles to retrieve the first aid kit near the bottom of the pack.

I'm about to hand the kit to Dad when I freeze.

"Allison…"

Rising, I hold up a hand for silence. I peer down the tunnel from the direction we came, listening. At the edge of my perception, I detect the dull patter of footfall and even a muffled voice.

I turn back to the others, careful not to look directly at the blood, and toss the first aid kit to Dad. He nearly fumbles it but manages the catch.

"People are coming up behind us. We need to hurry."

"How many?" Radcliffe asks.

I shake my head. "Don't know. More than one."

Dad uses gauze from the first aid kit to stanch Haji's wound. "Could it be Dalia and the others?"

"I will call and find out," Radcliffe says, raising a walkie-talkie. "Dalia, can you hear me?"

After a few seconds her voice comes over the walkie-talkie all staticky and loud. "I hear you. Barely."

Radcliffe fiddles with the controls, lowering the

volume.

"Are you all still heading down the mountain?"

"Yes." Dalia's voice quieter over the speaker this time.

Dad places a square bandage over Haji's wound and uses the remaining gauze to clean the blood from his face. I wish the blood was less distracting and that I can still call myself human.

"We're being pursued," Radcliffe says. "Be careful."

Static comes from the walkie-talkie. After several beats, Radcliffe lowers the device.

"I hope they're okay," I whisper and turn my attention back to listening to the approaching footfall.

"Ahhh, yes, I hear our pursuers now," Radcliffe says. "How far away are they? Can you tell?"

I frown. "Not far? We need a game plan. We don't have much time."

Haji stands, swaying. He places a hand against the wall to steady himself. "We keep moving forward. Up the mountain."

"Into the ambush?" Dad says.

"They might not realize we know they're in there," Haji says. "It's like a warehouse or something, right? There will be cover to get behind. We stay here, we're like fish in a barrel. We won't last long if they're armed with those fancy blasters."

"We're going to end up surrounded," I say.

Haji shrugs. "We already are."

"I don't like this." Dad looks at Radcliffe. "How many exits from the cavern?"

"I only saw one. A steel door that appears to be sealed by a combination of magic and technology. We will have to cross the entire room to reach it. If we are going through with this, we need to move now. Whoever is approaching us from behind is getting close."

"What about other exits?" Dad says. "We passed intersections. Maybe we can backtrack—"

"According to Orion Nash, those paths either terminate in more storage areas or dead ends." Radcliffe cocks his head to the side and holds a finger to his lips for a few seconds. "If I'm not mistaken, the pursuers are between us and the closest intersection."

I nod. "Radcliffe's right. They're nearly on top of us. Six people, at least. Probably men and definitely armed. Is there enough room for me to transform in the cavern?"

"I believe so," Radcliffe says. "It will be cramped. You will not have room to maneuver. You will need to act fast or risk grave injury. Those blasters—"

"I know." But acting fast won't be an issue. The sleeper and I are backed into a corner and ready to fight, although it's the desire for fresh meat overcoming the beast's trepidation of the burning blasters. "I have a plan. It's not a good one, but it can work."

Chapter 39

I'm rounding the bend so close to Radcliffe I'm nearly stepping on his heels. From behind us comes the dull footfall of the force closing in. Dad and Haji take up the rear, each holding a hand of mine in a death grip. Dad still carries the lantern, but it's off. Without that light, I imagine they experience something approaching absolute darkness. As we continue around the bend, dim light spills across the floor and walls.

The shaft continues for another fifteen feet or so, then opens into the large cavern Radcliffe told us about. The illumination from the room is bright enough that it takes my prosthetics a second to adjust. The equipment stored in the cavern makes me stop dead in my tracks and squeeze the hands of my companions.

"Ouch," Haji says, but at least his voice is hushed.

I loosen my grip on their hands. My breathing becomes rapid. A glass vat with tubes attached to the lid sits on a pedestal. I remember standing next to Bria, staring into a cavern much like this one, only larger and with hundreds of the same vats full of fluid and containing infants. "Brainless sacks of Juice," Gore had called them. "Not really alive," Dr. Kihl had claimed. Maybe the infants weren't alive, but that didn't change the horror of what was being done on Golden Shoal. Bria cried tears of sorrow and rage as we watched the helpless faery infants burn.

"Allison," Radcliffe hisses.

I shake my head, clearing the cobwebs left by my dreadful reverie. The footfall of the people approaching us from behind is like the war drum of an army. Soon even Dad and Haji will hear our pursuers.

I nod, releasing my companions' hands. "Give me a second." Pulling off my shoes and socks, I glance at Dad and Haji. "Turn around."

The light might be poor enough they can't see much, but I still don't want them watching me strip. Haji gives me a sheepish smile before turning away. The muscles in my abdomen tense. For a moment, he is the boy I kissed after rescuing him from the wrecked beater.

I strip under the watchful gaze of Radcliffe's humanoid form. As best I can tell, his draconic head observes our opponents in the cavern. Under different circumstances, I might've found his scrutiny unbearably embarrassing and old geezer icky. But he is a dragon, and I know he could care less whether I or any other human wears clothing or not.

I meet Radcliffe's gaze. "Ready."

"Remember, I am relying on you to be fast. My golem will not survive long under a barrage from those blasters."

I nod, only needing to look at the right side of his head to know the golem is far from indestructible. "Understood."

Radcliffe smiles crookedly. "I must admit, I'm looking forward to a real fight."

He turns away and strides into the cavern as if he has no concern in the world.

"Stop right there! Don't move!" A man's gruff

shout.

"Why ever would I do that?" Radcliffe says conversationally.

Then the old professor charges, and blaster fire lights up the cavern. I run inside, the sleeper ready to explode. Somehow Radcliffe avoids the opening volley of blaster fire. He grabs a man crouched behind a crate by the arm and flings him overhead. The man spins upward like a straw doll, his blaster flying from his grip, and slams into the ceiling with a sickening squelch before falling limply to the floor. A second salvo of blaster fire brightens the room, concentrated on Radcliffe. The plan is working. The mercs focus on the golem while ignoring the naked girl, the real threat.

The vat stands twelve feet tall, at least, which would be an excellent launching point for my leap into the air to give me enough clearance to transform, but I bypass it. I can barely stomach looking at the vat and refuse to touch it. Instead, I make for a stack of innocuous-looking crates.

A man blubbers incomprehensibly and then emits a death scream. Half a heartbeat later, more blaster fire crackles, lighting up the room. This time, I feel the super-heated air, smelling smoke and ozone. I'm about to climb the crates when I glimpse a mech in my peripheral vision. The sleeper cowers inside me, expecting to be burned to oblivion. I throw my arms in front of me as if my skinny appendages can provide any protection from the suit's arm cannon or fractal-encrusted sword.

I stare at the armor, expecting to see Bergman's hatchet-carved face behind the ballistic glass. "Oh, thank God."

The mech is powered down, the gun arm pointing at the ground and the black sword lacking the orange fractal glow. Still, the sleeper trembles, and goose bumps rise all over me. Bergman is here on Mauna Kea and has a mech available to her.

Blasters roar, and the air sears the goose bumps from my skin.

"Allison!" Radcliffe bellows.

I poke my head out from behind the stack of crates. Radcliffe lurches for cover, a blackened, smoking crater at his left shoulder. Smoke snakes from his left arm lying on the floor. Overhead, his draconic head glowers at me with narrowed, accusing eyes.

"You could've warned me about the mech." I scramble up the crates. At the summit, I gaze down on our remaining opponents—six mercenaries, four men and two women, all decked out in black and armed with high-tech blasters. Two more mercenaries are splayed on the floor, one in a pool of blood and the second with their neck at an unnatural angle.

For now, the mercs concentrate on closing in on Radcliffe, communicating with hand signals. They have no idea they're about to die by my hand. Guilt rockets through me, but I remind myself that they are willing to murder children and, given a chance, will slay Dad and Haji without a second thought.

Live by the gun.

Die by monster.

I leap from the pinnacle of the stacked crates, soaring upward and gaining the clearance I need to transform. I brace myself for exquisite pain that never comes. I reach the peak of my trajectory and plummet.

What are you doing? Emerge. Emerge!

A mercenary glances overhead, spotting us. She raises her blaster and takes the shot. An arc of white-hot plasma shoots past, close enough to redden the right side of my body. The scent of burned hair clogs my nostrils.

If we don't transform right now, I'm going to splatter on the ground, then be burnt to a crisp by blaster fire!

The all-encompassing agony of transformation makes the burn along the right side of my body seem as tepid as warm tap water. A maniacal master chef slices and dices my organs, rearranging them as they please. Hydraulic jaws crack my bones, shred my muscle, and tear my sinew. As my body expands, it crashes against crates and equipment, crushing them or sending them flying into the walls. My transformation completes before I smash into the floor, but not before I squish one, two, or maybe three mercenaries under my bulk. It's hard to tell as my long eel-like body undulates, smacking aside objects I brush against as I levitate mere inches from the ground. Men and women scream, clearly caught off guard by my skaag form and traumatized by watching their compatriots burst underneath my bulk. Fear thrums through me—my own and the sleeper's. Already electrical arcs roil over my body. The sleeper intends to kill before tasting the burning pain of blaster fire. Radcliffe's dragon form flickers all around me. I try to track translucent draconic body parts back to his golem, fearing I might've crushed it along with the mercenaries.

I glimpse the golem staggering away from me as the electricity running over my body reaches a fever pitch.

Wait!

The sleeper blasts electricity indiscriminately throughout the cavern. Radcliffe leaps behind a crate, barely avoiding a yellow arc that blackens the ground where he had stood. The smell of burned flesh and fabric fills the air.

I rise toward the ceiling to gain a better vantage point. As I suspected, all the mercenaries are broken, smoldering corpses or smashed to mush. The once neatly arrayed boxes are strewn around the place, the mech is overturned on its side, and the vat is shattered, glass sprayed across the ground, catching Radcliffe's golden glimmering light. The one-time professor navigates between the debris and fallen bodies to retrieve his smoldering arm. His back is pockmarked with smoking black craters, probably the result of my electrical attack.

I'm honestly relieved Radcliffe's golem isn't completely destroyed. The sleeper, on the other hand, doesn't share my satisfaction. It's a reminder of the half-skaag's dragon-slaying heritage.

Shouting and crackling come from the tunnel. The distinctive odor of ozone joins the stench of smoke in the air. A sizzling white bolt shoots into the cavern from the tunnel, hitting the far wall above the steel door, leaving behind a smoking hole the size of a watermelon.

Haji and Dad sprint into the cavern, diving out of the line of fire seconds before more plasma bolts belch from the tunnel's mouth.

"There's at least six of them," Dad shouts. "They're all armed with blasters."

I battle the sleeper's desire to immediately lash out

with lightning. All it will take is a stray bolt or two to fry Haji and Dad. But the beast is confident, reminding me of the precision it demonstrated at the field on the military base by taking out dozens of opponents without harming a single civilian.

That was outside and with more space. The tiniest miscalculation will kill Haji and Dad.

The half-skaag's consciousness batters me like a rogue wave. I'm knocked off my feet and swept by the riptide toward the vast storm that is the sleeper.

I won't let you. You can't.

More plasma bolts burst from the cave mouth, superheating the air and filling the cavern with the smell of ozone. Footfall follows the shots, along with muffled voices. The mercenaries are closing in. Soon, one might have a clear shot at us. The sleeper is having none of that. It fears being burned to near death again. Electricity buzzes over my body, and I see jagged yellow light in my peripheral vision.

I try to swim for shore, but the sleeper is winning the battle of wills. The beast moves our body of its own volition toward the cave mouth. I want to scream at Dad and Haji to flee, but their attention is focused on the entrance, and the beast won't allow me to utter a warning shriek.

Screams and crackling echo from the tunnel. An unarmed mercenary runs into the cavern. The sleeper is ready to discharge electricity when a plasma bolt strikes the man in the back. He collapses face-first to the ground, smoke rising from a hole burned between his shoulder blades.

Chapter 40

Dalia struts into the cavern, stopping inside the cave mouth, with a blaster, smoke spiraling upward from the barrels, gripped in her right hand, and my clothes jammed in the crook of her left arm. The electricity arcing over my body buzzes in my ears like angry bees.

It's Dalia. You can back off.

"Is that all of them?" Dalia looks around, oblivious that the sleeper nearly toasted her, and raises the blaster to the ceiling.

The sleeper calms, allowing the electricity to dissipate, but does not relinquish control of our body. Haji lurches to Dalia and throws his arms around her in an awkward embrace.

"Thank you. Thank you," he gushes. "Between the mercenaries and Allison's electricity shooting everywhere, I thought we were dead."

"Careful. The blaster's barrel is hot." Dalia looks up at me, flashing a cocky smirk. "No need to thank me. Just keeping everyone safe."

She shot an unarmed man in the back and is basking in the spotlight like an action movie hero. I want to chew her out, but I can't, obviously because I'm still in skaag form, the sleeper preoccupied looking for an exit that will accommodate our supersized bulk.

The only ways out are back through the tunnel or

through that door.

Neither is large enough for us to fit through, but the sleeper is desperate to find a way out of the cavern that doesn't involve surrendering control of our body back to me. It's a chilling realization to know the skaag doesn't want to fade into the background and is strong enough to force the issue. I hope the beast doesn't try to shoot through the tunnel or bust down the steel door. I have no desire to become lodged in an opening again like we had on Golden Shoal.

"Seriously, Haji, you can let go of me," Dalia says.

I can't see if Haji complies because the sleeper's hunt for escape becomes increasingly frenetic as its frustration grows. We shoot upward, stopping short of slamming into the ceiling. The beast scours the rock for any opening.

The only way we're leaving this cavern is in human form. You need to give me back control.

What if the sleeper can maintain control while we're human? I don't even want to consider such a terrible fate, losing all my agency to the inner beast. Isn't it enough I feel my humanity slipping away?

"What's going on with Allison?" Dad asks.

"I fear Allison might not be in control," Radcliffe says.

Frustration grows to anger within us, along with the desire to lash out at anyone and everything. A growl escapes our throat as an ear-piercing shriek. Dalia drops the blaster and throws her hands over her ears. Haji and Dad fall to their knees and throw their hands over their ears too. Their expressions are grimacing masks of pain. The one-armed Radcliffe is unaffected by the sonic attack. He stares at us, seemingly as detached as a scientist examining bacteria in a petri dish. His draconic form watches us, too, neck stretched to the ceiling so he can stare into our eyes.

That only incites the sleeper more. The beast wants to electrocute the dragon, pry up its armored scales, and deliver the death blow. A familiar electric tingling courses over our oily hide.

Don't! You'll hurt or kill my friends. My dad.

"Allison. Take control of yourself right now. You are the skaag, and the skaag is you. Your needs are one. Your desires are one," Radcliffe says. "Stop this nonsense at once before you do something you will regret."

Oh, I've done plenty of things I regret both as a skaag and as a human. I don't want to toast my squad or Dad, but I'll make an exception for Dr. Radcliffe. For how he used me as bait on the windswept beach in a failed attempt to ambush the skaag, Mark Cassidy. Or how he squeezed my friends and me nearly to death in his draconic hands. Or his real crime: unlocking the magic imprisoning the sleeper in the first place and stealing from me a normal life.

Keening escapes our lips, and anguish at rejection gushes into my consciousness from the sleeper. It's a feeling I know well from when Jason, my first crush, chose Leslie over me. I'm nearly swept away by the tidal wave of the sleeper's topsy-turvy emotions, but I manage to stand strong and sense the beast losing control. The electricity arcing over our body falters, not dissipating but losing much of its intensity.

I never wanted you.

The sleeper recoils. I squeeze our eyes shut, concentrating on transforming back into human form.

Our body implodes, collapsing in on itself like a dying star. The pain is enough to last ten lifetimes as I fall, body morphing into a mashup of human and skaag parts.

I scream as I rush to meet the floor, a date with death. Radcliffe watches me, his gaze resigned. Dad staggers up next to the professor, glowing blue hands extended overhead. My descent doesn't slow so much as it is suddenly arrested by a mountain of invisible fluffy pillows. I continue transforming, thrashing and screaming as organs contract, muscles shrivel, and bones compress. I slowly descend until my feet touch the cold, rough textured floor at the same time my transformation completes.

My legs have all the strength of overcooked spaghetti and fold underneath me. I collapse onto my hands and knees, and completely exhausted, curl onto the floor into an oblong ball. Dad and Dalia race to my side and kneel beside me.

"Haji, bring her clothes," Dalia calls.

"Allison, are you all right?" Dad asks.

"I'm…I'm so tired." My words come out mushy, and my eyelids flutter.

"You almost lost control of yourself, did you not?" Radcliffe asks pointedly.

I force my eyes open and crane my neck to stare at the professor. He looks down his nose at me, both the dragon and the man. At one time, I would've found his disapproval scary, but I don't any longer.

"You nearly lost control and attacked us." Radcliffe's condescending smirk lights a fire in my belly.

"Only you."

"Only me? Hmmm…"

"Can't you leave her alone for a minute?" Dalia says. Haji has set my clothing down next to her and has the decency to keep his eyes averted. "Let's get you dressed. Can you sit up?"

As Dalia helps me up, Radcliffe gives me a disapproving frown, then his gaze shifts. "Come, young Haji, we have a magically secure door to unlock."

Haji follows Radcliffe to the steel door.

Dad gently rests his hand on my shoulder. "If he's right. If you almost lost control…" Dad draws a deep breath. "I know you don't want to hear this, but remember your mother's training. It will help."

"Gee, thanks, Dad." I roll my eyes at him and my tired mind's inability to come up with a better retort.

Dad squeezes my shoulder, then stands and releases me. "I'll go help Dr. Radcliffe and Haji."

"Daddy, thanks for catching me."

"Anytime, Allison." He follows Radcliffe and Haji.

Dalia offers me my underwear and bra. "Can you dress yourself?"

"I hope so." The last thing I need is the embarrassment of being dressed like an infant. My mind is sharper by the minute, but my body is worn ragged, arms leaden and fingers sluggish. I pull on my underwear without too much trouble, but my fat fingers don't possess the fine motor skills to clip the bra. "Dammit."

"Do you need an assist?" Dalia asks.

My cheeks flush with frustration. "No…Okay, yes. Please."

Dalia moves behind me. She fastens the clasp. "There. Can you manage the rest?" I nod and start pulling on my pants. "I saw the backpack in the tunnel. I'll go get it. You look like you need some water."

After retrieving a blaster from the ground, she stands and heads for the tunnel. The muscles across my upper back painfully tighten. Lying on the ground before the mouth of the tunnel is the man she shot in the back, smoke still rising from the wound. An unarmed man. My bestie had shot an unarmed man in the back. A man running for his life. She shouldn't have done that.

Stirring, the sleeper brushes against my consciousness, its hunger for the burned flesh in stark dichotomy to my revulsion. I fight the urge to gag when I start salivating.

Go away. I tell the beast as I finish pulling on my pants.

I feel its hurt alongside my self-loathing. Maybe I'm going about this all wrong? How can I run from myself?

I'm sorry. Maybe...

Too late. The half-skaag already retreats from my awareness. Sighing, I pick up my T-shirt and pull it on. My nose crinkles from the stale sweat stench, but even wearing this disgusting rag is better than going half naked. I pull on one sock and have the other halfway on when Dalia returns with the backpack slung over one shoulder and the blaster held casually in her right hand. Kneeling beside me, she fishes out a water bottle from the pack and offers it to me.

I finish pulling on the sock and take the water bottle. "Why did you come back?"

Dalia's lips form a straight line, and her eyes are hooded. "Because I knew you needed me."

My BFF gives a synopsis of being pursued by two blaster-wielding mercs through the tunnel. "After the confab with Radcliffe, I set an ambush while the others escaped. Turns out I'm a pretty good shot. I figured you all might need help"—she shrugs—"so here I am."

I take a long drag from the water bottle. Setting the empty canister on the floor, I'm about to demand why Dalia shot the man in the back when Haji says boisterously, "Wait. I've seen this kind of spell before on Golden Shoal. I can unravel it. I can. Let me try."

Dalia zips up the backpack and swings it over her shoulders. "Sounds like it's almost time to head out." She stands up and offers me a hand.

I slip on my sneakers, then take her proffered hand. She tries to pull me up, but my strength is returning, and I yank her down, forcing her to take a knee. "Don't you feel a little bit bad about killing them?"

Dalia scoffs. "No. It was us or them. I'd do it again and again and again. Now, do you understand why you need me?"

Dalia pulls away, and I let her go. She grabs a second blaster lying on the ground beside a burned corpse. I stand and follow Dalia to the steel door, wondering if my best friend is losing her humanity just like me.

Chapter 41

Haji, Dad, and Dr. Radcliffe gather around the door. The lanky boy stands between the adults, his hands faintly glowing orange with an occasional pulse of blue. Fractal patterns are etched into his hands.

I come to a halt behind the men next to Dalia. "Should Haji be doing magic again?"

Haji glances over his shoulder, giving me a killer glare. "I can do it."

Haji faces the door, and Dad drops back beside me.

"Why can't you let everyone do their part?" Dalia says under her breath.

"What? So it's okay for him to be a strung-out junkie now? Are you okay with that?"

Dalia heaves a sigh. "No, I'm not saying that, but we're trying to save the world. That's bigger than any of us. It's going to require sacrifices. By everyone. Not just you."

"I guess that's what I should expect from a cold-blooded killer."

I regret the words almost before they leave my lips. I'm such an idiot.

Dalia blanches. "Is that what you think I am? A—"

"Girls, girls…" Dad says.

We turn our angry glares on him. Dad raises his hands to the side of his head and smiles nervously.

"If we're going to save the world, we must work

together as a team. Otherwise…" Dad shakes his head.

Disgusted and worried about everyone, I turn my attention back to Haji. The fractals covering his hands are streams of lava. The patterns flow up his arms and neck, terminating below his jawline, and flare beneath his T-shirt.

"This isn't right," I say. "He's going to end up comatose again or worse."

"He'll be fine, Allison. Trust me." Dad tries to take my hand, but I pull away.

I look Dad up and down, then brush past Dr. Radcliffe for Haji. "You're so obsessed with finding Mother, you don't care if Haji gets hurt or not."

"Allison, no, that's—"

Haji screams, his entire body flaring an orange and blue radiance that even overwhelms the lambent light of Radcliffe's dragon form. The shriek of shearing metal pierces the cavern air. Fractals fading from his skin, Haji staggers backward and falls into my arms. His skin is scalding. Our legs tangle, and I stutter-step to keep from falling over. I lower him to the floor, and he stares at me with listing eyes. The heat radiating from him dissipates as the orange and blue glow fades from his skin, and the fractal patterns disappear.

"I did it. I broke the spell." Haji's voice is weak, but he smiles.

"Yeah, I think you did," I say.

Radcliffe inspects a long crack in the steel running crosswise from the top left to the bottom right.

Haji's eyes flutter. "Good." He yawns. "I'm tired."

Radcliffe pushes on the door, but it doesn't budge.

"No, Haji, keep your eyes open." I'm afraid if he falls asleep, he'll slip into a coma again. I gently place his head in my lap and shake his shoulder to keep him awake.

He weakly paws at my hand. "Let me sleep. I'm beat."

"The spell is broken, isn't it?" Dalia asks.

"Yes, but the door is still secure by mechanical means," Radcliffe says. "I need assistance forcing the door, given my golem's physical condition."

"Maybe I can burn through the door with the blasters," Dalia says.

"Be my guest," Radcliffe says.

A roar and light blazes from up ahead. The familiar ozone scent hangs in the air.

Dad kneels beside Haji and me, producing a vial containing faintly glowing blue liquid from his fanny pack. Dad unstoppers the vial and lowers it to Haji's mouth. Haji twists aside and tries to push away the vial.

"No, no. I don't want it," Haji mumbles and shakes his head.

Dad brushes aside Haji's resistance with his free hand, forcing the vial to the boy's lips. "Haji, you need to take this. Otherwise, you'll have withdrawal symptoms."

"Please, I don't want it." Haji throws his head to the side, burying his face in the back of my thigh.

From Dalia's string of creative epithets, burning through the door must not be going well.

"Hold his head so I can administer the potion," Dad says.

Haji begins trembling, his head thrashing side to side in my lap.

"Allison!" Dad says. "Hold his head!"

I've seen this before. He's going to slip away

again. I grab hold of either side of his head, holding him steady. He writhes, legs bucking.

"It's okay, Haji. It's okay," I say, not knowing if he can hear me.

Dad presses the vial to Haji's lips and upturns it. Haji swallows some of the fluid and coughs. He breathes deeply and his eyes open, unfocused.

"Did I try to refuse the potion again?" Haji asks, voice weak.

"Yes." Dad nods. "Do you want to sit up? Orient yourself?"

"Yes." Haji blinks, gaze focusing on me. "Allison…gosh. Did you…I wasn't myself. It's part of the withdrawal."

"I'm glad you're okay."

Haji starts sitting up, body quivering. With help from Dad and me, he's able to sit. Another blaster shot rings through the cavern.

"Awww," Dalia cries. Something metal clatters to the ground.

"This is not working," Radcliffe says. "All you have done is overheat the weapon."

"Look at the metal. It's cherry red. I need to use a different blaster."

"Allison, you should go help them," Dad says. "We can handle this from here."

Haji's face is dripping with sweat, and a shiver runs through his body.

"Will you be okay?" I ask my friend.

He smiles wanly. "No worries."

I take Haji's clammy hand and squeeze. "I'm glad you're still with us."

The door is indeed a molten, cherry red, and still

standing as impassible as ever. Dalia squeezes off another blaster shot into the hot metal with no visible effect. By her feet is the discarded blaster, the tips of the smoking barrels glowing orange.

Dalia huffs in frustration. “How can the door still be standing? Look at it.”

I shrug and glance at Radcliffe. “Any ideas?”

“I suspect Haji failed to dispel all the magic infused in the door.”

“Can your dad help?” Dalia asks.

“He’s busy.” I would throw my shoulder against the door, but that’s out of the question given that it’s glowing red. Maybe I can throw something against the door to bust it down? I glance around the cavern. “I know.” I snap my fingers. “Do you think a bigger gun or a sword might work?”

Radcliffe raises his eyebrows. “Perhaps. But we have no idea how to operate it.”

“Ms. Bergman can pilot it,” I say. “How hard can it be?”

I lead Radcliffe and Dalia across the debris-strewn cavern to the mech toppled on its side. My body chills as I freeze up. “I don’t think I can pilot it. Even if I could figure out how to get inside.” I shake my head. “I can’t do it.”

Dalia shrugs off the backpack, which falls to the floor with a clunk from the metal water bottles inside. She gently rests her current blaster on the pack. “No problem. I got this.”

Smiling, Dalia scrambles over the mech, pausing to admire the arm cannon and black sword. Moving to the faceplate area, she begins probing the armor with her fingers.

I shake my head. “There must be some kind of security, right? So not anyone can climb inside?”

A clank echoes through the cavern, followed by loud hissing. Dalia scrambles away from the mech as the torso cracks open, swinging upward toward the ceiling to reveal a compartment inside its chest.

“I guess not,” Radcliffe quips.

“Dalia, wait—”

“I got this.” Dalia scurries into the compartment. “I’m a natural with these high-tech weapons.”

I chomp on my lower lip and, for once, keep my opinion to myself about how I fear this is a horrible idea. Dalia situates herself inside the chest cavity.

“Weird. There’s like no controls that I can see,” she says.

Without warning the door clangs shut, entombing Dalia inside the compartment.

“Oh, crap.” I’m about to go to her side when the mech shifts.

“Wow!” Dalia’s voice comes from near the faceplate, sounding tinny. “Can you hear me?”

We nod.

“Good. Say something.”

“Are you okay?” I ask.

“I can hear you.” Behind the faceplate, Dalia is grinning wider than I have ever seen. “The armor is adjusting, I think. It’s tightening—don’t worry, it’s not crushing me. I feel something. Gooey. Like a gel. Oh!” Dalia gapes. “Wow!”

“What? What happened? Dalia, talk to us.”

Dalia laughs gleefully. “I’m the armor!”

The mech’s arms and legs spasm.

“We need to back up,” Radcliffe says. “She might

be the armor, but she still needs to adjust to her new body."

I follow Radcliffe back ten feet or so as Dalia slowly rises, sending crates and rubble shooting across the floor. Standing at full height, the mech is at least twelve feet tall. It wobbles on its feet, arms flying out to the sides and windmilling. Radcliffe indicates we should keep backing away. I can't agree more.

Dalia finally steadies herself, face screwed up in concentration. "I think I'm getting the hang of this. Stay back. I'm going to try walking forward."

The mech staggers forward several steps but remains upright. Dad, supporting Haji, joins us in staring at Dalia inside the armor. They're both slack-jawed.

"Easy." Dalia laughs. "I'm not sure how to use the weapons yet. But…"

We collectively retreat as Dalia raises a leg as thick as a tree trunk and performs a front kick. Haji and I gasp, Dad curses under his breath, and even Dr. Radcliffe makes a startled sound.

"Stay out of the way. I'm going to kick the door down." Dalia lurches across the cavern, knocking aside obstacles on her way to the steel door that still glows red.

Chapter 42

Dalia thumps through the cave, taking up position before the resilient door. Already most of the glow is gone from the metal. With the whir of gears, an armored leg lifts from the floor. Dalia delivers a kick.

Boom.

The door shudders but stands firm. The armored foot thumps to the floor.

Dalia delivers a second kick.

Boom.

A depression forms where the blow lands.

This time Dalia doesn't lower her foot to the ground. Instead, she delivers a third and fourth kick in rapid succession.

Boom. Boom. Metal groans and shrieks. The edges of the door curl away from the wall.

Boom.

The fifth kick snaps the top hinge. Dalia lowers her leg. When her foot thuds to the floor, the sound is softer. She backs up, her footsteps echoing like a titan's. Objects in her path are knocked aside or crushed underfoot.

"Wow! This is so cool," Haji says.

I wish I could share his enthusiasm. But all I can imagine is the damage Dalia can cause with the mech, not just to our enemies but to herself. Maybe she's right. Perhaps it was us or them when she gunned down the mercenaries from behind. They were gunning for us, and her actions saved Dad and Haji. I don't doubt that. If I had discharged electricity into the tunnel, I would've electrocuted them. But she didn't have to shoot that last unarmed merc. She didn't. Maybe she didn't know he was unarmed, but honestly, I don't think she cared.

But she will.

When he starts haunting her dreams, she'll care.

I know that all too well.

Dalia comes to a stop about fifteen feet from the door.

"Is she going to blast it with the cannon?" Haji bursts with enthusiasm. I'm glad. It means he's recovering. "Dalia, blast the door with the cannon!"

"I wish," Dalia says. "I haven't figured out how to use the cannon yet, but when I do, those mercs better watch out!"

"Do we know what's behind the door?" Dad asks.

"A small room," Radcliffe says. "The only exit is a ladder leading up a narrow shaft."

I glance at Haji, who still leans heavily against Dad. I wonder if he can make the climb.

Thuds reverberate through the cave. Dalia charges the door like a supersized linebacker. She smashes into the steel portal with a thunderous clang. The door collapses, and she staggers into the doorframe. Crouching, she turns sideways to negotiate the passage, metal grating against rock. The door scrapes along the floor as Dalia drags it aside with giant armored hands, moving it out of the doorway.

"Come on." She drops the twisted metal and waves to us.

The room is cramped with the mech taking up most of the space. As Radcliffe described, a ladder built into the rock leads up a narrow shaft.

"Are you sure this is the only way out?" Dalia says. "There's no way the mech is going to fit. Even if I could figure out how to fly."

"You'll have to leave the mech behind." I point up the passage. "Bria must be up there, and so is the opening in the slipstream."

"I don't want to leave the mech behind." Dalia stamps her foot. The thud reverberates in the chamber. "There must be another exit Dr. Nash didn't tell us about."

We all back up as far away from her as possible. I'm glad she didn't start swinging the sword around in frustration.

Dad steps forward, leaving Haji to use the wall to support himself. "Dalia, listen. If you're coming with us, you'll need to leave the mech behind. You can look for another way out if you want, but we don't know how long that will take. If you leave the mech here, you'll know where it is. When we make our escape, maybe we'll use the tunnel. The mech will be here, waiting for you."

Dalia frowns, then her face lights up. "You're right, Mr. Lee. Now, I have to figure out how to get out."

"Are you able to climb with one arm?" I ask Radcliffe.

He nods. "It will be slow going, but yes. I will go first. I can reconnoiter as we go using my dragon form."

"Okay." I look at Haji. He's still pallid. "Can you climb?"

Haji flashes a sheepish smile. "I don't know. Probably not."

I roll my eyes. Oh, boy. "I think I've recovered enough to carry you. You'll have to hold on to me, though. Can you do that?"

"I think so."

I put a hand on his shoulder. He is trembling. "There's no thinking about it. If you can't hold on, you should stay down here."

He straightens, and there is steel in his voice when he says, "I can hold on."

A clank followed by a long hiss precedes the mech's torso popping open. Dalia stumbles out covered in translucent goo and smiling from ear to ear. She points at the mech.

"That is awesome! I'm going to go grab the backpack and a couple of blasters. I'll be right back."

****

Our slow ascent up the ladder grinds to a halt. I look up the shaft and wince. Haji clings to my back like a baby koala, putting strain on my neck. All I glimpse for my effort are Dalia's legs and butt. What a view.

"What's the holdup?" I want Haji off my back. Being in such close proximity means my every intake of breath is rife with his BO, an almost deadly reminder he is one hundred percent teenage boy. I've tried breathing through my mouth, but his stench tastes as bad as it smells.

"Can't tell." Dalia moves up a rung. "Mr. Lee, what's going on?"

"Not so loud." Dad's voice is barely above a whisper. "I think we're near the top. Radcliffe is checking things out."

"Finally," I murmur.

"What?" Haji's voice seems insanely loud in my ear.

I jerk my head to the side, away from him. Big mistake. Pain lances through my neck. If his voice ringing in my ear isn't bad enough, he has a serious case of bad breath.

"Am I too heavy? I weigh one hundred thirty pounds, maybe one twenty-five. I swear. I can climb off you if you're getting tired. I think I can make it the rest of the way."

No wonder his cheeks are nearly as hollowed out as a holocaust survivor's. He easily stands over six feet now. I think he needs at least another forty pounds to fill out his frame. "Don't you dare try climbing off me. The last thing I want is you falling."

"What's wrong then?"

"Honestly, you smell horrible."

Haji giggles, the sound so genuine I can almost forget we're dangling from a ladder where one misstep will result in our innards splattered on the floor. You could almost call it a date. What can I say? My standards are plummeting to new lows.

"Quiet," Radcliffe says.

Haji stops giggling, but I miss most of what the dragon says. Like a game of telephone, Dad relays the message to Dalia, who relays it to us. I catch everything Dad says, but I listen attentively to Dalia anyway; plus, Haji needs to know what to expect when we exit the shaft.

"Will you be able to walk? Run?" I ask Haji.

"I think so. No problem."

"Good." I worry that if I carry him on my back

while running our legs will tangle up.

Dalia starts up the ladder, and I follow.

"Bria, hold on. We're coming," I murmur.

****

The shaft ends at a hatch opening onto the mist-shrouded peak of Mauna Kea. A loud hum fills the air. A tremor runs through my body at the sight of red dirt everywhere except in the crater's bowl. In the crater is a gaping opening into the slipstream, a massive black maw surrounded by eerily glowing yellow tendrils.

"Come on." Haji pulls on my hand and points to a single-story building about fifty feet away, the observatory's bulbous dome looming behind it.

The dome is split open to reveal the massive telescope inside pointing toward the opening in the slipstream. From the telescope's front lens emits a ray of orange light shooting the gateway at its edge. Several similar structures sit along the edge of the crater, telescopes aimed at the opening in the slipstream and blasting the same orange rays. There must be more, lost in the fog, because more laser light cuts through the murk to the gateway.

"Do you see this?" I ask. "I'm not imagining it?"

"You're not. We need to go." Haji tugs on my hand again.

Reach the building and get inside, I remind myself. Radcliffe and Dalia have covered about half the distance to the building. But I've become a statue, and so has Dad. Faeries and mercenaries, or maybe super magicians, are everywhere, but they don't notice us. Instead, their attention is focused on the three skaags descending from the low clouds to hover above the gateway. A half dozen or more skaags, it's hard to tell with the low clouds, undulate about one hundred feet above the gateway, their attention also fixed on the three skaags.

The skaag in the middle is larger than its escorts and a prisoner. Chains looping around its long body are held by the guards with their short yet powerful forelegs. A muzzle covers the beast's mouth.

"Druk. Fight back," Dad says.

I reach out with my consciousness and scream into the void. *Mother!*

Her awareness crashes into me like a hypersonic fighter jet. I double over, falling to my knees and ripping my hand from Haji's, so I can throw both hands to the side of my explosively throbbing head.

Run, daughter, run.

Chapter 43

Battling the pain that feels like it is literally ripping my mind asunder, I tell Mother, *We're here to save you. Dad is here and—*

They can hear you, daughter. Mother's voice resounds in my skull like a struck gong. *Run, now.*

"No! Druk! Fight back!" Dad screams as Mother and the two guards descend into the slipstream's ravenous mouth.

Dad's screaming draws the attention of a faery standing no more than fifteen feet from us with her dragonfly wings extended from her back between her shoulder blades. Faery dust swirls around her, a kaleidoscopic blizzard. Our gazes meet, and her indigo eyes, highlighted with glowing orange veins, narrow. I tense, reaching for the sleeper, and to my relief, brush against the half-skaag. My perception goes supersonic, and the beast's dread intermingles with mine. It's a heady concoction. After a second or two, the faery turns back to the crater, not knowing how close she came to being torn to pieces wing by wing.

Why didn't the faery alert her comrades of our presence or move to detain us?

"Allison, Mr. Lee, we need to go. Like now." Haji's voice is tremulous. "Look overhead."

Bloated, serpentine shapes ripple through the fog. Clearly, the skaags are agitated.

I take Dad by the hand. "We need to go."

He doesn't so much as acknowledge me, his face a mask of horror and grief. I follow his gaze to the crater in time to watch Mother's bulk disappear into the slipstream.

Gone.

She's gone.

I don't know what to feel. It's one of my greatest dreams come true, but there's no denying she's left her indelible mark on me. No matter how much I might want to, I won't be flying under the radar anytime soon.

"Druk…why?" Dad says.

"Come on, Dad." I yank on his hand, and he reluctantly stumbles along behind me.

Haji is a few feet ahead, moving with a lurching gait. Radcliffe waits for us at the door to the observatory, waving at us to hurry. A blaster held in her right hand, Dalia runs back to help Haji.

"Hurry, Allison, we need your help…oh, no." Dalia slows to a halt, and so does Haji. They stare into the crater.

"We need to keep moving." A shriek draws my attention to the crater. Rising like cobras out of the slipstream's black maw are at least twenty skaags. I trundle to a stop, and so does Dad. All I can do is gawp at the writhing monsters in open-mouth terror.

"It's an invasion." Dad squeezes my hand.

Without preamble, the hum of the lasers from the observatory domes fade. The orange beams flicker and go out. With the dying of the lasers, the gateway to the slipstream collapses in on itself. As the gateway shrinks, the yellow tendrils on its edge slice like sawblades through the skaags. The beasts screech as the tendrils dismember them, ichor and body parts falling through the black pit or plopping to the crater's floor. Three skaags near the center of the gateway escape and are greeted by a withering barrage of blaster shots and fireballs. The beasts cry in rage and shoot toward the clouds. More shrieks come from the clouds, and yellow bolts arc through the sky.

I don't know exactly what happened or why, but I know what's about to happen. The sleeper sends me images of lightning striking all along the crater's edge, killing indiscriminately.

"Run! We need to run!"

Tightening my grip on Dad's hand, I drag him along. With my free arm, I sweep up Haji like a sack of potatoes. Sprinting for the observatory, I hope Dalia follows us. Yellowish light flares and explosions resound from all around the peak, and tremors shake the ground. The stench of ozone and burned meat fills the air, along with the screams of the wounded.

As we reach the door, it swings open, nearly clipping Radcliffe, who retreats a few steps. Men and women dressed in black and carrying blasters stream from the open door, leveling their weapons at us. Bringing up the rear is a faery with his wings retracted surrounded by a storm of colorful dust that doesn't entirely hide the twisted scar along his right jaw. My heart palpitates, and heat floods me. Even maimed, he's still as beautiful as an obsidian David.

"Ah, Allison, so wonderful of you to join us." Jett's smile makes the mangled flesh along his jaw squirm.

****

I walk beside Jett as he leads us through the

observatory building with an escort of two guards. The rest of the force under his command had joined the fighting, which judging by how often the building shakes and the number of explosions rattling the windows, isn't going well for the faeries.

"I really am pleased you're here to witness our great victory." Jett leads us past cubicles where prisoners cower under the watchful eyes of rifle-toting mercenaries.

"More like your greatest defeat," Dalia says from behind us. She might have been disarmed but she is pugnacious as ever.

Jett smiles, his hideous scars of puckered pink flesh twisting like a worm behind the dusting of tiny, colorful pompoms obscuring the wound. "Ah, Dalia, I forgot what a positive personality you have." Jett winks at me. "You know, I think you've become quite proficient with the blasters. You possess a knack for killing." He looks over his shoulder. "You should consider joining us. We're always on the lookout for competent battle armor operators. In fact—"

I shake my head. "Stop. Just stop." Unbidden tears well up in the corners of my eyes. It's just like him to have surreptitiously observed what happened in the cavern and use it to torture me.

Jett halts at the door, continuing to speak as if I hadn't pleaded with him to stop. "—I'm certain Ms. Bergman will be happy to teach you all the ins and outs of the armor, including how to operate its weaponry. Imagine what you can do with an arm cannon powered by faery magic."

"Go to hell," Dalia says, undoubtedly remembering the torture she suffered at Bergman's hands.

Haji speaks up. “Leave her alone!”

“Don’t worry, Initiate 935,” Jett says, using the designation given to Haji on Golden Shoal. “The super-magician training program will welcome you back with open arms.” Jett gives me a broad smile and opens the door. “Please, after you. Continue to the open door across the room.”

A thump reverberates from outside, and the floor shakes like we’re in the middle of an earthquake. I lose my footing, stumbling into Jett’s rock-hard torso. His right arm wraps around my waist, tugging me close to him. My body reacts against my will, pressing closer and desiring his tender caress everywhere. I draw a quick breath, sucking in faery dust.

No.

I flush, and my breathing becomes rapid, drawing in more dust.

No. I can’t do that. The dust will make me more susceptible to his will. I purposely cough, trying to hack out any dust I aspirated.

“Leave my daughter alone,” Dad says.

Jett tenses, and his smile grows wider, showing off his triangular serrated teeth.

“Stay out of this, Dad.”

“Yes, Archmagus, mind your own business,” Jett says, but he only has eyes for me.

“How—”

“Easy, Raymond,” Radcliffe says. “You were observed helping Haji in the cavern.”

“Yes, Raymond, listen to the dragon.” Jett blows in my face, colorful spindles spilling from his mouth. I sneeze, spraying spit all over his face.

“Stop it.” I pull myself free of his arm and walk

through the doorway.

"You can't blame me for trying." Jett wipes the spit from his face with the back of his hand.

I stride across what appears to be a storage room to the open doorway that leads to steep stairs heading down lit by evenly spaced oval light fixtures in the walls.

"Go down the stairs and wait for me at the door," Jett calls.

Not wanting to be separated from my friends, I wait for everyone to catch up. Jett glides past me down the stairs. Any temptation to turn the table on him evaporates at the sight of the mercs bringing up the rear with their blasters leveled at our backs. I can probably take them out without getting shot, but I doubt all of us would survive a scuffle.

The staircase is insanely steep, like we're heading down into a bunker deep underground. I keep glancing over my shoulder, half expecting I'll need to carry Haji, but he navigates the stairs without any issue. Regardless, Dalia is ahead of him and is even more concerned about his condition than I am, if her solicitousness is any indication. Dad, expression turning stormier by the second, and Radcliffe are next followed by the soldiers.

Soon I can barely hear the explosions shaking the ground. I wonder how long the faeries and their pet humans will last against the collective wrath of the enraged skaags. Not long, I imagine, and the sleeper agrees with me. Few monsters in the multiverse are the match for a full-grown skaag, and I estimate fifteen are on the rampage outside.

Finally, we reach the bottom of the stairs that

terminate at a metal door with massive heavy-duty hinges, almost like the entrance to a bank vault. Next to the door is a keypad.

"Bria better be down here. She's the reason I'm here," I say.

"Of course, she's the reason." Jett positions himself so I can't see the keypad and enters the code. "It has nothing to do with the fact my guards will turn your friends into smoking slag if you don't do as you're told." A loud mechanical thud comes from the door. Jett pushes on the door, which glides soundlessly until it abruptly stops about a third of the way open. "Plavio, it's me. I bring prisoners."

"Prisoners?" The deep voice is reminiscent of boulders grinding together. "Why bring them here?"

"Elder Noxima will want to see them." Jett smiles at me over his shoulder. "One is Allison Lee."

"You may enter." The door swings inward, revealing a towering brute of a faery nearly as wide as he is tall. Faery dust swirls around him in a cloud denser than even Jett's. He lumbers aside so we can enter. He wears the same form-fitting jumpsuit as the other faeries I've seen that has an opening along the back, allowing his massive dragonfly wings to be on full display.

We are ushered inside a conference room with a long rectangular table. Sitting at the head of the table is an elderly faery with her wings retracted. Her jumpsuit is unlike any I've seen, its riotous color matching the vibrant faery dust floating around her. Sitting at her right is a man in a blue suit and dark tie. On the wall to the left are three forty-plus-inch flat screens displaying different views of the battle outside. As I suspected, the conflict is decidedly one-sided in the skaags' favor. On the right wall is a closed door.

Once everyone is inside, the giant faery closes the door with a dull thump. The elderly faery stands, razor-sharp nails extending from her fingers, and points at us.

"You!" She snarls the word like it's a curse.

"I never thought to see you again, Noxima," Radcliffe says. "I was under the impression I killed you…what was it? Three hundred years ago?"

Chapter 44

Radcliffe strides by me to stand at the table opposite Noxima. The elderly faery still points at him, arm trembling, her lips curling into a sneer. Seems someone might feel more negative about Radcliffe than I do. What a surprise.

Plavio, the brutish faery—Noxima's bodyguard, maybe—shadows Radcliffe, bumping into me, which is like being smashed into by a boulder plummeting at terminal velocity. I stumble into Jett's chest, which doesn't seem so rock-hard compared to Plavio's body. Jett takes the opportunity to caress my hips and spew faery dust in my face.

I back away, blowing the dust right back in his face. Jett glares at me and smirks. Apparently, he doesn't appreciate his tricks being used on him. Arching an eyebrow, I sidle away from the faery boy.

More than the general ambiance of this end-of-the-world bunker or Noxima looking prepared to order us executed sets me on edge. Plavio accidentally knocked me around like a crash test dummy. He seems way too oblivious to have run into me on purpose. Still, I would've done a face-plant if I hadn't collided with Jett. He had done that to me, despite the sleeper's prowess coursing through my veins. If it comes to a fight, I might've met my match.

Noxima lowers her hand. She grips the top of the

chair, nails puncturing the back. “I should have Plavio tear your golem to pieces.”

Radcliffe looks over his shoulder at the hulk, his dragon form flaring bright. “He could try.”

Plavio grunts, faery dust pouring from his mouth to join the flurry around him. I’m not sure if the grunt was merely meant to intimidate or if it was an expression of amusement too.

Radcliffe turns back to the elderly faery. “Do you know what I believe, Noxima?”

The room shudders. Dalia and Haji exchange worried whispers.

“If you wanted to destroy us, you would have already tried.” Dr. Radcliffe sweeps an arm toward the screens along the wall. Faeries and humans under a continuous assault of lightning bolts arcing down from the clouds. They return fire with no obvious effect. “You have an army, but not for long.”

The suit at the ancient faery’s left tugs on his tie, glaring at the professor. On his lapel is a pin, a visored helmet with a stylized wand spraying golden glitter above it. That must be a reference to Knights of Magic.

“You don’t think we prepared for this moment?” The suit’s accent is thick, probably Eastern European. “The arrogance.”

Radcliffe chortles and smiles at the man. His dragon head, though, peering down from the ceiling, stares unblinkingly at Noxima. “If you think you can prepare to battle skaags, you are a fool.”

The suit goes beet red in the face, and he opens his mouth to speak. Noxima raises a hand, silencing him.

“Kozlov, my dear, the dragon is baiting you. Don’t allow him to raise your blood pressure with verbal jousting."

Taking a deep breath, Kozlov nods and remains quiet. Noxima looks ready to speak when the room rumbles and shakes so violently we're all stumbling, even Plavio. Chairs overturn, and the table shifts. The feed on the leftmost LCD goes to static.

"It's time, Elder. Allow me to signal the airship," Kozlov says.

"Airship?" Dalia whispers.

"Not a clue," Haji says.

Maybe the faeries do have a gambit to play. But judging by the death and destruction playing out on the LCDs, they need more than one trick to turn the tide.

Noxima nods. Lurching to his feet, Kozlov walks to the rightmost LCD, opening a compartment below it built into the wall, and pulls out a phone—like a landline. I haven't seen one of those in ages except for on old-timey shows on TV.

"This is Director Kozlov, authorization code 9-6-A-Z-0-0-B. Deploy the armored battalion." Kozlov slams the phone down and glowers at Radcliffe. "You'll see how prepared we are."

The professor ignores the human, speaking to the faery Elder. "I can help."

"You would help us?" Noxima laughs, and it sounds genuinely mirthful.

"If the skaags win, they will end humankind as we know it."

Noxima's smile turns to a frown.

"Are you too prideful to accept my offer?"

"We don't need your help." Kozlov points to the center screen.

The camera angle has shifted skyward. Darting in

and out of the clouds are dozens, no scores, of humanoid figures with flames shooting from the heels, wielding glowing fractal-encrusted swords and blasting skaags with arm cannons. One of the great beasts covered in smoking wounds plummets to the crater. Seconds later, several mechs tumble from the sky, spewing black smoke. Two are dismembered.

My throat constricts. I had no idea so many mechs existed. I hope Ms. Bergman is dead inside a dismembered suit.

Noxima stares at the screens, expression grim. "What will your aid cost?"

"We don't need his help," Kozlov grumbles but is ignored.

"You closed the gateway. That is what I intended to do. The skaags are a clear and present danger. My aid costs nothing. But I do have an ask."

"Ah, yes, this is the Radcliffe I know. Pure doublespeak. Everything has a cost," Noxima says.

She does know the dragon well.

"I will help regardless of how you answer." Radcliffe indicates me with a languid turn of his hand. "Allison is here to free her friend, the faery child Bria. All I ask is you consider freeing Bria in good faith."

"That is a price I can pay." Noxima's indigo eyes bore into me, and she smiles, revealing serrated teeth. "I'm sure the half-skaag and I can negotiate an equitable exchange for Bria's freedom."

I guess being called a half-skaag is preferable to being named the monster girl, but why can't they call me Allison? That is my name.

"What about Druk?" Dad strides forward to stand beside Radcliffe.

"One issue at a time, Raymond," the dragon says lightly.

"No!" Dad pounds the table with a fist. "I want to know what happened to my wife. Why is she a prisoner? Did closing the gateway collapse the slipstream? Is she even alive?"

Noxima pulls out the chair and sits. "Ah, you are her partner. The father of the half-skaag and a powerful magician for a human."

"An archmagus," Radcliffe says.

Noxima smiles. "Jett told me. So you failed to eliminate all of them too?"

"Seems I have failed at many tasks." Radcliffe waves at the screen. "May I join the fight?"

"Jett, take Radcliffe to join the battle. Then return here," Noxima says.

Jett inclines his head. "Of course, Elder."

Radcliffe turns to follow Jett out of the bunker. I grab him by his remaining wrist. "That's it? You're going to abandon us here with them and go join the fight?"

Radcliffe gives me an avuncular smile. "It is for the greater good, Allison. Somebody must save the world. Besides, you are all more than capable of handling yourselves without me."

I let go of him. Jett opens the door to the bunker and steps into the stairwell. Radcliffe follows, his dragon head looking down at me from the ceiling and winking. Plavio trundles over to the door and shuts it with a thump.

"Are you going to answer my questions about my wife?" Dad demands.

I give Dalia and Haji what I hope is a reassuring

smile. They both need reassurance, especially with the mercs standing behind them with blasters leveled at their backs. I turn back to the table. Noxima gives Dad an exasperated look.

"I will answer your questions in good time. First"—she raises a pointer finger to the ceiling—"I have something to discuss with your daughter."

"I'm only interested in you releasing Bria," I say.

Plavio walks up behind Dad and places a hand on his shoulder. "Come."

Reluctantly, Dad allows himself to be led away from the table by the brute.

"Sit." Noxima indicates the chair nearest to me.

"I prefer to stand." If it comes to a fight, I don't want to be hampered by a chair.

"Suit yourself. Our discussion won't take long."

"The dragon has joined the battle," Kozlov says.

On the rightmost screen, a massive golden beast takes to the air on green wings. Radcliffe quickly gains altitude, flames lancing from his mouth into the clouds.

"I will release Bria as long as you allow my scientists to take samples from you."

"Samples?" I turn to the faery elder. She smiles guilelessly. Deep in my bowels, the sleeper swirls. We don't trust her. But I'm willing to do anything to free Bria.

"Blood samples. And we'd like to run some tests. I don't know the specifics. Agree to this, and I will free the child. You have my word as an Elder."

"Allison, don't agree to anything," Dalia says.

"You can't trust her," Haji says.

"As if I don't know that," I say.

"Be careful what you agree to," Dad says.

I failed to keep Bria safe once. I won't fail her again.

The sleeper thrashes, images of betrayal flashing through my mind.

No, I have to do this. Don't you dare deny me this. You do, and I'll never speak to you again.

"I agree. Take the samples and run the tests. Just free Bria."

"Excellent." Noxima looks at Kozlov. "Kozlov, be a dear and bring Dr. Rah to meet her new patient."

Vertigo assails me, and the room blurs. "Dr. Rah…"

She's dead.

Jett ripped out her throat.

Chapter 45

Crow's feet extend from the corners of Dr. Rah's eyes like she's smiling behind her mask. She lowers the bone saw's spinning blade between my breasts. I want to break the restraints binding me to the surgical bed, but my body won't respond. I don't know if it's drugs or magic or both locking me in place.

The whirring blade is mere millimeters from biting into my skin and slicing through bone.

Help me. Do something. I scour my awareness and body for the sleeper. I can't find even a hint of the half-skaag.

"No, please, don't!" My pleading words are distorted like my tongue is a bloated banana slug.

The saw carves into my flesh, and I scream. A red mist rises from my chest, leaving droplets across Rah's mask. Over my wails and the saw's buzz, the doctor hoots like a madhouse clown.

"Dr. Rah? What are you talking about? She's dead."

Dalia's voice shatters the other sounds.

A warm hand envelops mine. "Allison. Allison, what's wrong?"

"Haji?" My vision smudges like a giant eraser plows through it. The immense pain in my chest fades.

"Wait! We want to see Bria first," Dalia demands.

I blink, the nightmare holding me splinters, and

reality comes into focus, which is almost as bad. My chest isn't cracked open, which is a major plus. However, Noxima staring at me from across the table, her unblinking indigo eyes highlighted with glowing orange veins, is enough to give me the heebie-jeebies. Kozlov stands halfway between the table and the door along the right wall, staring at me while opening and closing his hands at his sides. I know Plavio is behind me by his heavy breathing. I don't like that one bit, and neither does the sleeper.

"Are you okay?" Haji whispers.

I squeeze his hand and give him a cocky smile. "Thanks to you, I am." I release his hand and, taking a deep breath, step up next to Dalia. Hands on her hips, she stares at Noxima. I can do this. I'll do whatever it takes to set Bria free. Of course, Rah is dead, so something isn't adding up. Did the maniacal doctor survive her wound? No, that's impossible. "Dalia is right. I want to see Bria first. Then I'll submit to the tests. I need to see Bria."

Noxima sighs, then smiles, flashing teeth. "That is an acceptable condition. Do you have more demands?"

I glance at Dalia, who shrugs. "No."

Kozlov grimaces. "We don't need to…"

Noxima silences him with a raised hand. "Kozlov, inform the doctor to prepare for Allison Lee and bring the girl."

Kozlov straightens his tie and stalks from the room, leaving by the door on the right wall, which I assume leads deeper into the bunker. His passage leaves behind the scent of his cologne, which is as appealing as a compost pile baking in the desert sun. I stifle a groan but can't keep my nose from crinkling.

"You have caused us a great deal of trouble, Allison." Noxima's eyes narrow. "Our operation on Golden Shoal was on the cusp of reproducing Bria's blood before you destroyed it."

"You shouldn't have sent Gore to kidnap me," I say.

The bunker shakes. Dalia stumbles, catching herself against me. I grab the table for support. On the screens, the battle continues to go south for the faeries, even with Dr. Radcliffe's assistance. The golden dragon intertwines a skaag nearly as large as he is. Tumbling through the sky, they snap and claw at each other, bodies stained with ichor. On the ground are dozens of burned and broken humanoid bodies, but only one additional skaag corpse.

Noxima cracks a mirthless smile. "What is it you humans say? Hindsight is twenty-twenty."

"You could say the same thing about opening the gateway for the skaags," Dalia says.

"We didn't open the slipstream for those fiends." Noxima's expression darkens.

Haji walks up to the table and pulls out a chair. He sits down heavily. From behind us, the door to the bunker opens, and Jett enters, shutting the door behind him.

"Why did you open the slipstream?" Haji asks.

Jett strides to the head of the table. "You should tell them, Elder. It will help them understand us."

Frowning, Noxima glances at Jett. "You think I should share our peoples' tragedy for their amusement?"

"I don't think they will find the story amusing," Jett says. "It will help them understand."

"Will it? Do I even care about their understanding?" Noxima raises her white eyebrows. "I suppose it can't hurt, if it fosters understanding." Noxima leans forward, folding her arms on the table. "This wasn't the first time we opened a gateway to the slipstream, although the one you saw today is by far the largest. We made our first portal to the slipstream nearly thirty years ago. As you have learned, we discovered how to meld our magic with human technology. As human technology advanced, what we could accomplish by augmenting it grew."

The bunker shakes as another volley of lightning bolts crash into the ground from the clouds. Explosions erupt along the crater's rim throwing up debris and bodies. Ignoring the tremor, Noxima continues the tale.

"We learned we could use the powerful telescopes of these observatories to focus our magic, amplify its power until we could tear a hole into space-time itself, and access the slipstream between universes."

"But why?" Haji asks. "You invited the skaags here and then killed them. Now you're locked in a life-and-death battle. Why?"

Noxima smiles sadly. "That was not our intent. Not at first. We desired to reunite our people. We sought the lost ones."

"So the stories are true." Dad comes up beside me. "Druk spoke about rumors of your kind spread throughout the multiverse, hidden from the dragons."

My shoulders tense. I shouldn't be surprised Dad and Mother knew all about the faeries, but neglected to say anything about them to me.

"Hidden? Why?" Dalia asks.

"From persecution," Noxima says, faery dust blasts

from her mouth with her words. The colorful spindles swirl around her with increasing speed. “The dragons hunted us for sport for centuries, pursuing us from planet to planet. When we finally learned how to fight back effectively, they sent their slaves, the skaags, for us. So we scattered across the stars and the universes.” Noxima takes a deep breath, clearly trying to regain her composure. The faery dust spinning around her slows. “All we tried to do by opening gateways into the slipstream was to communicate with our brethren. Alas, when we finally received a response, it was from the dragons. We count ourselves lucky we had captured Druk by then—a treacherous skaag. A prize they desired even above our extinction.”

“So you traded my wife to them to ensure your survival.” Dad’s voice is bitter.

“Of course. She had been nothing but a thorn in our side since attacking the base on Golden Shoal. When the dragons answered our call through the slipstream, we immediately offered her to them. We agreed to open a gateway to the slipstream large enough to allow skaags to come to Earth and take possession of her. Druk in exchange for our safety. Of course, the dragons and their slaves betrayed us. The force we collapsed the slipstream on was meant to wipe out my people. We always suspected we’d be betrayed. Dragons only care for themselves. But we needed to rid ourselves of Druk. Her magic was too powerful for us to safely imprison her. Threatening her daughter kept her in line, but we feared if we moved to execute Druk, she would fight back and free herself.”

The door on the right side of the room opens.

“Excellent. Kozlov has brought Bria,” Noxima

says.

Bria stands in the doorway with her wings hidden from view with a smattering of colorful spindles floating around her. Kozlov rests his meaty hands on her shoulders, perhaps holding her up because she looks listless, drugged. But that's not what turns my joy, my triumph to ash in my mouth. No, it's the woman standing behind Kozlov at his shoulder who is responsible for that. Suddenly, the drone of air forced through the ceiling vent sounds reminiscent of a bone saw.

"Dr. Rah," Noxima says. "You are ready for Allison Lee, I assume?"

Chapter 46

"No way," Haji murmurs.

"If I had a blaster…" Dalia whispers.

I stare at the woman, trying to sort out her presence in the bunker with memories of her lying on my abdomen, bleeding out from a gash in her neck. "You're dead."

The woman steps around Kozlov and Bria, extending a hand as if she wants me to shake it. "You mistake me for my twin sister, Dr. Clarissa Rah. I'm Marissa Rah." She smiles. "Our parents weren't the most creative regarding names."

She glances at her hand, moving her wrist up and down. There's no way I'm taking her hand. This is way too freaky. Inside me, the sleeper coils like a snake ready to strike.

It's not her.

The sleeper projects an image of me strapped to an industrial-strength examination chair with Dr. Rah standing over me. Honestly, this woman looks exactly like the maniacal doctor. Except…I blink to clear away the sleeper's projection from my mind's eye.

Marissa gives me a quizzical look. "Is something wrong?"

I shake my head. *What about the hair? It's a bob haircut. Dr. Rah always wore hers in a bun.*

The sleeper sends an image of me sniffing the

woman like a dog. She smells like the doctor from Golden Shoal.

Okay. You're right about that. But what about her speech? She doesn't have as strong an accent, and she doesn't clip her words.

A horrifying gif plays in my mind of me pounding her face into a bloody pulp. The accompanying wave of emotion tells me to kill her, or I will regret it.

No! I'm not going to kill her. This isn't the Dr. Rah from Golden Shoal. Look at her. She doesn't have a stick rammed up her butt. If I try anything, the guards will open fire. I might be able to take them out before they roast me, but not before they kill my friends and Dad.

Disapproval of the decision palpable, the half-skaag settles itself. At least the beast didn't try to force me to transform. Still, I don't know if I can allow this woman to take samples and run tests on me. She might not be the sadistic doctor who tortured me, but she could be a mad scientist.

Rah lowers her hand. "You can call me Dr. Rah or Dr. Marissa or just Marissa. Whatever makes you most comfortable. I want you to feel relaxed and…"

I blow past Dr. Marissa Rah for Bria. Dropping to my knees, I throw my arms around the faery girl. Kozlov releases her, and she falls against me, quivering. Taking a deep breath, Bria returns my embrace. I don't think I've ever felt her so weak.

"C-c-careful," she whispers into my ear, teeth chattering.

"I know." As I speak, I realize I will allow Dr. Rah to take the samples and run the tests. Inside me, the sleeper paces and shrieks, but I ignore the half-skaag.

This is something I have to do, that we have to do despite our irrational and rational fears. "You're safe now. We're going to take you away from here."

The ground quakes, rattling the furniture. Bria teeters, and I squeeze her tighter, holding her upright. Dalia whimpers and Kozlov stumbles backward into Plavio.

Kozlov straightens and shakes off the brutish faery's hands. "Should I send in the second wave?" Kozlov asks.

"No, we hold them in reserve," Noxima says.

"Elder, if we commit Bergman's shock troops now, they might turn the tide of the battle," Jett says. "If we wait until the dragon falls—"

Noxima hisses. "Then he falls. We will not commit the second wave. Not yet. Escort Allison to the operating theater. See that she upholds her side of the bargain."

"Of course, Elder."

I face them, still holding Bria's trembling body. "Wait. Something is wrong with her. What have you done to her?"

Jett strides along the length of the table. "She's drugged, that's all. To keep her docile. You know how she can be. We wouldn't want a repeat of what happened to Dr. Kihl."

Jett stops before us, smiling toothlessly. I look to Dalia for help with Bria, but she shakes her head, eyes wide. Their first meeting on Golden Shoal was an all-out brawl, leaving Dalia's forearms ripped to bloody shreds by Bria's claws. The white scars haven't completely faded from my BFF's skin. Haji starts to stand, but Dad waves him to stay seated and comes to us. Jett takes a step back to give Dad room to kneel beside Bria.

"This is Bria?" he says. "I'm Raymond, Allison's father."

Clutching me tighter, Bria looks him up and down.

"It's okay. My dad will take care of you."

I gently push Bria toward Dad. Reluctantly, she releases me, then nearly collapses into him.

"Whoa! Gotcha!" Dad bundles the faery girl up in his arms. He looks at me with an intense gaze. "You're sure about this? What if they drug you?"

"I'll do whatever it takes to win Bria's freedom," I say.

Dad nods, expression grave. "Be careful. Bria, can you walk with my help?"

Bria nods, her face screwing up in extreme concentration. She mouths, "Be careful."

I give her a thumbs-up and wait until Dad has her in a chair before standing. "I'm ready."

"Excellent." Jett smiles, this time showing disconcertingly sharp teeth. "Do you remember the data Dr. Rah collected when you transformed?"

I ball my hands into fists. Of course, I remember.

"It was saved." Jett's smile widens. I'd like to punch him in the face. "We are closer than ever to unlocking how your body works. Closer than ever."

****

Dr. Rah leads Jett and me down a narrow hallway deeper into the bunker.

I whisper to Jett, "Does she know what you did to her sister?"

Jett grabs my wrist and pulls me close. Stumbling, I brush against the sleeper, summoning its power.

Breaking his hold on my wrist, I'm ready to thrash his face when I catch Marissa slowing and turning toward us in my peripheral vision. I drop my fist to my side and scuttle away from Jett. We must look like kids caught red-handed pilfering from the cookie jar.

"Is something wrong?" the doctor asks.

My tongue is tied. I can't even meet her gaze.

"Nothing," Jett says sullenly.

Marissa's eyes narrow. She opens her mouth as if to speak, but the hallway shakes. Yelping, she catches herself against the wall. "Come on. We best hurry."

As the doctor starts down the hallway, Jett whispers, "What Dr. Rah doesn't know needn't concern her."

"Last time I saw Bergman, she was hellbent on revenge for what you did to Rah."

"Bergman is a pragmatist. She chose to maintain our alliance."

Marissa leads us to the end of the hallway, where it T's. We take the right-hand corridor that terminates within twenty feet at a double door guarded by two men with blasters. At our approach, they step aside, and one pushes open the rightmost door. We enter a room with an operating table near the center beneath a powerful overhead light. Along the back wall is a door.

The astringent scent of harsh cleaners hangs in the air that don't completely mask the underlying aroma of blood—human and faery. The enticing scents awake the sleeper's interminable hunger.

Marissa raises an eyebrow and smiles when my stomach growls. She taps the table. "Please, make yourself comfortable while I go prepare. After the samples are taken, I'm sure I can find some snacks for you."

Jett is a dark blur highlighted by colorful dust in my peripheral vision. I spin toward him, and he catches my right forearm in a viselike grip and pulls me off balance. Before I can free myself, cold steel punctures my neck. The effect of the injection is immediate. The room twirls around me, my vision blurring.

"Don't fight it," Jett says. "It's a custom tranquilizer. Made just for you."

"Why? Why did you do that?" Marissa demands. "She was cooperating."

"Do you think she'd agree to go under? After what your sister did to her?" Jett scoffs. "Call your assistant. I need his help getting her onto the table the way she's struggling."

"Darius! We need an assist."

A white blur floats across the room, almost ghostly, to the door at the back wall.

"Darius!"

A muffled response comes from somewhere… maybe beyond the door. I can't tell.

"Calm down, Allison. Relax. This will all be over soon."

Something dark looms over my head, spewing kaleidoscopic dust. Faery dust!

Help me. Help me!

But the sleeper doesn't respond.

"Darius, hurry!" Jett yells. "The way she's fighting, I think the tranquilizer is already wearing off. Dammit! Guards! Guards! Get in here."

The next thing I know, I'm lifted bodily off the floor. I writhe, kicking and flailing my arms, but my strength is infantile. My head slams against something hard, and I see stars. I jerk my right leg free and kick, connecting with someone. A weight presses down on my chest, making it hard to breathe.

"Where's the gas!"

"I'm here! I'm here. Keep her head steady, so I can put on the mask."

Something green flashes in my vision, disappearing as quickly as it came. What the…?

Calm yourself, slave!

Those words vibrate my skull from the inside out, and I go limp. A covering is fitted over my mouth. Vaguely humanoid shapes stand over me, bleeding together at the edges. I reach for the covering, but the voice reverberates through my head again.

Don't touch the face covering.

The covering is tightened over my mouth. Green light flares again, this time directly in front of me. I squint, but the light fades before I can tell what it is.

"Turn on the gas."

Chapter 47

I dive through the gluttonous mouth of the collapsing gateway into the slipstream. The yellow tendrils around the opening bite like gnashing teeth through skaags exiting the pathway through the multiverse. My body wiggles through before the mouth clamps shut, severing a final skaag in two. The lower half of its body joins the gory debris leaking blood and viscera, floating alongside me. For once, a banquet of raw meat and hot blood doesn't stir the sleeper's hunger.

With the roar of wind I do not feel filling my ears, I undulate down the glowing path to escape the leaking body parts. Soon, I leave the gore behind. Beyond the translucent wall of the cylindrical passage is the void between universes, a black vastness that might stretch for meters or to infinity.

Good. You come. You obey.

I'm dreaming, at least, I think I am. This must be a dream, right? The sleeper isn't any help in deciding if I'm conscious. The half-skaag claws its way from the backwater of my mind to the forefront, not to offer advice but to leap to obey the voice.

Come. Obey. It is your purpose. Your only purpose.

Screw that.

This is a dream.

I can wake up.

Laughter vibrates my skull.

Wake up! I will my eyelids to open.

Nada.

Your eyes are open. You are obeying. You are fulfilling your purpose.

My body undulates, and I accelerate down the path. I'm not doing this on my accord; it's the sleeper acting every bit like a well-trained dog summoned by its master.

Stop! We can't trust the voice.

The sleeper ignores me, continuing to accelerate our body farther into the slipstream.

Marshaling my willpower, I command the beast, *Give me back control. Now.*

My "willpower" splatters against a storm wall. I've been consigned to a rear-facing child carrier. Real or not, this is a ninth circle of hell nightmare. All my agency is gone, like all it's ever been is illusionary.

No. Don't give up.

I thought we were a team. You know I don't want this. Can you at least tell me why? Why are you listening to the voice?

An image flickers in my mind, but the voice shatters it before it resolves into something discernible.

Stop resisting. It's against your nature. Obey and discover joy.

That voice. I heard that voice or one similar to it just before…just before the face covering was put over my mouth. I fought back. Maybe not effectively, but I tried. Then I heard the voice in my mind, and my body went as flaccid as a dead fish.

This is a dream. In reality, I'm in an operating room with Jett, that sicko doctor, and…and whatever made the flickering green light. What was the light?

No, it can't be. How is that even possible?

The voice says something, but I ignore it. I concentrate on my memory of the light and the shape it formed. What shape did it form?

"Darius, what are you doing?"

A female voice.

The sizzling crackle of electricity.

"Blast it! Blast it!"

I recognize Jett's voice.

Blaster fire. A scream. Indecipherable shouting.

Open your eyes. But the sleeper won't let me. Before us is the wall of darkness at the slipstream's terminus. The half-skaag must reach it, must discover what is on the other side.

"Allison! Allison!" Hands shake me.

The sleeper slams our head into the dark wall. The impact rings my bell, but undeterred, the beast strikes again. Cracks form, leaking white light. When that radiance bathes our hide, we feel ecstatic pleasure and desire to obey. As we batter our head against the wall, our consciousnesses begin to merge.

Good. Now you know what it means to obey.

No. What am I doing? I'd flip the voice the bird if I had the fingers to do it. Forget this. I make my own decisions, thank you.

"Wake up!"

Gasping, my eyes shoot open, and I lurch up on the operating table.

"What?" My tongue stumbles over the word.

"Run!" Jett pulls me off the operating table.

My feet touch down on the floor, and my legs fold underneath me. A roar fills the chamber, ringing my ears. The air around me superheats, and the scent of ozone permeates the air. I will my legs to support my weight, but I can barely feel my appendages. I'd fall, except Jett wraps a strong arm around my torso and underneath my left armpit, supporting me. He drags me toward Marissa Rah, who stands in the doorway, frantically waving at us. Her eyes are wide with terror, and tears roll down her cheeks.

In my peripheral vision, I glimpse blood splattered across the floor and something glittering green. Only what I see isn't insubstantial green light. It's the sparkling scales of a dragon that has passed out of the slipstream onto Earth. How in the hell can a dragon fit inside this room?

We reach the doorway. Jett pushes Rah through with his free hand into the hall. From inside the room, fire crackles, and a man screams.

"Shut the door!" Jett yells.

Rah slams the door shut, cutting the flames off from the hallway.

I need your help, I call to the sleeper. *There's a dragon trying to kill us.*

Kill them! They are the enemy! Kill them all!

The voice, the dragon's voice I think, resonates inside me. Prowess gushes through my body, and the sleeper barges into my consciousness. It's like being clipped by a runaway freight train. The half-skaag seizes control of our body, tossing Jett into the wall and lunging for Marissa Rah.

But a foot catches our ankle, and we go airborne, then bellyflop onto the floor. The impact knocks the wind out of us. We try to scramble to our feet, but Jett grabs us from behind, wrapping an arm around our neck.

Faery dust blows across our face. “What are you doing? You’re going to get us killed!”

Inhale. Inhale the dust. Don’t sneeze. Don’t cough. I suck in a breath against the will of the sleeper.

“Stop fighting. We need to run.”

Jett’s words batter the half-skaag. It’s enough for me to reassert control.

“Let go of me. I’m in control.”

Jett releases me, and we scramble to our feet. We sprint after Rah, who waits for us where the hallway T’s.

“Run!” Jett screams as the doors to the operating room burst open.

The dragon squeezes his bulk through the doorway. The beast is many times smaller than Dr. Radcliffe or any of the other dragons I’ve encountered, instead being about the size of a draft horse. Its membranous black wings are pressed close to its sides. Flames flicker inside its gaping mouth.

We reach the T, the air superheating around us. As dragon fire crackles through the hallway, we dive down the adjoining corridor. Flames and smoke fill the space we had just occupied. Scrambling to my feet, I grab hold of Jett by the wrist and yank him up. We follow Rah, who has kept running.

“Keep going to the conference room! Tell Plavio to prepare for a dragon!” Jett calls.

There’s a fifty-fifty chance Rah hears Jett over the dragon’s roar. He didn’t have to call after the doctor since we overtake her before she reaches the conference room.

I dare to glance over my shoulder. The dragon

hunches down on all fours, squeezing through the hallway, shoulders, hips, and wings scraping against the walls and ceiling. I'm tempted to grab Dr. Marissa Rah by the shoulders and throw her to the dragon. An even greater temptation is to do the same to Jett. This is a golden opportunity to rid myself of the faery boy. It's too good a chance to pass up…almost. Lucky for them, I don't want to be that person or half-person.

Kill the faery. I command it.

The disembodied voice rumbles through my mind. The sleeper hears the command and pines to obey with nearly every fiber of its being, but almost being rendered to ash by dragon fire is enough to make the beast think twice about blindly obeying incorporeal voices.

Jett reaches the door to the conference room first and throws it open. Bringing up the rear, I push Rah through the doorway and follow her inside. Behind me, the air sizzles, and I swear my hair and clothing are catching fire. I turn in time to watch dragon fire shooting through the hallway toward me before Jett slams the door shut.

The roar of fire resonates from beyond the door. In the conference room, multiple people talk at once. The fractals covering Plavio's body flare and the fairy dust swirling around him intensifies into a variegated blizzard.

"What is happening?" the brutish faery demands.

Everyone falls silent, looking between Plavio and the door turning cherry red along the edges.

"Darius…he's a dragon," Jett says.

Chapter 48

"Dragon?" Plavio's brow furrows as he looks between Jett and the door. He lumbers to the door and throws the heavy deadbolt. Backing away, he points to the mercs, who look ready to piss their pants. "Blast anything that tries to come through."

The guards exchange worried glances. There is a thud against the door, which vibrates but holds. Next comes the crackling roar of dragon fire. Wisps of smoke twirl into the conference room from around the door's edges.

The brute turns to us. "The rest of you should leave. Try to find—"

A resounding crash, followed by the shriek of shearing metal, cuts off the faery. The door slams to the floor. Black smoke puffs through the doorway around draconic body parts. Blaster fire erupts—it's impossible to know if the energy bolts do any damage with the smoke permeating the air. Aglow in fractal patterns and surrounded by vibrant faery dust, Plavio charges like a sumo wrestler.

Jett is a blur. "Elder, get down!"

Plavio slams into the dragon. His hands flare with orange light, and he presses them into the dragon's torso. The dragon shrieks in pain, lashing out with a foreclaw. Talons rip into Plavio's abdomen, and the big faery bellows. A well-aimed blaster shot sears the dragon's foreleg, and it releases its grip on Plavio. Blood gushes from the gut wound, but it is quickly stanched by faery dust.

"Stay back!" I warn everyone while looking for an opening to join the melee.

Only there isn't one. Even the mercs have stopped firing. The dragon and faery are lodged in the doorway, muscles and sinew bulging. If anything, I'd say the faery is winning the battle of the titans, except the dragon squeezes its head and long neck through the doorway below the top of the frame.

"Get down!" I shout, reaching for Dalia, who is closest to me.

I'm too late. Dragon fire explodes into the room, turning the two mercs into little more than charred bones, and engulfs Plavio. The faery dust swirling around him catches fire. As the roaring firestorm rushes toward us, I'm paralyzed by hopeless fear.

The flames never reach us. A translucent blue barrier silently lowers from overhead to the floor. When the fire hits, the shield flickers but holds.

"Oh my God." Dalia has a hand over her heart. "I thought we were going to die."

The inferno courses over an oblong blue dome reminiscent of the one Dad created to protect the civilians at the military base from the faeries' magical fireballs and blasts from the mechs' gun arms. Dad stands behind me, his right hand held overhead. From the palm of his upheld hand shoots a pillar of blue light. The pillar travels upward for about three feet, then spreads out to form the blue dome protecting everyone around the conference table, including Noxima, Kozlov, Rah, and Jett, huddling together at the table's head. On the wall, the three LCD screens smoke and bubble like boiling mud. The one in the center falls to the ground with a crunch and spray of debris.

Bria sprawls in a chair near Dad, looking even more listless than earlier. Haji stands over her, leaning against the table for support.

"Your blood. I need your blood. I know what to do." Haji points to the battle between Plavio and the dragon.

The dragon fire has dissipated, but Dad remains as still as a statue, face locked in concentration, keeping the barrier up. That's probably a good thing, especially since Plavio looks like he's on the losing end of the fight. Most of the faery dust surrounding him has burnt to a crisp. Smoke curls from his skin. The fractal patterns covering his body fade like flashlights running low on battery life. The glow around his face and neck is gone, the fractals indiscernible against his dark skin. Even the fiery magic engulfing his hands sputters, and his touch no longer appears to cause the dragon pain.

Centimeter by centimeter, then inch by inch, Darius forces his way into the conference room. The exit to the stairs leading to the surface is ten feet or so away, but reaching them means crossing the dragon's path. I doubt even I could cover the space between the barrier and the exit, open the door, and escape to the stairwell before Darius toasts me up. The others could not move fast enough, not even Jett. If we made it to the stairs, we'd be fish in a barrel. All it would take is Darius sticking his head through the doorway to roast us with dragon fire as we ascended the stairs.

Unless Dad's barrier is mobile.

"Ahh!"

Haji's yelp breaks my concentration.

"Haji, what are you doing?" Dalia asks, voice shrill.

"Haji, Bria, no," I say.

Haji kneels beside Bria. His T-shirt is rolled up to expose his deltoid, which leaks blood from a deep gash. The claws of Bria's right hand are extended and bloody. She leans toward the wound, glowing orange faery blood sloshing from her mouth and running over her lips.

I'm ready to spring forward to prevent the rite they're about to perform when the room quakes. Dalia stumbles into me, and instead of preventing Bria from clamping her bleeding mouth over Haji's wound, I'm stumbling.

At the same time, the table scrapes over the floor, the corner jamming into Dad's hip. He grimaces, and that brief break in his concentration is all it takes for the barrier protecting us to collapse, starting with the pillar of light shooting from his palm shattering into sparkling blue glitter. In a matter of heartbeats, the glitter fades like ephemera, and so does the shield. Dad slumps against the table, obviously spent from his exertion.

The dragon shrieks, and Plavio bellows. I spin toward them in time to watch Plavio knocked backward. Darius's neck shoots forward like a striking snake, mouth going impossibly wide and snapping shut over the faery's face. When the dragon withdraws, Plavio's head is jaggedly bisected. The giant faery teeters and falls to the ground with a thump. Darius shrieks again, a trumpet of victory, and inexorably continues squeezing his bulk into the conference room.

It's now or never, I tell the sleeper, *maybe we can*

force the dragon back into the hallway. Give the others a chance to escape.

Clenching my hands at my sides, I'm ready to charge and fill in my half-assed plan along the way. Maybe I can transform once I force the dragon into the hallway. Transforming will surely lodge me in the hall, maybe even collapse the corridor. But that's okay if it keeps Darius from killing my friends.

A hand grabs my wrist. "Allison, allow me. I know what to do."

My jaw goes unhinged. Haji releases me. His eyes are aglow with orange light, and orange vapor rises off him like mist as he strides confidently toward the dragon spilling through the doorway.

"What's going on?" Dalia asks.

"Faery blood," I say.

Darius practically falls into the room, coming down on his forelegs, talons sinking into Plavio's corpse. His head tracks toward us, mouth hanging open. Deep in his throat, acrid black smoke rises and flames crackle. Fire spews forth, meant to burn us all.

People scream.

I scream.

This is the end.

Haji throws himself into the fire's path. The flames lick at him, but orange light shoots from his body, consuming the fire and blasting directly into the dragon's gaping mouth. For an instant, the brightness is so intense my vision goes white, and I cringe, throwing an arm before my eyes. The light is gone as quickly as it came. Something heavy thuds to the floor.

I blink until my vision clears. Darius is sprawled on the floor, his serpentine neck ending in a charred stump. His head is conspicuously missing, and the scent of cooked meat intermingles with the smoke's stench.

Haji still stands before me, swaying precariously. I run up behind him as he falls and catch him in my arms. He stares at me, the orange glow gone from him.

"I did it," he says weakly and smiles.

Chapter 49

I sit on the floor, carefully lowering Haji as I do. I arrange my legs cross-legged and rest his head on my lap. His hair is matted down with sweat, and he trembles, but at least he's conscious.

I smooth back his wavy dark hair from his forehead to keep it out of his eyes. "You're going to be okay."

Haji coughs, chest heaving violently. Dark smoke fogs the air. The smoke's acrid stench clogs my nostrils, along with the residual scent of ozone from the earlier blaster fire, the distinctive aroma of burned meat, and a hint of blood. My stomach rumbles and clenches.

"Someone open the door to the stairwell to let out the smoke," I call.

"I will," Rah replies from the back of the room.

I tense at the sound of her voice. She's probably anxious to escape the argument that has broken out between Kozlov and the faeries. Kozlov rants at Noxima and Jett in English and what might be a Slavic language. I do my best to ignore them, concentrating on the gangly boy in my arms.

"Am I alive?" Haji asks between coughing fits.

I narrow my eyes. "Of course. You killed the dragon. Its head is gone."

"Now we don't know what's going on above ground!" Kozlov screams. "I can't communicate with the airship from here. The communication equipment is destroyed."

The argument is escalating, and I wonder if I'll be forced to intervene. On the plus side, Rah has the door to the stairwell wide open. She's walking back toward us—not good, I don't want to deal with her right now—when the bunker shakes. With the door to the stairwell hanging open, the boom of the explosion is audible. It's a not-so-gentle reminder that there is a battle that might decide the fate of the world and that I need to join it sooner rather than later.

"I can't feel it. I can't feel it at all." Haji's tone possesses a mixture of curiosity and trepidation. "My…my…I don't understand."

"You're not making any sense," Dalia says. "Hey, Mr. Lee, I think Haji needs your help. He's confused and talking nonsense."

Shouts come from the back of the room. Claws and wings extended, Jett positions himself between Kozlov and Noxima. Kaleidoscopic faery dust swirling around him is a blur backlit by the orange glow of the fractal patterns etched into his exposed skin.

"Can I help?" Dr. Rah asks.

I face the doctor, who kneels next to Haji's feet. Being so close to her makes my skin crawl, and the sleeper cowers, ready to lash out with deadly intent. I can hardly believe I had the fortitude to allow her to take samples and run tests. I suppose Darius might've done the human race a favor since he probably prevented Rah from taking any samples, or at least, destroyed any she managed to take. Whatever she and the faeries planned to discover or create wasn't in humanity's best interest. "I don't think there's anything you can do."

"Yeah, back off, doc," Dalia says.

Rah smiles. It's an expression I don't think I ever saw from her twin. "I disagree. Your friend has burned himself out. He will never use magic again. If my lab is not entirely destroyed, I have medicine there that can help him."

"Burned out?" Haji's voice is tremulous.

"It's true." Dad approaches, leaning against Bria, who seems to have overcome her listlessness and regained strength. "I don't sense any magical potential in him. Honestly, he's lucky to be alive and might still be in danger. Magicians who burn themselves out often die."

"I can help," Rah repeats.

"I can't feel the magic. It's gone. I never thought it would be gone." Haji grabs my hand. "I learned magic for you at first. I wanted to impress you. To prove I was special too."

"Haji, you are special with or without magic." But I can tell from his expression he doesn't believe me.

"You don't understand! Once I had magic…it's…it's wonderful. I don't know if I can go on without it." His grip tightens. "Don't let them use magic on me or give me drugs…let me go."

My jaw works, but no words come out. All I can do is squeeze his hand back. I know where he's coming from. I've been drugged and magicked more times than I can count—it's terrible. I'd do anything for things to return to the way they were before The Incident, but that's never going to happen, and I have to accept that. Haji needs to do the same when it comes to magic. If he's burned out, he's going to have to live with it. He can't die. He can't.

Dalia slaps Haji across the face hard enough to make him tear up. "I don't want to hear any more talk about dying. No one is dying today. Not you. Not me. Not Allison. None of us."

"You don't under—"

Dalia winds up for another strike. "Do you want me to slap you silly? Because that's what's going to happen if you say one more word about dying because you don't have magic. What good has magic ever done for you anyway? It got you kidnapped, brainwashed, and nearly killed more than once!"

"You're right," Haji concedes.

"He needs treatment. I've never known a magician to survive burning out without treatment," Dad says. "I'm too weak to help him, at the moment. If Dr. Rah has medication to stabilize his condition, we should accept her offer. Otherwise…"

Dad shakes his head.

I'm aghast. "No." I point at the doctor. "She can't be trusted. The things her sister did—"

"I'm not my sister," Marissa Rah says. "Given what you've been through, I know that's hard to believe. All I want to do is help."

I glare at the doctor. "I don't believe you."

"I don't know what to believe," Dalia says. "But I trust Mr. Lee knows what he's talking about. Haji needs help"—she points at the gangly boy—"whether he wants it or not."

"Al…Al…Allison," Bria says.

I turn to the faery girl. "Wha—"

The room shakes. From the back of the room, Kozlov screams, and there is the roar of blaster fire.

Dad and Bria half duck, half fall to the floor. Jett and Kozlov struggle, both holding the grip of a small blaster. The faery wrenches the weapon from the man's grip and tosses it aside. In a flurry of rapid slashes almost too fast for the eyes to track, Jett's claws rip into Kozlov. Tie shredded and suit stained with blood, Kozlov falls to the floor.

At the same time, a resounding crash comes from the stairwell. Dust puffs through the doorway.

"Is there another way out of here in case the stairway collapses?" I ask.

"Yes," Rah replies tremulously.

"Allison." Jett strides across the room, Noxima following. Blood drips from his extended claws, and he holds the blaster in one hand and a cell phone in the other. "We need to join the fight. I'm going to call the reserves, Bergman's shock troops. If the battle is not already lost..."

The room shakes again, more violently than ever before. Jett windmills his arms to stay upright, and Noxima falls against the table.

I know Jett is right. If the battle is not lost, now is the time to join it to win the day. We must triumph because failing means humankind becomes food stock for ravenous skaags. I know this truth from the sleeper.

Still, I hesitate. I don't want to leave my friend, the first boy I ever kissed. Not when he's compromised and might die. I know that's self-centered. I know if the skaags win, everyone will suffer. But the greater good isn't enough for me to leave Haji in the clutches of Dr. Marissa Rah.

"Dalia." Jett hefts the blaster.

Dalia stands, and Jett throws the blaster to her. She

catches the weapon, a smile lighting her face. Pink hair disheveled, clothes stained with sweat, and nose ring glittering, she looks one hundred percent pure badass.

"Go," Dalia says. "I'll keep everyone safe."

"Are you coming or not?" Jett demands.

When I don't respond, he shakes his head in disgust and stalks to the stairwell.

If only it was that easy. The Dr. Rah I knew was sly, predatory. Her twin could be the same. I trust Dalia, but can she protect Haji, Bria, and Dad from Rah and Noxima?

"Al…Al…Allison," Bria says. "Rah…is not…her si…sister. Safe." Bria nods. "Safe."

I look from Bria to Rah and back to Bria. The faery girl nods.

"Okay," I say.

After helping Haji sit up, I hug Dalia and whisper, "Don't trust Rah and Noxima."

"I don't," she breathes into my ear.

We break our embrace. I hug Bria.

"I won't lose you again," I promise her.

"I…tr…try not to get lost."

Finally, I face Dad and we awkwardly embrace.

"I love you. Be careful." He kisses me on the forehead.

"I will be." Breaking free of his hug, I chase after Jett before I change my mind and let the world burn.

Chapter 50

I take the stairs two at a time. The lights are out, and dust fills the air, but the stairway hasn't collapsed, at least not yet. Up ahead, light streams onto the stairs from an open door. Sounds drift down the stairs from that doorway: sizzling, roaring, shrieking, and death screams. Gulping, I stop on the stairs and stare into the light. I'm not sure I'm ready for this—to face death and to deal it.

The sleeper, though, quivers in anticipation of joining the battle. To fight, to kill, to feed. That is the half-skaag's purpose. But I don't want it to be my purpose, not now, not ever. An explosion echoes beyond the open door, and I swear the step rolls like a wave beneath my feet. From above me comes the crack of splitting rock, and my heart gallops up my throat into my mouth.

"We can do this. We have to do this," I whisper and continue the climb.

I'm unsure if I'm climbing to join the battle or to avoid being buried under tons of rubble. At the top of the stairs, I find the storage room in disarray, equipment and shelving overturned, and the contents of boxes sprayed across the floor. From a jagged hole in the ceiling large enough for a compact car to fall through comes the discord of battle, revealing the cloudy sky aglow with yellow lightning and red flames. Mechs and faeries flit in and out of view like darting mosquitoes. A crack pierces the air, and a yellow bolt strikes a faery, blasting the creature into orange mist.

I don't know why I should help the faeries and their human allies. They are no friends of mine, not by a longshot. By association, they are responsible for me being tortured by Ms. Bergman and Dr. Rah. I owe them nothing, and if I help them to victory, I'll be shocked if they don't turn on me. But doing nothing means dooming humanity and all the other life on Earth to the cruel dominion of the skaags. But I don't know the faeries' endgame. Is it any better than the skaags'? They have already proven they can superpower and enslave human magicians.

A deafening roar rings in my ears, and I flinch. I see a small section of Radcliffe's massive golden-scaled body streak by overhead. Black pockmarks mar his scales. A huge wound along his side leaks purple blood.

I see the dragon for a few seconds, maybe less, but it's enough to shame me. He risks everything to keep humanity safe. He could enter the slipstream and flee, but he fights despite the long odds. How can he have the conviction to fight while I'm ambivalent, at best?

"Kozlov is dead. An enemy agent killed him."

Jett stands in the doorway leading out of the storage room into the observatory proper with the cell phone to his ear. I go to his side and glimpse what made the bunker seem like it would collapse.

"No, I don't have his authorization code," Jett says. "Put me through to Bergman."

Most of the building's outer wall facing the crater and the roof have collapsed. The cause is a skaag, dark eyes open wide yet lifeless, strewn across the floor. I suspect about a third of the beast's bulk is inside the building, the rest outside, on the crater's slope. It's unclear what killed the skaag, but the stench of acrid smoke and burned meat lead me to suspect dragon fire.

Poking out from beneath the skaag's body are the limbs of crushed humans and pooling ponds of blood. The gore entices the sleeper, and my stomach clenches, whether from disgust or desire, I'm not sure. But I do know that the skaags battling overhead possess the same ravenous appetite as the sleeper. Preventing them from farming humans for meat is reason enough to join the fight, isn't it? Or do we humans deserve to be treated the same way as chickens and other domesticated animals we raise for the slaughterhouse?

"Bergman! Deploy the shock troops," Jett says. "Kozlov is dead. Allison is about to join the fight." Jett faces me. "I will rally the others." He lowers the cell phone from his ear. "Allison, you must transform and help Radcliffe."

Jett picks his way through the rubble toward the collapsed wall and the outside. Scrambling up fallen debris, he watches the battle unfold.

"There are only six or seven skaags left. We can do this, Allison. We can win." The fervor in his voice grows with each word. "Allison?" He faces me, a mask of disappointment clouding his expression when he sees I haven't budged. "What is your problem?"

His dragonfly wings buzz, moving so fast they are a blur. Leaping into the air, he flies, touching down in front of me. The fairy dust around him is so thick his face is obscured by swirling color, but I can still see the mangled flesh along his jawline.

"What's wrong?" Jett demands.

I shake my head. He doesn't want to hear my reasons or excuses. He wouldn't understand, and I don't want to confide in him.

Jett points at me accusingly. "Why did you even come here?" He throws his arms out to the side. "Why? You came to rescue Bria, didn't you?" He lurches into my personal space, so close the faery dust tickles my nose. "Didn't you?"

I take a step back and nod. "Yes, okay. Yes."

"Then saving her must be enough, Allison. I know you don't care about the greater good. Such high-mindedness is for fools like that dragon." He thrusts an arm behind him, pointing to the demon sky flashing orange and yellow. "You're like me. You only care about your people. I don't mean the humans." He scoffs dismissively, and I remember how he justified killing that poor nurse on Golden Shoal by declaring she was only human and easily replaced. "I mean Bria and your friends. If the skaags win, they will die. You have to decide if you will let them die due to your inaction."

Jett turns and strides toward the outside.

"We're not alike. I'm not a cold-blooded killer."

Jett looks at me over his shoulder, laughing. "Tell yourself that if it helps you sleep at night."

Clenching my jaw so tight my teeth hurt, I follow the faery past the fallen skaag, battling the sleeper's desire to feed on the human appendages sticking out from the beast's bulk and lap blood. Jett is right. I might not be inspired by calls to sacrifice for the greater good, but I can't doom my friends. I can't allow Dalia becoming a killer and Haji burning himself out be for nothing. I won't allow them and Bria and Dad to be eaten alive by skaags.

I carefully navigate the debris from the fallen wall onto the crater's rim. The racket of battle rings in my ears. Everywhere I look is the red earth of my nightmare. I feel small and helpless. Am I destined to die here? Maybe, but that doesn't bother me, not anymore. It's the dread my squad will die on these volcanic slopes that turns my insides to ice water.

Jett grabs me by the shoulders and shakes me from my reverie. "Help Radcliffe. I'll organize my people and the humans. We can win, but only if you fight."

I pull free of his hands. "I'll do my part."

Wings buzzing, Jett shoots skyward, flying along the rim to a group of faery and human fighters near an observatory building remarkably untouched by the fighting. Shrieks come from the flashing clouds. A golden body entwined by a skaag dips below the clouds and then is lost in the low-hanging mist. Fire crackles, and the clouds flare orange.

Trusting the sleeper to do its part, I leap off the section of collapsed wall I'm standing on. For a few seconds, I'm soaring over the crater as a human with the wind in my hair, which is pretty cool, but the experience lasts long enough for me to wonder if I made a mistake and that I'm plummeting to my death. Then the sleeper goes supernova, exploding my body and reforming it in an instant of agony longer than a lifetime.

Rising over the crater's rim, I take in the devastation. There might only be five or six skaags left, but that doesn't mean the battle has been going well for the faeries and their human allies and slaves. Scores of broken and burned faeries and humans litter the rim and the crater. Two dozen or more mechs are smoking ruins. The wounded are too many to count. But to the defenders' credit, nine skaags lie dead in the crater and along the rim.

An agonized shriek of pain I recognize as Radcliffe comes from the glowing clouds. I shoot upward toward my date with desolation. Faeries, occasionally hurling fireballs, and mechs blasting away with their gun arms zip in and out of the cloud cover. The faeries don't concern me, but I hope the mechs don't mistake me for the enemy. Their weapons can do real damage to me in skaag form.

I burst into the flashing orange and yellow clouds. I sense rather than clearly see the writhing forms around me: faeries maneuvering like fighter jets, a mech in an uncontrolled spin spewing black smoke from where the face plate should be, golden scales glittering in yellow light, a green wing of leathery membrane, and oily black hides appearing and disappearing in the clouds like leviathans of the ocean deep.

I speed to where I saw the glint of scales, a fireball smacking against my midsection along the way. Shrieking more in annoyance than pain, I remind the sleeper we're here to help the faeries, not slay them, and hope that the fireball was an errant one and not thrown at me on purpose. My hide can absorb dozens, maybe hundreds of fireballs, but each one exponentially decreases my ability to keep the half-skaag's baser instincts in check.

When I reach where Radcliffe should be, he's already gone—I don't know if that's good or bad. Summoning electricity, my body tingles as I dive through the clouds hoping to find Radcliffe and the skaag or skaags killing him. Instead, I run face-to-face into a full-grown skaag. It's like smashing into a battalion of tanks all at once. Stars flash in my vision, and my spine feels like it's been ripped from my body and each vertebra snapped in half one by one.

The clouds and skaag are all topsy-turvy and out of focus. My head throbs, and if my stomach had any food in it, I'd projectile vomit all over the massive beast in front of me. Somehow, don't ask me how, I'm levitating in front of the skaag, staring it down. For its part, the skaag stares at me with fathomless dark eyes, electricity sparking over its body that winds in and out of the clouds. Slowly, its mouth opens wide enough to bite my head off in a single snap.

Head spinning like a top and heart pounding so hard it will explode from my chest, I try to use my electrical attack, but my body won't respond. At least not to my command, because a bolt shoots from somewhere near my head straight into the beast's gaping maw, frying the monster from the inside out. Surprise flashes in the skaag's eyes, then the beast plummets listlessly from the sky.

Thanks. I tell the sleeper. *Find Radcliffe. He needs help.*

We quickly move through clouds, but not at the frantic, helter-skelter pace when I was at the controls. My muddled mind realizes we move with a hunter's grace. Slowly, my vision sharpens until I can distinguish between the faeries and mechs swarming through the clouds. There are more battle-armored figures than before. The memory of Jett calling Ms. Bergman belches into my forethought. The sleeper and I wouldn't mind committing a friendly fire incident, ending with Bergman a smoking wreck on the ground, but it's impossible to know if she's present, let alone pick her out from the swarm.

Suddenly, we change direction, diving downward or shooting upward, I don't know. The electrical tingling coursing over our body builds. Ahead is an oily black hide with electricity arcing over it. Faeries and armored forms dive bomb the skaag, but even the mechs' cannons have little effect. Electricity sizzles from our head, striking a smoking wound on the skaag's body. An earsplitting shriek fills the air.

Why?

The question crashes into my mind like a meteorite, pulverizing my gray matter to mush. Without warning, the sleeper retreats like it was struck. Still murky from having been concussed, I'm left in control of a body I barely know how to operate when my faculties are running at one hundred percent.

Chapter 51

The skaag's question makes my skull vibrate like a struck gong.

I stop undulating. For a moment, I'm floating weightless then I'm falling through the clouds.

Help! I call to the sleeper, but the half-skaag remains cowering at the edge of my perception.

The combatants flash past in my peripheral vision, occasionally a faery or mech shoots before me. I try to regain control of my body, but it's like I've been thrust into the pilot seat of a jumbo jet. All the controls are familiar from images I've seen on the Internet, books, or movies, but I don't know what the hell I'm doing.

I need help.

The sleeper might as well be deaf to my pleas.

This is so stupid and frustrating I want to scream.

This is my body.

Mine.

I don't need the sleeper. I know how to control my half-skaag body. I can do this.

I try to concentrate on that. I really do, but trying to focus makes my brain feel like it's been plopped into an industrial-strength food blender that's turned to the max.

I burst from the clouds expecting to see the red earth rushing up to meet me. Instead, I crash into a writhing coiled mass of oily black bodies and golden scales. The world, the sky, monstrous body parts, and everything spin like I'm on a carousel possessed by Lucifer himself. Roars and shrieks stab my eardrums. Something beats against me.

The air superheats. From somewhere in my swamp-mired mind comes the warning: dragon fire.

An inferno flashes as bright as the sun. I clench my eyes shut and still see it as an indecipherable brightness. I don't think the flames touch me, but still, my hide burns. The pain shocks the sleeper into action. The half-skaag doesn't reassert control of our body. Instead, the beast guides me, and for the first time in a long time, perhaps ever, I feel our synergy. We are more together than we are individually, and we both know it to our marrow.

The world still spins when we open our eyes, but our head doesn't. Our vision clears and comes into focus. Undulating our body, we break away from the writhing mass, gaining altitude but not passing back into the clouds.

Emerald wings beating furiously, Dr. Radcliffe is locked in battle with three skaags. The beasts coil around him like kaiju-sized anacondas, trying to pry up his golden scales to expose the vulnerable flesh underneath with their claws and fangs. The dragon fights to keep a skaag's hooked talons from the bloody gash along his side. Smoke rises from their hides where dragon fire licked them, and in places, their tough skin is burned away, exposing damaged pink flesh.

Around the monsters throng faeries with blurring wings and mechs with flames jetting from the soles of their feet. They concentrate their cannon fire and fireballs on the pink wounds dotting the skaags' hides.

A brave human dives in close, thrusting a fractal-encrusted sword toward a wound leaking fluid. Yellow bolts arc over the skaag's body. One discharges into the dive-bombing human. Electricity courses over the armored body that goes limp, foot thrusters sputtering. The armor bounces off an oily hide as it plummets.

Radcliffe's wing beats become less powerful and frantic with each heartbeat. The dragon is inexorably losing the battle. Even if the skaags fail to pry up his scales, they are squeezing his life out with their corkscrewing bodies. It's a technique we instinctually recognize. By squeezing the dragon around the chest and neck, they make it difficult for the beast to breathe fire by applying pressure to the organ that produces combustible vapors. They leave the dragon's wings untouched, knowing the panicked beast will fight to the bitter end to stay airborne, ensuring it tires itself more quickly.

Youngling! Help us kill this dragon, and we will allow you to feast on his flesh with us!

Yes, youngling! We need your aid. The faeries and humans are weak individually, but in great numbers they can harm us.

Why do you hesitate?

The skaags' voices crash into our mind and echo through our skull. This time the sleeper doesn't retreat. Instead, we shoot toward the combatants, intent on aiding the skaags.

No, we don't have to do that. We're free to make our own choices.

We pull up, hovering in the air right above the fight. Faeries and mechs fly past us, concentrating their fire on the skaags curled around Radcliffe.

Youngling, help us!

Again, we feel the pull to aid our kind.

We're not a skaag.

Remarkably, the sleeper agrees.

You don't have to fight, I tell the skaags, remembering Mother flying away before the battle against Radcliffe and his followers at Mt. Rainier. She had left her boss, Mark Cassidy, to die. *I know you have oaths you cannot break, but you can choose not to fight.*

We live to obey! We must fight! You must fight! Join us now!

The words resonate in our mind so loudly we quiver. Again, we feel the tug to obey.

No, you don't have to obey. We don't.

The sleeper speaks its language of imagery, projecting our memories of encountering the dragon Darius and resisting the beast's commands. To our surprise, a skaag starts to untwine from Radcliffe.

Traitor!

The word ricochets so loudly around our head that we wince. A second skaag releases Radcliffe and lunges for the first, mouth gaping. A lightning bolt blasts from the hindquarters of the withdrawing skaag, striking the lunging beast in the head.

The electrical attack dazes the skaag, and the beast stops undulating for an instant. The skaag drops from the sky for fifty feet or more before it ripples again. That halts the beast's uncontrolled descent but does not save it from a swarm of faeries and mechs. The faeries swirl around the giant alligator eel, hurling fireballs. The mechs land on its dark hide and stab their glowing, fractal-encrusted swords into its body. The beast shrieks and thrashes as it meets its demise under the magical blades.

A celebration breaks out amongst the faeries as the giant beast plunges to the crater below and the mechs leap to safety, foot thrusters firing. We have no time for the jubilation, for Radcliffe still falters in the grip of the remaining skaag. His forelegs barely keep the skaag's snapping jaws from his neck.

Shrieking a battle challenge, we summon our electrical attack. Body tingling, we allow the electricity to charge to maximum capacity. Even so, it will take a lucky shot directly into the mouth of the massive skaag to disable or kill it. Ready to strike, we wait for an opening clear of draconic body parts, faeries, and mechs to take our shot. A green wing rises, giving us a clear view of the smoking oily hide.

Electricity arcs from near our head. The bolt zips through the air, striking the skaag with a resounding crack. Body arching back from Radcliffe, the beast shrieks in agony. As soon as the tension on his body slackens, Radcliffe spews fire indiscriminately, nearly scorching us. We retreat from the burning heat and acrid smoke, but a handful of faeries and mechs are not so lucky. The fairies are rendered to ash, and melting armored figures fall from the sky.

Wings and tail lashing the air, Radcliffe breaks free from the skaag's deadly embrace with a roar that's part cry of pain and part scream for help. He had failed to score a direct hit on the skaag with his flames, and the beast shoots after him. Without hesitation, we dart forward, throwing ourself onto the massive skaag, burying our talons and fangs into the wounded hide.

To our surprise, the skaag writhes and shrieks but cannot throw us off. We bite off a chunk of flesh, swallowing blood and meat without savoring the flavors. Seeing the bloody wound, we know what to do and blast a lightning bolt into it. The stench of ozone and frying meat fills our nostrils and the monster shudders against us.

Exalting in our victory, we pull away as the gargantuan skaag falls, but something lashes us with such force our vision goes blood red, then black. We're falling and being crushed at the same time.

Chapter 52

My eyes flutter open, but my vision is blurry as all get-out. Just brightness and shadow. My ears ring and buzz. Ring and buzz. A thick animal musk fills the air, nearly drowning out the stench of smoke and blood and so much more.

Skaag. I smell skaag…

****

"Miss Lee. Wakey! Wakey! Come back into Earth's orbit, Miss Lee. Heh, heh."

My insides go icebox cold at the sound of Bergman's voice. I must be dreaming. Wake up. Wake up!

"You haven't died on me, have you, Miss Lee?"

Bergman sounds distinctly tinny—that means she's in a mech. An involuntary tremble vibrates my body.

"Ahhh. So you are alive."

A whirl of gears is followed by something sharp and searing pricking my throat. My eyes shoot open. My vision is fuzzy, but I can still see the glowing, fractal-encrusted sword pressed to my gullet. The weapon is held by a giant armored humanoid. What must be Bergman's face is a pinkish-white smudge between armored shoulders.

I reach for the sleeper and shimmy across the ground at the same time. Moving ignites terrible pain throughout my body, overwhelming my attempt to touch the half-skaag. My ribs feel like they've been crushed by a steamroller. I can move my left arm, but it doesn't work right from below the elbow. My face throbs like a powerlifter uses it for a piñata. The pain is enough to bring tears to my eyes, but that's not what makes me feel like a giant hand is squeezing all the air from my lungs.

It's my legs that cause that reaction. I'm in human form, and I can't feel my legs.

Help! I cry to the sleeper, and the half-skaag is with me. The beast is as pitifully weak as I am.

"What's wrong, Miss Lee? A skaag crush your legs? I'd love to put you out of your misery. Heh. I'm not supposed to. I'm supposed to let you live. But I'll tell you what, if you say the word or nod, if that's all you can do, I'll kill you right here, right now. Think hard before you answer. Because this is a one-time offer. You can say no, but I'll—"

"Bergman! Did you find her? What are you doing?"

"Dammit!" Gears whining, Bergman backs up, becoming even more indistinct, and withdraws the sword from my neck. "I found her! She's alive, but the poor girl's legs are crushed underneath this dead skaag."

A buzzing fills the air, reaching a fever pitch as a dark form highlighted with flecks of color appears over me. I squint—Jett. Great. He's the last person I want to be my savior.

He kneels beside me. "Allison, don't worry. We'll get you medical attention."

"I can't feel my legs. I can't feel my legs!"

****

"She's waking up!"

My eyes flutter, gummy. Someone stands over me. Wavy hair, lanky, dark skin, and a bandage around his forehead from where he smacked into the cave wall—Haji.

"Allison, you are awake!" Dalia shoulders in beside Haji. She has dark bags underneath her eyes but appears unharmed.

Slowly, I become aware of my surroundings. I'm on a makeshift bed, more of a cot, and covered by a warm blanket. Tubing runs from my right wrist to an IV stand next to the head of the cot. An array of smells assaults my olfactory organ: human and faery blood, harsh cleaners, and painkillers.

"I'm in a hospital again?" I groan. "That makes me want to go back to sleep."

Are you there? I query the sleeper. There's always a chance I'm so drugged up I'll be cut off from my other half. The beast stirs, drowsy and weak, at the edge of my perception, but it's there. I'm surprised by the immediacy and amount of relief I feel.

I interrupt Haji. "What? Sorry, I missed that."

Haji's eyes go wide. "Do you need more rest? Should I get a nurse?"

"No, no. My mind wandered."

Haji and Dalia exchange a look that says they're worried and don't think I can be trusted to evaluate my condition.

"Of course, I'll have to be seen by a nurse and doctor and whoever else. But I'm fine for the moment. You can continue your story. I'm listening."

Dalia smiles lopsidedly at Haji and shrugs.

Haji grins. "I was saying this is a field hospital set

up by the military. Not just the US military either! The Canadian and Chinese military helped out too! How cool is that? Fighter jets took out the last skaag! It was wild. I can't wait to write an article for *The Cascadia Weekly*!"

"General Lovelace is here and tons of other military types from all over the world. They're having endless meetings with Radcliffe, Noxima, and Bergman," Dalia says.

My jaw tightens. I recall Bergman pressing the sword to my neck. I don't think that was a dream. The sleeper projects an image of the maniacal spook with a sword tip against my throat—it's like the perspective you have in a first-person shooter.

"My legs," I murmur and try to move my toes. I let out a breath. "I can move my toes!"

"That's awesome!" Haji grabs my hand and gently squeezes. His skin is warm. "I'm going to find your dad. He'll want to see you right away."

Before I can reply, Haji darts away, dodging between nurses, doctors, and cots with patients. Watching him nearly trip over his own feet and bump into an orderly, a goofy smile plastered on his face the entire time, makes me feel warm inside. I have my friend back. For such a long time, I thought he was lost. Forever. And now he's not.

"He's recovered." I smile. I must be grinning ear to ear like a complete idiot, especially since that hurts my face. But that's okay. I don't want to stop. "I thought I'd never see him like this again."

Dalia nods. "His recovery is amazing. Your dad made some kind of potion with Bria's blood and other stuff. I was skeptical, but he recovered and can't use magic. I thought he'd be depressed about not having magic, but he seems okay. For now, at least. He hasn't left your side except to relieve himself. They even let him sleep on the ground next to your cot."

"Wow." My squad. What would I do without them? "Where's Bria? Is she okay?"

Dalia looks at the ground. "Bria is great. Your dad and her have almost been at your side as much as Haji. I have to warn you…"

"What is it? Did something happen to my dad or Bria?"

"No, it's not that." Dalia meets my gaze. "It's…you don't always get along with your dad. Not since he admitted to being an archmagus. He and Bria…they've struck up a friendship. They're practically inseparable." She holds up her hands. "It's not like weird or anything. At least not in a bad way. Radcliffe—he survived, by the way, and tells everyone, I mean everyone, he owes you his life—thinks the relationship is a good thing."

Before I fully process what Dalia said, a nurse holding a clipboard approaches the bedside.

"Allison Lee, you're awake, and I've heard you can move your toes. That's great. I'm going to take some readings, and the doctor will be over in a minute."

****

The doctor has concluded I'm making a speedy recovery all things considered before Haji shows up with Dad and Bria in tow. I catch the aroma of freshly brewed coffee and realize Dad holds a sixteen-ounce cup of brew. Bria is standing beside him, so close their arms touch, and she is smiling. Actually smiling. She's not showing any teeth—maybe she realizes her serrated teeth make people nervous—but I can tell the expression is genuine.

"This is for you." Dad proffers the cup.

I struggle to sit up, and Dalia, Haji, and even Bria come to my aid. The faery girl wears the same dark jumpsuit, leaving most of her back exposed, as I've seen Jett and other faeries wearing. With their help, I'm soon sitting up with only minor stabs of pain from the movement.

"It took us a little while to get here because Mr. Lee insisted on stopping by the mess hall to get you coffee," Haji says.

"Dark and fl…flavor…ful." Bria points to the cup, smiling even broader, exposing a hint of teeth.

I take the offered cup, which nearly slips from my hand. Only Dad holding the cup keeps me from spilling it all over myself.

"Careful there, Allison," Dad says.

"I keep forgetting how weak I am." I take the cup in both hands and breathe in the steam rising through the small opening in the plastic lid. It smells so good I can forget that the brew is in a disposable cup—almost.

"Allison had a visit from the doctor," Dalia says.

I barely take a sip of coffee when the questioning starts. I do my best to answer their questions between sips, which is pretty easy since it's all good news. By the time the interrogation ends, I've downed about three-fourths of the coffee because the brew tastes even better than it smells. With each sip, I revitalize a bit and can imagine everything being right in the world, at least for a little while.

"Maybe we should give Allison and Mr. Lee some space," Dalia says.

My eyes go so wide I'm surprised they don't pop out. Just because Dad brought me coffee and I can tolerate his presence doesn't mean I want to be alone with him right now.

"G…goo…good idea," Bria says.

Before I get a word in edgewise, Haji adds, "That's a grand slam of an idea."

Dad doesn't say anything but looks as excited as a golden retriever puppy reunited with his master after being separated for an hour. It's going be hard to say no, but still, I'm tempted to, but then the sleeper butts in with images of all the times Dad gave me sound advice, intervened on my behalf with Mother, and was simply present.

Thanks for the reminder, I say dryly, but my defenses are breached.

My squad individually hugs me before leaving. Bria is first, and her hug is fierce.

"I won't lose you again. I promise," I whisper.

"I kn…know."

Next is Haji, who hugs me maybe a little too long for comfort.

"I hear the military might give us medals for saving the world! Is that cool or what?"

"A little embarrassing, maybe?"

Last is Dalia. Our embrace is the longest, and we don't need words to communicate what is needed.

Dad and I stare at each other like we're the last people left in the universe. I can't help seeing the archmagus when I look at him, but I also see my dad, who is always looking out for my best interests—for the most part.

Dad breaks the silence between us. "I'm proud of

you. You saved the world."

"You helped my friends."

Dad kneels beside me and gently embraces me. I don't return his hug.

"I'm sorry it took me so long to do the right thing," Dad says.

I throw my arms around him, the IV tugging at my wrist.

****

Two weeks later, I'm leaning against Radcliffe's golem, otherwise I might fall on my butt, on the podium at the medal ceremony. A three-piece suit covers most of the damage to his humanoid body, but can't hide the fact that a good chunk of his head and an arm are missing. The massive golden dragon, the real Radcliffe, flickers in and out of existence around the podium and beyond. If I concentrate, I can see the half-healed wounds scarring the golden scales. Haji and Dalia are on the platform with us, looking out across the crater of Mauna Kea. Pavilions have been erected around the fallen skaags to preserve the bodies and allow government scientists to inspect them.

Assembled in folding chairs before the podium are dignitaries from the United States, China, Canada, Europe, and who knows where else. Dad sits in the front row, looking like he might explode with pride. Jett, Noxima, and Bergman have seats near the back. I clench a fist at the sight of Bergman. She notices me watching her and smiles like a homicidal clown. I wish she was under arrest or dead.

General Lovelace introduces the secretary of defense. Looming behind them hovering above the crater is a massive aircraft that looks similar to an aircraft carrier. The Knights of Magic airship is kept aloft by dozens of supersized whirling fans arrayed along its sides and unseen magic.

"You know," Radcliffe whispers. "A skaag survived the battle. We are trying to locate it."

"Really? I spoke to several skaags during the battle. One withdrew. I think. I lost track of it with everything going on."

General Lovelace steps aside, and the secretary of defense takes position behind the podium, adjusting the microphone to accommodate her shorter height.

"We will need to speak of what you said to the skaags later," Radcliffe whispers and falls silent.

The secretary of defense begins her speech. I try not to listen to the parts that reference me, but I'm happy to hear all the complimentary things she has to say about my squad and even the dragon.

I'm glad we all did our part to save the world, but I'm not looking forward to having a medal pinned to my chest.

I hope we don't have to save the world again.

A word about the author…

Dan Rice pens the young adult urban fantasy series The Allison Lee Chronicles in the wee hours of the morning. The series kicks off with his award-winning debut, Dragons Walk Among Us, which Kirkus Review calls, "An inspirational and socially relevant fantasy."

While not pulling down the 9 to 5 or chauffeuring his soccer fanatic sons to practices and games, Dan enjoys photography and hiking through the wilderness.

To discover more about Dan's writing and keep tabs on his upcoming releases, visit his website: https://www.danscifi.com and join his newsletter.

Thank you for purchasing
this publication of The Wild Rose Press, Inc.

For questions or more information
contact us at
info@thewildrosepress.com.

The Wild Rose Press, Inc.
www.thewildrosepress.com

Milton Keynes UK
Ingram Content Group UK Ltd.
UKHW022051110624
443988UK00015B/632

9 781509 254675